Robert Douglas retired, aged fifty-five, in 1994. He intended to paint, write short stories and lie about the house watching old films. A one-off article he wrote about six weeks spent with a condemned man in Bristol prison led to him being told 'You should write.'

The bestselling *Night Song of the Last Tram* is centred around his Glasgow childhood and became the first book in the popular trilogy detailing his life as a miner, dock worker, doss-house resident, soldier, prison screw – and survivor. For this, his debut novel, he returns to his first love: the lost Glasgow of trams and tenements.

He hasn't painted for years.

Praise for *Whose Turn for the Stairs?*:

'An outstanding novel with a cast of characters so beautifully drawn that turning the last page feels like flitting out of 18 Dalbeattie Street'   *Daily Record*

'Douglas's prose is simple and charming . . . this novel will appeal to fans of Douglas's previous trips down memory lane'
                                                          Scottish Review of Books

'*Whose Turn for the Stairs?* echoes the bygone charm and ingrained hardship of growing up at a time when rationing and families living in single end tenements were commonplace, yet laughter never seemed in short supply'   *Evening Times*

'Pure dead brilliant, so it is . . . a rare old read for folk that were round and about in the Forties and Fifties'   *Edinburgh Evening News*

'It's a braw read!'   *Hexham Courant*

Praise for Robert Douglas's previous books:

'Exquisite'   *Sunday Times*

'Engaging, deftly written and honestly remembered'   *Herald*

'A natural-born writer . . . convincing and entertaining'   *Scotsman*

'This will make you laugh, cry and buy copies for everyone you've ever known'   *Daily Record*

Also by Robert Douglas:

At Her Majesty's Pleasure
Somewhere to Lay My Head
Night Song of the Last Tram

Whose Turn for the Stairs?

ROBERT DOUGLAS

hachette
SCOTLAND

First published in 2009 by
HACHETTE SCOTLAND, an imprint of
HACHETTE UK

First published in paperback in 2010 by
HACHETTE SCOTLAND

4

Cataloguing in Publication Data is available
from the British Library

ISBN 978 0 7553 1892 6

Typeset by Ellipsis Books Limited, Glasgow
Printed and bound by Clays Ltd, St Ives plc

Hachette Scotland's policy is to use papers that are natural,
renewable and recyclable products and made from wood grown
in sustainable forests. The logging and manufacturing processes
are expected to conform to the environmental regulations
of the country of origin.

HACHETTE SCOTLAND
An Hachette UK Company
338 Euston Road
London NW1 3BH
www.hachettescotland.co.uk
www.hachette.co.uk

ACKNOWLEDGEMENTS

With many thanks to Bob McDevitt and Hachette Scotland for wanting to publish my books; my editor Wendy McCance (aka Southern Softie) for being a wiz at her job; Jane Selley for being a knockout copyeditor, Myra Jones for her top-notch proofreading and Michael Melvin for such a good cover. What a team!

Then there's my darling Patricia (The Manageress) who gives me loads of input – whether I want it or not. I usually take it.

A SHORT GLOSSARY

of the more obscure words and phrases used in this novel, for the benefit of those who have never been to Glasgow – and for those who have.

Freens: Friends.

Heid the ball (or baw): A rather dumb person.

Knock yer pan in: Work yourself to exhaustion.

Lintie/Linty: A linnet. 'Up like a linty!' – up early.

Lowse: To finish work.

Morn's morn: Tomorrow morning.

Murder polis: A rowdy, fraught situation.

Pan loaf: To affect a posh accent. A type of bread.

Pig's melt: A nasty, irredeemable person.

Wally close: A beautifully tiled close/entrance.

You'll get yer heid in yer hands tae play wi': You'll be in trouble.

The folk in this book lived up a tenement close at 18 Dalbeattie Street, Maryhill, Glasgow, NW. Just north of Queens Cross.

It is a work of fiction. That should mean that these people and their street never existed. Yet I knew them.

And if you were around in the '40s and '50s, so did you . . .

THE RESIDENTS OF 18 DALBEATTIE STREET IN THE YEAR 1949

'The Top Landing'

Archie CAMERON, aged 32.
Ella CAMERON, aged 30.
Archie jnr., aged 9.
Katherine, aged 3.
Archie served in Paras during Second World War. Captured at Arnhem 1944. Metal turner by trade.

Donald McNEIL, aged 66.
A bachelor. Born on the Isle of Barra. Served in France in First World War. Retired. Formerly worked for the Clyde Navigation Trust.

Agnes DALRYMPLE, aged 41.
Shop assistant at the City Bakeries. Was in the Land Army during the Second World War.

'Two Up'

Richard SNEDDON, aged 33.
Marjorie SNEDDON, aged 35.
Richard is a clerk in Glasgow Corporation Rents Department. Marjorie works part-time at the Fairy Dyes Company.

Billy McLAREN, aged 35.
Drena McLAREN, aged 29.
Billy jnr., aged 9.
Billy was captured at Dunkirk in 1940. Spent 5 years as a POW. He is a painter and decorator.

James PENTLAND, aged 49.
Irene PENTLAND, aged 51.
Brother and sister. Both unmarried. James works at N.B. Loco in Springburn. Irene keeps house for her brother.

'One Up'

Dennis O'MALLEY, aged 48.
Teresa O'MALLEY, aged 46.
Rhea, aged 21.
Siobhan, aged 17.
Dennis and Teresa are southern Irish. Lived in Glasgow since 1920s. Dennis is a brickie's labourer.

'Granny' THOMSON, aged 74.
Long a widow. Everybody comes to Granny for advice. The 'wise woman' of the close. She has lived there since 1910.

Andrew McDERMOT, aged 63.
Lena McDERMOT, aged 63.
Andrew served in World War One in the Highland Light Infantry. Have a grown-up son and two daughters. All married and living in city.

The Close

Bert ARMSTRONG, aged 29.
Irma ARMSTRONG, aged 22.
Bert is from Newcastle. Served in Durham Light Infantry during war. Irma is German. Bert is a taxi driver.

George LOCKERBIE, aged 32.
Joan LOCKERBIE, aged 31.
Both served in RAF during war. Joan is English. George works in factory assembling prefabs.

Samuel STEWART, aged 47.
Mary STEWART, aged 49.
Robert, aged 21.
Samuel built Spitfires during war. Now works at Singer's factory. Robert is apprentice at Beardmore's Motor Works.

CHAPTER ONE

A Night for Staying In

A late September evening in 1949. In the countryside just beyond Glasgow's city boundary, a fine mist is beginning to come down. The kind that most folk would look on as being part of that 'season of mellow fruitfulness'. A few miles away, inside the city, the same low pressure and damp air is causing the smoke from a few hundred thousand coal fires to swirl down from the tenement chimneys and mix with this mist. By half past eight, it has turned it into a blanket of throat-catching green fog. A peasouper. The first this year.

The further into town you travel, the worse it becomes. Beams of light from the tall lamp standards barely reach to the pavements. Shop lights shining out of windows become diffused, illuminating the fog and making it worse. Vehicles find their headlights totally inadequate as they bounce off it, seeming to turn it into a solid wall. With visibility down to six feet, Glasgow's motorists do what they always do at this time of year – follow the trams. Long streams of cars, buses and lorries trail back behind every one. Unable to overtake because of the limited distance they can see, they wait patiently as their tram stops every hundred yards or so to drop off or pick up passengers. Almost certainly, tomorrow's newspapers will carry their annual news items on motorists who blindly follow trams all the way back to their depot – right into the sheds.

Dalbeattie Street in Maryhill lies fog-bound like every other street in the city tonight. If it was possible to see the length of it, it would appear to be deserted. The residents of number 18 are staying close to their fires. As coal is rationed, these fires aren't very big. Some enterprising lads were round this afternoon, twice, selling coal briquettes from a horse and cart. Everybody at number 18 bought a large bag of these nuggets of compressed coal dust to supplement the meagre ration of one bag of coal per week.

In each of the twelve houses that make up this close, some of the acrid fog has seeped in through gaps in window frames and underneath doors. Every kitchen has a haze round the main light which hangs from the centre of its ceiling. As they sit, hugging the range, most folk listen to the wireless; perhaps a play or a variety programme. A few are absorbed in books borrowed from the Maryhill Library up at Gairbraid Avenue. Children read, for the second or third time, this week's *Beano* or *Dandy*.

Because it's such a dismal night, attendances are down at local cinemas like the Roxy, the Star and the Blythswood. Customers are few and far between in nearby pubs and snooker halls. It is, most definitely, 'a night for goin' naewhere'.

CHAPTER TWO

Purely for Pleasure

It is two nights later. A Saturday evening in the second-storey flat of Richard and Marjorie Sneddon at 18 Dalbeattie Street. If, as is unlikely, a stranger was invited to enter their home, there is no doubt he, or she, would be impressed by this well-furnished room and kitchen, and by the Sneddons. It is the most stylish of the twelve flats that make up this typical Glasgow close. The good impression won't last long if the visitor has any contact with their neighbours.

None of the women who live at number 18 are envious of Marjorie and her nice home. Not if it comes with Richard Sneddon. All the other residents up this close know he is a nasty piece of work who treats his wife badly. No one, however, is aware of just how much he enjoys it.

It has just gone eight p.m. The Sneddons sit at their small dining table. As they eat dinner they listen to the radio. *Variety Bandbox* is on. The guest comedian is Vic Oliver. Marjorie spent forty minutes this afternoon queuing at McGregor's, the fishmonger on the Maryhill Road, to get the nice piece of cod they are eating. The prospect of a pleasant evening lies ahead. Then Marjorie spoils it. Her timing couldn't be worse. Vic Oliver is in the middle of an amusing anecdote. As Richard eats and listens he makes contented snuffling noises now and again. The crux of the tale is imminent when Marjorie's fork slips from her fingers and clatters on to her plate. 'Oh! I'm sorry, Rich—'

'You stupid fucking bitch!' With his open right hand, Richard Sneddon slaps his wife hard across the face. 'Of aw' the fucking times tae drop your fork you huv tae drop it just as a comedian's aboot tae reach his punchline!' In spite of her fright, Marjorie has noticed he's forgetting to talk with his posh accent. She holds a hand to her cheek. Although she's used to being hit, the suddenness has shocked her. She sits very still, hoping he won't hit her again. Once usually isn't enough.

'Ah'll bet you fucking did that on purpose.' She can tell he's working himself up again; knows she'll almost certainly get another one. Sneddon looks at her. He likes to see the fright on her face. He begins to get an erection. Should he fuck her? Och no. There isn't time. *Saturday Night Theatre* is on soon. He'll wait till later. 'Right, you! Get yerself tae bed oot o' my sight. There's a play oan next. I don't want ye spoiling that too, yah dozy hoor. Go on, fuck off!'

'Will I do the dishes first, Richard?'

'What have Ah just told ye? Get oot o' ma sight!' He half rises to his feet. Marjorie stiffens in expectation. He feints with his left, then gives her another hard slap with his right as she leaves herself open. He feels pleasure at how clever that was. Marjorie is too frightened for tears.

She rises from the table, takes the key for the shared lavatory on the landing, and leaves the flat. Upon her return she hangs the key back on its hook, quietly closes the kitchen door and walks along the short lobby to the bedroom. Only after she has shut its door do the tears start. They stream down her face as she undresses. She looks through the net curtains of their second-storey window into the street. Across the way one or two folk have their lights on but haven't yet pulled their blinds, or in some cases their blackout curtains, even though it's four years since the war ended. From the shadows of the bedroom she watches in envy as people enjoy their evening: short conversations, laughter now and again; children in pyjamas wander in and out the room or sit playing at the table. What would things be like if Richard and I had children? Would he hit me in front of them? Probably. He enjoys it. Never, ever apologises. It's always my fault.

She steps nearer to the window, looks down into the street. It's almost dark. The tall green lamp standards cast pools of light on to road and pavement. Three women stand outside one of the closes, obviously enjoying a good blether, and the sultry weather. There are regular hoots of laughter. I'll bet they're talking about men, Marjorie thinks. I never have conversations like that with the neighbours. Richard wouldn't like it. Not with him working at the Corporation Rents Department. Goes to work in a suit, thinks he's a cut above everybody else in the close. In the street. We have to talk proper. His older brother, Alan, didn't half take the mickey out of him last time we visited his parents . . .

'Hey, Ma. Are you sure he belongs tae us? Ye did'nae find him under a bush in Hillhead by any chance?' Alan turns to Richard. 'Where dae ye get aw' this talking pan loaf? We were brought up in Parkheid – no' Park Lane!'

Richard bristles. 'There's nothing wrong with trying to better yourself, Alan. Speaking properly is part of that.'

'Naebody's bothered aboot your pronunciation, Richard. But you don't leave it at that. You've started putting oan this refained Kelvinside accent. It's so phoney. You weren't brought up tae talk like that – and you make poor Marjorie dae it as well.' He turns towards her. 'But you keep forgettin' noo and again, don't ye, hen?'

Marjorie recalls how embarrassed she felt as everybody looked at her. Alan was spot on. She hates being pressured into speaking with this acquired accent; often gives the show away when she becomes enthusiastic about something – and falls back into Glasgow vernacular. She sighs. Richard is obsessed with us bettering ourselves. Now he says he isn't happy with my part-time job in the office at the Fairy Dyes factory . . .

'It's an office job at one of the big companies down the town you should be looking for.'

'But it's only a couple of tram stops away, Richard. There are practically no fares. If the weather's good I just walk down to Trossachs Street. And old Mrs Grant will be retiring next year, so I should get the chance to go full time. I'll be making nearly four pounds a week!'

She closes the curtains, switches on the bedside light and climbs into bed. The sound of the radio drifts through from the kitchen now and again. Her tears have dried. She finds her place in her book and begins to read. She's really enjoying *The Third Man*. They went to the Blythswood Cinema down the Maryhill Road to see the film a while back. It was very good: Orson Welles, Joseph Cotton and – what's his name? Was In *Brief Encounter*. Aye, Trevor Howard. That was a lovely film. Too soppy for Richard. Still, he must have enjoyed Celia Johnson in it. Talked very cut glass, she did. It's a marvel she got through the picture without cutting herself.

She hears movement from the kitchen, then his footsteps as he comes into the lobby, opens the outside door and descends the short flight of stairs to the half-landing to make a final visit to the lavatory. She puts the book down and switches the light off. Not that it will make any difference. God! How I hate him. But what can I do? My mother would be delighted if I left him and came back home. But she'd never let me forget it. She disliked him right from the start. Marjorie sighs. Ma was bloody right. It would be so humiliating if I left him. And it would take years to get a divorce. Then imagine having to state in open court what he makes me do . . . The front door is banged shut, the big key turned. She turns so as her back is to the room door. Not that that'll stop him.

Richard Sneddon comes into the bedroom, switches the main light on. She feels a pang of fear in her stomach. He quickly undresses, then climbs on to the bed, kneels astride her. 'C'mon, don't lie there kidding on you're sleeping.' He forcibly turns her over so she lies on her back.

'Mmmm?' She pretends to be coming awake. Knows she's just delaying the inevitable. She opens her eyes, looks up at his kneeling figure.

'I'll teach you to spoil my programme. Open your fucking mouth.'

CHAPTER THREE

A Day of Rest

Donald McNeil steps out of the close at 18 Dalbeattie Street and heads for Ken's, the newsagent's. When he reaches the corner shop he stops for a moment, looks up and down the almost deserted Maryhill Road. The shops are all locked and shuttered except for a few newsagents, and they only open until noon. He loves Glasgow Sundays.

The bell above the door gives its usual welcoming 'ding' as he enters. Ken is cutting the string round a bundle of *Sunday Pictorials*. 'Good morning, Mr McNeil. How are ye this fine morning?'

'Chust grand,' says Donald in his soft Highland brogue. 'I'll have my usual two, Ken.' The newsagent takes a *Sunday Post* and a *Sunday Mail* from adjoining bundles – the two largest. The bell gives another 'ding'. Donald turns to see who's coming in. The smile leaves his face when he recognises the tall figure of Richard Sneddon. Donald lives on the landing above him. 'Right, I will be on my way, Ken.' He makes no acknowledgement of his neighbour as he exits.

Outside, Donald pauses again on the corner, takes a few

deep breaths of relatively fresh air. Once more he looks along the length of the Maryhill Road. Just four folk to be seen, three women and one man, going to or coming from a newsagent further along the way. In the distance a solitary tram, en route from Airdrie, makes its indolent Sunday-service way up the incline from Queens Cross. What a contrast with the other days of the week: trams, lorries, cars and the occasional bus going to or coming from the city, pavements thronged with folk – mostly women with bairns in tow – shopping for the rations.

The sun beats down, warming the walls of the tenements opposite, and a slight movement catches his eye as an eddy of breeze breathes momentary life into a discarded sheet of newspaper, causing it to glide a few yards along the pavement. Behind him the shop bell sounds again. That will be that Sneddon man.

Och, it's too nice to go straight back home. Donald sets off down the road at a good pace, arms swinging. He passes one of the women coming from the other newsagent. Like most housewives who go for the papers on a Sunday morning, she has also bought a bottle of Irn Bru. Three decades of living in Glasgow since leaving the Isle of Barra have taught him to read the signs. At this moment, back in her house, her husband will be lying in the recess bed 'at death's door', suffering from a near-terminal hangover. There is only one remedy that can pull him back from the brink – two Askit Powders washed down with copious draughts of the Irn Bru. Neat. As the woman enters her close, Donald gives a slight shake of his head. These Glasgow boys. Until he retired last year he'd worked with them for thirty years at the Clyde Navigation Trust. Oh, fine fellows. But the drink. Man, man, they guzzle down the beer and the whisky – blended whisky at that – as quick as they can on a Saturday night. Got to get as much into themselves as they can before the pubs shut at nine thirty. He contrasts that with his own Saturday nights at the Gaelic Speakers Club in Windsor Terrace. A couple of drams of Laphroaig single malt. Oh! You can taste the peat. Then an entire evening conversing with old friends in the Gaelic, and even though he doesn't smoke, the aroma of good cigars adding to the ambience of the wood-panelled, book-lined lounge. Now that is how a man should take his pleasures. Civilised.

Donald has walked almost as far as Queens Cross when he decides to turn and head back home. It's ten past twelve. Now that the paper shops have closed, the Maryhill Road is deserted. As he's about to retrace his steps, a number 11 tram hoves into view. It's an old tram. An 'auld caur', as Glasgow folk call them to differentiate them from the streamlined 'new caurs' which appeared in the late 1930s. A bunch of youngsters have commandeered the upstairs front cubicle, directly above the driver's compartment. They've closed the sliding door, isolating themselves from the other passengers. One of the boys is in the process of lowering the railway-carriage-type front window by its leather strap. Donald smiles. They'll be heading out to Mulguy to play amongst grassy fields and trees for a few hours. Later on, perhaps, they'll draw sweet water from the Allender to boil on a makeshift fire and brew tea. He sighs as he remembers such boyhood days on Barra. By 1918, three of his pals had perished in the trenches of the Western Front. So how could I serve four years in the Gordon Highlanders and never get a scratch? And finish up with a DCM – though no one knows about it. Never wear it.

Not even on Armistice Day. Och, it's all in the past. Been another war since my day. Aye, another 'war to end all wars'! Hah!

Arms swinging, perhaps more than before, Donald heads back the way he came. What a pity there are not two Sundays in a week. He decides to get even more exercise by taking a longer route. He turns left into Blairatholl Street, walks along to its end then turns right into the far end of Dalbeattie Street. Some boys are having a kick-around with a ball in the middle of the road. Three girls, barely school age, fuss around a doll's pram. One wears an old pair of her mother's high heels. She teeters about, scliffing the shoes along the pavement so as not to step out of them. As he passes by, he catches a snatch of conversation . . .

'Huv ye been for your messages yet, Mrs Telfer?'

'Naw, Ah'm gonny gie the house a good clean before Ah go tae the shops, Mrs Rafferty.'

'Ah did mine yesterday, so Ah did. Ah might go tae the pictures the night. Ah huv'nae been . . .'

When he reaches number 18, he takes the six flights of stairs up to his top-floor single-end with ease. There you are. He may be sixty-six, but a lot of young fellows would be hard put to match that. Donald's door is the middle of the three on the landing. As he climbs the last flight, he finds the right-hand door is open. Agnes Dalrymple kneels on a cushion placed on top of her doormat. She is chopping sticks. Donald always thinks of her as 'the spinster'.

'Good morn— no, good afternoon, Miss Dalrymple.'

Agnes stops work, sits back on her heels. Reaches into the pocket of her floral-patterned peenie for an embroidered hankie. Dabs her nose. 'Donald McNeil, if you're no' gonny call me Agnes, Ah'm gonny start calling you Mister McNeil!'

'Och! Now you know I am always forgetting. It's a terrible memory I have. Anyway, how were things at the City Bakeries yesterday?'

'Oh! Murder polis, so it was! Run off oor feet we were. Jist non-stop the whole day.'

'It's a grand morning out there, Agnes. I've chust had a good walk to myself. Blew away the cobwebs. You should take yourself for a wee walk later on.'

'Aye, ye hav'nae half been for a good donner. Ah heard ye go oot for your papers. You've been away for an hour or more.'

'Yes. And it's ready for a bit breakfast I am.' As he speaks, Donald inserts his Yale key into the lock. 'I'll see you later, Miss, ah, Agnes.'

He steps into the small lobby of his single-end and gently closes the door. 'Ahhh!' He opens the inner door and looks into his one room. The early-afternoon sun slants in at an angle through the double windows. Dust motes float in its beams. It won't be long until he loses the sun. He walks over to the table and places the two newspapers on the red chenille cover, then hangs his jacket on a hook in the lobby. He closes the inner door behind him. Agnes is still chopping her sticks. Now and again there's a metallic 'clang' as she lays the steel-headed axe on the slate landing. After filling the kettle at the solitary brass tap, Donald pauses for a moment to enjoy the warmth of the sun through the windows. He lights a gas ring. The walk has keened his appetite. A couple of scrambled eggs, I think. He reaches a hand into the chipped enamel bread bin, squeezes a Milanda Bakeries plain loaf through its greaseproof wrapper. Not as soft as yesterday. Och, it'll toast.

His good cheer evaporates as the sound of a raised voice drifts up from the Sneddons' flat. That bloody man is starting on that poor woman again. So full of himself. Sneddon's voice increases in volume, then stops as his wife cries out. 'Bastard!' says Donald. It's common knowledge in the close that he mistreats her. Poor lassie.

He walks over to the sideboard and switches on the Pye radio that stands on it. It's already tuned to the Third Programme. While the valves warm up there comes another brief cry from downstairs. Donald taps a foot in impatience. At last the music swells out from the large, wooden-cased receiver: 'Che gelida manina' from Puccini's *La Bohème*. Soon it takes him away from his single room on the top floor at 18 Dalbeattie Street. Banishes thoughts of man's inhumanity to man. And woman.

CHAPTER FOUR

Over the Top

Everything is sharp and clear. The colour of the stones embedded in the wall of the trench, the pitter-patter of dried earth trickling down from the parapet as he leans on it to look across no-man's-land. The two-hour bombardment of the German lines has just stopped. Ears still pop, nerves jangle. Andrew McDermot sighs. How many times can you go over the top before your number comes up? The best you can hope for is you'll get a 'Blighty one'. Preferably in the leg. Missing the bone. Then you'll be out of it all: a hospital in southern England. Clean sheets, no more lice. Bonny nurses.

'Have a gasper.' Billy Strang holds out his battered baccy tin. As Andrew takes one, he glances at his best pal. Is he as calm as he looks? Andrew flicks his trench lighter, watches the shower of sparks from the flint ignite the petrol-soaked wick, feels the touch of Billy's mud-caked hands as he cups them round his to protect the delicate flame while he lights his fag. They joined the HLI on the same day at Maryhill Barracks. September 1914.

Andrew looks along the trench at the long row of waiting men. Sergeant Murray seems to be raring to go. Anybody who's keen to start walking into machine-gun fire must be fucking mental. The officers stop looking at their watches, then, in unison, start blowing whistles.

'C'mon, lads! Up and at the bastards!' bawls Murray.

Andrew and Billy, side by side, clamber out of the trench. Andrew feels himself tense as he clears the parapet. Whuzzz! Whuzzz! Whuzzz! The bullets flying past sound like bees heading somewhere, no time to stop. Phitt! Phitt! Phitt! They begin to kick up earth all around him. Bastards are getting the range, coming nearer . . .

'Hah!' Andrew sits up in the recess bed. He's sticky with sweat. Oh, thank Christ! Thank Christ! It was jist that dream. Oh! Thank God.

Lena is hanging socks on the brass rail under the mantel-piece. 'Have ye been havin' yer dream, Andra?'

He remains sitting up. Stares at the wall at the foot of the bed. It's always so vivid. Even now it hasn't quite left him. He can still feel the touch of Billy's hands, the dried mud. It's only two minutes since he was with him. Naw it is'nae. He works it out. It's thirty-three years.

'The kettle's boiling. Do ye want a mug o' tea?' asks Lena.

'Aye.' His throat is dry. 'Aye, Ah would'nae mind, hen.'

A small table stands against the wall between the recess bed and the room door. He turns on his side, reaches for his baccy tin. Lena busies herself masking the tea. Their three grown-up children, Andy, Sheena and Maisie, are all married and living in other districts in the city. Lena and Andrew could sleep in the empty bedroom if they wanted. But they don't. They like the kitchen. Especially in winter. It's nice to snuggle up together in the recess bed on a bitter cold night. Lie in the dark, talking, while the dying fire in the range flickers on to walls, ceiling, and the washing that hangs from the pulley.

'Here's your tea, Andra.' Lena stands holding the pint mug until her man props himself up on two pillows. She likes the smell of the Old Holborn tobacco he uses to roll his cigarettes. 'Will Ah dae ye a bacon sannie and an egg yin, tae?'

'That wid be great.'

'Right. Ah'll put the gas on a wee peep while Ah go doon tae Ken's for the papers.'

'Aye, and make sure it is a wee peep, jist in case ye come back and find me – and the bacon – done tae a crisp!'

'Will Ah jist get the usual two?'

'Aye, the *Sunday Post* and the *Whore's Gazette*, hen.'

Lena sniffs. 'And mind, if ye read anything in that *News o' the World* that gets ye randy, ye need'nae think you're gonny have me hoppin' intae bed wi' ye. Far too auld for that game nooadays.'

Andrew looks fondly at his wife. 'Who are ye kidding? You're no' averse tae a wee bit slap and tickle noo and again.'

She gives another sniff. 'Aye, but there's a time and place.'

'And tell me,' says Andrew, 'whit better time or place is there than a Sunday morn'?' He laughs. 'Remember when the weans were wee? We'd jist be enjoying oorselves when, withoot fail, the door would open and wee faces start appearing. Usually when Ah was jist approaching the vinegar strokes!'

'Oh! Andra McDermot, you're turning intae a dirty auld man so ye are!'

'Whit are ye blushing for?' He begins to laugh heartily.

'We've been merried for thirty years. Anywye, Ah was alwiz a dirty young man – so noo Ah'm a dirty auld man. Ah grew up.' He watches as Lena puts her coat on then picks up her purse and brown Rexine shopping bag. He pulls the bed covers to one side, pats the sheet covering the mattress. 'Don't be long, darlin'. Ah don't think Ah'll be needing any inspiration fae the *Whore's Gazette* this morning.'

'Ah'm away. It's no' the papers Ah should be going for – it's the doctor. For you!'

As she steps on to the landing and closes the front door behind her, Lena is pleased to find there's no one on the stairs. She feels certain her cheeks must be burning.

Andrew stubs out the last of his cigarette, leans against the pillows. No, it's no good. Ah'll have tae go. He rises, puts his bare feet into his shoes, then walks into the small lobby. He puts his overcoat on over his pyjamas, presses an ear to the front door. Silence. He turns the Yale lock, remembers to put the snib on so as not to lock himself out. He slowly turns the handle on the big, old-fashioned main lock, then peers out on to the landing. All is quiet. He takes the lavvy key off its hook then, on tiptoe, makes his way down the short flight of stairs to the half-landing. He chaps the door with the key. 'Anybody in?' No answer. Great. He quickly lets himself in, bolts the door, raises the seat. Ahhhh! If a bean's a bean – what's a pee? A sweet relief! He flushes the toilet. Waits until the cistern has refilled and quiet descends. He opens the door a fraction. Nobody about. Smashing. He is just three steps away from doing a clear run when the middle door on his landing opens and Granny Thomson emerges from her single-end. 'Oh, hello, Andra. It looks like a grand mornin' oot there. Have ye jist been for a wee walk?'

'Naw. Ah've, eh, jist been paying a visit.' He nods in the general direction.

She looks down, sees the pyjama trousers under the coat. 'Oh, goodness me, aye. You'll hardly have been for a wee donner dressed like that. You should get yerself yin o' these.' She holds up a china chamber pot. 'Very convenient during the night, let me tell ye.' She gives him a playful dig with her elbow. 'As long as ye dinnae miss in the dark!'

'Aye, Ah'll bet ye it is, Granny.' He watches as she takes hold of the banister rail with her right hand and carefully makes her way down to the lavatory, chuckling all the while. He shakes his head. 'You're an awfy wumman, Granny Thomson.'

CHAPTER FIVE

A Delight in Small Things

Irene Pentland empties the soapy water down the sink, then rinses the enamel basin under the tap. The wooden draining board and windowsill are wiped dry with the dishcloth – one of brother James's old cotton semmits – then that in its turn is wrung out and hung over the edge of the sink. She glances at the clock on the mantelpiece. Ten to ten. Och, it's time for a wee cuppa. Then I'll get a few things rinsed through. Then round tae the Maryhill Road for the rations. The sun blazes down into the back courts. She raises the bottom of one of the two windows about six inches; the yellow linen curtains move lazily in the warm air. The sound of bairns playing drifts up. They must be on holiday. She loves mornings like this. Once she gets James off to work at the locomotive works in Springburn, the house is hers.

As usual it's the boys who are making most of the noise. But rising above their cries come the rhythmic voices of the girls as they play 'ropes' while singing one of their many songs.

Down in the valley where the green grass grows,
There sat Margaret, sweet as a rose.

Irene moves the damp dishcloth to the right, then leans on the draining board so as to look down into the back court. As two girls swing a length of clothesline, wee Margaret Hutchinson from number 20 concentrates on her skipping. Another four girls wait their turn. They all join in.

She sang, she sang, she sang so sweet.
Along came James Murray and kissed her on the cheek.

The girls begin to giggle. 'He's *no'* ma boyfriend!' protests Margaret, without missing a skip. 'Aye he is!' shouts someone. The girls are convulsed with laughter.

How many kisses did she get?
One, two, three, four . . .

The count reaches twenty-three before Margaret mistimes a jump and the rope catches on her ankle. She steps away from the centre. The inert rope lies on the ground. Without a word, Margaret relieves Jessie Brown at one end. Jessie replaces her in the middle.

'Eeeeh! Imagine kissin' James Murray twenty-three times,' says someone.

'Huh! Ah wid'nae kiss James Murray wan time, never mind twenty-three. Even if it wiz his birthday. So there!' Margaret begins to swing the rope. There is a collective 'Ooooh!' from the rest of the girls.

As she looks down from her second-storey window, Irene

smiles. Then sighs. It would've been nice to have married and had a bairn. A wee lassie. Aye, well, it never happened. And at fifty-one it never will. She gives the draining board a wipe it doesn't need. Looks out of the window again. From up here in Dalbeattie Street she can see along the back of one side of Cheviot Street. Four back courts, divided by iron railings, stretch the length of it. Each one is allocated to a close and the families who live up it; a mixture of back green and playground. A few boys have climbed up on to one of the wash houses. This is their castle and they are valiantly trying to repel invaders. Imaginary sword fights are going on as their foes, who have clambered up the middens at either end, engage them in battle. Now and again Irene catches some of the dialogue . . .

'You're deid! Ah've stabbed ye three times in the heart!'

'Ah'm wearin' armour, so it's no' gettin' through.'

'Gonny stoap firing bullets, they did'nae huv six-shooters in them days, ya eegit! They jist hud yon auld flintlock things that only fired wan bullet at a time.'

'Oh!'

Irene remembers. There was a pirate film on at the Roxy last week. That'll be the cause. They'll all have been to the matinee on Saturday. Who was in it? Aye. Tyrone Power. She looks along to the furthest of the back courts. Smoke rises straight up in the air from a wash-house chimney. Old Mrs Aitken from 16 Cheviot is stretching her clothes rope from a hook on the wall of the wash house to the metal pole in the middle of the grassy green. Irene watches as she winds it time and time again round the hooks at the top of the pole. Jeez-oh! she thinks. Ah'll bet when they're tying up the *Queen Mary* they don't wind the rope that many times roond a bollard. Anyway. Better get them few things rinsed through. She reaches down to open the door to the narrow cupboard under the boxed-in sink. On its small shelf stands a tin of Brasso, a ball of steel wool, emery paper, shoe brushes and a tin of Cherry Blossom boot polish. On the cupboard floor lie a pair of pliers and two screwdrivers. Behind them, at the back, are the items used every three weeks when it's Irene's turn for the stairs – a couple of floor cloths, a block of pipe clay, a cake of Sunlight washing soap, and a scrubbing brush. Not that *she* does them nowadays. Since her knees became too painful to kneel on for any length of time, James told her to get Mrs Geoghan from Rothesay Street to come and do them when it's her turn. Aye, it's two shillings well spent. Irene bends down to look in the cupboard, then reaches in for the brightly coloured box of Oxydol soap powder. She shakes the detergent into the water, swirling her hand through it to help it dissolve. A satisfactory lather is created.

She is almost ready to start when her outside door is knocked, then opened. 'It's jist me!' Irene turns to watch as the kitchen door opens to reveal Drena McLaren, her next-door neighbour.

'Aye, in ye come. Ah'll put the kettle oan.' She places the box of Oxydol on the draining board. Although Drena is twenty-two years younger than her, Irene gets on well with her neighbour and her husband, Billy. She also takes a great interest in their son, William junior. Since childhood he's called her Auntie Irene.

As she brews the tea, Irene chatters away. 'Ah've jist been watching auld Mrs Aitken starting tae dae her washing. Ah don't know why she diz'nae go tae the steamie. Aw' that bother when ye want tae use the wash hoose: lighting the fire under the boiler, waiting till the watter boils. Jist a shilling for the public wash hoose would save her aw that palaver.'

'That's probably why she does it – tae save a shilling.' Drena is sitting at the table. She pours some milk into her cup. 'Anywye, somebody of Mrs Aitken's age. They're in the habit of using the wash hoose. It diz'nae bother them.'

'Aye, you're probably right. And she'll no' have that much washing tae dae, anywye.' Irene stirs the freshly brewed tea, puts the lid on the pot then places it on the mat in the centre of the table. 'We'll let that mask for a wee minute. Dae ye fancy a custard tart, Drena?'

'Oh, that wid be nice.'

'Is your William in the hoose?'

'Naw. He's playing oot the back.'

Irene walks over to the windows and opens one wide. She spots him. 'William! William!'

'Aye, Auntie Irene?' The duel to the death he's involved in is suspended for the moment. He feels a little tingle of anticipation in his stomach. If she wants him to go a message for her, he knows it's a guaranteed threepenny bit.

'Go and get yer mammy and me a couple o' custard tarts oot the Scotia, will ye, son? Ah'll throw ye doon the money.'

'Aye.' He stands looking up at the window. Irene reappears. A two-shilling piece, folded in a torn piece of last night's *Evening Times*, lands in the back court.

'Don't be long, son. Ah've masked the tea.' William sprints through his close and hares across to the shop that is attached to the Scotia bakehouse. Minutes later he knocks, then opens, Auntie Irene's door. Feeling proud of himself, he enters the kitchen holding a cream-coloured paper bag at arm's length. Quite out of breath, he anticipates what will come next. Irene turns to Drena. 'Eeeeh! There is'nae a laddie in this street can run a message faster than your William. Jesse Owens could'nae dae it quicker – and he's got three gold medals!' William basks in the praise. But not for long.

'Huh! Ah don't get the same speedy service when he goes a message fur me. And there's alwiz plenty moanin' beforehand!' William gives his mother a dirty look. His face lights up again, though, when Auntie Irene, as expected, takes a threepenny bit from her change and presses it into his hand.

'Right, away and play wi' yer pals, William,' says Drena. 'And remember – don't stray from the street or back court unless Ah know where you're going. You're warned!'

'Ah'll no'. We're huving good fun oot the back playing pirates. Thanks, Auntie Irene.' Threepence richer, William rushes off, anxious to get back to his pals.

Drena puts her cup down. Looks at her friend. 'That bugger through the wall from us wiz hitting her again last night. Could hear it plain as day.'

'Dae ye think she'll ever dae anything aboot it? It's been going oan fur years.'

'Huh! How many times have we hud this conversation, Irene? Her and him huv set themselves up as being a cut above the rest of us. If she was tae get the polis tae him it wid aw' come oot, widn't it? Be a right showing-up. So for the sake o' appearances she lets him get away wi' it.'

Irene draws her shoulders back, sits up straight. 'Well, more fool her! But whit annoys me most aboot him is aw' his bloody airs and graces. He's nothing but a jumped-up rent man, so he is. When folk see him going alang the street they probably think, whit a smart-looking big fella—'

Drena interrupts her. 'Aye, an' little dae they know whit a

bad article he really is.' In unison they both stop and take a sip of tea. Their cups chink back into the saucers as one.

'My Billy gets fair mad when he hears him gettin' oan tae her,' says Drena. 'Especially when we hear a slap, then her greetin'. A couple of times Ah've had tae stop him going and knockin' oan their door. "Bloody conchie!" he'll say. "Made sure he never seen an angry German, but he's a big tough lad when it comes tae knockin' a wumman aboot!" Ah jist hope Billy never starts oan him, 'cause he'll forget tae stop!'

Irene laughs. 'Aye, and ye know whit would happen if he did, dain't ye? Your Billy would be the one that would get intae trouble wi' the polis. She'd swear blind that her man never touched her. So for God's sake, Drena, tell Billy no' tae get involved. S'no' worth it.'

CHAPTER SIX

For You the War is Over!

'So fuck that for a game of sodjers!' Archie Cameron stands, stripped to the waist, washing himself at the kitchen sink. Ella, his wife, kneels by the range.

'Dae you huv tae use that language in the hoose? The weans will hear ye through in that room.' As she speaks, little avalanches of fine ash fall from the shovel she's holding. 'See whit you're making me dae. There's bloody stoor everywhere!' She delicately tips the ash from the shovel into an open newspaper lying on the floor. 'Anywye, whit are ye moaning aboot?'

Archie is in the middle of having a good slunge at the sink. He's already splashed water under his oxters and now, using both hands, he's rinsing his face in cold water from the tap. 'Whit am Ah oan aboot?' he splutters. 'Ah jist telt ye two minutes ago. Wur ye no' listening? Jesus wept! Right, Ah'll try again. The foreman's wantin' me tae go oan piecework. The more Ah produce, the more Ah earn. Oan paper it sounds good – but in practice it is'nae. The valves Ah'm turning oot at the minute huv tae be produced tae a fine tolerance. If Ah go oan piecework Ah'll be pushed tae get the same money Ah'm making at the minute – never mind earn any bonus.' As he speaks, he has turned to face Ella.

She shakes her head. 'Will ye jist look at the state o' that linoleum. You're drippin' watter everywhere. Ah hope ye intend tae wipe that flair when you're done.'

'It's aw'right. Jist a couple o' drops.'

'Couple o' drops!' exclaims Ella. 'There's mair watter lying therr than there is in the Boating Loch doon the Great Western Road!'

Archie is about to reply, but at this moment the kitchen door opens. He and Ella turn to watch as three-year-old Katherine, dummy in mouth, makes her entrance. Still sleepy-eyed, she pauses in expectation of her usual big welcome.

'Hello, darlin'. Have ye had a nice wee sleep?' asks Ella.

'Uh-huh.'

'It's ma wee princess! Come and gie yer daddy a cuddle, hen.' Archie gives himself a last quick rub with the towel, then hangs it on the hook at the side of the sink. He squats down, arms outstretched, and sweeps Katherine up into them. He hugs her tightly while smothering her with kisses, then leans back. 'Phew! Somebody's ready tae sit oan her po-po. In fact, Ah think we're mibbe too late. Huv you clonged yer nappy?'

Katherine nods. 'Uh-huh.'

Archie stands her back on the floor, walks over to the recess bed, lifts the valance and reaches underneath for the child's chamber pot. As Katherine sits on it, her parents regard her. 'Is Archie still sleeping, Katherine?'

The ever-present dummy is moved to one side. 'Leadin' comic.'

Archie senior smiles. 'Jist like his faither used tae be. Always got his nose in a comic.' He looks at his daughter. 'Are ye finished, darlin'?' She answers by rising to her feet. 'You see tae her, Ella, while Ah get rid of this doon the lavvy.'

'Jist wait a minute.' Ella reaches for last night's *Evening Citizen* and tears one of the broadsheet's pages into four. When she's finished wiping Katherine, she puts the used paper into the chamber pot. Archie lifts it up. 'Oh, pooh! Whit an awfy smell. Quick! Where's the lid? Ah cannae stand it. Help!' He pinches his nose between finger and thumb. His wife and daughter go into fits of laughter as he staggers toward where the lavatory key hangs from a nail in the door jamb.

As Archie emerges from his top-floor flat, Donald McNeil, in shirtsleeves and braces, steps out of his door. 'Oh, good morning, Archie.'

'Mornin', Donald. Ah'm jist going tae empty the wean's po. Ah'll only be two seconds, then it's aw' yours.'

'Yes, yes. On you go.' Donald watches his neighbour descend the short flight of stairs to the half-landing, open the toilet door, lift the wooden seat and decant the chamber pot into the Shanks Superior patented toilet bowl. Archie pulls the long chain by its wooden hand grip and is rewarded with the usual strong flush. Leaving the toilet door open, he climbs back up the stairs.

'Therr ye are, Donald. It's aw' yours.'

As Archie rinses the po at the kitchen sink, Ella, still carrying Katherine, walks over to the sideboard and clicks on the Ecko radio. While the valves warm up, she turns the pointer from the Scottish Home Service to the Light Programme. Perry Como singing 'A – You're Adorable' swells out from the Bakelite set and fills the room. 'Aw! Ah love this, Archie.' She begins to sing along, then to dance round the small kitchen with Katherine held in her arms. 'Will we huv a wee dance, hen?' At thirty years of age, Ella still misses going to the dancing.

'It's a good job Ah've got you, sweetheart. It's a while since yer auld daddy gave yer mammy a dance.'

'Dancin', is it? Ah'll gie the pair of ye a dance,' announces Archie. He skips over and takes his wife in his arms, their daughter snuggled between them. As they slowly traverse the limited space, Archie looks at his wife and child. Tears come into his eyes. He tries to blink them back.

'What's the matter, darlin'?' Ella looks intently at him.

He clears his throat, tries to keep his voice steady. 'Sometimes when we have wee moments like this, Ah look at you and the weans and, well, it's like pictures flash intae ma mind. Jist like snapshots. From when Ah wiz a POW. They're alwiz from February and March '45. Nae Red Cross parcels gettin' through. And that's when the Germans decide tae start marching us tae the west tae get away fae the Russians. The worst winter for years. You've nae idea, Ella. Bitter cauld, deep snaw, and we're aw' bloody starving. Every day another two or three lads jist gave in, drapped at the side o' the road. Left tae die.' He looks into Ella's eyes. 'There wiz times Ah wondered if Ah'd see you and wee Archie again.' He nods toward Katherine. 'And this wan would never huv been born, would she?'

Ella's eyes also glisten. They move slowly now, not really in time to the music. Move to their own beat, their own mood. The record ends. Their daughter looks up into their faces. She can sense something is going on. Archie kisses his wife. 'Ah know it's four years since it aw' ended, but there's times it seems jist like four months. When Ah look at the three of ye and tell maself it's aw' behind me. Ah survived it. Whenever Ah dae that, you've nae idea how happy Ah feel. Ah could almost burst!'

'Don't you dare, Archie Cameron. Ah jist black-leaded that range yesterday!'

CHAPTER SEVEN

From Far and Wide

You could have taken a bet that Granny Thomson would be the first to spot the newcomers. By three o'clock on that Thursday afternoon she's cleaned her fire out and reset it, swept the floor, dusted everything in sight in her single-end, and put a new mantle into one of the twin gas lights that are fixed either side of her chimney breast. *And* been round to the Maryhill Road for her rations.

She sits at the table with a cup of tea and surveys her tiny kingdom. She could put the wireless on, but the accumulator is getting low. It'll have to be taken round to the cobbler's soon to be charged. It's getting difficult nowadays to find somewhere that still does them. If he stops doing them Ah'll have to buy a portable battery set, she thinks – or rent one from . . . what's their name? Aye, Radio Rentals. Ah couldn'y dae withoot my wireless. Sitting at the range every night, a bright fire chuckling away to itself and the soporific hiss of the gas lights regularly making her doze off as she listens to a good play or a comedy programme: *Happidrome* or *Much Binding in the Marsh*. She likes a laugh.

Granny looks at the clock on the mantelpiece. Ten past three. She reaches out with both hands and smoothes the multicoloured chenille tablecloth. Och, Ah'll have a look oot intae the street. See who's aboot. Granny sits at her window at least twice a day. If the occasional warm summer evening comes along, she's been known to do the treble. From the vantage point of her first-floor flat she can see all of Dalbeattie Street. Along to her left, a hundred yards away, the street ends in a T junction with Maryhill Road. Corporation trams and buses trundle past all day long. Just twelve feet below her, folk make their way up and down the pavement. Many stop for a few minutes to have a wee blether with her – until their necks begin to ache with the continual looking up. As Andrew McDermot next door often says, when he comes along the street and finds her leaning on her windowsill, 'Ah see you're oan sentry duty again, Granny.'

'Aye, somebody's got tae keep an eye oan things.'

And that's how Granny becomes the first to see the new tenants. The Armstrongs.

It is almost four o'clock. She's had a couple of brief conversations with passers-by. Teresa O'Malley, her neighbour on the other side, leaned out of her window to take the air and the two women chatted for a while. Granny enjoys talking to Teresa, and her husband, Dennis. They're both southern Irish, and she never tires of listening to their brogue. Just like Barry Fitzgerald in the pictures. They've lived next door for twenty years. Aye, Ah've got good neighbours. The O'Malleys on one side, and Andrew and Lena McDermot on the other. They've been in their room and kitchen for nearly thirty years. When did Ah move in here? Eeeeh, it diz'nae bear thinking aboot. She works it out: 1910, it was. Thirty-nine years. My God! Where has it all gone? Ah wiz jist thirty-five when Ah came intae the street.

She leans forward on to the cushion on her windowsill, lets it take her weight. She reaches a hand back and adjusts the pillow she's using as a cushion on one of her wooden dining chairs. 'Ah! That's better.' Old bones get sore easily nooadays.

Granny has been thinking it's maybe about time to withdraw into the house when the removal van turns in off the Maryhill Road. It comes slowly along the street. Are they looking at numbers? Could it be? The single-end in the close has been empty this last two months. The big van stops, then cuts across the street at an acute angle; parks with its back doors directly in front of the close. Aye, 18 Dalbeattie Street's gonny get some new tenants. All thoughts of going back into the house are dismissed. Granny plumps up the cushion on the windowsill. She looks at the side of the van – Speedy Removals, 22 Market Street, Newcastle upon Tyne. Michty me! She watches in interest as four men and a slim, pretty young girl climb out of the roomy cab. While the men stretch, yawn, then light cigarettes, the girl looks around her. One of the men reaches into his pocket and produces a key.

'Well, will we gan and tak a look at it?' he says.

'Oh yes,' says the girl. As they approach the close, she looks up. Smiles.

Granny smiles back. 'Hullo! Are you gonny be oor new neighbours?'

The girl looks uncertain. The young man speaks to her. She looks up again. 'Yes, thank you very much. Yes, we are going to live here.'

'And have ye come aw' the wye fae Newcastle?'

Once again the girl looks nonplussed. The young man

answers. 'Aye. We left Newcastle this morning. Ah've got meself a job up here.' He points to the van. 'So we've moved, lock, stock and barrel.' He laughs. 'Though mind, there's not much stock.'

'When you've got yer stuff intae the hoose, just come up tae the first landing and Ah'll make youse a wee cup o'tea. It's the middle door. Thomson's the name.'

'Right ye are, hinny,' he says. 'It'll no' tak us ower lang.' The couple vanish into the close. Granny brings her cushion in off the windowsill, then slides the lower sash down. Don't want them thinking Ah'm hanging oot the windae to see what sort of furniture they've got. She fetches the kettle, fills it at the sink, puts it on the gas ring. With great care she sets the circle of flames at a low peep. The cold tea in the teapot is gently poured down the sink so as not to disturb the mass of tea leaves inside. These are decanted into a galvanised bucket that stands under the sink. Right. It's a wee bit dark. She turns the gas on at the first of the two wall lamps. As it hisses up into the mantle, she strikes a match. Plop! The small tap is turned until the mantle glows with a greenish-white light. Then she lights the second lamp.

Best cups and plates, Ah think. These are taken from the sideboard and the table is quickly set. The biscuit tin is also brought from the sideboard. She removes its lid. Digestives, Rich Tea, a few Gypsy Creams. Aye, plenty of biscuits. Mind, they've been there a while. Ah hope they're no' starting tae go foosty. She selects a Rich Tea, bites into it. Fine. She eats the rest of it.

It is fifty minutes later when a knock on her door wakes Granny up. The gentle hiss of the gas lamps has worked its magic again. The kettle sings softly on the ring. Eeeeh, that's them bairns. Now wide awake, she stiffly hurries to the door, opens it wide. The newcomers stand in the shadows of the landing – the wee Leerie hasn't been round yet to light the gas lamps in close and stairs. 'In youse come. Away through.' She gestures with her hand. The couple, rather shyly, walk through into the room, then stand waiting for her while she shuts the outside door.

'Jist sit yersels at the table. The kettle's biled, Ah'll soon mask the tea. Where's the removal men? Are they no' having a drink o' tea afore they go?'

'They've gone, Mrs Thomson. It's a lang run back tiv Newcastle. Soon as they emptied the van they were off.'

'Och, well. Aw' the mair biscuits for us. Noo, for a start ye can forget the Mrs Thomson. Everybody calls me Granny. Ah've been Granny the last twenty-five years or mair.' She looks around the room, as though about to divulge some great secret. 'Ma first name,' she screws her face up, 'is Isabella. Yeuch! Ah hate it. And even worse, when Ah wiz young Ah always got called Bella. So don't forget,' she points a finger at them in turn, 'it's Granny!'

The couple laugh. The young man speaks. 'Well, I'm a bit like yerself. I'm Albert Armstrong, but I'm glad to say I allus get called Bert. And my wife . . .' He turns toward her, places a hand on top of hers. 'This is Irma. Irma's from Germany.' He pauses; perhaps expecting a reaction. 'Ah met her when Ah was in the army oot there.'

Irma blushes. Granny feels it isn't just because she's meeting someone new. Probably does it every time folk are told she's German.

Irma holds out her hand. 'I am very pleased to meet you, Mrs Thomson.'

Granny wipes her hand down the front of her floral peenie, shakes Irma's. 'And Ah'm pleased tae meet you, hen. Only whit did Ah say aboot Granny?'

'Oh yah. Yes. I'm sorry.' She gives a deferential, very continental, nod of her head. 'Of course, Granny.' She smiles. Obviously relieved the introductions have passed with the minimum of embarrassment.

Granny goes straight to the point. 'Ah would imagine you'll have come across some nasty folk who haven't made ye feel very welcome.'

Bert snorts. 'Aye. And not just here. We got wed three years ago, '46, in Paderborn. Ah was stationed there. Lots of Germans against it, too. The army wasn't pleased either. It's a good job Ah was due oot, otherwise the buggers would've posted me tiv Hong Kong or somewhere t' try an' break us up. Dae ye mind if Ah smoke?' Granny says nothing, just passes him an ashtray. 'Irma's parents were fine with it. One or two uncles weren't.' He lights his cigarette. 'It was just as bad when Ah brought her ower tiv Newcastle.' He pauses, takes a deep draw. 'My older brother, Arthur, was killed a month after D-Day, fighting in Normandy.' He takes another draw on his cigarette. 'Ah can see their point. They lose their oldest son fighting the Germans – and a year after the war's finished, their youngest marries one!'

Granny refills the cups. 'Aye, there's only wan thing that'll cure that problem, son. Time! And,' she leans over and gives Irma a nudge with her forearm, 'Ah think you'll find that when the wee bambinos come along, Bert's mother and faither might find it hard tae resist seeing their grandweans.'

'Aye, we hope you're right,' says Bert, 'and we've already decided that if we have a wee boy, he'll be named Arthur after me brother.'

'Oh, now that wid be nice,' says Granny. 'That wid be a nice thing tae dae.' She scratches her chin. 'Wait a minute. Bambinos is Italian, in't it?' She laughs, turns to Irma. 'Whit's German for weans? Babies?'

Irma blushes again. 'Kinder. Kinder means babies.'

'Aye, when the wee kinders come alang. That'll melt their hearts.'

CHAPTER EIGHT

Blues in the Night

The noise of the midden men doing their rounds on a Thursday night always wakes Agnes Dalrymple. Usually around eleven thirty. Yet she never resents it. Somehow – she doesn't know why – she finds it comforting.

'Ach!' She sits up in the recess bed, throws the covers back and climbs out. The linoleum feels cold under her feet. She slips them into her old plimsolls, then walks round the table to unhook her cloth coat from the back of the door. Not bothering to button it, she wraps it round herself and holds it closed. Scliffing her feet along the floor to keep them in her makeshift slippers, she makes her way towards the windows, the last few glowing coals in the range lighting her way. Holding the coat shut with one hand, she uses the other to tuck the net curtain up behind the wire from which it hangs. Folding her arms, she leans on top of the coal bunker so as to look down into the back courts.

The corporation midden men, wicker baskets on their backs, miner's helmets and lamps on their heads, appear as pools of light as they trek in and out the closes. Three of them stop

at one of the brick-built middens for a moment to light cigarettes. Not for the first time, Agnes looks at their strange
uniform. Strapped to their backs and shoulders are metal-
studded leather protectors – the same type as coalmen wear
when making their deliveries. They all have ties round the
bottom of their trouser legs to stop the rats running up. All
this is topped off by the miner's helmets. They always remind
her of medieval knights.

One of the men nips his cigarette. The red tip lands on
the tarmac amid a shower of sparks, then lies glowing for a
few seconds. Agnes sees him place the stub in his shirt pocket.
Illuminated by his workmates, he reaches into the midden
for one of the square dustbins. Dragging it out, he empties
it into his basket then, enveloped in a cloud of ash, in one
unbroken movement lifts it, swings it behind him and up on
to his back. He pauses for a moment before shrugging it
higher. As he does so, one of the other men reaches deeper
into the midden and begins to drag out the second of the
four galvanised bins. There comes a shout, 'Get the bugger!'
She watches the two unencumbered men stamp their feet in
a frenzied tap dance as a rat, disturbed as it goes about its
nightly business, makes a dash for safety from the back of the
midden. Somehow surviving the gauntlet of tackety boots, it
runs off into the night. The men laugh. Agnes shivers. Horrible
bloody things! Yet she has never, ever seen a rat during the
day when she empties her rubbish into the midden.

Ten minutes later, the men are further along the street. As
the railings dividing the back courts are still in good order,
there are no short cuts through any gaps. They have to progress
in and out the various closes to gain access. Eventually they
pass out of Agnes's sight as they exit into Rothesay Street,

though she can still hear them. She straightens up, pulls the curtain loose and lets it fall back over the window.

Shuffling over to the sideboard, she switches on the lamp that stands there, half shutting her eyes at the instant brightness. When she opens them, the framed photo of an RAF sergeant stares up at her. She looks at that once-so-familiar smile. From distant back courts she can still hear the dull, drum-like boom as the midden men sling the now empty bins back into their brick enclosures. It reminds her of bombing heard from a distance. She gives her attention once more to the sergeant. Arnold Webb. She knows that inside the frame, on the back of that photo, is written in blue ink: 'To my darling Agnes, with much love.' 'Oh, Arnold!' she whispers.

Agnes had hardly been out of Glasgow until, in 1942, she volunteered for the Land Army. She was posted to Cumberland. Kettlesham Farm. What lovely folk they were, Mr and Mrs Forrest. They looked after Agnes and the other three girls so well. It turned out to be the happiest time of her life. My God! It's now seven years since she first set foot on the farm. Four since she left. How exciting it was, mixing with all those English folk for the first time. She expected everybody to talk like Margaret Lockwood and Rex Harrison. Hah! Not in Cumberland they didn't. She had to learn to temper her broad Glasgow accent; slow it down. It was hard work on the land, but rewarding. She really felt she was contributing to the war effort, replacing the men on the farm so they could go into the forces. Then, at a dance in Keswick, she met her fella. She looks at the photo again. Agnes was thirty-four, Arnold thirty-two. He was Corporal Webb then. An aircraft fitter at one of the many bomber fields just over the border in Yorkshire. But that wasn't enough for him. No, he wanted to be air crew. By late '43 he'd done it – sergeant navigator. By October '44 he was getting near the end of his tour of operations. Three more trips and that would be it. Get a nice cushy number with some training squadron and sit it out until the end of the war. He promised her he wasn't daft enough to volunteer for another tour, so they became engaged. Agnes's eyes stray to the little jewel box near the photo. She hasn't looked inside it now for almost a year. Just one week after that, he took off on what he called a milk run. Neither crew nor plane were ever found. Must have come down in the sea.

She wrote to his family in Brighton for the next two years. By the third year their letters had become intermittent. Must be a year gone since she last heard from them. Agnes reaches out to the photo and touches his cheek. 'Good night, Arnold. God rest.' She switches the lamp off. The luminous hands on the clock on the mantelpiece show ten to twelve. C'mon, Agnes, you'll be sleeping in for your work in the morning. Carefully making her way across the kitchen in the near-dark, she climbs into the recess bed. Lying on her back with the covers pulled up to her neck, she knows what to expect next. As she waits, her thoughts go back to Arnold. We'd have been married by now. Probably got wed in '45 with the war finishing. I'd have been thirty-seven. Wonder if we'd have had any bairns? She is about to take her thoughts further when, as expected, they are interrupted.

It's faint at first as it comes echoing through the night. Always is. The last tram, speeding down the Maryhill Road heading for its distant depot. So it must be five minutes to midnight. She lies in the dark, listening to the metal wheels sing, louder and louder, bouncing off the silent tenements, echoing down the side streets until the once-quiet night is filled with this beautiful Last Post. She can almost see it, this moving beacon making haste down the darkened road toward Queens Cross and thence on to the city. Occasionally someone will want off, or on, and the song will be interrupted as it slows to a halt. The reverberations almost fade, but just as the night is about to be still, the tram pulls away from the stop, gathers speed, and resumes its Glasgow nocturne.

Agnes lies without moving, hardly breathing so as to hear it for as long as possible. As the tram progresses further down the Maryhill Road, its lullaby decreasing in volume, she strains to catch the last of it. She never, ever does. Long before the last note fades into the night, Agnes Dalrymple is fast asleep.

CHAPTER NINE

Secrets

'Dae my seams need touching up, Ma?' Rhea O'Malley is late for work. She's always late for work. Her younger sister, Siobhan, left the house twenty minutes ago.

'Jayz! If ye'd stand still for a second I moight be able to tell ye.' Teresa O'Malley sits at the table with a cup of tea, watching her daughter go through her frenetic morning routine.

Rhea takes another bite of toast as she passes the table. She looks at her face in the mirror that hangs between the double windows. 'Is ma make-up okay?'

Her mother sighs. 'Since when did I have the X-ray vision? Do ye think I can see through the back o' yer head?' Rhea giggles, crosses over to the table, takes a mouthful of tea followed by another bite of toast. 'Right, Ma. How's the make-up?' She leans forward.

'It's hard to tell when yer gob's going!' Rhea stops chewing for a few seconds. Her mother peers at her through narrowed eyes. 'Yeh, it's foine. And what about yer seams?'

'Oh aye.' Rhea turns round, leans forward, lifts her skirt a few inches.

'Come nearer.' Rhea shuffles backwards. Teresa bends down, carefully examines her daughter's calves. 'Pass me the eyebrow pencil. And a cushion.'

'Hurry up, Ma. Ah'm gonny be late.'

'Sure an' yer always late. Should've been yer middle name.' Kneeling on the cushion, Teresa begins to carefully restore the eyebrow-pencilled lines on the backs of Rhea's legs where the seams of stockings should be. 'You'll have to put some more o' that leg tan on tonight. It's beginning to fade.'

'Ah know. Oh Ma, when are we ever gonny be able tae jist walk intae a shop and buy a pair o' fully fashioned stockings? Or better still, a pair o' nylons? It's over four years since the war finished. Why are so many things still rationed? Huh! If this is us efter winning the war, it's a bloody good job we did'nae lose it!'

'Will ye mind yer language, please.'

'Ma! Bloody is'nae swearing.'

''Tis in this house. If yer father was in, ye'd get a clip, so ye would.'

Rhea gives an exaggerated sigh. 'Naw Ah wid'nae. Ma daddy dis'nae hit me. Ah don't know why ye alwiz say that. Ye know fine well Daddy only ever skelped me wance. Yon time Ah took money oot yer purse tae buy sweeties in Mary's.'

'Well I'll give yer a clip meself, so Ah will.' With one hand on the table, Teresa gets to her feet.

Rhea gives her mother a quick hug and a kiss on the cheek. 'Ma, the next time you hit me it'll be the first!' She opens the door to the lobby, takes her new swagger coat off the row of hooks. 'Right, Ah'm away. Don't forget, me and some of the girls are going straight tae the pictures efter work.'

'And what about yer dinner?'

'Ah'll no' need any. We're going tae the café for something tae eat.'

'What are ye going t' see?'

'Don't know yet. We're going tae wan o' the big picture hooses doon the toon.'

'You'd better not be late or yer daddy won't be pleased.'

'Aye, Ah know, Ma. And if Ah am, Ah suppose Ah'll get another imaginary clip!'

Teresa looks heavenward. 'Jaysus, are ye listening? Is this to be me reward for bringing this child up? Nothing but check?'

Rhea also looks heavenward. 'Jesus, don't pye any attention tae her. The wumman's no' right in the heid!'

Teresa blesses herself then puts her hands together. 'Holy Mary, do ye hear the way this spalpeen's talking to yer only begotten son? Can ye intervene on me behalf?' She tries to continue but becomes convulsed with laughter, as does her daughter.

Rhea leans against the door jamb. Dabs her eyes. 'Ma! Will ye stoap it. You're making ma mascara run. Ah'm away. Cheerio.' Before she shuts the outer door, her mother has managed to control herself and has launched into another prayer.

'It's the next number 23 tram coming down the Maryhill Road. Could ye mibbe arrange a small bolt o' lightning? Just enough to give her a . . .' She stops. She can hear the clatter of her daughter's high heels fading as she runs down the two flights of stairs then gallops along the close. 'Ah, now ye can just forget that, 'cause ye know Ah didn't mean it.' She blesses herself again.

As Rhea crosses the Maryhill Road towards the tram stop,

she knows exactly where to look. There he is! Robert Stewart stands a few feet away from the queue, leaning on the wall next to R.S. McColl's sweetie shop. She feels a tingle of excitement. Can't help it. Robert lives with his parents in a room and kitchen in the close at 18 Dalbeattie Street. Rhea lives one up. Her parents are Irish Catholic. Robert's are Glasgow Protestant. The twain are not supposed to meet. Or go to the pictures.

'Hi yah!' Rhea casually stands beside him. Glances at the dozen or so folk at the tram stop to see if anybody's looking. No one is. She touches his hand. For a moment he intertwines his fingers with hers, then lets go.

'Ah was beginning tae think ye were'ny coming. There's been three 23s come and gone.'

She laughs. 'Ah jist could'nae get oot o' ma bed this morning. Ah heard you leaving yer house.'

'Aye, Ah gave the door a good bang so as ye'd hear it. Are we aw'right for the pictures?'

'Ah've telt Ma Ah'm oot wi' the girls. Where are we going? What's oan?'

'There's a good picture on at the Paramount—'

She interrupts. 'Oh good! Ah jist *love* the Paramount. It's so plush – and dead modern. Whit did you say they call that style?'

'Art Deco. It was aw' the rage in the 1930s. Ultra modern.'

'It is'nae half. Ah alwiz think it's like being oan board an ocean liner when we go tae the Paramount. Can we have something tae eat in the restaurant before the picture?'

Robert holds a hand to his chest; staggers as though shocked. 'Dae you think Ah'm made o' money?'

'Aw, go on. We'll go halfers. Sitting in yon restaurant is lovely. We can jist huv an omelette. That should'nae be dear. Anywye, whit's showing this week?'

'*Samson and Delilah*. Victor Mature and Hedy Lamarr. It's in Technicolor.'

'Right, that'll suit me.' She looks up at him. 'Whit time will we meet?'

'Mmmm, better make it six if we're gonny have something tae eat.' He turns his head. 'Here's oor caur coming. Will we sit doonstairs?'

'Oh, aye. Ah hate up on top, it's alwiz too smoky.'

As the tram heads citywards, they sit close together on a double seat. Robert waves a hand to draw her attention to the decor of the saloon. 'These Coronation trams are in the same style as the Paramount. These were built in the late thirties. Art Deco was aw' the rage then.'

She looks around. 'Eeeh, you're right, Robert. It jist shows how ye can go aboot and no' really look at things. Ah know there are auld trams and new trams, but now you've said it, it actually sticks oot a mile.' As if seeing things for the first time, her eyes range round the saloon. 'Ah'm jist lookin' at the style o' the lights and the design oan the ceiling, even the pattern of the upholstery. Ah've been walkin' aboot wi' ma eyes shut, Robert!'

All too soon the tram enters West Nile Street. A short walk from here will take Rhea to the offices of Macready and Co., the solicitors for whom she's worked since leaving school. She squeezes Robert's hand. 'See ye ootside the Paramount. The Renfield Street side. Cheerio.' She steps off the tram, then stands for a moment on the pavement. As it glides away from the stop, she gives him a smile, watching as it takes him off to Beardmore's Motor Works, where he's about to finish his apprenticeship. Decisions will have to be taken. Soon.

*   *   *

It's a few minutes to six, turning dusk and starting to rain. Robert hurries along and takes shelter under the Paramount's canopy. He looks at the lurid poster: Victor Mature with a head of thick black curls. He smiles. Hedy will have wheeched them aff by the end o' the picture. He feels warm as the mass of lights blaze down. And conspicuous. Even on a Monday evening, the city is busy. He stands for a moment watching the world go by. Outside this neon haven, the cobbled setts of Renfield Street glisten in the rain, tram lines turned to strips of tinsel. Lights from shops, many of them coloured, reflect off the rounded cobbles, turning them into a mosaic on which trams and buses glide, their steamed-up windows refracting their interior lights, bathing the passengers in gold. And all for tuppence. Passers-by hurry along pavements, collars turned up, anxious to get out of the rain. Those with umbrellas move to a different drum.

'Hi yah!' Rhea comes up behind him. Links her arm through his. He squeezes it to his side.

'Hello, pal.' He looks into her brown eyes, at her bonny face. 'Ah don't care if anybody sees us.' He kisses her on the lips.

CHAPTER TEN

The Welcome

As Drena McClaren comes down the last flight of stairs into the close, she is pleased to find Irma Armstrong polishing the brasses on her front door. Irma turns, smiles. So does Drena.

'Hello! Ah'm Drena McClaren.' Drena points upwards. 'From two up, ah, the second floor. Granny Thomson was telling me we have new folk in the close.'

Irma offers her hand. 'I'm pleased to meet you. Yes, Granny Thomson. She is very nice.' It's obvious both women want to talk, but there is a pause as they try to think of something to say. It becomes a little uncomfortable. Finally, Drena opens her mouth and says the first thing that comes into her head.

'My husband, Billy, will probably be practising his German oan ye first chance he gets. He spent five years as a prisoner of war in Poland and Germany.' Immediately she thinks, Oh God! Why did Ah say that? She rushes on. 'Aye, he, eh, found it dead interesting being a, whit were they called? Aye, a kriegsgefangener. Aw his letters had that printed alang the top.' Whit a stupid thing tae say! Will ye shut up, Drena.

'Oh, goodness!' Irma looks embarrassed. 'I would think that wouldn't be a very nice experience. Five years. To be a prisoner all that time. He must have bad memories of his—'

Drena interrupts. 'Oh, but he dis'nae dislike Germans. You would think he would – but he dis'nae.' She just stops herself from saying, 'Honest.' 'Ah've never heard ma Billy say a bad word aboot the Germans.' That's a bloody lie! she thinks. She begins to break out in a cold sweat. Can ye no' stop talkin', ya stupid wumman? You'll never be able tae look this lassie in the face again. Just then, mercifully, Bert Armstrong enters the close.

'Ah! Here is mein man. This is Mrs Mc— How do I say your family name, please?'

'Ah'm Drena McClaren. From two up.'

'Ah'm Bert. Pleased tiv meet ye, pet.' They shake hands.

'Ah'm afraid Ah've been babbling oan tae yer wife. Telling her that ma man, Billy, was a POW in Germany and Poland during the war. His time wis'nae wasted, though. Efter five years he finished up speaking really good German.' You're daeing it again, Drena. Will ye shut up! She feels the sweat trickling down her armpits.

'Ah'll have tae gan, pet. Ah'm up tiv me neck. Got a lot on.' He smiles. 'Divn't be shy, mind. If tha has the time, pop in for a bit crack. Irma will allus mak tha welcome.'

Drena smiles and nods. What with Bert's strong accent and habit of speaking quickly, she hasn't caught any of that. It's obvious his wife speaks the better English. As he vanishes into the house, she decides to extricate herself. She reaches out a hand and squeezes Irma's arm.

'Well, Ah really must go. Just going tae the shops. Ah'm glad Ah've bumped intae ye. Tae welcome ye tae the close. Oh! That reminds me. Has anybody told ye yet about how the tenants take turns tae keep the close clean?' She points down. 'You know, scrubbing and washing the floor and using pipe clay along the edges?'

'No. I would like to know how it is done. Then when it is my day, I can do it very good.'

Drena laughs. 'Billy said that. He said, the German lassie will show ye all up. Said German housewives are famous fur being awful clean.'

'Awful?'

Drena blushes. Oh God! Can ye no' jist open up a hole in the grund . . . 'Naw, Ah don't mean awful. When we say something is awful, we actually mean the exact opposite. Like awful clean, means *very* clean. Or we say something's awfully good; that means it's *really* good. It's hard tae explain. It's like awful has two meanings.' Drena feels certain the sweat will start running down her legs any second now.

'Mmmm, I think I understand. But please, I would like to know about the washing of the close.'

'It's really simple. It's washed and scrubbed once a week. As you know, there are three houses in the close – so your turn comes round every three weeks.'

'I do this, too?' Irma points to the stairs.

'No, no. The folk on the first landing do that. You and your neighbours just do the close. From the front all the way through to the back. Anyway, if you'd like to come up for a wee cup of tea this afternoon, Ah'll explain it all tae ye. And Ah'll also tell you about the wash house in the back court that you can use – and taking turns hanging oot washing in the back court tae dry. Though mind, Ah'd advise ye tae take your washin' tae the steamie, or the bagwash. It's a lot easier.'

Irma drops her Brasso. 'Steamie? Bagwash? Goodness, what are these things?'

Drena decides to make a run for it while the going is good. She feels the need for some fresh air. She reaches out again, squeezes Irma's hand. 'Well, as Ah say, come up tae my house this afternoon. Ah'll invite Granny Thomson as well. About two thirty. We'll have a nice wee cup o' tea and hopefully Granny and me will be able tae tell ye aboot aw' these things ye have tae know when ye come tae live up a close. It's the second landing, the middle door. Okay?'

Bert emerges from the house, the lavatory key in his hand. 'Ah'll have tae gan tiv the netty, girls.' He makes his way along the back close to the lavatory door.

'So, until two thirty. That will be good?'

'Smashing! See ye then.'

'Smashing?'

'See whit Ah mean?' says Drena. 'Awful! Smashing! Sometimes they don't mean what they usually mean. It's awfy complicated. Anywye, Ah'd better go and get the rations in before the shops sell oot. See ye this afternoon.'

Two minutes later, the cold sweat still drying on her, Drena is just yards away from the Maryhill Road when the familiar figure of Granny Thomson turns the corner into Dalbeattie Street. 'Jeez-oh, Granny! You've nae idea. Ah thought Ah wiz aboot tae start World War Three there! Ah'm no' kidding. Talk aboot huvin' the best o' intentions. Ah wiz jist trying tae make the German lassie feel welcome. But every bloody time Ah opened ma mooth, Ah put ma fit in it!'

Granny laughs. 'So whit were ye saying?'

'Ah'll tell ye later. Ah'll huv tae dive tae the shops. Ah've invited her tae come up tae the hoose at half two for a cuppa and said that you'll be therr tae.' She pauses. 'Ah'll tell ye something else, mind. Ye never told me the *two* of them were German!'

CHAPTER ELEVEN

Melting Point

The late-September sun beats down from a cloudless sky into streets and back courts. The heat, as though liquid, seems trapped between the high tenements. As the day wears on, the temperature rises remorselessly, until by late afternoon it is into the high eighties. Every flat in Dalbeattie Street has its windows thrown wide open, but in the hot stillness, not a curtain moves.

Three women from number 18 – Drena McClaren, Teresa O'Malley and Granny Thomson – sit on kitchen chairs on the pavement outside their close. The same scenario is repeated here and there along the street. Drena and Teresa have rolled their stockings down to their ankles. Granny, a mob cap on her head, has opened the top button of her blue shantung blouse. That is her only concession to this Indian summer.

'This is the bloody life, girls, in't it?' Drena stretches her arms and legs out in front of her.

''Tis an' all,' says Teresa.

'Ah think the elastic oan ma knickers huz melted!' announces Granny. All three hoot with laughter.

'Jayz, I've got a mountain of ironing waiting for me up in that house,' says Teresa. 'Dennis is needing a shirt. He's at a meeting of the Knights of Columbus at eight o'clock.'

'Ach! If it's the *nights* of Columbus, naebody will notice in the dark it's no' ironed!' Drena sighs at the lack of response. 'Have youse two no' even got the strength left tae raise a wee laugh? Talk aboot falling oan stony ground.'

Granny yawns. 'Now everybody knows sitting in the sun takes it oot of ye. It's a fact.'

'That's why I went out extra early this morning and got me offices done,' says Teresa. 'The forecast said it was gonna be warm. I was finished by nine.'

'That's a rerr wee job you've got,' says Drena. 'It's jist two hours a day, in't it?'

''Tis. Monday till Friday. It's a wee bit extra money coming inta the house.'

Drena takes a Capstan cigarette packet out of her apron pocket and lights one. The spent match is put back into the Bluebell box. She smokes half the cigarette, then nips it and puts the remainder back into the packet. 'It's funny, but Ah never really enjoy smokin' a fag in the open air. Ah wonder why?'

There is no reply. The trio lapse into silence as the sun continues to blaze down. A few minutes later Drena catches Teresa's eye by waving a hand, then points at Granny. The old woman has dozed off, her chin sunk on to her chest. As though by some sixth sense, Granny raises her head, opens her eyes. Looks around. Her two companions smile at her.

'Are you twa buggers making a cod o' me?'

Drena laughs. 'Naw, we were feart in case ye toppled aff that chair oan tae the pavement.'

'Nane the fear o' it,' says Granny. 'Ah've got this sunbathing game doon tae a fine art.'

There's movement along the end of the street as children, in twos and threes, turn the corner off the Maryhill Road. William McClaren spots his mother and runs along the street to join her.

'Hi yah, Ma!'

'Hello, pal. You're jist in time, we're aw' dying o' thirst. Away alang tae Ken's paper shop and get yer mammy a bottle o' ginger. Irn Bru.' She reaches into her apron pocket again and this time extracts her purse. 'Therr's a shilling.'

'Can Ah huv something for maself?'

'Ye can have a Penny Dainty – but keep it till efter yer tea. And don't run oan the wye back in case ye fall.' The three women watch as he races away.

'That's a good idea, Drena. I've been t'inking of going up them stairs this last half-hour for a drink o' water, but I havna the strength.'

A man enters the street from its junction with Blairatholl Street. 'Oh, here's Donald McNeil from the top landing,' announces Granny Thomson. The other two turn to look. 'He's a lovely man, so he is. He comes in noo and again for a wee cup o' tea and a blether. But no' very often. He's wan o' them folk that likes tae keep themselves tae themself.'

'He is indeed,' says Teresa, 'but he never goes past without a word. Sometimes even stops for a minute or two.' The three women fall silent as Donald comes within earshot.

'Hello, Donald. How are ye the day?' enquires Granny. Teresa and Drena also greet him, but call him Mr McNeil. He stops for a moment.

'Oh, fair to middling. I have chust been along to have a wee refreshment with an old workmate. Lives in Gairbraid Avenue. Retired from the Clyde Trust same time as myself. We were both on the dredgers.'

'So how is this weather suiting ye?' asks Granny.

'Man, man, I am afraid it is far too hot for me. There was not a breath of air to be had last night. Very uncomfortable.'

William arrives with the bottle of Irn Bru. 'Here ye are, Ma.'

'Right, son. Noo mind whit Ah telt ye aboot that Penny Dainty.'

'Ah know. Ah'll keep it till efter ma tea.'

Donald ruffles the boy's hair. 'Hello, William. My, what a big boy you are getting to be.'

William blushes. Then, 'Can Ah go and play wi' ma pals until it's time fur ma tea, Ma?'

'Aye. But don't stray from the street or the back court. If Ah've got tae shout and bawl for ye – or come lookin' for ye – you'll be in trouble. So mind!'

'Well, ladies, I think I'll away up. Make myself a wee bite to eat. I suppose I'll find the milk's turned sour again. You cannot keep it ten minutes in this weather. I stood it in a basin of cold water before I came out, but I have no doubt it'll still be off.' He touches his cap and enters the close. The trio turn their faces back to the sun and listen to Donald's footsteps fade as he slowly ascends the six flights of stairs to his top-floor flat.

Drena breaks the silence. 'Look who's jist came intae the street! It's that pig's melt Richard Sneddon.' She turns to Teresa, 'Did you and Dennis hear him at her again oan Sunday night?'

'We'd nae option. Even turnin' the wireless up could'nae droon it oot. 'Tis getting worse.'

'Ah really cannot understand that lassie,' says Drena. 'Whit is the matter wi' her? Putting up wi' being knocked aboot like that. If he wiz mine, Ah'd huv put the bread knife intae him by noo!'

'Eeeh, ye wouldn't,' says Teresa.

'Wid Ah no?' replies Drena. She turns to Granny. 'Could you hear any of it?'

'Ah heard a bit of it noo and again, but you two are better placed. It definitely was louder than usual.'

Drena shakes her head. 'It went oan for aboot half an hour. Ye could hear the yelps of her. Anywye, he's coming. Kidding oan he's reading the paper. Jist ignore him as he comes past us. And if the bastard huz the cheek tae speak – leave it tae me tae answer him.'

Richard Sneddon, supposedly engrossed in the *Evening Citizen*, runs the gauntlet of dirty looks and makes his way briskly past the three women.

Drena looks towards the close after he's entered. 'She never went tae her work oan Monday, ye know. Ah think he'd gave her such a hiding she wiz'nae able.' Yet again she shakes her head. 'Ah mean, whit is the matter wi' her? If she's no' gonny get the polis tae him, why no' leave him and go tae her mother's?'

Teresa sighs. 'Poor girl! It cannot go on like this. 'Tis every weekend now, and ye can tell 'tis getting worse. It'll finish up one of us neighbours will be sending for the garda – eh, the polis.' She turns to Granny. 'It's frightening listening to it. Wondering what he's doing to her. Me heart was in me mouth Sunday night.'

Granny sits very still, eyes shut against the glare. 'From what Ah could hear, Ah don't think it can be long afore things come to a head. And somehow – don't ask me why – Ah feel Richard Sneddon will be the loser.' She nods her head as though in affirmation. 'Aye, something tells me that man will get his comeuppance.'

CHAPTER TWELVE

To Better Oneself

It has just gone ten past six as George Lockerbie approaches number 18. Same time every evening. He is just a couple of paces from the close when he hears hurried footsteps. He pauses. Seconds later, Billy McClaren steps out into the street. 'Hello, George. That you jist getting hame fae yer work?'

'Aye. Another day, another dollar.'

'Ah'll tell ye what. It's a while since we hud a pint the gither.'

'In't it? Must be the best part o' two months.'

'Are ye still gettin' intae the Thistle Bar?' asks Billy.

'Oh aye. The nearest pub tae Dalbeattie Street.' George laughs. 'You'll no catch me wasting time and energy. Ah'm nae fool.'

'Well, Ah'll tell ye, whit aboot say a week come Setterday, Ah'll see ye in the Thistle roon' aboot eight o'clock and we'll huv a couple o' pints?'

'Okay. Ah'll try and get along, Billy. Anywye, where are you going at this time o' night? Yer surely no' away for a pint as early as this.'

'Naw. Ah jist got hame fae work maself, ten minutes ago.

Ah got off the tram wi' James Pentland. We were that busy blethering as we walked roon' fae the Maryhill Road, Ah clean forgot tae go intae Ken's for ma *Citizen*. So this is me jist nipping along tae get yin. Ah wid'nae enjoy ma dinner withoot the *Citizen* propped up against the milk bottle.'

'Hah!' George shakes his head. 'That's two things you'll never see oan oor table – a paper, or a milk bottle.'

'Aye, well, that's wi' you huvin' a posh English wife, George. Ye huv tae mind yer manners. Anywye, Ah'll away for ma paper. Don't forget, see if ye can get alang tae the Thistle a week come Setterday. See yah!' With a wave, Billy sets off along the street.

George enters the close. As he makes his way into the gloom – the lamplighter hasn't been round yet – he is conscious of the smile leaving his face. He turns the door handle and steps into the small lobby. There is the smell of dinner cooking. Dinner. He instantly recalls how long it took him, at Joan's insistence, to stop calling it tea.

'Hiyah!'

'Helloooh!' comes from the kitchen.

He takes his old RAF small pack off his shoulder and hangs it from a coathook in the lobby. This is followed by his gaberdine mac and his jacket. He undoes a buckle on the small rucksack and extracts a brass tea and sugar tin and the folded-up piece of greaseproof paper in which his piece was wrapped. Putting on a smile, he turns the doorknob and enters the kitchen.

'Hello, dear.' Joan stands at the range. A couple of pans give off steam. Wooden spoon in hand, she is poised above them, ready to pounce when needed. 'Have you had a good day at work?'

'Aye. No' bad. Jist like every other day, Ah suppose.'

'Now, when you think of it, George, you are actually doing a worthwhile job. There was that little bit on the Movietone News, I think it was when we were at the Roxy, saying that prefabs are making a major contribution to solving the housing shortage. I thought, my George does that.'

'It definitely is. But you've nae idea how boring it is oan a production line. Ah've spent better times wi' the toothache!'

'Oh, George. Really! Anyway, wash your hands, dear. I'm about to put the dinner out.'

He walks over to the Belfast sink, turns on the single tap and manages to unstick the red tablet of Lifebuoy soap, which is welded to the dish. As he lathers his hands under the flow of cold water, the familiar smell of the soap rises to meet him. He's always liked Lifebuoy. Joan wanted to change to Knight's Castile.

Fifteen minutes later, just the ribs of the chops are left and none of the mashed potato substitute. He takes another mouthful of tea, looks at the remnants of the chops. He's tempted to lift the bones and suck the marrow out of them, but knows that will be a cause for complaint. Instead: 'It makes aw' the difference mashing that Pom up wi' butter instead o' margarine, dizn't it?'

'Yes. I always try to keep some butter for it.'

George puts his cup of tea, his second, back in its saucer. He rises from the table and sits on a fireside chair. Looks at the fire, then reaches down to the coal scuttle. Using finger and thumb, he selects a couple of pieces of coal and places them carefully on the fire. Rubs his hands together to brush off any dust.

'George! I do wish you would use the tongs.'

'Do ye fancy going tae the pictures? *All the King's Men* is oan at the Blythswood. It's supposed tae be smashing. Broderick Crawford got the Oscar for it.'

'Mmmm. I think I'd rather go Friday or Saturday night.'

'Well, okay. But the trouble is, we'll probably need tae queue them nights. That's when aw' the winching couples go. Midweek ye can usually walk right in.'

'Not really in the mood for the cinema tonight.'

He decides to try again. 'It's not a bad evening oot there, considering it's October. Fancy a good walk doon the toon? It's a while since we had a nice donner tae oorselves. You like tae dae a bit window-shopping, don't ye?' He smiles at her.

'Hmmm! I don't see the point, George. Looking at all that furniture and carpets and curtains,' she waves her hand around, 'and trying to imagine it in a room and kitchen. Would be different if it was a flat in a red sandstone in Kelvinside or Hillhead. No matter what we do to this house, whenever we have visitors they still have to use the lavatory in the close – the lavatory we share with two other families! Really, George. It's impossible.'

He shakes his head. 'Here we go. Every chance ye get, back on your auld hobby horse. Look, this is a good wee hoose – and we've got good neighbours. The last year or so you've got this bee in yer bonnet aboot moving tae somewhere posh. It's got tae be a wally close, bay windows an' aw' the rest o' it. This hoose is only seventeen and six a week. A one-bedroom flat in the sort o' building you're talking aboot is at least thirty-five bob a week. Double! We jist cannae afford it.'

'We could if you got yourself two or three nights a week doing bar work like you did when we first got married and left the RAF.'

'Joan, Ah'm already working six days a week. We've nae kids. Why don't *you* get yerself a wee job? You've never worked sin—' She interrupts him.

'I didn't get married to spend the rest of my life working. My mother's never worked since the day she married my father. I look after the house and I look after you.' She draws her shoulders back. 'That's what a wife's supposed to do. I keep my side of the bargain.'

'So, Ah knock ma pan in six days a week but it's no' enough. All of a sudden Ah've tae fit in a couple of evenings a week tae, so's you can get back tae living like ye did in Camberley. But it's me that has tae dae aw' the graft; you're no' gonny contribute. Jist a part-time job would make aw' the difference.' He sits back in the chair, folds his arms.

Without another word Joan rises, clears the table, pours hot water from the kettle into the sink and begins to wash the dishes. George continues to sit at the fireside. As he watches her, his thoughts go back to when he met her: RAF Scampton, 1942. She was a sergeant in the WRAF, he an RAF corporal. Even then she bloody outranked me! He quite liked the fact she was so posh. Born in Camberley, Surrey, she was brought up in a detached four-bedroom house. Her parents would probably look on Hillhead as a slum. She'd never known life without a family car. He was totally in love with his English girl, as she seemed to be with him. Married in April '45, she was well warned as to what life in Glasgow would be like. Said it didn't matter; love would conquer all.

So it had – most of the time. Until last year. As 1948 changed to '49, increasingly she became dissatisfied with life in their room and kitchen. In a way, he doesn't blame her. He knows that having to share the toilet in the close is her main complaint, and no bathroom in the house, either. She grew up in far better surroundings. She's also made no close friends amongst their neighbours. Hasn't fallen out with any of them, but neither is she in and out their houses for a cup of tea and a natter. He knows they call her 'English Joan'. Sometimes he wonders if it was mainly the excitement, the romance of those wartime days that attracted them to one another. Folk, male and female, from all walks of life thrown together. All wearing the same uniform. That was the great leveller. The intensity, the highs and lows of working at a major bomber airfield. With Joan, there was also a strong element of opposites attracting. She was surprised to find out how well read he was, almost patronisingly so. Those days are now four years into the past. Life has become mundane. For the last two years they've been trying to start a family. But Joan just hasn't fallen pregnant.

He looks at her again. Well. He's the one who'll have to do something about it.

'Joan!'

'Yes?' She half turns towards him, keeps her soapy hands in the basin.

'Ah'll get the *Evening Times* and the *Citizen* on Friday night. That's the best night for the Situations Vacant. Ah'm not wanting tae work in jist any auld pub. Ah'd like tae get a place in one o' them lounge bars down the town or maybe in the West End. The experience Ah had working in the bar in the officers' mess at Scampton should stand me in good stead. The pay will be a wee bit better than a pub – and there should be the chance o' tips. Ah might earn enough in just two nights if Ah dae Friday and Saturday, the busy nights.'

'Oh! Darling, that would be wonderful. It really would.' As she turns back to the sink she is smiling. But it isn't the smile of a year or two ago. The one that used to light up her face and melt his heart. A great wave of disappointment sweeps over him. A sadness. Her smile now was . . . aye, a 'cat that got the cream' smile.

CHAPTER THIRTEEN

The Hard Man

———

A cold wind is blowing along the terraces at Firhill Park. Archie Cameron turns the collar of his mac up; knots his red and yellow scarf round his neck. He looks again at the scoreboard. Partick Thistle 1 – Third Lanark 0. Glances at his watch. Just over ten minutes to go. He turns to the man beside him; he knows him only as James. They always stand in this spot.

'Ah'm beginning tae get a bad feeling aboot the way this is going, James.'

'So Ah'm Ah.'

'We'll be lucky if we can hang oan tae this lead till full-time.'

'Thirds are beginning tae look dangerous.' James stamps his feet to get a bit of circulation going. 'It's a good job big Tommy's oan form. He's saved oor fuckin' bacon a couple o' times this efternin.'

Archie takes his eyes off the play for a moment to glance at Thistle's goalkeeper, Tommy Ledgerwood. The big man is a template of how a goalkeeper should look: yellow woollen jersey, black shorts, tweed cap pulled low to keep a wintry sun out of his eyes. His leather gloves lie by the right goalpost – ready for use if it rains and the ball becomes slippery.

'Mind ye, we've no' half missed Johnny Mackenzie oan the wing the day,' says Archie.

James snorts. 'We'd huv been three up if Johnny had been playing. You've got tae be honest, we're only moderate withoot him. Ah hope tae fuck that ankle o' his is better for next Setterday. We're away tae Motherwell. If he's no'—' The conversation is cut short as they watch, hearts in mouths, as Third Lanark put in another spirited attack.

'Aw, fuck me!' they say in unison. The opposition have equalised. The cheers of the few hundred Thirds supporters are drowned out by the synchronised groans of eight thousand 'Jags' fans.

'That fuckin' diz it fur me,' says Archie. 'There's aboot eight minutes tae go. We'll be lucky if we can hing oan tae a draw. Ah'm no' stying here tae watch a wan-nuthin' lead turned intae a two-wan defeat. Ah'm away, James. Ah'll see ye at the next home game.'

'Right. Aw' the best, Erchie. See ye in a fortnight.'

Archie, along with a few more of the disenchanted, makes his way up the terrace then down the steep stairs behind it to the exits. He pushes hard on a turnstile until, with a few clicks, it reluctantly allows him out into Firhill Road. Ach! Ah'll away for a quick pint. He walks along the length of the road then cuts across Garscube Road into Hinshaw Street. As he enters this short street he glances at number 20. Wish Ah had a penny for every time Ah've been in and oot that close. Next, his eyes are drawn to a barn-like wooden building sandwiched between two tenement blocks. The Rag Store. It still looks as if it doesn't belong. The two large doors are wide open. Inside the gloomy interior he can see the various heaps of rags: woollens, cottons and linens. Ah guess auld Mr Goldstein's still making a living. He turns his eyes again to number 20. Should Ah nip up and see Ma and Da for a couple o' minutes? Och, if Ah dae, Ah'll never get away. Anywye, Ah jist seen them last Monday night.

He comes to the end of Hinshaw Street, where it forms a T junction with Maryhill Road. Facing him, with a frontage no bigger than the shops either side of it, is the 419 Bar. He stands at the kerb while a couple of trams, a Milanda Bakeries van and a few cars go by. Walking out to the middle of the road, he pauses to let an Alexander's Bluebird single-decker bus rumble past on its way to Dumbarton. As he walks the last few paces, he takes in the pub's blue-painted front. The name, the 419 Bar, is emblazoned in gold above the premises. As a boy, that name never failed to catch his eye. He thought it was dead smart. All the other pubs on the Maryhill Road had names, proper names – the Queens Cross Vaults, Ye Olde Tramcar Vaults. They liked that word, vaults, in Glasgow. But to call your pub the 419 Bar, that showed real imagination. Sounded American. And why 419? Why no' the 336 Bar? Or the 555 Bar? Actually, that would be quite a good yin. It must mean something tae the owner. Symbolic. He never thought to ask his da why it was called that. Only he, Archie Cameron, and the owner knew it was special.

He pauses for a second, looks up again at the gold letters. Smiles as he recalls the day the mystery was solved. Just before he pushes open the swing door to enter the bar, he looks up to his right. It's still there. Always has been. A small enamel plate, probably four inches square, with 419 in black on a white background. A similar plate is fixed outside every shop, close and premises on the Maryhill Road. On every one in the city. And all supplied by Glasgow Corporation. It's dead simple – the pub's postal address is 419 Maryhill Road.

Placing a hand on the brass door plate, he pushes. Ahhhh! The smell of beer, sawdust and tobacco smoke embraces him. Conversation is approaching full volume. Like all of Glasgow's pubs, the 419's bar is men only. There is a wee, very wee snug if anyone is accompanied by a lady. Three barmen, all with long white aprons down to their boot tops, stand behind the bar. Archie manages to slot himself into a space on the far right of the long scrubbed counter. He orders a pint. As he reaches into his pocket for some change, he glances at the customers. The majority wear trench coats. A few like himself run to gaberdine macs. Nearly all sport cloth caps. The subjects under discussion are various aspects of football. The only acceptable alternative is boxing. Every third or fourth word is 'fuck', 'cunt' or 'bastard'.

Still depressed after Third Lanark's equaliser, Archie looks at the pub's clientele. He feels even more depressed. At thirty-two, he is beginning to look like these old guys. He takes his bunnet off and stuffs it into his mac pocket. Looks along the line of middle-aged men again. Jeez! To try and cheer himself up, he takes a long draught of pale ale, then thinks back to the Archie Cameron of five short years ago. Early '44. Sergeant A. Cameron, Argyll and Sutherland Highlanders, just transferred to the Paras. Jeez-oh! The infantry training had been tough enough when he'd joined the Argylls in 1940. He takes another mouthful of beer. But it wasn't a patch on the Airborne's regime. He thinks back to how fit he was just five years ago. Fit to drop – into Arnhem!

As he comes out of his reminiscing, and his eyes refocus, he becomes conscious that a young man on the other side of the bar is staring hard at him. Archie looks at him. Immediately recognises the type. He's in his early twenties. Double-breasted suit. Hair Brylcreemed and combed straight back, no parting. One of the local hard men. Archie also takes in the fact that he stands alone. Isolated. The other customers anxious not to crowd him. He must think I've been staring at him this last few minutes. Dozy bugger! Archie shakes his head and reaches for his pint, a half-smile on his lips. That's the final straw: Archie smiling. He watches the young man lift his whisky glass, down it in one gulp, then begin to make his way purpose-fully through the crowd at the bar. From the corner of his eye, Archie sees one of the barmen nudge another, whisper, then nod in his direction. He reads the signs. This bugger's coming for me. He straightens up, is gratified to feel that tingle once again. The buzz as the adrenaline starts to surge through his system. He begins to take slow deep breaths. The last time this feeling kicked in was in the Dakota over Arnhem – as the red light changed to green. He almost smiles at the realisation that just as on that day, he feels calm. Confident.

'Who dae ye think you're fuckin' staring at? Dae ye fancy yer chance?' He's pushed two customers out of his way and suddenly appears at Archie's left side. From the corner of his eye Archie sees him slip a hand inside his jacket, and keep it there. He has a knife; or more likely, a razor. Ready to draw it. No point trying to explain he wasn't staring. Be taken as a sign of weakness, of trying to avoid a fight. Without turning his head to look at the other man, or speaking, Archie flashes his open left hand upwards and catches him across the throat with the edge of his palm. The tough guy, as expected, makes a choking, rasping sound. Archie spins a quarter-turn on his heels to face him, his right fist half clenched so that just the knuckles face forward. He punches upwards twice, rapidly, again at the man's throat. Feels the Adam's apple split. This guy is now his! With his left hand he grabs a handful of shirt front; with his right he grabs his opponent's testicles. Hard. The young man yelps. His hand comes out of the jacket, a half-open razor falls to the floor, lies amongst the sawdust. With both his hands, the young man makes a weak attempt to push Archie away. His testicles are squeezed very hard. He tries to scream. It comes out as a rasping gurgle. Blood flecks his lips.

'Put your fuckin' hands by your sides,' he is told. 'Don't move them again!' The guy complies. The customers have fallen back to form a half-circle. They watch in silence.

Archie grasps the shirt front more firmly, increases the grip on the guy's testicles and lifts at the same time. He rapidly propels him backwards across the room in a macabre tiptoeing dance that ends as he slams him, full force, into the wall. There is now utter, pin-dropping silence in the bar. Letting go the shirt, Archie takes hold of the man's damaged throat. He speaks in a low, almost conspiratorial voice.

'Look at me, ya stupid bastard. You've jist discovered, the hard wye, you've picked oan the wrang guy. Ah'm an ex-Para. Ah could eat ye – and shite ye – before breakfast! Don't even think of coming efter me wi' wan or two of yer pals. If you come looking fur me wi' a weapon, Ah guarantee Ah'll take it aff ye – and insert it up yer arsehole. Look at me!' He shakes him by the throat, then stares into his eyes. 'That is a promise. Be warned.'

He suddenly propels the young man, still backwards, over to the door. Letting go his balls, he uses his free hand to swing the door open. 'Don't come back intae this pub. Ah drink in here. Now fuck off!' He ejects him into the street and lets the door swing shut.

Archie turns to face the rest of the customers. All is silence. Then it's broken.

'Ah thocht things like that only happened in the pictures!'

There is some nervous laughter, two or three cries of 'Well done!' then the customers slowly resume their places and restart conversations. The head barman wipes the counter round Archie's glass of pale ale. 'Will ye take a wee half? Of single malt, of course,' he adds.

'Aye, that wid be nice.' He looks at his watch. 'Ah'll huv tae be getting hame soon. The wife will huv ma dinner oan the table.' He smiles. 'If Ah'm late, Ah'll get ma head in ma hands tae play wi'.' They both laugh. The bar is almost back to normal, though the hubbub hasn't quite reached the same volume as before. Heads are frequently turned in Archie's direction. The barman places a shot glass on the counter and would have filled it if Archie didn't remonstrate with him. 'Oh, for God's sake, that's plenty!' He raises the glass. 'Slainte!' Takes a sip. 'Oh, mammy, daddy! Ye can taste the peat. That has got tae be an Islay malt.'

'It is indeed. Ardbeg. Fifteen years auld.'

'Anywye, who was the tough guy?' asks Archie.

The barman leans on the counter 'Ye mean former tough guy. Name's Billy Webster. A real nasty bastard. Slash yer face wide open as soon as look at ye. Maist o' the polis are feart of him. They'll be delighted when they hear aboot this efternin's work.'

'That reminds me,' says Archie. He steps back and looks around the floor. 'Therr it is.' He retrieves the half-open razor, blows the sawdust off, closes it and places it on the bar. 'Ah'll leave you tae get rid o' that.'

'Are ye no' wantin' tae keep it as a souvenier?'

'Oh, God, naw. No' ma style.' He looks at his watch again. Finishes the rest of the whisky. 'Right, Ah'd better away. Ah'll see ye another time. Aw' the best.'

Ten minutes later, Archie walks briskly down Dalbeattie Street. He still feels exhilarated. No' so much of an auld man as ye thought ye were, Archie. He takes the six flights of stairs to the top landing two at a time. Opening the door, he enters the small lobby, hangs his coat and jacket on the hooks then opens the kitchen door. As expected, Ella is at the range, cooking dinner.

'It's a good job fur you you've came in now. Me and the weans were aboot tae huv oor dinners. You've jist saved yersel' a good telling-aff.'

'Yes, darling.'

'Daddy!' Three-year-old Katherine waves her spoon in the air.

'Wiz it a good game, Da?' Archie junior raises his eyes from his *Film Fun* for a moment.

Archie walks over and kisses his wife on the cheek. 'It wiz aw'right. Could huv been better.'

'Ye won, didn't ye?' says Ella, 'Whit more dae ye want?'

He looks at her. 'Did we win? Are ye sure?'

'Ah thought ye were at the game.'

'Ah wiz. But ten minutes before time, Thirds equalised, so Ah got fed up and left. Ah went fur a pint. You're definitely sure the Jags won?'

'Aye. Ah hud the wireless oan listening tae the results. Thistle got a last-minute winner.'

Archie rubs his palms together. 'Great! That's made ma day.'

CHAPTER FOURTEEN

Interrupted Melody

It's a Monday morning. Frank Sinatra's just come on the Light Programme singing 'Sweet Lorraine'. Teresa O'Malley is sitting at the table. Rhea is late for her work.

'Aw, Ma. Ah jist love this record.' She takes a mouthful of tea to wash down a bite of toast, then pauses to listen to the music.

'Ye havna time to listen to the wireless. I put the wireless on to hurry ye up – not slow ye down, ye spalpeen that ye are!'

'Aw'right, Ma. Aw'right.' Rhea finishes her tea then dashes into the lobby for her coat.

'I don't know why that firm put up wit' ye. If I was the boss I'd have given ye yer jotters long ago, so I would.'

'Ah'm the best shorthand-typist in the office. There's nae fears of them getting' rid o' me.'

Rhea snatches the remaining half-slice of toast off the plate and takes a bite. 'Right, Ah'm away, Ma. Don't forget, the girls and me are going tae the pictures the night. Ah'll no' be hame till efter ten.'

You're not going to be showing me up walking along the street eating that toast, are ye?'

'Aye!'

Teresa shakes her head. 'What a sight! Got its posh coat on, and walks along the street eating its breakfast for all the world tae see. I'll be too black affronted to step outside o' this house today! Anyway, what are ye going to see?'

'Ma, we don't know. We never know until we leave the office and buy a paper and check whit's oan. And tae save time – seeing as Ah'm late – don't ask me "Whit aboot yer dinner?" 'Cause that's usually yer next question. We'll be going for something tae eat before we go tae the pictures.' She walks over and gives her mother a kiss. 'Cheerio, Ma. See ye the night.'

Teresa holds up a finger 'And remember! Don't be late or yer father will—'

Rhea interrupts. 'Give yer a clip!' She laughs out loud. Her mother tries not to. Instead she looks heavenward.

'Holy Mary. If ever a woman suffered, you know who it—' The outside door slams shut, and she hears her daughter's footsteps receding. Teresa sits for a moment, shakes her head. The record finishes on the radio. She rises, takes the few steps over to the sideboard and switches the set off. Quiet descends. She can hear the clock tick, the fire draw up the chimney. She lights a gas ring and moves the blackened aluminium kettle on to it. Time for a dish o' tay and a read at yesterday's *Sunday Post*. She gives a contented sigh.

'Hi yah!' Robert Stewart stands in his usual place, next to R.S. McColl's. A few yards away from the folk at the tram stop. Rhea strolls over and stands beside him.

'You're later than ever this morning. Ah've been here nearly twenty minutes. Ah've lost count of the number of 23s that've gone by.' He's turned the collar of his coat up; there's a spit of rain.

Rhea brushes her fingers against his hand. 'Sorry. Ah cannae help it. Ah'm murder polis in the mornin'.'

He turns slightly so he can look at her, face on. 'Ah was hoping Ah might have bumped intae ye ower the weekend.' She feels a chill in her stomach; knows what he's about to tell her. 'Ah got ma letter on Saturday morning. I've tae go for ma medical oan the twenty-first of this month.'

'Oh, Robert! We knew it hud tae come, but it's still a sickener.' Her eyes brim with tears. 'Whit am Ah gonny dae without ye? Two years! It'll be a lifetime. Why can they no' leave us alane?'

He hears the steel song of a tram approaching; turns his head. 'Here's oor caur. Dab yer eyes, pal, or folk'll wonder whit's going on.'

They sit on a double seat at the front of the lower saloon. Close together as always. 'When dae ye think you'll be away?'

'Ah've been trying tae work it oot. Ah was asking some of the boys who've done their two years. Right. Medical on the twenty-first of November. While Ah'm there, they'll ask me whit branch of the forces Ah'd like tae go intae. It'll probably be the end of the second week in December when Ah get the result.'

'Whit urr ye gonny ask for?'

'Well, wi' me just finishing ma apprenticeship and being a time-served motor mechanic, Ah'm gonny ask for the REs or the REME.'

She looks at him. 'And whit urr they when they're at hame?'

'The REs are the Royal Engineers. REME stands for Royal Electrical and Mechanical Engineers.' He laughs. 'Though from whit they tell me, they've got a great habit of giving ye the exact opposite of whit ye've applied for!'

'They'll no' take ye before the New Year, will they?'

'Ah don't think so. We should get oor last Hogmanay in aw'right. Most of the boys say it'll be the first or second week in January before Ah'm away.'

Rhea sits silent for a moment, then, 'So if ye go in January 1950, you should be oot January 1952. Is that right?'

'Aye, that should be it.'

'Oh, Robert. It'll never pass. It might as well be for ever. 'Cause that's what it'll be like.'

Robert shrugs his shoulders. 'It cannae be helped. That's the way things are.'

'Well it's no' fair. Why can they no' leave us alane?'

For the rest of the journey they sit in silence, holding hands, lost in their thoughts, until . . .

'Rhea, the stop after next is yours and we hav'nae decided where we're going the night.'

'Oh!' She thinks for a moment. 'Ah don't think Ah want tae go tae the pictures. Ah need cheering up. Let's go fur a wee dance. Whit aboot the Locarno?'

'Aye, good idea. Ah'll see ye up the top o' Buchanan Street at six. We'll go for something tae eat, then wander along Sauchiehall Street and get intae the Locarno about eight. Okay?'

'Aye. That'll be fine.' She squeezes his hand. 'See ye at six.'

As ever, she stands on the pavement by the tram stop for a last smile before the tram takes him off to Beardmore's.

She lingers longer than usual this morning. Watches the tram until it is lost to distance and traffic as it takes her love away from her. That's what it feels like. She tries not to think about it. Fails. It's constantly on her mind. Seven or eight weeks from now there will be no Robert waiting faithfully at the tram stop on the Maryhill Road every morning. She'll sit alone every day going into the city. No last secret smile as it pulls away. Two long years.

It's just after eight thirty. Robert stands in the vestibule while Rhea checks her coat into the cloakroom. On her return, she gives him her ticket. 'Put that in yer pocket for me.' Hand in hand they walk towards the ballroom, then, on entry, pause for a moment at the edge of the floor. The glitter ball revolves, casting flurries of light over silhouetted dancers. At the far end of the large hall the band sits high on a stage, their leader conducting energetically. None of the musicians pay any attention to him. As the dancers glide by, he nods and smiles at some of the regulars. Without speaking, Rhea takes Robert's arm and presses it close to her side. The dance finishes, the floor clears. Two minutes later, the band leader approaches the mike, leans into it and speaks in that confidential manner that seems to be mandatory.

'Ladies an' gennelmen. The next dance is – a quickstep.' He spins round to face his players. 'Ah one! Ah two!' The band launches into 'Yes Sir, That's My Baby'.

'Oh, c'mon, Robert, ma favourite. You know Ah love a quickstep.' For the first time that day, Rhea brightens up.

It's dark as they enter Dalbeattie Street. The tall lamp standards beam down separate pools of light along empty pavements. Nothing is visible in the darkness above their slender columns.

Robert looks at his watch. 'Nearly twenty past ten. Time for aboot ten minutes' winching, eh?'

'Aye.'

Just before they come to number 18, they turn off right into the lane known as the Gap. A few paces over the grass bring them to the empty outbuildings once used for storage by a furniture shop. They disappear into the shadows where two of the units meet. Rhea leans against the wall; Robert puts his arms round her and they kiss for a few minutes without speaking. Rhea breaks the heavy silence. 'Robert, Ah knew when ye finished yer apprenticeship that that would be yer deferment ended. But since ye told me this mornin' . . .' She pauses. 'It's been oan ma mind the entire day. Ah've no' been able tae think of anything else. It's gonny be awful.'

He hugs her even tighter; kisses her again. 'Ye know what Ah was thinking?' He doesn't wait for a reply. 'Imagine this was only ten years ago. The war just started. All the guys wi' girlfriends and wives getting called up, and little do they know it, but they are gonny be away for *six* years! And there's a chance of gettin' killed intae the bargain! So at least we know Ah'm only going away for two years, and there's nae war oan at the minute. Mibbe we should be thankful for small mercies, dae ye no' think?'

She puts both arms round his neck, kisses him all over his face. 'Naw, Ah don't! It should be a help – but it is'nae. Robert, Ah don't know whit Ah'll dae withoot ye.' She is on the verge of crying. He kisses her passionately a few times more. Then speaks.

'Do ye know whit else Ah've been thinking?' He carries straight on. 'We know Ah have tae dae ma two years. So at the moment there's nae point confronting oor parents about gettin' married. Especially oor fathers. And even if we did, and miracle of miracles they said it was okay, we're no' in a position tae get married. National Servicemen get paid washers, aboot a pound a week. We'll no' be able to afford tae get married until Ah'm oot and workin' at ma trade.' He hugs her close and kisses her again. 'What aboot this? We get secretly engaged before Ah go away? And Ah *mean* secret. You don't even tell your sister. We'll be the only ones who know. It'll be oor bond. Oor link with one another while Ah'm away. Then,' he squeezes her tight, 'when Ah'm demobbed – and remember we'll both be twenty-three by then – that's when we'll face up tae them. Tell them how long we've been going out, how long we've been engaged. Tell them we want tae get married, hopefully with their blessing, but if not, well, it'll have to be without. What dae ye think?' He brushes his hand against her cheek; knows he'll touch tears. 'What dae ye think, Rhea?'

She laughs through her tears. 'It's the best idea Ah've heard fur years!' She reaches for her hankie. Dabs her eyes then blows her nose. 'But dae ye mind if Ah point oot something – you huv never, ever actually asked me tae marry ye.'

'Oh God! Ah hav'nae, have Ah? Ah've just always taken it for granted tha—'

'Ah know. So huv Ah. But it would be nice if ye proposed tae me, Robert.'

They both begin to laugh. He cuddles her in close; kisses her forehead, her cheeks, her lips. She hears him swallow hard. 'Rhea O'Malley. Ye know Ah love every bit of ye. There's never been anybody else. Would ye please marry me? If ye don't, Ah'll just pine away withoot ye.'

She stands on tiptoe and kisses him. 'Ah always knew Ah'd marry you, Robert Stewart. It'll be nice tae huv oor engagement ring, even though naebody will get tae see it till God knows when.'

Robert speaks again. 'Now, what you'll have tae try and do this Saturday, Rhea, is think up some excuse tae get away on yer own. We'll meet outside the Argyle Arcade. It's full o' jewellers' shops. Ah've got fifteen pounds saved up, so we should be able to get a really nice ring for that.'

'Oh, no' half. She pauses. 'Imagine, Robert. Oan Setterday we're goin tae pick oot oor engagement ring.' She bursts into tears. 'Isn't it jist wonderful?'

CHAPTER FIFTEEN

Dumbstruck!

George Lockerbie emerges from Hillhead subway station into a rainy Byres Road. He lingers for a moment in the shelter of the subway entrance, not only to keep out of the rain, but to look up and down the road, enjoy being in the area again. It's funny. Maryhill is only a mile away, yet the contrast with Hillhead is striking. Like chalk and cheese. Or should that be chalk and Brie? All my life Ah've considered this is where the toffs live. Even now, thirty-two years old, Ah still feel I'm trespassing. Soon as Ah open my mouth Ah'll be recognised as 'not one of us'. Can't blame Joan for wanting to move here or somewhere like it. At first glance a stranger might think it's like any other Glasgow district: cobbled setts and trams, tenements all the way from Great Western Road to Dumbarton Road and in all the streets running off to left and right. But there are no shared lavatories in these blocks. No need to make your way, rolled towel and soap dish under your arm, to the Public Baths and Washhouse for a bath. No painted and distempered closes. This is 'wally close' territory. Beautiful Art Noveau tiled entrances welcome you. The flats are self-contained with bathrooms and toilets. It must be great getting up during the night and not having to put a coat on over your jammies to visit the lavvy on the half-landing – especially in the winter when it's below zero. Trouble is, the rent is gonny be at least double. Maybe more. Jist tae huv a pee in comfort? Anyway, if that's what it takes to get Joan back to how she used tae be . . .

He steps out from the shelter of the subway entrance and walks the few yards to where a guy is managing to sell newspapers in spite of his unintelligible cries: 'TIMESAHCITZEN! EVENINGTIMESAHCITZEN!'

'Do ye happen tae know where Franchetti's Bar and Lounge is?' He has asked at the same instant as a man is buying a paper. He waits while the brief transaction is completed.

'Aye, it's well doon the road. It's oan this side, mibbe aboot a hundred yards fae the Dumbarton Road.'

'Smashin'. Thanks very much.'

'Nae bother.'

He sets off at a good pace, arms swinging. Well, drizzling or no', Ah'm still gonny enjoy a walk the length of the Byres Road. Anyway, it's December. Whit dae ye expect. Sunstroke? His thoughts go back to late '45, when Joan and he first arrived in Glasgow after their demob. Still having a bit of their RAF gratuities left, they quite often took the subway over to Hillhead for an evening out. It usually included a visit to the Hillhead Salon. Maryhill had the Roxy, Star, Blythswood and Seamore cinemas. Hillhead had the Salon. Even the names over here are pan loaf. Still, it's the place to go if you want to see some good foreign films. Ordinary cinemas never show them; folk just won't pay out good money to see movies in which you have to read subtitles to find oot whit's going on. But the toffs do. And so would he.

Thoughts of evenings spent in Hillhead are still running through his mind when, hardly a hundred yards from the subway, he sees he is approaching the Bar Deco. Jeez-oh! Ah forgot about this. It's almost like running into an old friend. Joan and he regularly called in here back in those early days in Glasgow. He takes in the black-and-white-tiled frontage. All very stylised and 'moderne'. A prime example of Glasgow's love affair with Art Deco in the thirties and forties. It still looks good. He's about to move on when a printed card in the corner of the window catches his eye: 'Experienced Cocktail Barman wanted. Part time. Apply within.' The position at Franchetti's was in the Situations Vacant in Friday's evening papers. This wasn't. Might as well chance it. Why not? It's handy for the subway station. Save a lot of walking. He pauses for a moment. A couple of deep breaths, shoulders back. Try and look as if you're not bothered whether you get it or no'.

He pushes open the inner door with its Art Deco stained-glass window. Inside it's just as he remembers it. Discreetly lit. Discreet everything. On the right is the bar. Smoked mirrors on the wall behind it; subdued lighting softly spilling out from the shelves above them. Running along the left-hand wall are the semicircular red plush booths, each with its own small table lamp. On the right stand three men, all wearing expensive-looking top coats. Almost certainly businessmen having a little refreshment before going home. He catches a snatch of their conversation. Definitely businessmen. They all three look to see who has just come in. Nobody of interest. They look away, their conversation barely interrupted. A young couple occupy one of the booths, touching hands on the table.

George walks along to the far end of the room. The lone barman approaches. He's wearing black trousers and a short, well-fitted pale blue jacket with brass buttons. The jacket is reminiscent of RAF officers' mess jackets.

'Can I get you something, sir?'

George leans on the bar, not wanting everyone to overhear his conversation. 'I've come about the vacancy for the part-time cocktail barman.'

'Ah!' The barman also leans on the bar. 'Do ye mind if Ah ask ye. Ye definitely have cocktail experience? We've had a few came in quite frankly just wasting the boss's time.'

George smiles. 'No, you're quite right tae ask. My last two years in the RAF, towards the end of the war, Ah worked every weekend in the officers' mess at RAF Scampton. The bar was very much run as a cocktail bar. And the guy who taught me, Eddie Scarponi, was the former head barman at the Dorchester before the war.'

The barman pats him on the arm. 'Sounds good tae me, ma friend. Ah'll just go and tell the boss somebody's here aboot the vacancy.'

As he watches him make his way through the door into the rear of the premises, George has a good feeling. If Ah do get it, Ah feel Ah could work with this fella. Ah wonder how many other staff there are? The barman hasn't been gone two minutes when the door opens and he reappears. He reaches under the flap at the end of the bar and George hears a bolt slide. The flap is lifted. 'Just come through.' George walks behind the bar. He hopes it's the first of many times. The barman nods his head in the direction of the door. 'Straight along to the end of the corridor, the door facing you. It's got "Manager" oan it. Good luck!'

'Oh, thanks.' As he enters the corridor, he hears the flap gently close and the bolt slide home. Once again George takes a few deep breaths, braces his shoulders. Remember! Don't talk too posh, but don't talk broad Glaswegian either. Strike a balance.

As he approaches the office door, his footsteps have been heard. He raises his hand to knock.

'Just come in!'

It's a woman's voice! Somehow, he wasn't expecting a female boss. He takes hold of the handle and pushes the door open. Two steps inside the office he stops. He will forever describe himself at this moment as dumbstruck!

He looks at her, opens his mouth to say good evening. Nothing comes out.

Behind the desk sits a woman of, he will learn later, thirty-four years of age. She looks at him. He can't take his eyes from her. Dark hair, somewhere between brunette and black. Pale alabaster skin, dark eyebrows and bright red lipstick. She sits at a desk you'd expect to find Sydney Greenstreet behind. The only light source, a green glass table lamp, sits a few feet away. Hollywood couldn't have lit her better. She has a cigarette burning in a tortoiseshell holder.

'Good evening! You've come about the vacancy?'

'Hello. I have,' is what he says. It comes out as a sigh. She's taken his breath away. He holds a hand up, palm forward, as though to stop her saying anything else until he's caught up with himself. He moves that hand to his mouth, coughs gently, pats his chest with the other hand and, discreetly, manages to muster up a bit of saliva. 'That's better!' he says, in a reasonable impression of how he used to speak. Strangely enough, he doesn't feel embarrassed. He decides to play it for laughs. Looks to his left and right. 'Okay, where are the cameras? You have got to be a movie star!'

She laughs. God! Bette Davis or Joan Crawford would kill for that laugh.

'Anyway. Sorry about that – though it's your own fault. My name is George Lockerbie.'

She stands up. Everything she wears adds to the image. Black taffeta blouse, black pencil skirt, broad red belt. And when she walks round the desk to offer him her hand, it's in red high-heeled shoes. He takes her hand in his. It feels cool, soft. He looks into her eyes. They're hazel.

'I'm Ruth Malcolm. Alan tells me you have cocktail bar experience.'

'Yes. Two years in the officers' mess at RAF Scampton. With it being an important bomber base, we used to get plenty of high-ranking visitors – including many Americans. It was run very much as a cocktail bar. Not just the usual, shall we say British cocktails – Singapore Slings, Pink Gins – but my boss, Eddie Scarponi, taught me to make Highballs, Tom Collinses and all the Yanks' favourite drinks. With lots of Anglo-American co-operation going on during the later stages of the war, the officers' mess was the ideal place to learn the cocktail business.

'Sounds to me like you could be the man for the job. What sort of hours were you thinking?'

'I work full-time assembling prefabs over in Partick. I live in Maryhill. I'd prefer, if possible, just Friday and Saturday evenings – if that's all right with you. I work on Saturday mornings.'

'No, that's fine. It's only on Friday and Saturday evenings that I need a part-time barman. I pay a pound per evening.

Start at seven o'clock. We're supposed to close at nine thirty; by the time we have last orders, get the place cleared and cleaned up, hopefully you should be off home by ten fifteen to ten thirty. Now, what you'll also find is that many of our customers are quite generous. Especially when they get to know you. Some will give you a tip. Others will tell you to take a drink for yourself. If you wish, you can just mark on the pad at the side of the till how many drinks you've been offered. At the end of the night you can tally up, and provided the till balances, you can take these drinks in cash. I believe Alan can make a couple of pounds over the two nights. It pays to be popular!'

She sits back in her chair again. 'Anything else you'd like to ask?' She busies herself fitting another cigarette into the holder. As he watches her, he feels an air of sadness around her.

'Are there other staff?'

'Yes. Another barman. Stefan. He's Polish. Didn't go back home after the war. He's married to a Glasgow girl. He was in the Polish navy. If we are having an exceptionally busy night, or if somebody is off sick, I usually come behind the bar and give a hand. But mostly I sit on a stool at the end of the bar. Public relations, as it were.'

George laughs. 'I would imagine there will be many a customer calls in purely for that reason.'

'Yes. Unfortunately, one or two, especially when they've had a few drinks, can become quite amorous – sometimes bordering on lecherous! However, I can manage them. And most of my regular old boys will come to my rescue if someone's becoming a nuisance. You'll find it's quite a nice bar to work in. Trouble happens very, very rarely.'

'Right, ah, it's Mrs Malcolm, I take it?'

'Yes. In front of the customers it's always Mrs Malcolm. When it's just the bar staff and myself – that will now include you – it can be Ruth. I always call the barmen by their first names. So you'll be George.'

'Right, Mrs Malcolm. Well, it sounds as if you run a tight ship. I think I'll like working here. Do you want me to start this coming Friday?'

'Yes please. If you could come in between six forty-five and seven at the latest. Is that okay?'

'That's fine.'

She holds her hand out again. George smiles.

'See you Friday.' He tries not to hold her hand for too long. Or look into those hazel eyes.

The rain has slackened while he's been in the Bar Deco. He strides up the Byres Road towards the subway station feeling quite exhilarated. Jeez! Outside of a cinema screen Ah've never seen a woman as beautiful as that. She is just . . . just what? How could you describe her in one word? Well, classy for a start. But classy doesn't do her justice. He eventually exhausts his vocabulary and is left with two contenders. Delectable, or exquisite. It'll have to be exquisite. Just to be around her is going to be nice. Roll on Friday!

CHAPTER SIXTEEN

Alles Muss Sauber Sein

By now Irma Armstrong is well into her stride washing the close. She dips the scrubbing brush into the bucket a few times and lets the water fall on to the large slabs that make up the surface. She then rubs the brush on the block of red carbolic soap and scrubs the wet slabs. The floor cloth is used to mop up the excess water, the cloth being wrung out into the bucket when it can absorb no more. Finally she takes the block of pipe clay and rubs it along the edge of the slabs at either side of the long, narrow close where they meet the wall. She stops for a moment and looks along the length towards the back close. All nice and clean and bordered on either side by the broad white lines where the pipe clay has dried. She turns her head and looks towards the close mouth. Nearly finished. Maybe two metres. No! Think in feet. She looks again. Six feet? I must have clean water.

She puts the bucket by her side, then stretches forward to start scrubbing where she left off. She hears footsteps but knows she has left enough room for people to pass.

'Oh, for goodness' sake!'

The bucket clatters over and water swishes along the floor. Irma feels her knees becoming wet as it soaks into the folded-up old towel she is using to kneel on.

'Oh, I am sorry. I thought I had left enough room for . . .'

He neither stops nor speaks. She watches the tall, slim man wearing the blue overcoat start up the first flight of stairs. As he has his back to her, she can't see the satisfied smile on his face. When he turns on the half-landing and begins to ascend the second flight of stairs, he glances through the rails of the banister and is pleased to see that the spilled water has cascaded ten feet or so along the newly washed close. Good! She'll have to do that again. As he climbs out of Irma's sight, his smile gets wider. 'Nazi bitch!' he murmurs.

Irma stands up. Her skirt is wet as well as her kneeling pad. She looks towards the stairs; she can still hear his footsteps. Did he mean to do that? She has seen this man a few times since they moved in. He never speaks, never glances. Always walks quickly past. She looks along the close. It will have to be dried off. And more pipe clay put down. She turns her head towards the close mouth; then I can finish this part. With a sigh, she picks up the bucket and heads into the house for some fresh water.

It's just after six p.m. when Drena and Billy McClaren enter the close. Irma stands at her door polishing the brasses. Even though it's dark outside and there is only the gas light in the close to see by, Drena notices how clean the floor is. She stops and looks down. 'Ah'll bet it's been your turn for the close the day, Irma.'

Billy points down. 'Wie eine gute Deutsche Hausfrau – alles muss sauber sein!'

Irma gives a little curtsey. 'Oh, danke sehr.'

Drena turns towards Irma. 'Ah hope that's no' him sweering at you, Irma.' They all laugh.

'No,' says Billy. 'I said, "Like a good German housewife – everything must be clean!"'

'This bit is extra clean. I have done it zweimal, ah, two times.'

'Twice!' says Drena. 'Ah never noticed the close was dirty enough tae need doing twice.'

'No, one of the men who lives upstairs knocked my bucket over. That tall, quiet man. He never speaks when he comes in and out.'

Billy looks at Drena, then back at Irma. 'Did he say sorry?'

'Ah, no. Just, "Oh, for goodness' sake!" and carried on up the stairs.'

'Wearing a dark blue overcoat, was he?' asks Billy.

'Yes. I think maybe he lives up near you. I can hear his footsteps for a long time.'

'Well! We know who that'll be,' says Drena. 'Ye can bet yer boots that would be no accident.'

'Pardon?' says Irma.

Billy speaks. 'Vielleicht es war kein unfall.' He looks at Drena. 'Ah'm saying, "Perhaps it was no accident."'

Drena draws herself up to her full height. 'Ye can take a bloody bet it wid be nae accident. No' if that reptile wiz involved!'

Irma looks from one to the other. 'He is not a nice man?'

'Ye got that right first time,' says Drena, still bristling. 'His name is Richard Sneddon, lives next door tae us. Almost every weekend he hits his wife.' She says it in a loud voice, not caring who hears – especially the subject.

Billy starts laughing. Drena rounds on him. 'Whit urr you laughing at?'

'You! You're always stopping me going next door and intervening. Listen tae ye. Ah hope Sneddon diz'nae put in an appearance before Ah get you safely intae the house – you're liable tae banjo him!'

'Well nae wonder,' says Drena, 'picking oan a young lassie. That's jist typical o' that, that . . .'

'Scheisse!' says Billy. He and Irma laugh.

'Whit's "shyser"?' enquires Drena.

'Shit!' answers Billy.

'That's him! A big shyser!' All three go into fits of laughter.

'Well if you think it was deliberate, Ah'm sure Bert will sort him oot,' says Billy.

'Oh, Gott! No. Please, do not tell Bert. He will get into trouble. He is very, eh . . .'

'Protective?' suggests Billy.

'Yah. Yes. Very much so. You must not say to him what has happened. Really.'

'Yeah, okay. Don't worry.' Billy smiles, says it in German to reassure her: 'Keine sorge.'

'Oh, thank you.'

'So, Bert's out with the taxi, is he?' asks Drena.

'Yes. Working evening and maybe until two in the morning. This is the best time. Not enough people want a taxi during the daytime.'

'Right.' Drena reaches out and squeezes Irma's hand. 'We'll get away up the stairs. Come up aboot half ten the morra morning and we'll huv a wee cup of tea. Okay?'

'That will be nice. Bert will be sound asleep. I'll come after ten.'

Drena takes Billy's arm. 'We'll get away up the stairs. Good night.'

'Good night,' says Irma.

'Schlafen Sie gute,' says Billy.

'Whit huv Ah telt you aboot sweering at that lassie?' says Drena. She turns and winks at Irma.

Irma watches until they go out of sight, then resumes polishing her brasses, humming a tune as she does so.

CHAPTER SEVENTEEN

Stiff Upper Lips

———————

Sunday morning. Samuel Stewart sits at the kitchen table, pretending to read the *Sunday Mail*. Mary always has first claim on the *Post*. Son Robert lounges on a fireside chair, feet up on the range, absorbed in the *Sunday Pictorial*. The aroma of bacon and egg still hangs in the air.

'Put a few wee bits of coal oan the fire for me, son.'

'Right y'are, Ma.' Robert reaches forward, picks up the tongs and does so.

Samuel, one elbow on the table, leans his head on his hand and seems to be engrossed in the paper. Robert sits at right angles to him; Mary is busy at the sink. Neither of them can see how often he looks at his son. God, Ah'm no' half gonny miss him. Christmas next week, followed by Hogmanay. Then he's away on the seventh. The hoose'll be empty without him. That's the trouble wi' only having one of a family. Samuel looks at Robert again. He's never been a bit o' bother. Good at school, passed aw' his exams. And noo, just when he's become a fully qualified motor mechanic, two bloody years in the army! Ah bet it'll change him. He sighs. It was lovely when he was a wee boy. Every Sunday morning without fail, through he'd come fae the front room and climb intae the recess bed and snuggle in between Mary and me. It was great when he was wee, plenty o' hugs and kisses for his daddy as well as his mammy. Noo it's just Mary gets them. He must've been aboot twelve when Ah last got a kiss or a cuddle.

Only twice in his twenty-one years has he disappointed me. Diz'nae like fitba. Never played it oot in the street and never comes tae Ibrox wi' me tae see the Gers. Then, just a few weeks ago, the second body-blow. No' interested in joining the Lodge. Says aw' that Orange Walk and dressing up in the regalia is'nae for him. Well, Ah cannae force him. He might come tae it eventually, in his ain good time. Anywye. Diz'nae alter the fact Ah'm gonny miss him something terrible. Jist Mary and me in the hoose. Nae Robert. Samuel sighs again.

'By, you're daein' a bit o' sighing therr, Sammy.' Mary steps back from the sink and nudges him with an elbow.

'Aye. Bored. Whit likes the weather oot therr, Mary?'

She pulls the curtain to one side and looks out into the back court. 'Well, it's dry. Ah think it's still quite cauld. It wiz when Ah went fur the papers.'

Samuel closes the *Mail*, stretches his arms up in the air. 'Fancy a good brisk walk, Robert? Blaw away the cobwebs.'

Robert takes his feet off the range. 'Aye, Ah'm game. Another five minutes o' this and Ah'll be dropping off.' He rises from the chair. 'C'mon then, Da.'

'Baith of ye put yer coats oan. There's a bit of a wind blawing, it'll cut right through ye's.'

As father and son emerge from the close and turn left for the Maryhill Road, coming towards them are the O'Malleys on their way home from chapel. Rhea and her sister Siobhan, arm in arm, are in front. Teresa and Dennis, also arm in arm, bring up the rear.

'Good mornin',' say Samuel and Robert, almost in unison.

''Mornin',' echo the O'Malleys.

Robert and Rhea catch each other's eye for a moment. Siobhan speaks. 'Somebody was tellin' me you're away tae the army efter the New Year, Robert. Is that right?'

'Aye, Ah'm afraid so. Seventh of January.'

'And do ye know what lot they're puttin' ye into?' asks Dennis O'Malley.

'Oh, aye!' Robert laughs. 'Ah've just finished my apprentice-ship, so Ah'm now a motor mechanic. Ah asked for the Engineers or the REME so's Ah can use my trade. But because Ah can drive, they're puttin' me into the Ordnance Corps. The RAOC.' As he speaks, Robert tries not to look at Rhea all the time.

'Jayz! Isn't that the way of it?' says Dennis. ''Tisn't the first time Oive heard a tale like that. Anyways, I hope yer going to be first-footin' us at Hogmanay, son. I'll give ye a wee half to send ye on yer way.' He turns to Samuel. 'And that includes yourself, mind, Sammy. Even Rangers fans are welcome at New Year in the O'Malleys'.'

'Ah think Ah'll take ye up oan that, Dennis. Ah'm no' ower happy at losing ma boy oot the hoose for the next two years. Ah could dae wi' a bit o' cheering up.'

'Well, don't ye's be forgettin',' says Teresa. 'As soon as them bells ring, our door will be open till yon time.'

They all say their cheerios, and father and son set off at a good pace. 'Ah like the O'Malleys,' says Robert. 'Rhea and me have played the gether since we were weans, and we often used to be in the same bunch in DiMarco's café when we were in our teens. She's a nice lassie.'

'Aye, he's not a bad lad for a Catholic, Dennis.'

Robert laughs out loud. 'God, Da! Whit difference diz that make? Dennis O'Malley is a good-living, hard-working man. His two lassies think the world of him, and Ah'd imagine he's a good husband tae Teresa. See, that's why Ah did'nae want tae join the Lodge.'

'Well,' says Samuel, 'there's a lot mair tae it than that, ye know.'

'That Sneddon fella that lives up the stairs uses his wife as a punchbag. Ah'd imagine he's a Proddy. Are ye telling me, Da, that simply 'cause he's no' a Catholic he's a better man than Dennis O'Malley?'

'Well of course Ah'm no', Robert. Anywye, for the minute let's get aff the subject. Ah'm no' wanting us tae fa' oot jist before ye go intae the army. Ah want tae enjoy your company as much as Ah can afore ye go away.'

They walk together in silence for a few minutes, then Robert breaks it. 'How far are ye thinking of going, Da?'

'Ah'm for a real stretch o' the legs. Whit aboot doon Queen Margaret Drive tae Great Western Road, aw' the way alang tae St George's Cross then back up the Maryhill Road?'

'Sounds good tae me, Da. Ah'd think by the time we get hame we'll be ready for a lie-doon.'

'Be ready fur some oxygen, more like!'

Side by side, arms swinging, father and son set off companionably together.

They are on the last stretch of the Maryhill Road when Samuel, at last, makes himself bring up the subject of Robert's going away. He clears his throat. 'So what dae ye think about going intae the army, son?'

'Just one o' they things, Da. Every lad knows he has tae do it. So Ah might as well knuckle doon and jist get on wi' it.'

'It wid'nae be sae bad if Ah'd been in the forces during the war,' says Samuel. 'But Ah was in a reserved occupation, building Spitfires oot at Paisley. So it's no' as if Ah can gie ye any tips aboot basic training or stuff like that, like maist faithers could.'

'Da, Ah always get the impression you feel a bit guilty 'cause ye did'nae go intae the forces.' Robert laughs. 'You were doing more for the war effort in 1940 by building Spitfires than you could have done in any o' the services.'

'Dae ye think so?'

'Ah know so. Whit if you'd been in the army and sent tae France – then captured at Dunkirk? You could now say you'd been in the army, for aw' the good it would have done ye. You're a skilled tradesman, Da. Working oan aircraft production was essential. Far more important than being a soldier. It would have been a waste of your skills.'

'Oh! Ah always thought that mibbe you were a wee bit disappointed 'cause yer da did'nae serve abroad like maist of yer pals' dads.'

'Naw, not a bit of it. My da was building the Spitfires that won the Battle of Britain. Ah think that's more important than you spending months oan guard in a trench near Dover – for an invasion that never happened. Never happened because of the fighter planes you built!'

Samuel Stewart feels a lump in his throat. He swallows hard. 'Well, it's nice tae know ye feel like that, Robert.' He just manages to keep his voice steady. They walk on for a while, then Samuel speaks again, 'Ah did'nae know ye were so well up oan the Battle of Britain and aw' the history of that time, Robert.'

'We got it at the school first of all. But in the last couple of years Ah've had two or three books oot the library. So Ah know that if we'd lost the Battle of Britain, the Germans would've tried tae invade us. But the RAF stopped them in their tracks. Thanks tae you and your workmates oot at Paisley.'

They walk slower now, up the last stretch of the Maryhill Road before Dalbeattie Street.

'How far dae ye think we've walked this morning, Da?'

'Jeez! Aboot five miles. At least.'

'Well, Ah'm no' bothered aboot having a lie-doon. Ah think Ah'd rather huv the oxygen.'

CHAPTER EIGHTEEN

The Hothouse

Ella Cameron and daughter Katherine emerge from their top floor flat on to the landing. It's ten past nine on a Monday morning.

'Wait there a wee minute, hen, while Mammy locks the door.' Katherine watches as her mother does just that, using the big key. As Ella places the old-fashioned key into the bottom of her shopping bag, there comes the noise of a door opening, then being shut, from the landing below. Ella leans over the banister, looks through the narrow well formed by the stairs and catches a glimpse of the bottom half of a dark green coat. 'Zat you, Drena?'

Three-year-old Katherine, dummy in mouth, pushes in front of her mother so she can look through the rails too. Drena steps on to the second step of the flight leading up from her landing, turns and looks up to the third storey. 'Auntie Drena!' Katherine waves her hand.

'Hello, hen!'

'Are ye going tae the shops?' asks Ella.

'Aye.'

'Jist wait a minute, we'll go the gether.' Ella lifts Katherine and they come down the two flights of stairs to join Drena. 'Are we going tae the steamie oan Wednesday morning?'

'Aye,' says Drena. 'We'll gie Lena a knock as we go by, see if she's going tae. And Ah'll tell ye who else. Irma wants tae come wi' us as well.'

'Oh my God!' exclaims Ella. 'Ye realise she'll probably give us aw' a showing-up? Ye know how clean the Germans are supposed tae be. She'll probably want tae wash the fireside chairs. Aw' the ornaments aff the mantelpiece.' She pauses. 'Mibbe starch the linoleum!'

Drena has to hang on to the banister as she grows weak with laughter. It takes her three attempts to say, 'That is absolutely stupid!' She wipes her eyes. Katherine looks from her mother to Drena, moves the dummy to the side of her mouth. 'Whit laughin' fur?'

Ella, still chuckling, puts a hand under her daughter's chin. 'Aw, ye wid'nae understand, hen – even Ah don't.' This sets the two women off again. Ella picks Katherine up and the trio descend the two flights of stairs to the first storey. Drena rattles Lena McDermot's knocker and opens the door. 'Lena, are ye therr?'

They hear Lena's voice from the kitchen. 'Aye?'

Drena opens the kitchen door. 'Ah'm gonny get tickets for the steamie oan Wednesday morning. Are ye going?'

Andrew McDermot speaks before his wife can. 'Whit dae ye mean, knockin' folk oot thurr beds at this unearthly 'oor o' the morning?'

'Pye nae attention tae him,' says Lena. 'He calls twelve noon too early nooadays.'

Drena pops her head round the door. Andrew is sitting up in the recess bed, reading the *Daily Record* and smoking a roll-up, a mug of tea nearby. 'Here, Ah'll gie ye the shilling fur the ticket,' says Lena. 'Wednesday mornin' at ten as usual?'

'Aye. Ah cannae stop. Ella's waiting for me, we're going fur the rations.'

Drena rejoins Ella and young Katherine and they descend to the close. Drena knocks and opens the Armstrongs' door. As she does so, Irma opens the kitchen door. She makes a 'sssshhhh' noise. 'Bert is sleeping. Night shift with the taxi,' she whispers.

'Oh, aye, of course. Sorry! Do ye want tae come tae the steamie with us oan Wednesday morning?'

'Yes. I have quite a few things needing to wash. What do I do?'

'Wrap all your dirty washing up inside a sheet. You have to carry it. Bring soap powder and a bar of soap; ye can jist put them inside your message bag. If you need bleach or anything you can borrow mine until you get yourself organised. We'll be leaving the close aboot half nine or jist after. Okay? Oh, if you have a pair of Wellingtons, or a strong pair of leather shoes, wear them, oh, and an apron. There's alwiz a lot of watter about in the steamie. Okay. If ye give me a shilling, Ah'll buy the tickets and book each of us a stall.'

'A stall?'

'Aye, a cubicle. That's, eh, that's the wee area where ye do your washing. You hire sinks, hot water, a boiler. Anywye, once we get there oan Wednesday, you'll see whit Ah mean.'

The first thing that strikes Irma as she enters the Maryhill steamie is the humidity. The large white-tiled room looks as if it should be cool. It isn't. It is filled with warm, moist air. It reminds her of the first time she and Bert entered the Tropical House in the big greenhouse at Kelvingrove Park. Instant humidity. What was its name? She turns to her companions.

'Drena, what is the name of that big greenhouse in Kelvingrove Park?'

'Dae ye mean the Kibble Palace?'

'Yes. This is just like when you walk in to the Tropical House. Yes?'

'Aye. So now ye know why this gets called the steamie. 'Cause it is.'

Irma watches as Ella and Drena park their 'transport' next to their cubicles. Ella's dirty washing is contained in a galvanised tin bath. This is sat in the middle of the chassis and four wheels – all that remains – of Katherine's pram. Drena's transport is young William's 'bogie' that his father made for him. She also uses a galvanised bath as her chosen container. Both women have pulled them along the Maryhill Road with pieces of string. There was a slight delay when Drena's string broke and the caravan halted while running repairs were made. Lena and Irma have their laundry wrapped in bed sheets, which they've carried over their shoulders.

''Mon, Ah'll show ye whit tae dae, Irma.' Drena leads her into the cubicle. 'It's really straightforward. You've got two sinks. Ah always huv wan full of hot soapy watter, the other wi' cauld watter, for rinsing.' She points to the metal sink in the corner. 'This is for boiling yer whites. Noo be really careful. Fill this wi' hot water and put yer whites in, then see this pipe that leads intae it?' She doesn't wait for an answer. 'When ye turn that round tap thing, this lets really hot steam intae the watter tae boil it up. Don't ever turn it oan unless you've got watter in the sink. You'll scald yersel. It's no' only very hot, it's also under high pressure. When ye huv it on it makes a bit of noise.' She takes Irma to the entrance of the cubicle. 'See that row of tall, thin doors. When ye pull them oot there are rows of sort of rails. If ye ever bring blankets or woollens, wash them first, spin them, then hang them up in wan o' them things. It's a really dry heat in there, so yer woollens will be drying while ye dae the rest of yer washing. Okay?'

'Yes, that is fine.'

'Now, last of all. The spin-dryers ower there.' She points to the row of large dryers. 'See that fella wi' the white coat. That's Andy. Ye let him load yer washin' intae the spinners. They have tae be balanced, loaded correctly wi' the weight spread evenly. If they're no' balanced they make a helluva racket and the drum inside can be broken. So alwiz let him dae it.'

'Right, okay. How much time do we have?'

'One hour. Well, aboot fifty minutes now. We've spent ten minutes talking. That should be plenty time for ye the day. If you're no' sure aboot anything, Ah'm jist in the next cubicle.'

'Right, thank you, Drena.'

Irma enters her cubicle. Already the sweat is running down her sides from her armpits. Her brow is beaded with it. She puts the plugs into the drains in both her sinks. Turns on the hot tap in the left sink and sprinkles a good measure of Oxydol from its black and yellow box into it. She swirls her hand through the water, until it becomes too hot, to help dissolve the detergent. She fills the right-hand sink with cold water. Bert's two white shirts she puts into the metal sink. She half fills it with water, adds some detergent, then tentatively begins to turn on the steam.

As she works, Irma finds it easy to fall into a routine. It is so good to have these facilities; far better than washing things through in the sink. Occasionally she looks through the grid-work of the partition and into the next stall. Drena is also busy, intent on getting all her washing done before the time is up. Irma looks out, across to the row of stalls on the other side. All but two of the cubicles are occupied: women with rubber aprons on top of their peenies, some with Wellington boots, others with rubber galoshes. A few have their hair tucked up under turbans, continually using the backs of their hands or forearms to brush away the sweat running down their brows, the sides of their faces and the backs of their necks. Looking through the gridwork at an angle, she can see the half-dozen or so women waiting to have their clean but wet washing loaded into the spinners. She gets the feeling this is the best time. Their washing as good as finished, the women seem in no hurry to be on their way. Some stand with arms folded, others lean on a couple of the spinners. This is, most definitely, a woman's world. Andy is ignored, outnumbered. He stands isolated at the end of the row of spin-dryers. Whatever the topic of conversation is, it is riveting for the women. A hefty-built woman holds their attention. As she tells her tale there is occasional laughter from her audience, or they show surprise – two or three of them are easy to lip-read as they enunciate 'No!' or 'Never!' When she finishes her soliloquy to gales of laughter, it is the turn of two of her listeners to either add to it, or relate similar experiences. These are also received with bursts of laughter. Irma's observations are interrupted when Drena's face peers at her through the cast-iron grid. 'Huv ye used the boiler?'

'Yes. I have two of Bert's shirts inside it.'

Drena moves away and seconds later comes into the stall. 'You'll need this tae transfer them from the boiler tae the sink. This is a boiler stick. Some folk use these, others use a pair of wooden tongs. Noo remember whit Ah telt ye. That watter is bileing hot. You've got tae transfer the shirts fae the boiler intae the cauld rinsing watter. Ah'll dae the first yin for ye.' Irma watches as Drena turns the steam off. The boiling shirts slowly subside. 'Right.' Drena dips the stick into the water and gently moves it under a shirt. She lifts the stick straight up in the air, and lets the almost boiling water run, then drip, off the shirt back into the sink. 'Noo watch whit Ah'm gonny dae.' Holding the shirt at arm's length, the stick horizontal, she begins to move the shirt in the direction of the sink full of cold water. She leans forward from the waist so that any drips on to the floor won't splash on to her feet. The shirt is succesfully transferred into the sink. She turns to Irma. 'Remember. Ye have tae hold the stick level. If ye hold it up at an angle, hot watter will run doon and burn ye. Bend forward and keep it well oot in front of ye so as any splashes on tae the grund will'nae scart back on ye. Okay?'

'Yes, I think so.'

Irma stands with her back against a spin-dryer. Ella, Lena and Drena, plus three other women whom they obviously know, stand together.

'So how's life treating ye, Isobel?' asks Drena.

'Och, no' bad. Jist have tae get oan wi' it.'

Drena leans forward, drops her voice. 'Wiz that big Margaret Ah seen when we first arrived?'

'Aye. She must huv taken an early ticket this morning.'

'That wee boy of hers will be gettin' big. Be at the school noo, Ah'd imagine,' says Drena.

'Aye.' Isobel glances round the steamie, adjusts her bosom in an upward direction.

'Whit wiz it she christened him?'

'Eugene.'

'Jeez-oh!' says Ella.

'Oh, but that wiz'nae the best of it.' Isobel carries out further adjustments. 'Her man wiz a POW the last three years o' the war.'

'Eeeeh, he wiz'nae!' says Ella.

'He wiz.' Isobel pauses for effect. 'And the bairn happens tae be coloured!'

'Bugger me!' exclaims Ella.

After order has been restored, Lena makes a few enquiries. 'How did she get away wi' it?'

'Well, when he got repatriated in 1945, she telt him that wan moonless night in 1942, during the blackoot, she wiz jist coming oot the subway at St George's Cross when somebody ran up tae her in the dark, shoved a bundle intae her arms and said, "You've got a kind face!" then vanished intae the night.'

'Fuck me!' says Ella. 'How could they tell?'

'And when she took it back intae the subway fur a look, whit did she find but two tins o' American lend-lease condensed milk – and a wee coloured wean!'

There's a longer pause to allow the audience time to recover, then Isobel continues. 'So she telt her man, "Ah wiz gonny hand it ower tae the authorities, but efter a few days Ah got awfy attached tae it, so wi' me being lonely Ah decided tae keep it. And the milk." An' he fell fur it!'

'He did'nae.'

'He did!'

Some thirty minutes later the Dalbeattie Street quartet sit round Drena's table. A foray has been made to the Scotia Bakery's shop for the purchase of two fern cakes and two pineapple tarts. Rich blue cigarette smoke drifts up into the air, a teaspoon chinks as sugar is stirred into freshly poured tea. Irma speaks. 'I think I am going to like the visiting of the steamie.'

CHAPTER NINETEEN

A Secret Shared

Rhea and Siobhan O'Malley lie reading in the double bed in the front room. Rhea is halfway through *Gone With the Wind*; Siobhan is absorbed in one of the stories in the weekly *Red Letter*. The light source is the lamp hanging from the centre of the ceiling. Book and magazine have to be held at awkward angles to avoid shadows.

Rhea is beginning to doze, the hardback book tilting towards her face. Her sister nudges her.

'Whit!'

'You're fawing asleep again.'

'Well, so whit?'

'If that book lands oan yer face it'll brekk yer nose!'

They hear the door from the kitchen open, their mother's footsteps traversing the short lobby. She enters the room. 'Right, c'mon, you two, quarter to eleven, time the light was out.'

'Aw, Ma, Ah'm jist at a good bit.'

'Don't you tell yer lies,' says Siobhan. 'She wiz fawing asleep, Ma.'

'Eee! Whit a wee clipe you are.'

'The light's goin' out. I'm the one has to suffer you in the mornin', Rhea O'Malley. 'Tis nine o'clock every night I should be sending ye to yer bed.'

Rhea gives a loud tut.

'Never mind tutting. By the time I get ye out that door in the mornin', 'tis fair exhausted I am. Why can't ye be like Siobhan? 'Tis a pleasure to get that child up. Like a lark she is.'

'Mair like a vulture!'

'Oh! Whit a cheeky bizzum!' Siobhan gives her sister a dig with her elbow; the two girls lie prodding one another. Their mother smiles.

'Right, the light's goin' out. Now if there's any noise or carry-on, it's your father I'll be sending through.'

Rhea gives a long sniggering laugh. 'Is that a threat?' The pair take a fit of the giggles.

Rhea has to make three attempts before she's able to say, 'And aw' Daddy ever diz is gie us a kiss and tuck us in.' This sets them off again.

Teresa stands, hand on the light switch, looking at her two daughters, both red-faced with laughing. She shakes her head. 'Ah, there *was* a time when he would hit you a skelp, 'specially if ye's wouldn't settle down in bed.'

'That's whit you think.' The two girls now go even more helpless. 'Oooh! Mammy! Daddy!'

Siobhan finally manages to gasp, 'Should we tell 'er?'

'Aye.'

''Member yon couple o' times, when we were wee, and ye sent him ben the room tae gie us a skelp 'cause of aw' the racket we wiz making?'

'Yes?' Teresa tries to look stern.

'Ye know whit he used tae dae?' The two of them once more become weak with laughter, Siobhan more so than Rhea. She manages to gasp, 'Rhea, you'll huv tae tell her.'

With an effort of will entirely foreign to her, Rhea says, 'He used tae batter the bolster hard wi' his hand and shout, "NOW! NOT! ANOTHER! SOUND!" And wi' every word he'd gie the bolster another skelp!' Rhea wipes the tears from her eyes. 'And then . . .' she manges to control herself, 'and then he'd promise us he'd give us a wooden threepenny bit each in the mornin', if we'd shut up and get tae sleep! Oooooh!' The girls now lie prone, weak, unable to get their laugh out, both having taken a stitch. Rhea manages to raise her head to see what her mother is doing. Teresa has had to sit down on the nearest chair. She holds her side with one hand, while with the other she wipes her eyes.

''Tis a madhouse I'm living in, so 'tis.'

Rhea sits up in bed. 'Ah'm gonny huv tae go tae the lavvy efter aw' that. Ah'll pee the bed if Ah don't.'

Siobhan also pushes herself up. She leans back on her arms, 'Me tae.'

The two girls rise, put on their coats and the nearest pair of shoes, then make their way down to the half-landing, lavatory key in hand. Minutes later they hurry back. 'Aw, Ma, it's freezing oot therr.' They take the shoes and coats off, shiver. 'And it's no' much better in here!' They jump back into bed. Lie together with their legs pulled up until the bottom of the bed begins to warm.

Teresa still sits on the chair, shaking her head as she looks at them. 'Never seen a pair like ye's. Lying there like two kippers in a box! Now, it's lights out.' She goes over to the bed, goes through the motions of tucking them in, gives each of them a kiss. 'Good night, girls.'

'Good night, Ma. Dae ye want tae hit the bolster a couple o' skelps afore ye go?' asks Rhea.

'Now mind.' Teresa points a finger at them. 'Enough!' She succeeds in keeping her face straight. The sisters watch her go over to the door, put her hand on the light switch again.

'Eh, that wiz a good laugh, Ma. Win't it?'

Teresa smiles, switches the light off, closes the door. They listen to her footsteps in the lobby, then the squeak of the hinges on the kitchen door. They hear their father's voice, 'You've been a devil of a time tonight gettin' them girls settled.'

'I've got a bone tae pick wit' you, Dennis O'Malley.'

Rhea turns on to her side, pulls the covers tight round her neck. 'Ah'm exhausted efter aw' that. Ah'll never get up in the moarning.'

'Huh! Tell me news, no' history,' says her sister. She also turns on to her side and cuddles into Rhea's back. The girls lie quiet for a minute. Siobhan moves her face nearer to the back of her sister's head. She takes a breath in, as though about to speak. Then, 'Are you seeing Robert Stewart?' She feels Rhea tense. It seems an age before an answer comes,

'Whitever gave ye that idea? Whit a load o' nonsense!' It sounds forced, put on.

Siobhan knows her sister too well. 'Rhea, Ah can tell that's no' true. Ye know you're the worst liar in the world. Anywye, you've been seen. Don't worry, Ah'll no' tell oan ye. Ah wid'nae dae that tae you and Robert.'

Rhea turns her head round to face her in the dark. 'Is that a promise?'

'Aye, cross ma heart and hope tae die.' Siobhan leans back so as to bless herself.

There's a pause. 'Okay. We've been going oot the gether for mair than a year.' She decides not to tell Siobhan about the engagement.

'Ah've always known you hud a soft spot for Robert. Whenever Ah used tae be in DiMarco's café wi' you and yer pals, Ah could tell. Ah'd sit in the booth and watch ye. Ye could'nae take yer eyes aff him. If ye were sitting beside him, you'd sit that close ye wur very near oan his lap.'

'Did not!'

'Did sot!'

Rhea sighs. 'Ah've loved him since Ah wiz aboot seventeen.'

'Whit aboot him?'

'Oh, it took him longer. He telt me, "Ah always liked you a lot, but that was aw'." It's jist aboot the last year or so wi' him.'

'So whit are ye's gonny dae aboot it?'

'There's nuthin' we *can* dae aboot it at the minute. He's away intae the army in aboot ten days' time.' Rhea sighs heavily. 'So we're jist gonny huv tae wait till he comes oot. There's nae good telling his parents or oor ma and da. We cannae afford tae get married till he's oot and working. Oh, Siobhan! You've nae idea how much Ah'm gonny miss him. Ah think Ah'm glad now that you know. Ah'll huv somebody tae talk tae instead of keeping it tae maself.'

'You should get secretly engaged before he goes away!' suggests Siobhan.

'Huuuh!' Rhea draws her breath in, then bursts into tears.

'Whit's the matter?'

'We have!' wails Rhea. She puts her head under the covers

in case her parents hear her. A second later it pops back out again. Pheww! Huv you pumped?'

'Aye. Mammy put beans in the mince, remember?'

In a combination of tears and laughter the sisters lie quivering, weak. Soon, arms draped over each other, foreheads touching on their shared bolster, they fall sound asleep to the lonely sound of someone's tackety boots echoing off the pavement, fainter and fainter in the night, as he walks the length of Dalbeattie Street.

CHAPTER TWENTY

Hogmanay

Dalbeattie Street is like any other street in Glasgow on the 31st of December. Especially when it turns dark. The lights are on in almost every house. Curtains are open, blinds not pulled, and light spills out from rooms and kitchens into back court and street. Preparations are under way for the greatest night in the year. Hogmanay! For the majority of working men this is *their* night. For the majority of wives and daughters, the 31st of December – the entire day – is nothing but hard work.

'Ah'm gonny have tae sit doon for five minutes. Have a wee blaw.' Ella Cameron lets herself fall on to a kitchen chair. 'Gie us yin o' yer Capstans, Archie.' Her husband obliges and supplies a light. She takes a long draw. Archie watches the blue smoke drift slowly upward. He looks at the clock. 'It's jist ten past seven. Time drags oan Hogmanay, dizn't it? Seems like the bells are never gonny come.'

Ella purses her lips. 'Well that's mibbe 'cause you've jist been sitting aroon' the hoose aw' day. It huz'nae been dragging fur me, sunshine! Been tae the shops, started getting the hoose tidy, and noo there's aw' the grub tae cook, prepare, lay oot.'

'Ah! But you alwiz make such a good job of it, Ella. Any first-footers that come tae that door know that you offer the best spread of any hoose in the close.'

'Oh, it's awfy good of ye tae say so.'

'Och, c'mon, Ella. It's only wan night in the year.'

'Aye. And it takes me aboot three months tae recover efter it!'

'So, whit huv ye got tae offer folk?'

'Two big ashet pies fae Guthrie's the butcher – God, ye should huv seen the queue at that shop – black pudden, sausages. Ah've got a nice pot o' stock from when Ah boiled the ham, so Ah'll be making a pan o' Scotch broth. There's black bun, clootie dumpling, shortbread, Dundee cake . . . you name it, we've got it.'

Archie leans back in the fireside chair. 'Ah'll bet ye the King, doon in Buckingham Palace, diz'nae get a better spread than that.'

Archie junior looks up from the *Beano*. 'Huv we got mair tae eat than the King?'

'Twice as much!' says his father.

'Can Ah stay up for the bells the night?'

'Aye. But jist tae bring the New Year in. Ten past twelve you'll be through that door and intae yer bed. The New Year is fur big folk. You had your celebration a week ago at Christmas. It's the mammies' and daddies' turn noo.'

As expected, three-year-old Katherine pipes up. 'Can me stye up?'

'Aye, you can stye up as well, darlin'.' Her father smiles at her mother. They both know she'll have fallen asleep long before ten, never mind twelve.

Next door to the Camerons, Donald McNeil sits by his fireside. Classical music from the Third Programme plays softly on his wireless. He's been dozing off and coming to for the last forty minutes or so. But that is all right. He knows that come midnight he will do his rounds. He always first-foots Agnes Dalrymple next door. Yes. It is supposed to bring good luck to a house if their first-foot is tall and dark. He smiles. Well, short and grey is the best I can offer. Still, it does not seem to have done Agnes, or any of the others, any harm. Then I will take myself down to the landing below. James and Irene Pentland. The brother and sister always insist I'm their first-foot, too. James gets a nice single malt in every year. And then Granny Thomson. If I do not go there, as she always warns me, 'You'll get yer heid in yer hands tae play wi', Donald McNeil!' She buys a wee miniature of whisky, alas just a blend, every year for my visit. The craic is always good. And, as ever, she will tempt me with something to eat as well. And finally, maybe about one o'clock, I'll wander back up the stairs and call into the Camerons' for five minutes. From midnight onwards their door is always open. Then back to my own house and have a last ten minutes looking out of the window before I take myself to bed. All the houses with their lights on, music, laughing and singing spilling out into the street. Folk in groups of two, three or more passing by. The men with bottles sticking out of their pockets, often stopping for a minute or two to toast folk they don't even know. Cries of 'A Happy New Year!' 'All the best!' drifting up to the top-storey windows. Then, watching as they all go their separate ways. Och, you cannot help but like the Glasgow folk.

And that's the way it will be at 18 Dalbeattie Street. In and out of one another's houses. Some folk, like James and Irene Pentland, welcome everyone who knocks on their door. But they don't like calling in on other neighbours – even though they know they'd be made welcome. It's not their way. Some houses, like the Camerons, McClarens and O'Malleys, open their front doors at midnight and they'll stay open till the last visitor leaves in the early hours. Bert and Irma Armstrong will join Robert Stewart and Rhea and Siobhan O'Malley and call in on most of their neighbours. The newcomers will have a wonderful time for their first Scottish New Year. Robert Stewart and Rhea O'Malley will pretend they are just part of the group. They will surreptitiously kiss as often as they can. They will fool no one.

The Sneddons are the exception to this outburst of pleasure. They have their evening meal at the usual time. As they eat it, they listen to the new hit show on the radio, *Take It From Here*, starring Jimmy Edwards. They will go to bed sometime after ten o'clock. Richard Sneddon ignores the New Year celebrations. He has no wish to kiss his wife, therefore he does not wish her a happy New Year! He hasn't done so for the last four Hogmanays. No first-footers will knock on their door. If they did, it wouldn't be opened. Richard likes it like that. It is *his* way.

That is how number 18 Dalbeattie Street welcomes in the new decade. There are few regrets for the passing of the forties. For years to come, the words 'the forties' will resonate with memories of war. As the day slowly brightens on the 1st of January 1950, not too many people stir at number 18. It is a morning for long lies. Especially amongst the menfolk. There will be time enough later in the day to contemplate the fact of a new year and a new decade. Much later. Anyway, the fifties have got to be better than the forties. Stands to reason . . .

CHAPTER TWENTY-ONE

First-Class Worrying

Agnes Dalrymple loves her Sunday mornings. But not this morning. Nor the last few Sundays. She lies on her back, staring unseeing at the ceiling. The sound of weans playing drifts up from the back courts; occasional laughing, shouts, girls screaming now and again, wee yins howling at regular intervals, usually because they feel like it, mammies raising windows to shout down to older brothers or sisters.

'Whit urr ye daeing tae that wean?'

'No' daeing anything.'

'Whit's he greetin' fur?'

''Cause he likes tae!'

'Noo Ah don't want any o' your cheek!'

'Ah'm no' gieing ye cheek. It's true. He's no' happy unless he's greetin'.'

'He is not. If Ah hear him greetin' wan mair time, yer comin' in.'

Agnes usually loves to lie and let it wash over her. Even though she's only listening to what's going on, in her mind's eye she can see it. That's the best thing about living on the top landing. Being up here keeps the noise at a certain level. She nearly always dozes off to the sounds of the weans at their games. But not this morning.

For the seventh time in the last hour her right hand reaches up to feel the lump. Just at the side of her left breast. It's definitely getting bigger. And more tender. She feels that stab of fear in her stomach again. That's 'cause you'll no stop touching it. Leave the bloody thing alane. You'll huv tae go tae the doctor. Touching it every day wullnae dae it any good. God! Forty-wan years of age; probably be lucky if Ah see forty-two. She feels near to tears.

Agnes opens the door to the newsagent's. Ken is leaning on the counter reading the *Reynold's News*. 'Good morning, Agnes.' He reaches for a *Sunday Post*. 'Just made it this morning, hen. Ten tae twelve.'

'Aye. Cannae seem tae get moving the day.' She lays the money on the counter. Ken looks at her. She seems distracted. 'Are you aw'right this morning? Seem as if yer miles away.'

'Och aye. Fine. Jist thinking of other things. Cheerio.' She manages a smile.

As she sets foot on the first landing, Agnes pauses; looks at Granny Thomson's door. She takes two steps towards it, raises her hand, then changes her mind. She has just turned away when she hears the door handle turning. The door opens.

'Well. C'mon then if yer coming!'

'Oh, Ah was jist, eh, jist . . .'

'Jist gonny knock ma door – then ye changed yer mind. In ye come. The kettle's bileing.' Agnes feels relieved. A decision has been made for her. She walks into the so familiar room, familiar smell. It's a dark January morning. One of the pair of gas lamps hisses quietly away on the chimney breast. She lays her paper on the table, then places her open palm on the comfort of the chenille cloth. Breathes in the smell. Lifebuoy soap, California Poppy . . . maybe, is that oil of cloves? Granny gets bothered wi' the toothache noo and again.

Granny stops on her way to the range. 'Happy New Year, Agnes.'

'Oh aye, this is the first Ah've seen ye. A Happy New Year tae you, tae.' Granny leans towards her and Agnes kisses one of her red cheeks.

'Did ye huv a quiet wan?' As she speaks, Granny puts three caddy-spoons full of tea into the china teapot, then, stirring all the while, pours boiling water from the black iron kettle into it. She puts the lid on, then carries the pot over to the table and places it on its matching stand. 'We'll jist let that infuse for a wee minute.'

Agnes watches as Granny fetches the Carr's biscuit tin from the sideboard along with two plates, then sits down opposite her.

'Whit's the matter?'

'Ah wiz just gonny come an' see ye, eh, wish ye a happy New Year.'

'Naw ye wiz'nae. Ye wur gonny go back up the stairs withoot coming tae see me. Ye'd changed yer mind.' Granny reaches for the tea strainer. When she finishes pouring, she puts the cosy over the teapot. Sits back. 'Spit it oot!'

In spite of her mood, Agnes smiles. Takes a breath in. 'Well, Ah'm jist a bit worried. Ah found a wee lump jist at the side of ma left breast.' Instinctively her hand goes to the area.

'Ah! So you've got yerself deid and buried, have ye?' Granny takes the lid off the biscuit tin.

'Ah suppose so.' Agnes gives an embarrassed smile. 'Ma sister Molly died wi' breast cancer. She wiz jist forty-two. That wiz how hers started. Wi' a lump. So when Ah found this one, well, that's the first thing ye think of, in't it?'

'Aye, right enough. Oh, Ah don't blame ye, Agnes. Ma mother died wi' a cancer. She'd jist turned fifty. Since that day tae this, Ah've been expecting tae find a lump oan a monthly basis!' She leans forward. 'Ah'll take a bet ye cannae stop touching it either, can ye?'

'Naw. Aw' the time.'

'Right! First thing tae do is leave the bugger alone. Whitever it is, you're jist irritating it. Hands off! Now, tomorrow's the third. The surgery will be open again, so get yerself along tae the doctor's. If he makes an appointment for ye at the Western or somewhere, Ah'll go with ye for company. Aw'right?'

'Oh, that would be good of ye, Granny. Ah don't want tae tell ma mother, get her aw' worried.'

Granny puts on her best stern face. 'Aye, nae good huving the two of ye demented!'

Agnes laughs, reaches out a hand to touch the older woman's arm. 'Ye make things seem so simple, Granny. Ah feel a lot happier already. Ah was fair getting maself up tae high doh.'

'And Ah'll tell ye something else, Agnes Dalrymple. Ye can bet yer boots you've been getting yerself up tae high doh aboot nuthin'. But the only thing that'll put yer mind at ease is a visit tae the doctor.'

'Of course it is. Ah wiz'nae thinking straight. That's jist common sense, so it is.'

'Ahh, but that's the trouble, Agnes. Common sense is'nae sae common nooadays.' Granny proffers the biscuit tin again. 'Anywye, let's get aff the subject. Was Donald McNeil your first-foot as usual?'

'Oh, aye. He always comes intae me straight efter the bells. Then he comes doon tae you, Granny, disn't he?'

'Aye. Did ye have anybody else in efter Donald?'

'Not on the Hogmanay. But New Year's Day Ah had Archie and Ella Cameron, and later oan Billy and Drena McClaren came up. Them two, Archie and Billy, baith had hangovers. They jist had a wee taste o' beer tae drink a toast. Did'nae have the stomach fur anything stronger. Whit aboot you, Granny?'

'Ower the Hogmanay and Ne'erday Ah've had maist o' the close in,' says Granny. 'Ah had the newcomers in as well. The new yins in the close.'

'Oh, aye. It's Bert and Irma, in't it?'

'That's right. He's a Geordie and she's a German lassie. Ah had them in for a cup o' tea the day they flitted intae the close. She's a nice lassie, mind. Very polite. They were telling me they went first-footing up the close. Everybody made her very welcome, seemingly. So that wiz good.'

'Ah!' says Agnes. 'That must huv been them that knocked oan ma door. Ah think it wiz aboot two in the morning. Woke me up.' She pauses. 'Here! Ah hope they did'nae go tae the Sneddons' door?'

'Naw. They were along wi' some o' the younger yins in the close.' Granny laughs. 'Jesus-Johnny! Can ye imagine a stranger knocking oan that door – and yon fella Sneddon opens it? Put ye aff New Year for life! Ah'd rether first-foot Hitler in the bunker!'

'Eeeh! Granny.' Agnes covers her mouth with her hands. She manages to rise from the table. 'Right, Ah'm gonny get maself away up the stairs.' Granny sees her to the door. 'And Ah'll go and see the doctor the morra' morning. When Ah come back Ah'll let ye know whit he says. Thanks a lot, Granny. You're always such a good help. Folk up this close don't know whit they'd dae withoot ye.'

'Och! Away and stop yer havering.' Granny waves a dismissive hand.

'It's true.' Agnes takes one of Granny's hands in both of hers. 'Ah hope ye have a smashing year in 1950.' She gives the old woman a peck on the cheek. 'Cheerio.'

'If Ah don't see ye through the week,' says Granny, 'Ah'll see ye through the window.'

Agnes shakes her head, smiles. With a lighter step she makes her way up the stairs.

CHAPTER TWENTY-TWO

Gone to a Soldier

As Robert and Rhea exit the Seamore Cinema they stop for a moment in the shelter of the main entrance. They look out on a blustery January night. Robert turns to her.

'Do ye want tae take the tram?' He knows what her answer will be.

'No. Ah'd rather walk. This'll be oor last date fur a while, Robert.' She links her arm through his. 'Ah want it tae last as long as possible.'

'Me tae.' They step out on to the Maryhill Road.

They are approaching Queens Cross. They have much to say, but have hardly spoken since they set out. Conversation has been desultory, stilted. Rhea clears her throat again; Robert wonders if she'll say what she wants to say, then maybe he'll be able to find his words.

'It wiz great tae see that wee polar bear cub again oan the newsreel. Jeez, it's no' half getting big, in't it?'

'Aye. Brumas. Ah think they'll soon stop showing it, mind. It's getting tae be too big. No' as cuddly as it was. Soon be as big as its mother.'

'Aye.'

They walk along in silence once more, their minds full of what they want to say. Rhea takes a breath in, presses his arm tight to her side. 'Oh, Robert, Ah wish Ah could see ye off at the Central the morra night.'

'Ah know. Me tae. But we cannae, Rhea. It would give the show away. My ma and da would wonder why you were there. We're just supposed tae be friends because we live up the same close. They'd be wondering why the rest of my pals aren'y there. Just you and naebody else.'

'Ah know, Ah know. Oh God! Isn't it bloody stupid? If we were both Catholic, or both Protestant, things would be fine. But we're no'.' He can feel her trembling with frustration, temper. She looks at him. 'Ah'll tell ye whit, Robert. When you're oot the army and we're merried – even before we're merried – religion is'nae gonny cause any more bother. Because we're no' gonny let it!'

He bends his head down and kisses her on the temple. 'You're bloody right we're not!'

They stand in the dark shadows of their usual winching spot, unseen. Many a time their love for one another has led them to the brink. Usually Rhea is the sensible one, fending off Robert's hands, keeping his passion, and hers, under control. But not tonight. Her mind is filled with the thought that tomorrow is the seventh of January. Twenty-four hours from now, a train will be taking him hundreds of miles away from her. Her arms are round his neck. Her blouse is open, his hand finds its way down inside her skirt. There has never been a night like this. 'Rhea, I cannae wait any longer. I want tae make love to ye.'

'Ah cannae wait either. Where can we go?'

Robert nods his head. 'The only place oot o' the way is the auld shelter. It still has some of the benches in it. The weans keep it clean, they use it as a den.'

'It'll have tae dae.'

Hand in hand in the dark, they pick their way over to the air-raid shelter.

'Well, Ah suppose we'd better be going, Robert. It's ten tae nine. Your train is nine forty, in't it?' Samuel Stewart rises and goes through to the lobby for his jacket and coat. His wife, Mary, follows him. Robert waits until they've come back into the kitchen to put them on, then goes to fetch his. 'Have ye got everything, son?'

'Far as Ah know, Da. Shaving kit, toothbrush, writing pad and envelopes.' Robert points to the small suitcase. 'That's all ma worldly goods. The men Ah work wi' who've done their two years say there's nae point taking things like shirts, socks and stuff like that. Ye have tae send aw' yer civvies back hame – they supply the broon paper and string – you're no' allowed tae wear your civvies until efter you've done yer basic training *and* yer trade training. So that's aboot four months doon the line. You don't get oot the camp for your first six weeks. Then, when you are daeing your trade training you can go oot, but only in uniform. Once ye get to whit they call your permanent posting, that's when you're allowed civvies.'

Minutes later they step out into the close. Robert watches as his mother shuts the door, locks it with the big key then turns the handle and pushes it two or three times. As they leave the close to walk along towards the Maryhill Road, he turns and looks up. As arranged last night, Rhea stands at her first-storey window. Her face is etched with sadness. Robert walks backwards for a few steps. 'Better just have a last look at the auld street, be a few months afore Ah see it again.' He purses his lips in a silent kiss; she blows one in return. Then he spins round and walks between his parents, resisting the urge to look at his love once more. The three of them quickly go out of Rhea's view. When she thinks they'll have covered enough distance, she quietly raises the lower sash window and leans her head out. Illuminated by the beams from the tall lamp standards, she watches them, Robert in the middle, walk the last few yards to where Dalbeattie Street joins the Maryhill Road. There they turn left and are lost to sight.

There aren't many passengers for the 9.40 sleeper to London. Robert and his parents stand on the platform trying to make small talk. Stamping their feet to keep warm. A cold wind is blowing straight through the station. Robert looks along the rows of parallel platforms. Another three, seemingly identical, locomotives stand impatiently steaming and occasionally sighing. The atmosphere is laden with the taste and smell of superheated steam and cinders.

'It looks like Ah'm gonny have a compartment all tae myself.'

'Aye, it's no' busy the night.'

'Try and hang on as long as ye can before ye eat your sandwiches, son,' says his mother. 'Goodness knows when you'll next get a proper meal.'

They watch as the guard starts to walk the length of the train, checking the doors and banging shut the few that are open.

'Right, Ma, Da. There's no good prolonging the agony. We're aw' freezing.' Robert smiles. 'Let's get it ower and done wi'. Dae ye no' think?'

'Aye, quite right, son.' His father sticks his hand out. 'All the very best, pal. Ah know you'll get oan aw'right.' As they shake hands, neither can speak. Their glistening eyes say it all.

'Cheerio, Ma. Ah'll write as soon as Ah get a minute.' They kiss and hug. Samuel envies his wife those hugs. 'Now, Ma! Ah'm only going intae the army for two years. There's nae war on. The lads tell me that once Ah get ma basic training done, it's a doddle.'

'Oh, Ah know, son. But even so . . .' Mary's voice trails off and she dabs her eyes again.

'Right, c'mon. It's gonny get aw' maudlin. Ah'm getting intae ma compartment. Now please don't wait until the train goes. Okay?'

'Aye, you're right, son.' His father takes his mother by the arm. Robert gives her another kiss. 'Aw' the best, son,' she says, dabbing her eyes again.

He opens the door, climbs up on to the high step and into the empty compartment. Just then the guard comes by and slams the door shut with a heavy clu-thunk! Robert lowers the window on its leather strap. 'Look! The compartment is lovely and warm. Ah don't want tae lose aw' the heat by having the windae open tae say goodbye another twenty-three times. We've said oor goodbyes. Ah'm gonny get ma coat off, put ma case up oan the rack and settle down tae read the *Evening Citizen*. Ah'm NOT gonny look oot the windae any more. You'll baith get your death o' cold. Goodbye!' He blows his mother a kiss, then pointedly closes the window and begins to settle himself into the compartment. From the corner of his eye he sees his father, at last, manage to propel his mother away from the vicinity.

Three minutes later there comes a loud blast from the

guard's whistle, and twenty seconds after that, Robert realises the train is moving. He feels butterflies in his stomach. I'm off! It's here at last. He sits back on the long bench seat. Sees the last of the station lights fall behind. Tries to analyse his feelings. He feels very grown-up. Manly. I'm going away to the army. As soon as he thinks that thought, the butterflies rise again. Well, that's because Ah'm sort of . . . going into the unknown. Anyway, Ah'm twenty-one. If Ah hadn't been an apprentice Ah'd have gone in at eighteen. Jeez! Ah don't think Ah'd have been ready at eighteen.

He looks out of the window for a while, watches the lights of Glasgow slipping behind, doesn't recognise one single place. Well, it is dark. He reaches into his pocket for his wallet, opens it and takes out a folded piece of blue writing paper. Smoothes it out: 'For the attention of Miss Rhea O'Malley, c/o J. Macready and Co. Solicitors . . .' Thank goodness her boss said it's okay for his letters to be sent there. He looks at her handwriting; runs his finger along it. Rhea wrote that. He's not used to seeing her writing. He folds the paper up carefully and places it back in his wallet. That's another thing to feel grown-up about. He's now twenty-one, he's engaged. And after last night, he's no longer a virgin. Rhea and he are lovers. All of a sudden, he's getting to be a man. He gives a rueful smile. And whether he likes it or not, this man's about to be a soldier.

CHAPTER TWENTY-THREE

The Making of Memories

It is just after eight thirty in the morning. Drena McClaren comes down the two flights of stairs from the second-storey landing to the first storey, and knocks on the McDermots' door. As expected, Lena answers it. Andrew will still be in his bed.

'Oh, hello, Drena. Is everything aw'right?'

'Ah'm sorry tae bother ye, Lena. Ma brother-in-law has jist called roon' tae tell me ma mother has got an appointment at the Western at three o'clock this efternoon – somebody has cancelled, so she got the vacancy – and she'd like me tae go wi' her. When Wil—'

Lena interrupts her. 'Do ye want William tae come tae us when he comes hame fae the school?'

Drena smiles. 'Aye, that's whit Ah was gonny ask ye. Ah should'nae be late back. Wi' a bit o' luck, by the time Ah see ma mother home Ah should be back for six at the latest. Hopefully Ah'll be back before Billy gets in from his work.'

'It diz'nae make any difference when ye pick William up. If he's still here at six ah'll gie him his dinner wi' Andra and me, so don't be breaking yer neck tae get back. Andra and me enjoy huvin' the laddie. Ye know whit Andra's like wi' weans. He cannae get enough of oor grandweans.'

'Right, thanks a lot, Lena. Ah'll see ye later.'

Drena sits down on a kitchen chair, pulls William over by his arm and manoeuvres him into position in front of her. She begins to comb his hair. 'Never mind screwing yer face up. Noo listen tae whit Ah'm gonny tell ye. Don't forget! When ye come hame fae school you've tae go tae Auntie Lena's doon the stairs till Ah get back. So come straight fae school. Don't go tae any of yer pals, or Lena will be wondering whit's happened tae ye. She's expecting ye at ten past four. If you're no' there she'll get worried. Dae ye hear me?'

'Aye. Anywye, Ah'll no' want tae go anywhere else. Uncle Andra's a rerr laugh, Ah like tae go tae their hoose.'

'Good boy.'

'Who wiz that at the door, Lena?' Andrew McDermot is sitting up in the recess bed rolling a cigarette.

'It wiz Drena. She wants us tae take William when he comes hame fae the school until she gets back. She's taking her mother tae the Western this efternin.'

'Aw great! Ah like wee William. Ah'll huv the life tormented oot o' him by the time Drena gets back. Is there anymair tea in the pot, hen?'

'Dae ye think you'll mibbe manage tae get oot yer bed by the time the bairn gets here?' As she speaks, Lena reaches for the brown china teapot.

'Excuse me,' says Andrew, 'but could Ah point oot that Ah'm retired.'

'Bedridden, mair like!'

'Haah!' Andrew draws a breath in, as though shocked. 'When Ah think of aw' they years Ah wiz up at six thirty every moarning tae go oot – in aw' weathers – tae work ma fingers tae the bone tae keep you and oor weans—' He is interrupted.

'Aye. And who had tae get up half an hour before ye every morning tae light the fire, put the kettle oan, start yer breakfast, and shout oan ye every five minutes until – aboot twenty tae seven if ma memory serves me right – you'd finally stagger oot o' yer bed?'

'Ah well, if you're gonny turn nasty . . .'

Lena laughs. 'Ah suppose any minute noo you'll be enquiring if Ah could find it in ma heart tae run alang tae Ken's tae get ye a *Daily Record*?'

'Well, darlin', whit a good idea. Ah never thought o' that. But it certainly would be appreciated. And if it's not an imposition, a half-ounce of Old Holborn wid be gratefully received.' He reaches down and rubs his right leg through the blankets. Winces. 'The auld war wound is giving me a bit of gyp this mornin', hen.'

'Oh, which wan o' your war wounds is it? The wan ye got when ye were fu' of rum and fell intae the trench?'

Andrew rubs his leg harder, screws his face up. 'Naw. It's the wan Ah got when Ah tripped oan the barbed wire and twisted ma knee. But it wiz German wire, mind.'

Lena tries to suppress a laugh; shakes her head as she goes through to the lobby for her coat. 'Right, Ah might as well go noo. Otherwise Ah'll never get a minute's peace.'

'Ah know whit ye mean, dear. It wiz four years before Ah got peace: 1918! He pointedly rubs his leg again.

'You're rubbing the wrang leg!'

He smiles at her. 'You're working well this morning, hen.' They both go into fits of laughter.

It's just after ten past four when the expected rattle of the letterbox comes. 'That'll be the wean,' says Lena. Andrew sits on a fireside chair. As the boy comes into the kitchen, Andrew looks surprised. 'Well, crickey jings! If it is'nae William McClaren. Have ye knocked at the wrang door, William? You live up oan the next landing.'

The boy knows he's being kidded, but he looks at Lena. She shakes her head. 'Don't pay any attention, William. He knows fine well we're expecting ye.'

'Could ye manage a drink o' ginger?' asks Andrew.

'Oh, aye, eh, yes please, Uncle Andra.'

'Irn Bru, Tizer or American Cream Soda?'

'Ahhh, American Cream Soda, please.'

'We huv'nae got any.'

William laughs. 'Well, Irn Bru will dae.'

'Huv'nae got any o' that, either. Dae ye like watter?' William can't answer for laughing.

Lena shakes her head. 'Stoap tormenting the poor laddie.'

Andrew goes to the press and returns with a bottle of American Cream Soda and a tumbler. 'Come and sit at the kitchen table, William.' He fills the tumbler, then sits opposite the boy. A draughtboard, already set up, lies in the middle of the table. He looks at William. 'Ah'm jist having a wee bit practice at the minute, 'cause Ah'm defending ma title in a couple of weeks' time. Did ye know that Ah'm the Scottish All-Comers Champion?' Lena is preparing veg at the sink. She shakes her head and looks heavenward.

'Eh, naw, Ah did'nae know, Uncle Andra.' William isn't too sure if he's being kidded or not.

'Oh, aye. Ah took the title aff Arthur Mometer efter a hard battle. Ah did'nae half huv him sweating. His temperature went sky high. He'd won the title the year before when he beat Ray Ling, the well-known Chinese fence.' Andrew shoots a glance at Lena. She's bent over the sink, shoulders shaking, holding her side. 'Ah take it ye know how tae play draughts, William?'

'Aye.'

'Oh, that's good. We'll huv a couple of games. It's very difficult fur me tae find anybody good enough tae play wi'. Ah usually jist play maself. Ye know, Ah move a white yin, then turn the board roon' and play a black yin. If it's a really fast game, Ah can get quite dizzy.'

'That's nuthin' new,' says a voice from the vicinity of the sink. Andrew ignores it.

'Noo, of course, William, as you'll soon realise, ye huv nae chance of beating me – me being a champion an' that. But it'll be good experience fur ye. Playing wi' the big boys.'

Five minutes later, Andrew has won the first game. 'As ye can see, William, Ah play tae a very high standard. Right, set them up again.'

Ten minutes later they each have just a few men left; it seems to be touch and go as to who could win. Andrew concentrates hard for a couple of minutes – then makes his move. William's face lights up. 'Got ye, Uncle Andra!'

'Well! That wiz a bit of a fluke. Ah must'ny have been concentrating there. Aye, ye were dead lucky there, William. Ah mean, tae take a game aff the Scottish Champ. There's no' many people can say that. Anywye, Ah'll set them up again. And Ah'm afraid that Ah'll huv tae put ye in yer place. There'll be nae mercy this time, pal.'

An excited William sits back 'Auntie Lena, Ah've won! Ah'm two-wan up.'

'Eeeh! Good for you, William. Imagine beating the champ. Ah cannae remember the last time somebody beat your Uncle Andra.' She puts on a serious face. 'Mind, Andra, you'd better watch oot. He could take yer title aff ye.'

'It wiz jist a fluke. He's a wee lucky-bag!'

'Ah beat ye fair and square,' says William, laughing and jabbing a finger at his opponent.

'Okay,' says Andrew, 'Ah'll tell ye whit Ah'm gonny dae. Ah'll let ye see how a champion can play when the chips are doon – in fact, even when the fish are doon! Set that board up again.' As William busies himself, Andrew winks at Lena. 'Now, William. We're about to start a new series of games. Ah'm gonny put ma title oan the line. We are gonny play whit's called "the best of five". The first wan of us tae win three oot o' the five is the winner. If you win you'll be the new Scottish Champion. But Ah can tell ye now,' he leans forward, 'you huv nae chance. Ah'm gonny spifflicate ye!'

Lena comes over to the table. 'Are ye sure ye want tae put your title oan the line, Andra?'

'Huh! C'mon, Lena. William's no' a bad wee player, but he's a boy playing a man. A champion. Ye know whit Ah mean?'

Twelve minutes later, Andrew wins his second game. 'Ah hah! See that, Lena. Two–nil up. Ah jist need wan game oot o' the next three, and that's me retained ma title. Wee boys should'nae try and play wi' the big boys.' He tries hard not to laugh as he looks at William, who leans on his folded arms, brow knitted in concentration. 'C'mon then, Ah'll just get another game won and that'll be the end of William McClaren.'

Quarter of an hour later, William makes a move. 'Auntie Lena! Auntie Lena! We're at two each.'

'Oh, goodness me! Ah'd better come and watch this last game.' She pulls a chair up to the table. 'So is this it. Whoever wins this game is Scottish Champion, is that right?'

'Aye,' says William, face flushed.

'Ah'm telling ye, Ah've never known such a wee lucky-bag. If he fell intae the canal, he'd come oot dry!' Andrew watches as the board is readied. 'Right, now you're gonny see how a real champion plays when his back's against the wa'.' He winks at Lena.

Less than five minutes later it's all over. 'Eeeh, Andra. You've lost yer title. William's beat ye.'

Andrew leans on the table, cups his face in his hands. 'This is terrible. Ah'll have tae write a letter tae the committee tae tell them Ah've loast ma title. William McClaren, 18 Dalbeattie Street, Maryhill, is the new champion. Ah'll never live it doon. Beaten by a laddie. Ah'll be a laughing stock. Put them draughts back in the box and put them in the sideboard drawer. They'll never see the light of day again!' As William puts the box away, Andrew and Lena smile at one another.

It's just coming up for quarter to six when Drena knocks the McDermots' door, then opens it.

'It's me, Lena.' As she enters, William goes to her side. 'Ma! Ma! Dae ye know whit—'

His mother interrupts. 'Wait a minute, William. Ah'm talking tae Auntie Lena.'

'Aye, in ye come,' says Lena. 'Everything go aw'right wi' yer mother?'

'Oh, aye. Fine. It wiz jist a wee op. Ye know,' she mouths, 'women's trouble. And whit aboot this yin?' Drena pulls William in close to her.

'Don't talk tae me aboot this laddie,' says Andrew. 'Ah decided tae play him a few games o' draughts tae pass the time. Did the dirty oan me. Never let oan he wiz a wee wolf in sheep's clothing. I am – well, Ah *wiz* Scottish Champion. No' many people know that, Ah'm no' the type tae brag, as ye well know. Anywye, Ah'm no' champ anymair. He's taken ma title aff me!' Andrew shakes his head. 'Oh! The disgrace!'

'Ah beat Uncle Andra, Ma. Ah won three games tae two.'

'Well, imagine that,' says Drena. 'We've got a champion in the family. Well, c'mon, champ. We better get up them stairs and get yer faither's dinner oan.'

Andrew looks at the new title-holder. 'Aye, ye might as well – hey! Stand still a minute, there's something behind yer ear.' He reaches out a hand and plucks something from behind William's left ear. 'In the name o' the wee man! Put yer hand oot.' William does as he's told. He feels a glow, a tingle, as Uncle Andrew lets a silver sixpence fall into his open palm then looks quizzically at him. 'How did ye dae that?'

William shrugs. 'Don't know.' The two women try not to laugh at the look on his face.

'Huh! Nae wonder he beat me. He's got the fairies oan his side!'

As they climb the stairs, Drena pulls her son in close. 'Did ye enjoy yerself at Uncle Andra's and Auntie Lena's?'

William has carried some of the glow with him from the

McDermots'. 'Oh aye.' He looks at his mother with eyes a-sparkle. 'Uncle Andra's great. Ah think he's ma favourite uncle.'

CHAPTER TWENTY-FOUR

Bad Things Happen
to Good People

Agnes Dalrymple steps out on to the top-storey landing, closes her door, then gives it its mandatory three pushes to ensure it's locked. She turns her head as she hears one of her neighbour's doors being opened. Ella Cameron appears. She's carrying a galvanised tin bath full of dirty washing. 'You no' at yer work the day, Agnes?'

'Oh, hello, Ella. Naw, Ah'm no'.'

'And aw' dressed up. Ah hope you're no' meeting a man.'

In spite of not feeling like it, Agnes smiles. 'Nae such luck. Ah've got a hospital appointment.'

'Nuthin' serious, Ah hope?'

'Oh, goodness, no. Jist a wee matter.'

Ella looks at her. That didn't sound like the usual Agnes. She decides not to pursue it. Instead, she nods her head in the direction of the bath. 'There's nae prizes for guessing where Ah'm going.'

'Off tae the steamie by the look of it. Are ye going wi' some o' the girls?' Agnes wishes she was going with them.

Going anywhere but where she is. She feels another pang of fear.

'Aye. Lena and Irma. Cannae keep Irma away fae it. If it's no' nailed doon, it's a cert tae finish up at the Gairbraid Avenue steamie. Bert says she's washin' everything in sight.'

As the two women step on to the first-storey landing, Granny Thomson's door opens. Granny, coat and hat on, her small Gladstone bag hanging from her arm, steps forth. 'Ah'm aw' ready, Agnes. Oh, hello, Ella.'

'Hiyah! Is Granny going with ye?'

'Aye, jist for a bit o' company.' Agnes fails to make this sound casual.

Granny shuts her door; which is also subjected to the three-push test. She turns to Agnes. 'C'mon, hen. It's efter half-nine. You've got tae be at the Western before eleven.'

'Your appointment's at the Western, is it?' Ella turns towards Agnes.

'It is, aye.' Agnes avoids looking at her.

As the trio descend the stairs into the close, they find Lena McDermot and Irma Armstrong waiting. 'Ah'll just nip oot tae the wash hoose and get ma transport, girls.' Key in hand, Ella dashes out to the back court to get the four pram wheels on their chassis, which she uses to take her washing back and forth to the steamie.

Five minutes later, the group turn the corner into the Maryhill Road; the parting of the ways.

'Right, we're away ower tae the tram stop.' Granny links her arm through Agnes's. 'See ye's later on, girls.'

'Ah hope they don't find oot you're three months gone, Agnes!' says Lena.

'Ah'll tell ye whit. If Ah am, it'll be one o' yon, eh, eman-cipated conceptions!'

'Put your bundle on top of mine in the bogie, Lena.'

'Are ye sure?'

'Aye. Nae bother. It's jist as easy tae pull. Ah'm sorry there's nae room for yours as well, Irma. Anywye, you're young and strong. You'll manage that wee bundle.'

'Oh, yes. This is not a problem.'

They walk along the quiet Tuesday-morning Maryhill Road in companionable silence. As Ella pulls the twine tied to the chassis of her transport, it yaws slightly from side to side. Ella glances back. 'Got a mind of its ain, this bugger.' She looks at Lena. 'Ah must say, Ah thought Agnes wiz a bit, eh, evasive therr. She's no' letting on whit she's goin' tae the Western for.'

'Aye. Ah was thinking she was awfy quiet this morning. Not like her.'

'Anywye, Ah'm sure it'll aw' come oot in the wash. Hah! Come oot in the *wash*! And we're on oor wye tae the steamie. Zat no' topical, girls, eh?' Ella looks at her friends. In vain.

'By! You're as sharp as a blancmange, so ye are,' says Lena.

Irma glances from one to the other. 'Sometimes I have great trouble with the Scottish English.'

Forty-five minutes later finds the three of them, sticky with sweat, toiling away in their stalls in Gairbraid Avenue's steamie. Irma, hair tucked under a turban fashioned from a headscarf, feet in a pair of rubber boots, a floral wrap-around peenie tied tightly at her waist, looks like any other Glasgow house-wife – from Paderborn. She has occasional short conversa-tions with Ella through the cast-iron grille that separates their cubicles. Lena is a few yards away in another row of identical stalls. Irma likes coming to the steamie. Enjoys the kameradschaft. What is that in English? The friendliness? Mmm, almost but not quite. She leans forward. The top of the washboard digs into her stomach as she scrubs, rubs and pummels one of Bert's shirts against the metal ribs. 'Phew!' She lifts a wet hand, holds it over the sink to drip while she rubs her perspiring brow along her upper sleeve.

'Aw' yah bugger o' hell! Trust me. Ah've forgot ma bloody washing soap!'

Irma stops, looks through the partition. 'What is the matter, Ella?'

Ella stands, arms akimbo. She turns. 'Ah had a wee bit of washing soap tae finish, and Ah had a brand new cake of Fairy. Ah could huv swore blind Ah put it in the bathtub this mornin'. Ah was in such a stramash getting them bairns ready, Ah must have forgot the bloody thing.'

'You can borrow mine, Ella. You know it is not a problem. Moment!' Irma takes her hands out of the sink and, still dripping with suds, reaches for the bar of washing soap. As she takes hold of it with her right hand, it slips through her fingertips and shoots up into the air in a slight arc. She attempts to catch it, but instead deflects it towards the corner of the cubicle. The corner where the metal sink used for boiling whites stands. Thirty minutes ago Irma filled this sink, then slightly opened the pipe to allow superheated steam to enter the bottom of it. The water, seemingly still but imperceptibly swirling, now simmers just below boiling point. The cake of soap bounces off the wall and slips, with barely a splash, under the clear, flat surface of the liquid. In a reflex action, before she can stop herself, Irma plunges her hand in after it.

The scream carries all over the large white-tiled room. The voices of the women are stilled instantly. Only the whine of the industrial spin-dryers disturbs the peace. And Irma's wailing.

'What the hell huv ye done?' Ella doesn't wait to find out. She drops everything, runs in a skidding, slipping half-circle into Irma's stall. Irma leans against the back wall, next to the metal sink. She holds her right arm out. Its hand, to a few inches above the wrist, is scarlet. She moans and sways from side to side, eyes near shut against the pain.

'Oh my God! Huv ye scalded yersel'?' Ella goes to her, puts an arm round her waist. 'Quick! Under the cauld tap.' She propels her over to one of the two Belfast sinks. Holding Irma with her right arm, she turns the cold tap on with her left, then uses it to force Irma's forearm under the gushing brass tap.

'Ohhh! Oh, Ella, es schmerzen. Es schmerzen so viel!'

'Diz that mean "sore", hen?'

'Yah. Yes.'

Ella looks to her left. Outside the cubicle is a sea of concerned faces. 'Wan of ye run tae the office, tell them we need an ambulance straight away. She's scalded her hand and wrist.'

A voice says, 'Ah'll go!' There comes the sound of someone running in clogs.

Ella turns her head, looks closely at her friend. Irma's eyes are almost shut. Involuntary tears, from the pain, run from them. She is very pale. 'Ah'm gonny keep yer hand under this tap till the ambulance comes, hen.'

'But this cold is also sore, Ella.' Irma's voice is weak. Ella hopes she won't faint.

'Archie did a first-aid course years ago. Ah remember him saying the sooner a scald is under a cauld tap – and the longer it's under – the better. It'll heal quicker and there'll hardly be a . . . mark left.' She doesn't want to use the word 'scar'.

Lena has pushed her way through. She enters the stall and stands behind her two neighbours. She gently strokes Irma's back. 'You'll be aw'right, hen. The ambulance will be here soon.'

'Ah'm gonny go wi' her tae the hospital, Lena. Dae ye think you'll be able tae get aw' oor washing the gether and get it hame? We were baith nearly finished.'

'Ah'll get it rinsed and spun for ye's if Ah can,' says Lena.

'Ah'll give ye a hand! Hello, Ella.' A woman pushes through and stands just inside the stall.

Ella turns her head. 'Oh, that would be great, Annie.' She turns to Lena. 'This is a friend o' mine. Annie Farmer. She's frae Fernie Street.' She nods her head towards Lena. 'This is Lena McDermot. We aw' live up the same close.' Ella turns her attention back to Irma. 'How are ye doing, kid? It'll no be long noo.'

Irma nods. 'It is little bit not so sore. But, oh, I do not feel very well, Ella. And my hand is so kalt.' Ella gently squeezes her close. Kisses her on the temple. 'Jist stick it oot. No' be long.'

'They're here! The ambulance men are here!' Three or four voices announce it.

'C'mon, girls. Clear the way. Let them through!' Annie Farmer takes it on herself to marshal the spectators. She and Lena then move to the back of the stall as the peaked hats of the ambulance attendants approach. 'We'll finish oor ain stuff first, ah, Lena,' says Annie, 'then we'll dae these two's bits and pieces. Ah'll gie ye a hand doon the road wi' it as well.'

Lena smiles. 'That's awfy good of ye, Annie.'

Agnes Dalrymple and Granny Thomson sit together in the busy waiting room at the Western Infirmary. Agnes looks again at her watch. 'Twenty past eleven. Ah'll bet ye if Ah'd arrived here at five past eleven, the buggers wid huv been shoutin' and bawling my name for ages.'

'Och, aye. It's always the same.' They both have their attention taken as the outer doors swing open and two ambulance men appear. They support a woman between them. Another one walks alongside.

'That's Ella fae oor close!' says Agnes. 'Huh!' She draws a breath in. 'And that's Irma! Something must huv happened. Whit's goin' on?'

'Ella!' Granny accompanies it with a wave.

Ella makes a slight detour. 'Ah huv'nae time tae stop. Irma's gave herself a bad scald. We were at the steamie this mornin' as ye's know. Ah'll see ye's later.' She speeds off.

For the moment, Agnes forgets her own troubles. 'Ah hope that wee soul's gonny be aw'right. She's a nice wee lassie, so she is.'

'She is that,' says Granny. She tuts. Reaches out and pats Agnes's folded hands. 'Why diz bad things happen tae good folks, eh? Ah've never been able tae understand that.'

CHAPTER TWENTY-FIVE

Loneliness

Artie Shaw's orchestra with 'Dancing in the Dark' floats out from the radio. It's one of Rhea's all-time favourites. Even now it's threatening to make her tap her feet. This time last week she'd have been dancing round the kitchen, her mother shouting she'd be late for work. It has got tae be the best quickstep number ever, she thinks. And his 'It Had to Be You' is every bit as good. When Robert and me get married, we'll huv a record player and whenever we feel like it we'll put oan aw' oor favourite records – they'll aw' be quicksteps – move the table oot the road and dance roon' the kitchen for as long as we want. Oh Robert! Ah weesh Ah could see where ye are at this—

'Rhea! Jayz! What is the matter wit' ye?'

Rhea comes out of her daydream. She's sitting at the table. There's a barely nibbled piece of toast in her hand; a cold cup of tea stands in the saucer. She feels like bursting into tears.

'Oh! Ah wiz miles away, Ma.'

'Miles away? This last couple of days you've been on the

planet Melancholia, I t'ink. Ye look like somebody's stole yer scone.'

Rhea tries to smile. She fails again. She places the toast on the plate. 'Aye.' She looks at the clock. 'Ah'd better be going, Ma.'

Teresa stops what she's doing, stands with arms akimbo, looks keenly at her daughter. 'Is there sum'ting the matter, Rhea?'

Rhea finds things to do so she won't have to look her mother in the eye. 'Naw, Ma. Jist a bit fed up. Probably 'cause we're right in the depths o' winter or something. And when we get rid of January, we'll huv sunny February tae look forward tae. Ah don't think!'

'Mmmm.' Teresa is unconvinced. 'Is that you going to work with hardly a bite of toast or a drink of tay in ye? And 'tis like a stepmother's breath out there this mornin'. You'll need your raincoat and your umbrella. Are ye goin' out wit' the girls tonight?'

'Naw. Ah'll be straight hame.' She comes over and kisses her mother. Wonders yet again if she should tell her about Robert. 'Cheerio, Ma. See ye the night.'

'Make sure ye get something hot for yer lunch. Cheerio.'

As Rhea descends the last flight of stairs to the close, she looks along it and out into the street. The close mouth frames a scene of winter at its worst. Great gobs of sleet are slanting down as fast as they can. It lies on pavement and road as slush. Rhea stops four feet or so from the mouth of the close, leans against the wall for a moment. The sleet tries to billow in and wet her shoes. She holds the umbrella forward, ready to open it as soon as she steps out into the street. God, if Ah wiz'nae already depressed, huvin' tae go oot in this wid make me.

She turns the corner into the Maryhill Road. Already the bottom of her coat is spattered with fast-melting sleet. Every step she takes splashes dirty slush on to her shoes and stockings. People should'nae huv tae go tae work when it's like this. She stands at the pavement, looks to left and right. A flash from her schooldays comes into her mind. A brand-new jotter with its glossy brown covers lies face down on her desk. The back is covered with all the times tables. Along the bottom, in heavy type, it says 'BETTER A MOMENT AT THE KERB THAN A MONTH IN HOSPITAL!' An Alexander's Bluebird bus comes along. She stands well back as its never-ending bow wave of muck spatters on to the pavement. Right. As there is nothing else coming, she crosses the road at an angle towards the tram stop. All the folk, who are normally in an orderly queue, are sheltering in closes and shop doorways. She's been trying not to look, but her eyes are eventually drawn to R.S. McColl's. Nae Robert. Nae Robert for the next two years. She feels she's about to burst out crying.

The number 23, a 'new caur', comes slowly towards them. In contrast to the bright livery of cream, green and orange on its sides, the entire front is bespattered with half-frozen slush, more being added as it butts its way through the swiftly falling sleet. The top third or so of the '23' can just be seen. The destination board is a complete whiteout. The driver's lone windscreen-wiper battles in vain to keep an increasingly smaller window clear for him. As the tram glides to a halt, folk rush out from close and doorway and gather at the stop. All the women – only one man – have umbrellas. They wait impatiently while a woman alights, then there's a scramble to climb aboard. Those first on try to stand for a moment on the small platform to shake the half-melted winter morning off their umbrellas before finding a seat. It's no use. Folk still on the pavement want out of the weather; they push and surge their way on. Those already aboard, unshaken umbrellas in hand, are forced to find a seat. The outer doors rattle shut. With a shiver, the tram pulls away from the stop.

Rhea has found a double seat downstairs. She sits alone. The coldness outside – and the humidity inside from wet macs and umbrellas – has produced more condensation than the usual rainy Glasgow day. With no Robert to talk to, Rhea would like to look out the window. She looks at it. Jeez, if Ah wipe that wi' ma hand or sleeve Ah'll be wringing wet. She compromises by clearing a 'letterbox' for herself. It'll have to do. It doesn't. Most of the journey is spent thinking about Robert.

It has just gone nine thirty. The typing pool at Macready and Co. is a haven as the central heating pumps warmth into the large radiators. Now dried out, Rhea sits at her desk twiddling her stockinged feet underneath it. The boss is at a meeting, won't be back until the afternoon. She threads a sheet of paper into her typewriter; looks out the window into what is now a wintry Wellington Street, pities the few pedestrians as they reluctantly make their way through the ever-deepening snow.

'Ah would imagine you've been waiting oan this, Rhea?' Janet extracts a letter from a bundle of newly arrived mail.

'Eeh, Janet. Ah never heard the postman come intae reception.' She takes hold of the blue envelope. 'Thanks.' Janet slips away. Rhea holds the envelope in both hands. It's nice and fat. She looks at the Portsmouth postmark cancelling the green penny-ha'penny stamp with the King on it. 'For the

attention of: Miss Rhea O'Malley, c/o J.Macready and Co. . . .'
She glances up to see if any of the girls are watching her; all
four manage to look elsewhere just in time. She takes hold
of the letter-opener. Extracts the six-page letter, unfolds it
and bends it until it's almost flat. Robert sent this! She looks
at his new address. The only familiar thing is his name, otherwise it's all army number and 'A Company' and 'Three
Battalion' and 'Hilsea Barracks' and 'RAOC'. Jeezus-Johnny,
he's nearly lost!

My darling Rhea,
This is the first time when I've had a minute to write.
Basic training is, in the words of the Immortal Bard,
'murder polis!' We're being drilled and worked to death.
Yet because me and the rest of the lads in the billet (hut)
are all in it together, you have no idea how pally and
close we've become. In spite of all the chasing and pressure we get from the DIs (drill instructors), there are
times when I've been totally helpless with laughter. Even
so, my greatest pleasure comes when I have one of the
few brief moments (like NAAFI breaks) when the sergeants
and corporals give us peace. Immediately my mind is
filled with thoughts of you. Not my ma and da. Just my
Rhea. You keep me—

'Seeing as the boss is away – the girls can play!' Elsie
reaches for her coat. 'Ah'm gonny risk life and limb going
oot tae the baker's fur a wee snaster. Anybody want anything?'
    Rhea looks up. 'Aye. Get me two sausage rolls and two
custard tarts, will ye.' She reads another line of Robert's letter.
Looks up again. 'Elsie! And bring me a bridie tae!'

CHAPTER TWENTY-SIX

Two Visitors

Agnes Dalrymple, wearing her best coat – and best every thing – climbs the two flights of stairs up to the first storey. She pauses a second at Granny Thomson's door, the middle of the three on the landing. Everything seems so sharp and clear, so beautiful, this morning. She reaches out to rattle the letterbox, looks at the '1. Thomson' above it. It'll no' be long until you'll no' be able tae read that, she thinks. Granny's got it just aboot polished away. The black paint on the door is also worn away in certain areas, especially round the handle and letterbox. She can see the brown paint that preceded it showing through.

Agnes gives the flap a few rattles, then opens the door. Granny'll be expecting her. The smell of the house starts at the small lobby. It's funny how some houses have their own individual smell. This is a mixture of gas lighting, mothballs, cheap perfume . . . and the musty smell of the old clothes Granny wears every day. 'It's Agnes, Granny!'

'Aye, come away in wi' ye. The kettle's oan.'

As she enters the one room that makes up Granny's

kingdom, the old woman is rising to her feet. She looks hard at Agnes. 'It wiz your follow-up appointment at the Western this morning. So were ye right when ye said ye did'nae need me tae go wi' ye?'

'Ah was.'

'Well?'

Agnes beams, throws her arms wide apart. 'All clear! Jist like the doctor said it would be – it wiz jist a cyst.' She does a little tap-dance on the linoleum. 'Aw, Granny. You've nae idea how relieved Ah am. It's . . .' She stops; bursts into tears.

'Aw, Agnes hen. Jist let it aw' come oot.' Granny goes over to her neighbour and puts her arms round her, rubs her back. 'It's wi' you being on yer own. You've had nothing tae dae but worry aboot it. Naebody tae talk tae.' She leans back so as to look Agnes in the face. Gives her a squeeze. 'It's aw' behind ye noo. Not a thing wrong wi' ye. Aw' yer worrying's finished, hen.'

Granny lets Agnes go, pulls out one of the kitchen chairs. 'Sit yersel' doon. We'll huv a nice pot o' tea tae celebrate the fact you've got another twenty-five years tae look forward tae behind the counter at the City Bakeries!'

Agnes laughs between the sobs, dabs her eyes with a minuscule hankie. Watches Granny masking the tea. Minutes later they sit companionably together. Agnes is still exuberant.

'Ah'm no' kidding. When he telt me it wiz jist a cyst, harmless, it wiz like huving the death sentence lifted. Ah could huv kissed him! Even though he'd said to me last time he wiz almost certain it wiz a cyst, Ah'd still got maself wound up intae such a state while Ah was sitting waiting this morning.' She pauses. 'Oh, and Ah'll tell ye who else was there. Irma! She wiz getting the last of her dressings off the day. It's no' half healed up lovely, Granny. She showed me it. Hardly a mark tae be seen.'

It's about an hour before Agnes has calmed down and decided it's time to go upstairs. 'Ah'll have tae get changed and get away tae the shops, get something for ma dinner.'

'Well, there wiz nae point buying anything this mornin'. Ye were aboot tae snuff it any meenit!'

'Eeh, God, Ah know.'

'Ah was gonny lend ye a book,' says Granny. '*The Grapes o' Wrath*. Then Ah thocht, there's nae point, she'll never finish it.' The pair of them become convulsed with laughter. Granny manages to say, 'Ah thocht, Ah'll just send her up a volume o' short stories!' This puts them into further kinks. Eventually Agnes manages to rise from the table.

'Ah'm gonny have tae go, Granny, otherwise Ah'll be back doon that Western for the second time the day – collapsed wi' laughing.' She kisses the old woman on the cheek. 'Thanks for being sae helpful and supportive. We don't know whit we'd dae withoot ye at number 18.'

'Och, that's whit neighbours are for, Agnes. Ah'm jist pleased your worst fears did'nae come true.' She sees her visitor out on to the landing. She is just on the point of closing her door, then she opens it again, sticks her head out. 'Ah'll send ye up *The Grapes o' Wrath* – and the short stories as well!'

Rhea O'Malley is half an hour earlier than usual when she enters the street. She keeps close to the wall just in case her ma looks out the front-room window. As she climbs the stairs and approaches the first landing, she stops for a moment halfway up the second flight, looks through the banister rails towards her door. If my ma happens tae come oot, ah'll jist say Ah've come hame early from work 'cause Ah'm no' feeling well. She steps on to the landing and tiptoes towards Granny Thomson's door, opens it, steps into the small lobby and knocks the inner door. 'Granny!' She opens the kitchen door. 'Granny! It's me.' She closes the outside door then stands just inside the single-end. Granny Thomson sits in her fireside chair, sound asleep. The twin gas lights hiss quietly to themselves up on the chimney breast. 'Granny!'

'Eh? Whit? Who is it?' She peers towards the door with heavy eyes.

'It's Rhea fae next door. Can Ah come in?'

Granny stretches her arms out in front of her. 'Mmmm, that wiz a lovely wee sleep. In ye come, hen. Whit are ye wanting? Have ye time tae take a seat?'

'Aye, Ah will.' Rhea sits herself down on the same chair occupied by Agnes Dalrymple a few hours ago. Granny looks at her.

'Huv ye time for a cuppa?'

'Aye, Ah wid'nae mind. Ah'm jist hame fae ma work. Ah hav'nae been in the hoose yet. Ma mother diz'nae know Ah'm here.'

'Ohhh! Is that so. Well, we'd better hae a wee drink o' tea, Ah'm thinking.' Rhea watches as Granny hoists herself stiffly out of the chair. 'Ah fair enjoy ma wee snoozes, Rhea. But Ah'm as stiff as an auld board whenever Ah rise. Takes me a wee while tae loosen up.'

'Will ye have a biscuit?' Granny asks when she brings the tea.

'Naw thanks, Granny. It wid put me aff ma dinner.' Rhea gives a nervous cough.

Granny Thomson looks at her. She's known her, and her

sister Siobhan, since they were infants. She could take a guess at what she's about to hear. 'So, whit's the matter, Rhea?'

'Oh, Granny. Ah think Ah might be in trouble. Big trouble!'

'Mmmm. Are ye late?'

Rhea nods her head. 'Aye. Eight days. Ah'm never, ever late, Granny.' She twists and turns a hankie between her fingers, looking down as she does.

Granny takes a sip of tea. Places the cup back in the saucer. 'Is it Robert's?'

'Hah! How dae you know that?'

'Ah'm no' Granny Thomson fur nuthin'! Ye can see an awful lot fae one-up, ye know.'

In spite of herself, Rhea laughs. Shakes her head. 'Aye, it's Robert's – that's if Ah really am,' she adds. 'The best laugh is, we've only done it wance. Jist wance!'

'Aye, well that's aw' it takes, hen. Jist takes wan match tae light a fire.'

'Whit can Ah dae, Granny?'

'At the minute, nuthin'! Ah know you're saying you're never late. But there's a good chance – a very good chance, that it's jist wi' aw' the emotional upset of Robert going away tae the army, the fact that ye, well, gave intae him, shall we say – aw' these things could huv combined tae upset yer rhythm. So it's no' quite written doon in black and white yet. There's still time for ye tae come oan.' Granny reaches out and squeezes her hand.

'God, Ah hope you're right.' Rhea looks up. 'And jist in case you're thinking Robert should get aw' the blame,' she blushes, 'Ah wanted to as much as he did. Ah love him tae death, Granny. Ah really do. When he comes oot the army, whether oor parents like it or no', we'll be gettin' married.'

'Good for you, hen. Now, as Ah've said, there's a good chance you're jist extra late. But, and you've got tae think o' these things, if ye *were* expecting, what wid ye dae? Or what wid ye want tae dae aboot it?'

Rhea shrugs her shoulders. 'Ah'd jist have tae face up tae ma parents, then Robert's. If Ah am expecting, well, Ah'll be having it. There's nae question aboot it. It's oor baby, Robert's and mine. We'll be having it – and we'll be keeping it!'

Granny's face breaks into a big smile. 'Good for you, hen!' She rises and goes round and stands beside Rhea. Gives her a hug and a kiss. 'And if you're getting a hard time from any of them, jist come and see me. Ah'll be behind ye aw' the way. But anywye, we're baith jumping the gun.' She returns to her chair. 'It's far to early tae say ye are. So don't breathe a word tae anybody. None of yer pals or the lassies ye work with. Have ye told Siobhan?'

'Naw. You're the only wan.'

'Well, Ah suggest ye don't even tell Siobhan. She probably would'ny tell yer mother and faither. But she might no' be able tae resist telling a pal at work or somebody like that. And it's surprising how these things get back. Keep it tae yerself. Anywye. Have another cup o' tea, Rhea. Because Ah'm going tae tell you something.' She places the tea strainer on Rhea's cup.

'Now, the first thing Ah'm gonny say tae ye is, keep this tae yerself. There is not another soul up this close, or in the street, who knows aboot this. Okay? Right, for a start, whit you'll have tae realise is – Granny Thomson wiz'nae always seventy-four years auld. Ah wiz born in Girvan, doon in Ayrshire. And Ah had a boyfriend, Alec McCrindle wiz his name. Ah wish Ah had a photie of him, Rhea. Whit a good-looking laddie he was. He wiz a fisherman. There wiz quite a few McCrindle families in Girvan back then and nearly all o' them were fisherfolk. This wiz, let me see, aye, 1899. Ah wiz born in 1875. Ah wiz twenty-four when aw' this took place. Me and Alec were as good as engaged. Betrothed it wiz called in them days. We were due tae be married on the tenth of May. Jist like you and Robert, we only had eyes for yin another. Jist a few days before the wedding, well, we could'nae wait either. It did'nae make any difference, did it? We'd be man and wife by the end o' the week. So off went the fishing fleet. Be back in four or five days' time.' Granny pours some more tea into her cup. 'And while they're at sea, up blaws the worst storm for twenty years or mair. There wiz eight men lost. And, of course, wan o' them wiz ma Alec. A month or so later Ah finds oot Ah'm expecting. Ah wiz pleased, and so wiz Alec's family. Oh, we were aw' hoping for a boy . . .'

'And was it?' Rhea is hanging on every word.

Granny sits back in her chair. Smiles. 'Aye, it was. But the wee soul did'nae live long enough tae be christened. Some fever thing or something. Got wan o' them big long names. He wiz a fine healthy wee laddie when he wiz born. Ten days later we were burying him.'

'Aw, Granny. That's really sad. But ye eventually got married, didn't ye?'

'Aye. Ah came up tae Glasgow in 1902. Ah went intae service at a big hoose oot the far end of Great Western Road. That wiz where Ah met Frank Thomson. Him and me got married in 1910. We moved in here the same year. We said that when we started a family we wid move tae a bigger hoose. But it did'nae happen. Ah had a couple o' miscarriages; Ah wiz thirty-five when Ah married Frank, so mibbe that had something tae dae wi' it.' She shrugs her shoulders. 'Then, Ah don't know if you've ever heard folk talk aboot it, there wiz a terrible worldwide outbreak of influenza in 1918. They called it a pandemic – no' an epidemic, a pandemic. It killed hundreds of thousands, mibbe even mair, all over Europe. And poor Frank went wi' that. So that wiz me left a widow, no' even any bairns. And that wiz it. Ah wiz forty-three, and Ah've been on ma own ever since.'

'Oh, Granny. That was sad. If that wee boy ye had tae Alec had lived . . . Well, anywye, if Ah'm expecting Robert's bairn, Ah'll be having it – and keeping it! Eh! Look at the time. Go and look oot yer door on tae the landing for me. See if it's all clear.'

Two minutes later, Rhea steps quietly out on to the landing. 'Thanks a lot, Granny. Ah'll let ye know if anything happens. Or diz'nae. Cheerio.'

Granny stands and watches Rhea open her door and step into the lobby. 'It's me, Ma.'

She hears Teresa, 'And about time too. Where the devil have ye been? Another two minutes and yer dinner will be ruined. Hurry up and get sat down at this table.' Rhea gives Granny a smile, then closes the door.

Granny shakes her head, shuts her door and walks back into her room. Och, who misses bairns when I've got all ma neighbours and their troubles to sort oot? There's never a dull moment up this close.

Next morning, just coming up for half past eight, Granny's kneeling at the hearth raking out the ashes. Her door is knocked and opened. The inner door moves slightly, and Rhea's head appears.

'Granny, thank God, Ah came oan during the night.'

'Oh! Isn't that grand. That'll save a lot o' bother – and explanations. Noo don't forget, when he comes hame oan leave, get him doon tae the barber's for, you know – them contrathingummys!'

CHAPTER TWENTY-SEVEN

A Bolt from the Blue!

Irene Pentland walks into Andrew Cochrane's, the grocer's on the Maryhill Road. Being mid-afternoon, it isn't busy. As she does on every visit, she breathes in. She loves it. A wee shop on a Glasgow street, yet the aromas immediately take you over half the world. Maybe more. Alec Stuart, the manager, looks up as the clip-clopping of her heels on the floorboards announces her. 'Hello, Miss Pentland, how are you the day?'

'Fine, Mr Stuart. And yourself?'

'Aye, grand. Grand. What can Ah do for you?'

'Ah'll have my four eggs and a quarter of the Australian butter, please.'

'Certainly, m'dear.' He reaches over for one of the blue cardboard egg boxes and places it on the marble-topped counter in front of her. 'There we are.' He takes a piece of greaseproof paper and lays it four-square on the scales. She watches him step over to the back counter, where the barrel-shaped slab of rich yellow butter stands on a piece of cold marble. He takes the wooden pats out of a bowl of water, shakes the excess off them, then digs them into the mound of butter. He comes over to the scales and uses one pat to topple the portion of butter off the other on to the grease-proof paper. They watch the pointer on the large Avery scales swing back and forth for what seems an age, till it eventually stops. 'There we are, Miss Pentland. Just marginally over. Ah think we're safe enough calling that a quarter.'

She smiles. 'Yes, Ah think so, Mr Stuart.' She now gives her attention to his dexterity as he lifts the quarter of butter back on to the wooden implements and proceeds to pat it into shape. When it is done to his satisfaction, he folds it into the paper. 'Ah don't care what anybody says, Ah know this Australian bulk butter is the cheapest, but Ah just love that tangy aftertaste it has. Now and again Ah'll buy some Devon or Cornwall farm butter, supposed tae be for a wee treat. Well, it might be dearer, but withoot fail Ah always finish up saying tae myself, "It's no' as tasty as Cochrane's bulk butter." '

Alec looks around as though not wanting to be overheard – even though Irene's his only customer.

'Ah have tae agree wi' ye, Miss Pentland. That's the only butter Ah'll have in the house. Ah long ago stopped taking home some "best butter" for a treat.' He leans forward, hands on the counter. 'Because it is'nae! *That*'s the best butter in the shop.' He points to the bulk.

Irene nods her head in agreement while she places her and James's ration books on the counter. Alec opens both books at the appropriate pages for eggs and butter. He lifts a stubby copying-ink pencil from the counter, places the tip between his lips and wets the point with his tongue. 'Riiiight, ah'll mark the eggs off your book, Miss Pentland, and the butter off your brother's.' He cancels the numbered squares in both books. Looks up. 'Is there anything else now?'

'No, that's fine, Mr Stuart.' She puts the items in her message bag. 'Well, that's about the only good thing you can say about the winter. The butter keeps nae bother in this weather. Ah just stand the butter dish near tae the windows. It keeps for a week or more wi' the cold air striking through the glass. Anyway, Ah'll say cheerio, Alec.' She blushes as she uses his first name.

Alec rubs his hands briskly together. 'Aye, cheerio, Miss Pentland.' He leans confidentially across the counter, says sotto voce, 'Ah believe Friday morning we're supposed tae be getting some nice Irish bacon in. Jist a word tae the wise, Miss Pentland.'

Irene smiles, pleased to be considered as a preferred customer. 'Right, thank you once more, Alec. Ah would think you'll be seeing me again on Friday. Mid-morning.' She makes her exit with Alec's parting 'Cheery-bye!' wafting her on her way.

Irene looks at the clock on the mantelpiece. Five past five. She reaches up to the washing hanging from the pulley. 'Ah, lovely! It's bone dry. She hates for James and her to eat at the table with a pulley full of washing reaching down towards them. Especially if it's still dripping. Unwinding the almost white rope from its double hook, she gently lowers the pulley until the questing shirtsleeves just touch the bright oilcloth that covers the table. She winds the rope round the hook a few turns so the pulley will stay where it is. A few minutes later the dry washing has been folded neatly and placed in a galvanised tin bath. She lifts the valance, slides the bath under the recess bed, lets the valance fall. It can all be ironed tomorrow.

As happens often, James Pentland and Billy McClaren step off a number 18 tram on to the Maryhill Road together. James, a rather quiet, taciturn man at the best of times, has hardly spoken a word during their journey, contenting himself with making the right noises in reply to Billy's attempts at conversation. As they approach Dalbeattie Street, Billy feels relieved that they are about to part company.

'Well, Ah'll huv tae nip ower tae Ken's fur a *Citizen*. Ah'll see ye around, James.'

'Yes, aye. Certainly will, Billy. Cheerio.'

Billy takes a last glance at his neighbour before heading for the corner newsagent's. Jeez! The big man's definitely got something oan his mind the night. He's miles away.

As James heads towards his close, he pulls a silver Waltham pocket watch from his waistcoat pocket. He doesn't really need to look at the time. He knows it'll be around ten past six. It's always ten past six, or thereabouts, when he comes home from his job as timckccpcr at thc North British Locomotive Company in Springburn. It's nine minutes past. He slips the watch into his waistcoat pocket, glances down to check the silver chain hangs right and the fob at the top of the chain is turned so as to show its best side – the red and blue enamel scrollwork and 'The Ancient Order of Oddfellows' in gothic script. Of which he's not a member. He saw it on a stall down the Barras one Sunday, about three years ago. Seven shillings and sixpence. He enters the close. The gas lamp is guttering. Needs adjusting. It'll do that all night now. The pale, greenish-white light flickers and flares. The shadows that are always there during the hours of darkness now move, seem to wax and wane in intensity. He climbs the stairs. The lamp on the first-storey landing burns as it should. As does the one on the second storey, his landing. He places his hand on the fluted brass doorknob. It'll have to be done tonight. He determines he won't put it off any longer. He opens the outside door.

'It's jist me, Irene!' The lobby light is already on. She always has it on for him coming home.

'Helloooh!' As ever, her voice comes from the kitchen.

He hangs the war-surplus, ex-army small pack on its hook. His mac and jacket now go on top of it, followed by his tweed bunnet. He extracts his piece tin, tea and sugar tin, and the already thrice-used Beattie's Bread wrapper from the khaki-coloured pack. He swallows hard before entering the kitchen. As expected, his sister Irene is floating between cooker and sink. There's the smell of something nice cooking; the table is set. 'Hello, James. Ah think you've just managed tae get hame afore it rains.'

'Aye, it looks like it. Still, it's February, so we should be thankful it's no' snaw.' He moves halfway towards the sink, stands by the sideboard so he's not in her way. 'Have Ah time tae gie ma hands a wee wash?'

'Aye, on ye go. Ah'm just aboot tae put the dinner oot.'

'Right.'

Minutes later he sits eating a piece of steak with a fried egg on top. It's accompanied by home-made chips. Next to his left hand sits a glass of stout. James looks at the steak.

'Have they been increasing the ration? This piece of steak looks bigger than normal.'

'No. Ah bashed it wi' the hammer oot o' the bunker. Don't worry, Ah washed it under the tap first.'

'Ah'm pleased aboot that.' They both laugh. For a second he glances at the meal, the glass of stout, the fire burning away cheerily in the range, the clean and tidy kitchen. His sister sitting opposite him. She's a good soul. He feels as guilty as hell. If you start thinking like that you'll never be able to tell her. You've promised you'll do it this week. Ah'll wait until we're drinking our tea, he decides. No longer

James takes his cup of tea, and saucer, over to the fireplace. Sits on his chair. His sister is filling the kettle at the sink. She'll be putting it on for the dishes. He looks at her back. At the way she knots her peenie. She always wears a turban made from a headscarf when she does her household chores.

'Irene! Would ye come and sit down a minute. Ah have tae speak tae ye aboot something.'

'Oh, goodness me! That sounds ominous, James.' She quickly unties her peenie, slips the loop over her head, and hangs the floral concoction from a nail next to the sink.

Ah wish she hadn't said 'ominous'. That's how she'll find it. James swallows hard. He's finding it difficult to look his sister in the eye. He forces himself to. 'Irene, Ah've got something tae tell ye. Ah'm afraid it's gonny be quite a surprise to ye. Totally unexpected, Ah suppose.' His throat has gone dry; he takes a sip of the almost cold tea. She's staring straight at him, looks frightened, probably thinks he's ill or something. Tell her! 'Well, Irene. You'll probably find it hard tae believe, But Ah have a lady friend . . .'

'Oh, God, James! Is that all it is? You've nae idea what Ah was thinking then. Ye had me worried tae death. Ah thought ye were aboot tae tell me ye were desperately ill or something.'

'Well, there's a wee bit more tae it than that, Irene.' Now he's started he wants to get it all out. Wants her to know everything. 'Ah've been seeing her this last year or so, once or twice a week.'

'Oh!' Irene takes this in. 'A whole year! So when you've been oot for a pint, you've really been seeing this . . . eh, lady friend.'

'Aye.' James starts again. 'And – this is gonny be an awfy surprise for ye – we're, eh, well, sort of engaged!' He feels a wave of relief. Right, now she knows. He looks at his sister. She sits back in her chair. She has gone quite peely-wally. 'Are ye aw'right, Irene? Do ye want a wee brandy?'

'Aye. Ah think Ah do.'

While she sits staring into the fire, he hurriedly pours her a goodly measure of cognac – and an even larger one for himself. He watches her take a mouthful. She screws her face up as it burns her throat. She immediately takes another gulp. 'James, have ye any idea what a shock this is for me? Ah thought ma life was settled.' He can tell she is thinking aloud, not just speaking. She looks at him. 'You're a grown man, nearly fifty. Of course ye can have a girlfriend, but . . .' She pauses. 'Why aw' the secrecy? Nearly a year – in fact mair than a year – and not a word aw' this time.' She looks into the fire. Thinking. Looks up. 'Why are you telling me now? Ah take it there's a reason?'

'Well, aye. There is. We're thinking of. Well, no' thinking, we're intending tae get married soon!'

Irene shakes her head. She raises the glass and takes another gulp of brandy. Looks at him, gives a smile that is anything but. 'Ah cannot understand why ye did'nae tell me, right from the start, that ye had started to see somebody. Aw' this secrecy. And whit's her name, by the way? Am Ah allowed tae know her name? Or is that still a secret?'

'Aw, come on, Irene. It's no' as bad as that. She's a woman

who works in the pay section at the loco works. Her name's Mary Anderson. She's a widow-woman. Got a grown-up son. She lives in Springburn. She's really nice. When ye get tae know her, you'll like her. Really.'

Irene sits for a moment. 'So whose decision was it no' tae tell me?'

'Oh, don't blame her. She's been telling me, almost right from the beginning, "You'll have tae tell yer sister." It was me that had the idea tae wait a while. The way Ah was thinking was, well, if it dis'nae last there'll be nae harm done. If Ah stop seeing her there'll be nae need tae tell ye about it. Ah suppose it sounds stupid now.'

'It diz! How do ye think Ah'll feel the first time Ah meet the woman? She'll be thinking, this is the sister that he feels did'nae have tae know about us.'

'Ah know, Irene. All of a sudden it seems tae be such a stupid idea. But for the first couple of months when Ah was seeing her, ye know, Ah just thought it would'nae last, it was only a friendship sort of thing.' He looks closely at his sister. He can tell she's near to tears.

'And what's going tae happen tae me, James? Ah'm fifty-two next birthday. Since oor mother died, over twenty years ago, ma life has been keeping house for ma brother. That's what Ah dae. Ah look after you. Ah take it you'll be going tae live at her house – or do ye's plan tae live here? Maybe want me tae move oot?'

'Aw' Irene. It's no' like that at all. We've been talking about it. About what we should do.'

'Ahhh! So youse have been talkin' about whit you'll dae wi' me. Am Ah supposed tae be grateful that you and your girl-friend – who's only been in your life this last year – are interested in what's tae happen tae your sister, who's looked efter ye for mair than twenty years?'

'Irene, Ah know it's been an awfy shock to ye. And Ah know Ah should have done things different. But please listen.' James reaches over and places a hand on top of Irene's. 'Ah'm sorry Ah've made a mess of things. You're ma sister, and Ah love ye, and Ah'll always dae ma best for ye. You know Ah'd never let ye down. Now if, or when, Mary and I get married, I intend tae carry on paying the rent on this place for ye – and the other bills as well, ye know, gas, electric and anything else. And so's you'll have some money by ye, Ah intend tae put two thousand pounds intae a bank account in your name, so's as you'll have money and you'll no' have tae take a job. And if, in years tae come, the money in the bank is getting low, all ye have tae do is tell me and Ah'll top it up. It's the least Ah can do for ye, Irene. You've always looked after me well. So Ah'll be looking after you as best Ah can.'

Irene sits back in her chair. Finishes the last of the brandy in her glass. James reaches for the bottle. 'Would ye like a wee drop more?'

'Oh, goodness, no.' She sighs heavily. Looks at her brother. 'This is the biggest shock, upset, call it what ye will, that Ah've ever had. Ah thought my life was so settled. You've no idea how much pleasure I get keeping house for the two of us. It's my life. When Ah get talking tae strangers, in queues or things like that, if they ask me what Ah do, what Ah work at, that's what Ah tell them – "Ah keep house for ma brother." Ah'm not gonny enjoy living on ma own, James. It's gonny be a terrible wrench tae know you'll not be coming through that door every evening at ten past six. You'll be all right.

You'll have company. Anywye. There's nae good talking about it any more. There's the table tae clear and dishes tae wash.' She rises from her chair. 'As Ah've heard other folk say for years, life must go on! Well, Ah'm about tae find oot.'

CHAPTER TWENTY-EIGHT

Contrasts

It's five to six on a Friday evening as George Lockerbie strides into the close at number 18. He opens the outside door. 'It's me, Joan.'

'Hello!'

As he enters the kitchen he sees she has a sandwich waiting for him. 'Hiyah!' He picks it up from the plate, takes a large bite. Goes back into the lobby and hangs his jacket up.

'Would you like a cup of tea, dear?'

'Aye, go on. Ah'll probably only have time to drink half of it.'

Joan rises and reaches for the teapot. 'Have you had a busy day at work, dear?'

'Mmm, so-so.' He takes another mouthful of sandwich. As he chews it, he takes off his overalls, puts on the trousers that are hanging over the back of a chair, ready for him. As Joan pours the freshly brewed tea into a cup, he puts a clean shirt on, then stands for a moment in front of the mirror with the tips of the collar pointing up as he knots his tie. Satisfied with it, he turns the collar down, gives the tie a few tweaks until the knot is centred. He takes a mouthful of hot tea.

'It makes Friday an awful long day for me when you're just in and out like this,' says Joan.

'Well, you want to move to a better place, dear.' He again has the passing thought: if you got yourself a wee part-time job during the day – instead of sitting round the house reading and listening to the wireless – you might find the time goes in better. He takes a last mouthful of tea, then goes over to the sink and gives his teeth a quick brush. 'Right, that'll have tae do. Ah'd better away.' He crosses over to where Joan sits to give her a kiss. She offers a cheek.

As he closes the door behind him and walks along the close, he feels that tingle in his stomach. Every Friday and Saturday night. Ah'll be in company with Ruth Malcolm in half an hour, he thinks. As he strides round to the Maryhill Road to take a tram to St George's Cross, he smiles. It's like when you were, what? Twelve? And had that crush on Miss Ogilvie at the secondary school. Just loved to be in her presence, to be able to look at her for as long as possible. Imagine! Nearly thirty-three years old – and got a crush on Ruth Malcolm. Hah! She probably wouldn't give you a nod in the desert. Anyway, that doesn't matter. She's never gonny know. So what if it's all one-sided? Ah just look forward to being in the same room as her two evenings a week. The pleasure, most definitely, is all mine.

It's a couple of minutes after seven when he steps smartly out of Hillhead subway station and heads along the Byres Road. Trams glide past, cars make a 'pitter-patter' sound as they drive over the wet cobbled setts. Shop lights on the other side of the road turn passers-by into silhouettes. Just a couple of hundred yards. The tingle stirs again in his stomach. As he approaches the Bar Deco, can actually see the façade, the tingle becomes almost unbearable, like an itch he can't scratch. This is bloody ridiculous! Calm yourself down. But it's almost a week since Ah last saw her. Saw her? Looked at her. He places a hand on the stylised brass door plate. Come on, get a grip of yerself. He pauses for twenty seconds or so, takes a few deep breaths.

As the door swings shut behind him, the ambience of the Bar Deco envelops him. Stefan and Alan look round. There are only three folk in. A couple and a lone man.

'Good evening, chaps,' he says.

'Hello.'

'Good evening.'

He makes his way along to the far end of the bar. As he does so, Stefan heads in the same direction. He undoes the bolt and lifts the flap, stands to the side holding it up.

'Thanks, Stefan.'

'My pleasure.'

'The boss in the office?'

'Yes.'

The tingle intrudes once more. He opens the door into the corridor and takes the few steps along it, towards the door marked 'Manager'. As usual it's ajar. He wonders what she'll be wearing this evening. Reaching out to knock, he doesn't quite make it.

'Come in.' Her voice.

He takes a deep breath. Opens the door. It's a green silk blouse, with a green and white knotted scarf. 'Good evening, Ruth.' Man! What a long five days it's been.

'Hello, George.' She sits at the desk, reading. Lays the book down. Smiles.

He walks over to the old-fashioned wardrobe in the corner, takes his jacket off and hangs it up. Puts on the short light-blue barman's jacket. As he buttons up, he turns his head at an angle to look at the spine of her book. 'Ah! *The Razor's Edge*. Are you enjoying it?'

'I am. Very much. I've been threatening to read Maugham for years.'

'Yeah, Ah did much the same. One of my pals in the RAF ran the library in the officers' mess. He let me borrow *Of Human Bondage* one weekend. That was it! Ah read them all one after the other. Finished with the *Collected Short Stories*. Loved them. Every one.'

'Goodness!' She sits back in her chair. He tries not to stare, drink in the sight of her. It's difficult. 'So would you recommend them, George?'

'Definitely. Great stories, great characters. And incidentally, it's surprising how many have been made into films over the years.'

'Do you like going to the pictures, too?'

'Oh yeah. They're my two favourite forms of entertainment. A good book or a good film.' He closes the wardrobe door. 'What about you, Ruth. Books or films?'

She reaches for a tin of Black Sobranie cigarettes. In what could only be described as a languorous manner, she extracts one and fits it into the tortoiseshell holder. God! Does she not know the effect she has on me? On most men. He finds himself stepping towards the desk to lift the heavy table lighter. She sits back; the blue smoke curls up beyond the desk lamp and vanishes. He can't take his eyes off her. 'I think maybe books before films.' For a second he wonders what she's talking about. Then he remembers he asked her a question. Hours ago. 'Yeah. Well, okay.' He clears his throat. 'Ah'd better show my face in the bar, Ruth. The boys will be wondering where Ah am.'

'They know where you are, George. You're talking to me.' She looks intently at him. He feels that glow; the same one Miss Ogilvie always gave him in class. A crush magnified ten times. All of a sudden, leaving the office becomes difficult. He doesn't quite know where to put himself. He backs up awkwardly to the door. 'Right, eh, Ah'll see you later on, Ruth.'

'Yes. I'll finish this chapter, then I'll come out.' She watches him leave. Smiles. Shakes her head.

When he's gone, she makes no move for the book. She sits for a while, tries to analyse what it is about George Lockerbie that she likes so much. He's obviously quite enamoured of me. Well, as the Yanks say, 'Get in line!' No, it's not because of that. I've had to handle that since I turned seventeen. I think I like the idea that he'd never, ever make a pass at me. Probably tells himself he wouldn't stand a chance. What else is there? Well, I like the look of him. There's something nice . . . no, good about him. He's intelligent. Well read. Better read than I am. For goodness' sake! Never mind him having a crush on you, Ruth Malcolm – you are attracted to him. She almost laughs out loud. All those businessmen and ex-officer types who come in here. Try their best to impress me, fawn over me, wine and dine me. Now, all of a sudden, there's this part-time barman. What was he? Yeah, a corporal in the RAF. She takes a draw on her cigarette. Who'd have thought it? I've been a widow seven years. Nearly eight. Impervious to all known methods of seduction. Now I can't wait for Friday and Saturday nights to come around. This big soft lump of a guy is gonna come into the office around seven o'clock and be all shy and gauche because he likes to be around me. And I have to put on this Oscar-winning performance, playing someone who is blasé, sophisticated and totally indifferent. She picks up the book. Wonder how long I can keep it up?

CHAPTER TWENTY-NINE

Friends and Neighbours

By midnight, Donald McNeil has had enough. Although his top-floor single-end lies at an angle to the Sneddons' second-storey front bedroom, he has lain in bed for the last forty minutes listening to the increasing distress of Marjorie Sneddon as her husband inflicts his almost weekly violence on her. In what would otherwise be a quiet Saturday night, the sounds carry in all directions for most of the neighbours to hear.

Shortly after the last tram has echoed its good nights from the Maryhill Road, the only sounds now disturbing the peace are the regular yelps and sobs of Marjorie Sneddon, counterpointed occasionally by the booming voice of her husband.

Donald lies on his back in the recess bed, eyes wide open in the dark, staring at the blackness where the ceiling is. Thoughts race through his mind. Pictures of what is happening to that poor lassie. Snatches of conversations with neighbours during this last year show all are in agreement that Richard Sneddon's treatment of his wife is worsening month by month. There come the sounds of another bout of violence, which ends as she screams. It's the scream that does it. Donald throws back the covers, switches his bedside light on and hurriedly pulls his moleskin trousers over his pyjamas, his braces looped over their jacket. In a cold fury, this normally slow-to-anger man descends the two flights of stairs and pounds on the Sneddons' door. In the silence of the night, the booming noise reverberates the length of number 18, from top to bottom. After what seems a long time, but in reality is less than fifteen seconds, he stops. Listens. All is silent inside and outside the house. Donald stands with his head bent forward and tilted to one side. He can hear no movement inside the flat, no footsteps in the lobby. He pounds the door again, then bends and opens the letterbox, 'Sneddon! If I hear another sound from this house, I will be going for the police!'

No sooner has he straightened up than there is the sound of a door opening. He turns. Billy McClaren, who lives in the single-end on this landing, emerges from his door. He has thrown his mac on over his pyjamas. As he steps on to the landing, Drena's face appears from behind the door. 'Don't you be gettin' yourself intae trouble, Billy McClaren!'

Billy smiles. 'Good man yerself, Donald. Ah've been wantin' tae dae this for Christ knows how long. If the snidey bastard opens the door an' he's lookin' fur trouble, jist leave him tae me. Ah've been longing tae banjo this bastard fur the last year or mair.'

'You will not, Billy McClaren!' says Drena. Only her head and one hand are visible as she looks out.

'Did ye know Ah hud a talking door?' says Billy

The two men stand in silence on the cold landing. The weak greenish-white light from the gas lamp casts pale shadows of them on to the floor. There is no movement from Sneddon's flat. They don't know it, but Richard Sneddon is just a couple of feet away, standing in the dark inside his lobby. He has tiptoed along from the bedroom to listen to what's being said. The cold from the linoleum is already chilling his bare feet. He leans back against the coats hanging from the row of hooks, tries to get some warmth. It is a cold April night. He has no intention of confronting them. He hears another door being opened. Recognises the voice of Irene Pentland, his other neighbour on the second storey.

Donald and Billy turn towards Irene.

'Ah! It's you two. Good for you! It's time that reptile was sorted oot. The man's a damn disgrace. Anyway, Ah'll leave the pair of you to it. Well done, boys.' With a smile, Irene closes her door.

Billy points to Sneddon's door, then points to his own ear, mouths, 'He'll be listening.' Donald nods in agreement. 'Right,' says Billy in a louder voice. 'Nae good wasting any mair of oor time. There'll be nae fear of that windy bastard coming oot tae play. If it wiz two wimmen oot here, he wid fancy his chance.' He winks at Donald. 'We'll get away tae oor beds.'

'Yes. Thank you ferry much for joining me,' says Donald.

'Och, it wiz ma pleasure. It wid huv been an even greater pleasure if the bully-boy had opened his door.'

'Naw it wid'nae,' says Drena, still in position.

Billy pretends he's been startled. 'Jeez! Ah forgot Archie Andrews wiz still therr.' Drena sighs.

'Good night,' says Donald.

'Good night.'

The McClarens close their door. Richard Sneddon listens to Donald McNeil climb the stairs, then hears his door shut. He sighs. He returns to the bedroom.

'See what you've fuckin' caused!' he says to his wife. In a low voice.

It takes Donald McNeil almost two hours before he is settled enough to fall asleep. Just before eight a.m., he wakens, then lies for half an hour thinking over the events of last night. He feels that, unpleasant as the incident was, he did the right thing. That poor lassie needs someone to stick up for her. It was good that Billy joined me – and Irene Pentland. He begins to feel better about it all. He rises, washes and shaves, then goes along to Ken's for the Sunday papers. When he returns he still feels unsettled. He looks out the window into the street. It's a drab scene. Since he returned with his *Sunday Post* and *Sunday Mail* it's started to rain; blustery rain. That'll be one of those April showers. Och, there's only one thing will shake me out of this mood. He goes into the cupboard and press, gathers the bowls, implements, trays and ingredients needed for baking. It always works, takes his mind off anything that is worrying him.

Two hours later, he opens his door and takes the few steps over to Agnes Dalrymple's. He gives a knock, listens to her kitchen door being opened then her footsteps in the lobby. Her outside door swings open. 'Ah, good mor—' Like one of the Bisto Twins, she sniffs the air. 'Huv you been baking, Donald McNeil?'

He smiles. The therapy of the last couple of hours has lifted his spirits. 'Yes, yes. Chust a few soda scones and . . .' He pauses. Agnes takes her cue.

'Treacle scones tae?'

'Oh, chust two or three. They are always at their best when they are still warm, as you well know. The kettle is on the boil. Would you like to come over for a dish of tay and sample the odd one. Or two?'

'Wid Ah no'! But huv ye seen the state o' me?' Arms outstretched, she looks herself up and down. She wears her peenie, her hair in curlers; on her feet are a pair of men's slippers.

'Och, now there's entrancing you are, Miss Dal— eh, Agnes.' He holds up a warning finger. 'The scones will be going cool and the butter not melting on them if you do not hurry up.'

' 'Nuff said!' Agnes steps out on to the landing, closes her door. 'Lead on, McDuff!'

As they enter Donald's house, the aroma of freshly baked scones surrounds them. 'Oh my God!' says Agnes. 'It's worth it jist coming in for the smell o' them.' She sits at the table. The rain swishes against the double windows now and again, making Donald's single-end seem all the more cosy, welcoming. Hot coals glow in the range. Agnes folds her arms, leans on the chenille-covered table. She sniffs. 'That sounded like a wee bit of a rammy going on last night doon at Snidey Sneddon's door. Ah thocht Ah could hear you. And Billy McClaren.' With both hands she smoothes out a non-existent wrinkle in the chenille. 'And jist toward the end, Ah fancied Ah could hear Irene Pentland?'

'Man, man! Now I neffer knew you had got the radar installed.'

'Never mind aboot radar. Ah've paid the penalty, so Ah have.' She turns her head and points to the wad of cotton wool in her left ear. 'Ah took the big key oot the door so's Ah could listen at the keyhole.' She gives the cotton wool a token push. 'Woke up this mornin' wi' a raging earache! Ah've hud tae put some warm olive oil in it. Good job Ah got some fae the chemist's last week.' She watches in pleasure as Donald pours freshly brewed tea from his brown china teapot into her cup. He brings two heaped plates from the oven, places them on the table. Soda scones and treacle scones. He slides the butter dish over.

'Now don't you be shy, Agnes. I am expecting you to have one of each. At least. And that is good butter. Don't be sparing. Most of the time it is the margarine I use.

He watches as she reaches for a soda scone, spreads it with butter, takes a bite, 'Oh my God! And Ah've still got a treacle yin tae come.' She takes another bite, speaks with her mouth full. 'C'mon then, Donald . . .' She pauses to take a sip of tea. 'Aboot last night? Oot wi' it.'

She leans forward. 'Every last detail, mind.'

CHAPTER THIRTY

No' Afore Time!

It's a Monday morning. Marjorie Sneddon looks at her face in the mirror. Touches the bruise on her right cheek, just below the eye. The discoloration has spread into her lower eyelid. There are other bruises too. Not all on her face. As she peers at herself, she thinks back to yesterday. That was a very quiet Sunday. Those neighbours gathering outside our door on Saturday night, especially that one shouting through the letterbox. She smiles. He did'nae half put the wind up Richard. For the first hour or two after we got up, every time he heard footsteps on the stairs or landing you could see him tense. Big cowardy bastard. Did'nae go for the papers until ten to twelve in case he ran into one of them who'd been at the door.

Look at your face, wumman! She does. Your neighbours are doing more about it than you. It's never gonny end, you know that, don't ye? You dread the weekends. Whit sort of a life is this? C'mon, get a bloody grip of yourself! She takes a final look. Ten minutes later she has packed a small leather suitcase and her shopping bag. She tears off a sheet of writing paper.

* * *

Granny Thomson, of course, is the first to know. She is tuned in to her close, especially the landings directly above and below – though she has been known to occasionally misread the top storey. Granny heard the Sneddons' door open and close at its usual seven thirty a.m. when Richard Sneddon went to his work. She should hear it again at eight fifteen when Marjorie leaves for the Fairy Dyes. Not today. It's five to eight – and Marjorie's footsteps sound different; heavier. This needs looking intae!

A few steps take Granny into her lobby. She stands silently behind her door as the familiar but heavy-sounding footsteps come on to her landing, turn, and start down the next flight of stairs to the half-landing. Granny bends, and with practised ease takes hold of the spring on the flap of her letterbox and slowly opens it. As expected, she sees the back of Marjorie Sneddon – with a suitcase and message bag – descending the stairs. She gently closes the flap just before Marjorie turns on the half-landing and starts down the next flight of stairs – it would never dae for Granny to be caught at 'Action stations! Periscope up!' To confirm her sighting, she now goes to her windows, waits a minute or so, then opens one and looks out. It's a late April morning, cool, with the sun making a bid to come out. For a minute Granny watches the forlorn figure with the two pieces of luggage walking slowly towards the Maryhill Road. She feels a sadness come over her. Poor lassie. If she'd jist married the right man she should be having a nice life. Instead she married that, that . . . pig's bastard! Well so he is! Whit else can ye call him? Granny watches until Marjorie Sneddon turns the corner and goes out of sight. She comes in from the window, closes it. 'Och, good luck, hen,' she says aloud. She adjusts her curtains. Anywye, business is business. Ah'll start at Teresa's. Spread the news.

Marjorie intended calling at her mother's first, then going to work. Halfway down the Maryhill Road, she changes her mind. Ah'll go at lunchtime. Alighting from the tram at the Post Office stop, she turns the corner into Trossachs Street and crosses the road towards the large red-brick factory. Amid sparks from hooves and nervous high-stepping, a carter is coaxing a young Clydesdale to reverse his cart into one of the loading bays. Big Jack Marshall, the dispatch foreman, stands talking to the man. His face lights up as he spots Marjorie.

'Good morning, Marjorie. You're early this morning, hen. Are ye going oan yer holidays?' His smile disappears as she comes nearer. He leaves the carter and comes towards the outside door to the office. Marjorie keeps her eyes cast down. Jack puts a hand on the door handle but doesn't open it. With his free hand he reaches for the suitcase. There's a pause; she lets him take it. He looks at her. It's common knowledge she has trouble with her man, but she never talks about it. 'Are you aw'right, Marjorie?' He can see the large bruise under the make-up. Feels the anger rise in his throat. 'Is there anything Ah can dae? Anything at aw'?'

C'mon, Marjorie urges herself. This is the new you. Starting today! She clears her throat. 'Ah've left ma man. Fed up gettin' knocked aboot. Ah'm gonny go back tae ma mother's.'

'Good for you, hen!' Jack lets go the door handle, places his big hand on her forearm, squeezes it gently. A surprising gentleness for such a big man. 'Ah'm awfy glad tae hear ye say that. Ye do realise everybody's known for a good while there's been something up. But it's . . . sort of yin o' they things people don't talk aboot.'

Marjorie gives a faint smile. 'Well, it's oot in the open at last.'

Jack bends forward so as to look the downcast woman in the eye. 'Marjorie, it's nane o' ma business, but Ah've known ye for quite a while, especially wi' me bringing ye aw' ma chits and receipts oan a daily basis. Noo, Ah've had something like this happen twice in ma family ower the last few years. Ah can forecast that yer man will try aw' sorts tae get ye tae go back tae him. He'll promise ye the world. He'll be greetin', pleading. Oh! It's aw' gonny be different. He'll never raise a hand tae ye again. So, if ye listen tae jist one bit of advice, listen tae this. If ye go back tae him, Ah'll guarantee the honeymoon will hardly last a fortnight. Ah've seen it before. Twice! He'll start knockin' ye aboot again worse than ever, but this time you'll no' be strong enough tae leave again. If ever there wiz a true saying, it's that yin aboot a leopard never changing its spots. Anywye, Marjorie. If Ah can dae anything tae help, you've jist got tae ask.'

Marjorie looks up at Jack Marshall. She's known him for all of the two years she's worked at the factory. That has been the longest unbroken speech she's ever heard from him. She feels touched. Near to tears. 'Thanks, Jack, I don't intend tae go back tae him. But that'll help me stick tae ma resolve.'

He smiles. Opens the street door. 'If ye want tae talk aboot anything, sort of get a man's opinion as well as a woman's,' he nods in the direction of the café on the corner, 'we can always go ower tae Cocozza's for a cup of tea or coffee – might even treat ye tae a plate of hot peas. Nae expense spared if Ah treat a wumman, ye know!'

She almost laughs. 'Okay, Jack. Thanks for the advice.'

'Will Ah jist put yer case in the cleaning cupboard, Marjorie?'

'Aye. Good idea.' She looks along the short passage to the office door. The lights are on. Once more she braces herself. C'mon! Lets get them told. Then there's jist ma mother tae tell. At least it'll please her. From the first day she met him she said he was a bad yin.

CHAPTER THIRTY-ONE

Starting off on the Right Foot

It's a lovely May morning. For the first time this year, Granny Thomson is able to put a cushion on the windowsill, a pillow on a kitchen chair, and take up her position on sentry duty. Never mind aboot swallows. To the residents of Dalbeattie Street, this is the sign that summer is coming.

'Jaysus! Does me old heart good t' see yourself hanging out that window, Granny.' Teresa O'Malley stops by the close mouth and looks up. She carries a bulging message bag.

'Aye. Summer's no' far away when Ah start sitting at the windae. Is that you jist back from your wee job, Teresa?'

''Tis. That's me offices all spick 'n' span for another day. And a bit o' shopping done for the night's dinner.' She sighs. 'Got a buggering pile of ironing to do. Them gurls! Every blessed t'ing gets worn just the once. I'm sure they t'ink they're royalty, them two. Mind, our Rhea, don't know what's the matter wit' her lately. Hardly goes out, just sits round the house.' Teresa looks down at the pavement, shakes her head, then looks up again. 'But the most worrying t'ing of the lot – she's up like a linty now in the mornings. Just one call and she's out o' bed. No more chasing her to get her out the house. Sumpt'ing wrong with that child.'

Granny smiles knowingly.

'Anyways, I'd better go and make a start. For the second time this day.'

It is nearly eleven o'clock when the woman, a stranger, walks into the street. Smartly dressed, she comes striding along at a brisk pace. Granny watches her. Mmmm, a well-set-up woman. Wonder who she is? Just as she nears the close, Mary Stewart emerges from it. Off to the shops, message bag in one hand, weekly letter to son Robert in the other.

'Morning, Mary.'

Mary stops, turns, looks up. 'Oh, hello, Granny. Is this the first time this year you've been able tae hing oot the windae?'

'It is indeed. That you sending a letter tae Robert? Where is he noo?'

'Aye. Ah enjoy writing tae him. Keep him up tae date wi' whit's happening in the street. He's doon Aldershot wye, noo.' She looks at the envelope. 'A camp called Blackdown. His basic training's aw' behind him; he's now daeing whit they call trade training.

'When will he get a spot o' leave?'

'He should be hame the middle o' this month for a week. His faither and me are fair looking forward tae it. That'll be four months since we seen him last.'

'Aye, Ah'll bet youse are, Mary.' Granny smiles. And, the thought passes her mind, Ah know somebody else who'll be fair looking forward, too.

Just then, the unknown woman speaks to Mary. 'Excuse me. Can you tell me which landing Irene Pentland lives on?'

Mary Stewart smiles. 'Yes, she lives on the second storey.'

'Thanks very much.' The woman enters the close.

Granny and Mary look at one another. Granny allows a decent pause, to make sure the woman will have started up the stairs. 'A visitor for Irene? Mmmm? Diz'nae get many visitors, Irene.'

As the woman steps on to the second-storey landing, she looks at the highly polished brass nameplate on the first door on the right; 'J. PENTLAND'. Oh, this is it. She breathes in, then reaches up for the bell. It's one of those bells that since childhood have always reminded her of winding a clock. She takes a hold of the butterfly-like winder and twists it, feels it grate and grind through her fingers. From behind the door comes a weak 'grinnntinkle, grinnntinkle'. Jeez! You would'nae hear that behind a tram ticket! This thought is about to make her laugh, probably nerves, when she hears movement behind the door. Composes herself.

This meeting is going to be very important. Crucial! The door opens. In the gloom of the landing she makes out a woman who looks pretty much as she'd imagined.

'Hello! Is it Irene?'

'Yesss? That's right.'

'Irene, Ah really hope this isn't too much of a shock for you. But Ah'm Mary Anderson. You know, James's lady-friend. James doesn't know Ah'm here. Ah've waited long enough to meet you and Ah really would like for us tae get tae know one another. Ah hope that's all right?'

'Oh, aye. Well, Ah suppose you'd better come in.' Irene stands back and gestures for Mary Anderson to step inside.

She ushers her into the kitchen. 'The kettle's no' far off the boil. Will ye take a cup of tea?'

'That would be lovely.' Mary sits down on the proffered chair. She feels nervous. She so wants this first meeting to go well. 'Ah, Irene – do you mind if Ah call you Irene?'

'No, that'll be fine.' Irene's glad she's got something to do, something to keep her hands busy. She puts dry tea into the teapot.

'Now, just in case there's any doubt, Irene, can Ah say that Ah've been at James right from the beginning to introduce the two of us.'

'Well, I can put your mind at ease aboot that. When he told me about you and him getting married,' Irene turns round to look at her visitor, 'and Ah'm sure you'll realise what a shock that was?' Mary nods. 'Ah played merry hell with him about never, ever being introduced to you.'

'Ah can imagine,' says Mary.

'So he did tell me himself, "That's aw' ma fault." '

There's a pause in the conversation while tea is poured and biscuits offered. Irene now sits herself at the table, opposite Mary.

Mary takes a sip of tea, returns her cup to the saucer, looks straight at Irene. Smiles. 'Ah've been rehearsing this meeting for weeks, Irene. Ah really do want us tae be friends. It's very important to me that you and Ah get on. Ah have a son, John, who's twenty-three and just got himself married. But Ah don't have any brothers or sisters, and Ah'd really love to have a sister-in-law who is also my friend. Ah really would. So that's why I've come tae see you, to tell you how I feel.'

Irene looks at her future sister-in-law. In spite of the anger, the hurt that's still just under the surface after her brother's shock announcement, she likes the look of Mary Anderson. Feels she is the sort of woman she would almost certainly become friends with if they worked together. She reaches out, lays a hand on Mary's forearm for a moment. Smiles.

'Och, Ah think you're right. Why should we let a silly man have the two of us at daggers drawn because he has'nae the sense tae introduce us tae yin another?'

Mary lets out a sigh. 'You've no idea how pleased Ah am tae hear ye say that, Irene. Ah'd have been really upset if James and Ah got married and you never, ever came tae visit us, or spoke to me if we happened tae meet somewhere. That would be just awful.'

Again Irene lookes closely at this woman who's about to marry her brother. Steal him away.

'Aye. Ah think you've maybe got the right idea. Ah'll not deny Ah'm gonny be really sad when James leaves. Ah never dreamed he would just up and get married. As ye know, Ah wasn't even aware he had a lady-friend. Ah thought we'd grow old the gether – bachelor brother and spinster sister. Ah'll also not deny, it's gonny take some getting uscd to, living on my own. Anywye. At the very least, it'll be good if you and me do get on with one another. But it'll be even better if we become friends. Things like meet now and again tae go doon the toon and round the shops, or maybe have a night oot at the pictures, or see a show. That really would be good, Mary. Something tae look forward tae.'

Mary visibly relaxes. 'Oh, Ah'm so glad Ah came, Irene. Glad we've cleared the air, as they say.'

It's more than an hour before Mary Anderson finally rises. 'Well, Ah'd better get myself away. Ah took the day off work tae come and see you, so Ah'd better get tae the shops before closing time.' She pauses in the small lobby as Irene is about to open the outside door. 'Ah take it Ah can leave it tae you to tell James ye had an unexpected visitor today?'

Irene laughs. 'Aye. Ah'll enjoy that. Ah'm gonny wait until he's in the middle of his dinner, then Ah'll say, "You'll never guess who called in the day."' The two women laugh.

'Well, Ah don't mind telling you, Irene, Ah'll be going home a lot happier than when Ah left the house this morning. Especially now Ah know that you and Ah are starting off on the right foot.'

CHAPTER THIRTY-TWO

Days that Fly By

Rhea O'Malley comes wideawake. She turns her head to see what time it is. The luminous green hands point to five past six. Robert's coming hame the day! A glow spreads out from her stomach to every part of her. Ah cannae wait. Well you'll jist huv tae! She runs over in her mind what he said in his letter. No need to see it. Since it arrived at the office, she's practically memorised it. Well, the important bits . . .

Arriving Saturday afternoon off the five past one at the Central. Told my ma and da I'm not sure what train I'll be coming off, so no point them coming to meet me. That means you'll be safe enough to come down (if you want!?). To be honest, I'm not looking forward to seeing you one little bit. Just one ENORMOUS bit!!! If you're not on the platform as the train pulls in it will spoil my arrival completely. Just remember all the times we've sat in the back stalls of some cinema, Rhea, and watched Judy Garland or Jane Wyman or Ann Sheridan standing on the platform, on tiptoe, looking over the heads of the other folk who are waiting, dying to catch that first glimpse of the returning hero (that's me!). It's just three days now until I see my wee darling. Is it EVER going to go in?

She sighs. It's today. Robert and me will be together again the day! She glances once more at the clock: nearly quarter past six. Siobhan stirs, turns towards her, drapes an arm over her.

Rhea lies for another wee while. There have been occasional noises from the kitchen as Daddy gets ready for his work. Well, as her mammy gets him ready for his work. The kitchen door opens, footsteps in the lobby, grunts as he puts his coat, then his mac, on. Subdued 'cheerios' and 'see ye the nights'. The outside door is closed. That'll be half past six. She hears her ma go back into the kitchen. She'll be huving a wee sit-doon and a cup o' tea now. Och, Ah might as well get up.

Teresa is in the middle of pouring her tea when Rhea pushes the door open and enters the kitchen. Rhea blinks and narrows her eyes at the transition from dark bedroom to what at first seems a bright kitchen.

'Jayz Almighty!' Teresa says. 'I could have scalded meself, so I could! What do ye mean by coming in here at half past six in the mornin'? Never been known. Have ye wet the bed?'

Rhea laughs. 'Naw, Ma. Ah'm wide awake, so Ah thought Ah might as well get up.'

'Wide awake!' Teresa splutters. 'Now and again I've seen ye maybe half awake when yer leaving to go to yer work at quarter to eight. But wide awake at half past six? Never been known in the history of mankind! It's the doctor yer needing to see. Do ye want a dish o' tay?'

'Aye, Ma. Ah might as well huv a slice o' toast tae. Anywye, Ah'll need tae go tae the lavvy.' Rhea slides her feet into her daddy's slippers, takes the lavatory key from the hook on the door jamb, slips into her mammy's coat and, after checking all is silent on the landing, makes her way down to the toilet. A couple of minutes later she returns and reverses the procedure. 'Aw, Ma, it's cauld oot therr.' She runs the solitary cold tap into the sink and washes her hands. 'Jeez-oh! That watter's freezin'.'

'You've got more complaints than a doctor's book, so ye have,' says her mother. 'Anyway, there should be no mad dash this mornin' to get ready for yer work. You'll likely be the first one in the office the day.'

'Aw, noo, Ah wid'nae go that far, Ma. Jist keep the heid, will ye!'

'Are ye coming straight home after ye finish? Or are ye havin' a Saturday afternoon in the toon wit' some o' yer pals?'

'The toon. Janet and me are gonny have a wee donner roon' the shops. So Ah don't know when Ah'll be in, Ma. We're thinkin' of going fur something tae eat late oan, then mibbe go tae the pictures. Probably early evening afore Ah'm back.'

'Right, that's foine. Sure, I'm just pleased you're takin' a bit interest in going out. You've been gettin' to be a right wee stay-at-home this last couple o' months. Gettin' worried about ye I was, no kidding.'

Rhea reaches out and squeezes her mother's hand. 'Naw, Ah'm aw'right, Ma. Jist wiz'nae much bothered aboot goin' oot ower the winter. Nae fun going oot in the bad weather.'

'Hah! Sure it never stopped ye before, so it didn't.'

As soon as the train enters the outermost edge of the Glasgow suburbs, Robert Stewart feels an excitement. Not only because he will be seeing Rhea soon – but he is back in Glasgow. He opens the sliding door of his compartment and steps into the corridor so he can stand at the window. He has no idea what district this is. But it *is* Glasgow. There are streets of red sandstone tenements. Most of the time he's looking at the backs of them, glimpses of grassy back courts, railings, washing hanging out, weans playing. At the end of each block he gets passing glances, snapshots, of the other side of the street, front views of identical tenements. Corner shops, sometimes pubs, folk walking past. Then, suddenly, his first tram. The green, cream and orange livery. Just a fleeting look, passengers sitting at upstairs and downstairs windows as it glides out of sight. He feels his eyes smart. Jeez-oh! Ah'm hame. Until he saw the tram, he didn't realise how much he'd missed his home town. His city.

As the train nears the aptly named Central Station, it travels slower. From a raised section of line he sees, for the first time, how grimy the fine city-centre buildings are. A century of soot and smoke from a zillion coal fires. Jeez! I never knew they were so mucky! There are now lines of Corporation trams and buses, punctuated by cars and commercial vehicles. He feels the excitement rise again in his stomach. Ah'm hame. Ah'll be seeing Rhea any minute!

He re-enters the compartment, buttons up his battledress tunic, puts his army belt on and slips his beret out from the epaulette that holds it. Knees bent, he looks at his reflection in the glass-covered adverts for holiday destinations that can be reached by rail. He adjusts the beret, his face superimposed on a reminder that 'Skegness Is So Bracing!'. Ready, he reaches up to the rack for the brown paper carrier bag that is his sole item of luggage.

'Cheerio,' he says to the airman and the young married couple who have been his travelling companions since London. 'Bye.'

'Have a nice leave, mate!'

He steps back into the corridor just as the train enters the Central and begins to glide along a lengthy platform. He opens the small ventilation window so he can smell the station. His need is instantly gratified by the aroma of steam and cinders plus a cantata of guards' whistles, shouts from porters, and the chuffs of a locomotive departing amidst clouds of steam, smoke and slipping wheels. His train comes to a halt. Right! Now to put his plan into operation. He has deliberately chosen the first carriage behind the engine and tender. He exits from the door next to them. As hoped for, Rhea has walked a few yards along the platform and now stands on tiptoe, scanning the faces of the three hundred or so passengers, many of them servicemen in uniform, as they exit the long train and swarm along the platform towards her. As he looks at her from behind, wearing that so familiar swagger coat, he feels like his heart might burst. He walks towards her, praying she won't turn round. Sometimes she stands evenly on both toes, other times she'll favour one leg or the other, seeming to teeter, straining her head up in the air to try and gain an inch. He comes close behind her, puts the carrier down. Passing passengers smile as they figure out what's going on. He takes a last step and wraps both arms round her waist. 'Rhea!' he says.

'Oh!' She is only able to turn her head and shoulders; leans back so as to focus. 'Robert! It's you! It's you!' He releases his grip so she can turn round, then pulls her close. 'Oh Robert. You're hame!' She starts to cry. He cannot trust himself to speak. He kisses her cheeks in turn, kisses away each tear as it appears, tastes the salt of them. Tastes her.

'Oh, God! Rhea, you've no idea how Ah've missed you. Four months.'

'You've nae idea how miserable Ah've been, Robert. But oh, look at ye in yer uniform. Ye suit it. You look really handsome. An' ye look that big. Solid.'

He laughs. 'Ah've put oan a stone, would ye believe. Aw' that exercise and steamed food. Anyway, let's find a nice wee café somewhere.'

They continue to hold one another. The last few dozen passengers move past on either side of them, a stream round a rock. Many look and smile, remembering when they were in love. Some wish it were them.

They find a café just a couple of hundred yards away, sit with a pot of tea and two cakes. Face each other across the table, hands clasped while their tea goes cold.

'How often are we gonny see one another this week, Robert?'

'As much as we can. Ah'll spend time wi' Ma and Da during the day and early evening, that'll keep them happy. But every night Ah'll tell them Ah'm going out tae meet ma pals – but Ah'll only be going to see one pal. Guess who?'

'When dae ye go back?'

'There's a train next Sunday morning, gets me back early evening. Ah'll get that one.'

She squeezes his hands. 'Oh, Robert! A whole week. It'll be jist lovely.' She suddenly remembers. 'Listen, in case Ah forget. There's a smashin' picture oan at the Paramount. It's been held back fur a second week. Wan o' the lassies at work went and seen it wi' her man. She says it's great! That auld silent movie star, whit's her name? She's in it. You'll know—'

Robert interrupts. 'Does it have a name, this picture?'

'Aye. Yon William Holden's in it. Aw! Whit's her name? Gloria Swanson! That's her. It's called *Sunset Boulevard*. Janet says it's terrific. Will we go and see it?'

He looks at her excited, sparkling-eyed face. Love for her just bubbles up inside him. He glances round the café. Nobody is paying any attention. He leans forward and kisses her on the lips. 'Yeah, we'll go and see it. Ah read about it in one o' the Sunday papers.'

'Whit's aw' this "yeah" business, Robert Stewart? You're no' gonny come back efter your two years talkin' like a Cockney, urr ye?'

He laughs. 'You've nae idea how easy it is tae pick up saying "yeah". Everybody says it – Taffs, Paddys, Jocks and, of course, all the English lads. Especially the southerners.'

She looks at him. 'Oh, Robert. A whole week.' She sighs. 'Ah'll bet ye it jist flies in.'

CHAPTER THIRTY-THREE

Good News

It's a Wednesday morning. Rhea O'Malley sits behind her desk in the offices of Macready and Co. in Wellington Street. Three of her co-workers, Elsie, Margaret and Shona, sit at their desks. Her other workmate, Janet, has gone to reception to see if the mail has arrived. It has. After four months of Robert sending his letters to Rhea c/o the company, it has now become a ritual. The girls await their arrival with almost as much enthusiasm as Rhea.

'When did he travel back, Rhea?' asks Shona.

'Sunday.' As she speaks, she is watching Janet sort the mail. 'Ah thought Ah might have got one yesterday. But there should definitely be something this morning. It's important, this yin. He's jist finished his trade training, that's why he got leave. They were gonny be told on Monday where they are being posted tae. This is whit they call their permanent posting. We're fair hoping it'll be somewhere in the UK, so as he can get hame regularly. If he wiz tae get Hong Kong or somewhere like that, we'll hardly see one another.'

All eyes are on Janet. 'Aha!' She extracts an envelope from

the bundle. Holds it aloft. It's the usual blue Basildon Bond. 'Is there a Miss Rhea O'Malley oan the premises?'.

'Oh! Gimme! Gimme! Gimme!' squeals Rhea. She takes hold of the envelope; hasn't the patience to use the letter-opener, tears it open with her index finger. His letters are never any less than four-pagers. Her pals watch as she races through it.

'Eeeeeeh!' Rhea's face is wreathed in smiles. 'It's good news!'

'Is he getting posted tae Maryhill Barracks?'. suggests Margaret.

'Naw. No' quite as near as that.' Rhea presses the now unfolded letter flat against her breast with both hands, fingers open wide. She looks around. 'One mair guess.' There's a brief silence.

'Redford Barracks in Edinburgh,' says Elsie.

'Naw! Ah'll have tae tell ye's.' She looks at the letter again to make sure she gets it right. 'He's gettin' posted tae CAD Longtown, Carlisle. CAD stands fur Central Ammunition Depot. He's going there as a driver.' She looks at the letter again. Begins to read from it. ' "One of the regular soldiers here at Blackdown used to be at Longtown. He says that two weekends out of four, if you're not on duty, you finish at five o'clock on the Friday night and you don't report for duty again until first parade on Monday morning. He says most of the Glasgow lads usually hitchhike hame on the Friday night, and take the late train back on Sunday. It's only four miles tae the A74 – that's the main Carlisle to Glasgow road. When you're in uniform you get lifts no bother. If you're lucky enough to get picked up by a businessman or sales rep in a car, you can be in Glasgow before eight o'clock. Isn't that terrific!"' Rhea looks around the office. 'Jeez! He could hardly get a better posting if he'd picked it himself. In't that great?'

Janet tries to keep a straight face. 'Rhea, you'll be fed up looking at him. Coming hame every second weekend? Be sick o' the sight of him.'

'Naw Ah'll no'. Nae fear o' me getting fed up seeing ma Robert.'

Elsie decides to join in. 'Now if he hud been oot in Hong Kong or Singapore. Aw' them field post office letters coming fae abroad – like Ah used tae get fae ma Ronnie, saying how much he missed me – now that wiz romantic. But Carlisle? And hame every fortnight! C'mon, Rhea. Where's the romance in that? Is it the *Salvation* Army he's in?'

They all, Rhea included, go into peals of laughter. 'Listen,' says Rhea, 'ye can keep yer field postal orders or whitever ye call them. Ah'll settle for ma Robert gettin' hame regular. Yon absence makes the heart grow fonder carry-oan. Ye can keep it!'

They fall silent as the door from the corridor that leads to the partners' offices is slowly opened. Young Mr Macready, dressed in his three-piece pinstripe suit, gold double Albert hanging from his waistcoat, takes two paces into the room and stops. He removes his half-moon reading glasses. 'Now as you know, ladies, we like to have a happy staff. However, there seem to be regular outbreaks of hilarity this morning.' He looks at all of them in turn. 'I take it the work isn't suffering as a result?'

'Sorry, Mr Macready,' says Janet. As the senior typist, she feels obliged to be spokeswoman.

'Sorry, Mr Macready,' echo the other four.

They watch as he steps backward and through the door. 'Good morning, girls.'

'Good morning, Mr Macready,' they chime. They watch his silhouette through the opaque glass of the door as he ambles back to his office. They are all frightened to look at one another. Whenever they receive their periodic tellings-off, it always gives them the giggles. Rhea, who is undisputed Giggler Number One, rises, half bent, from her desk. Keeping her eyes fixed on the floor, she makes for the door leading to the toilets. The heads and eyes of the other four swivel to watch her. The nearer Rhea gets to the door, the louder are the choking, gasping, squeaking noises she makes as she loses control. Elsie emits a prolonged low whine. 'Stoap it! Behaaave . . .' Janet makes a futile attempt to restore discipline, but she too succumbs and has to stuff a hankie into her mouth. Shona has been biting the side of her hand for the last two minutes. For the rest of the morning there will be occasional, unsolicited outbreaks of giggling. Shona says it's the best job she's ever had.

Drena McClaren joins the queue in Ross's Dairy on the Maryhill Road. She spots Irma Armstrong, who is well in front of her and next to be served. As Irma turns away from the counter, about to leave, Drena stops her. 'Hiyah, Irma.'

Irma's face lights up. 'Hello, Drena. I have not seen you since early in last week.'

'That's jist whit Ah wiz thinkin'. Huv ye much more shopping tae dae?'

'Just to the shop of the Scotia Bakery. Then I am finished.'

Drena opens her purse. 'Here's two bob. Will ye get two custard cakes and a pineapple cake and bring them up tae my hoose. Ah'm going straight hame efter this. Ah'll nip up and gie Ella Cameron a knock – she's daein' a stack of ironing this morning – and the three of us will huv a cup o' tea in ma place.'

'Oh, but I think it is maybe my turn for the cakes,' says Irma.

'You can get them next time,' says Drena.

Irma tuts. 'You said that the last time.'

Thirty minutes later they sit round Drena's table. 'Right y'are, girls. A cake each.' Drena turns to Ella. 'How urr ye gettin' on wi' the ironing?'

Ella screws her face up. 'No' quite halfwye. God! Ah hate ironing.' She finishes the last of her cake, wets the tips of a couple of fingers and uses them to pick up the last few crumbs. She reaches into her peenie pocket and brings out a five packet of Woodbine, places one in front of Drena. Looks at Irma. 'Ye want wan, Irma?'

'No thank you, Ella. I do not smoke.'

Drena pipes up, pointing a finger at Irma. 'Ah know whit that is in German. You're a nicht raucher. Is that right?'

Irma laughs. 'Good for you. A non-smoker. In German, a nicht raucher. You have learned that from your Billy?'

'Aye.' Drena looks from Irma to Ella. 'You've nae idea, wi' him being a POW fur five years, using German every day, the amount of words or wee phrases he comes oot wi'. He swears maist o' the time in German. Says it's stronger, helps ye tae get it aff yer chest better. But fur the last five years since he came hame ah've picked up loads of wee bits.' Drena laughs. 'Jist tae prove it.' She picks up the Woodbine, leans towards Ella. 'Haben Sie Feuer, bitte?'

'Yah!' says Ella. The three of them burst out laughing. 'Don't forget,' says Ella, 'Archie was a POW tae – but jist the last seven months.' She passes her box of Bluebell matches to Drena, then turns to Irma. 'My Billy was captured at Arnhem in September 1944.'

Irma looks at both in turn. 'Sometimes I feel so embarrassed when people tell me their husband or brother was taken prisoner, or even more terrible, killed in France or Germany.'

Drena pats her on the arm. 'Noo we've hud this discussion before, Irma. You were thirteen when the war broke oot. Ah don't think it hud much tae dae wi' you, hen.'

'I was very pleased when you said to come for a cup of tea, Drena. Because I wanted to see you and Ella, but as you know, with Bert working night-times with the taxi, and sleeping the daytimes, I cannot ask you to come to our house. Staying in the single-end is very awkward when your husband has to sleep daytimes.'

Drena speaks. 'Thank God Billy diz'nae dae night shift, or Ah'd be the same.' She looks at Irma. 'Ah'm coming up for eleven bloody years in this single-end of oors. Ah'm aboot demented, so Ah am.' She takes a draw on her Woodbine. 'Oor William's ten noo. Ah'm gonny tell Billy, if we don't get a room and kitchen there will be nae mair . . .' she looks at Irma, 'nae mair jigajig!' Once more, hilarity reigns supreme.

Irma dabs her eyes. 'So, please. I have something to tell you. I am expecting a baby!'

'Oh! That's wonderful. No. That's wunderbar, Irma!' says Drena.

'Eeh, Ah'm really pleased for you,' says Ella. 'When are you due?'

'The doctor thinks near to the end of November, maybe December.'

'What would you like? You know, a boy or a girl?'

'We both hope very much for a boy. If you remember—'

Drena interrupts. 'Aye. Ye told me aboot Bert's brother. He was killed, wasn't he?'

'Yes. He was called Arthur. He was killed during the fighting in Normandy. One month after D-Day. So Bert would like – and so would I – a boy. Then, of course, he will be called Arthur.'

'Och, well that's nice. Ah really hope it's a wee boy,' says Drena.

'Aye, me tae,' says Ella. 'Well, that's something tae look forward tae jist before the winter. Especially if it's a wee laddie.'

Irma smiles. 'I am now going down to see Granny Thomson, to tell her. She has always said that when Bert and I start to have children, perhaps his mother and father will want to, eh, be more friendly to us. They do not want to see Bert because he married a German girl.' Drena and Ella look at her. They can tell she's near to tears.

'Och, these things happen, Irma. There is always falling-outs in families. As the years go on, time often helps tae soften things,' says Drena.

'Ah think Granny Thomson is right. If ye have a wee laddie and he's named efter Bert's brother, that'll be a nice thing tae do. So let's hope it's a wee boy.' Ella squeezes Irma's hand.

It is ten to six when Irma leaves Granny Thomson's house after telling her the good news.

It is quarter past six when Rhea comes home from work bursting with her good news. But alas, there are only two folk whom she can safely tell about Robert's posting. Siobhan is one. And the other, of course, is Granny Thomson.

CHAPTER THIRTY-FOUR

The Unkindest Cut

Friday night. As George Lockerbie steps into his lobby, he calls out his usual greeting. 'It's only me, Joan.'

'Hello, dear. I'll just finish preparing your sandwich while you change. I'm afraid it's Spam again. Do you want some mustard on it?'

'Yes, please. It'll give it a bit of taste.' He hangs his small rucksack on one of the coathooks, then his jacket. Taking his flask, tea and sugar tin and folded-up piece of greaseproof paper from the bag, he opens the kitchen door, reaches in and places them on the table. 'Ah'll just nip through the room and change into my pub gear. Sure has been warm in the factory today.'

'Has it, dear?' Joan continues with his sandwich. 'Shall I pour your tea?'

'Yes please.'

Minutes later, he sits on the edge of the bed and, with difficulty, pulls his old RAF boots off, then the thick woollen socks he's worn all day. Ohhh! Lovely. Ah think Ah'll have a clean pair of socks on for the bar tonight. And Ah'll give my feet a quick wash under the tap. He walks over to the chest of drawers. Now, what drawer is it she keeps my socks in? He pulls open the top one. No. As he's about to close it, a small white cardboard box towards the back catches his eye. Haven't seen that before. He picks it up, turns it round in his hand. 'Ajax Contraceptives Ltd' is printed in bold letters. Underneath, in pencil, someone has written 'One Dutch cap. Batch: February 1946.' He gets a sick feeling in his stomach as he opens the box and looks at the rubber device inside. It's a pale pink colour. He's never seen one before, but knows what they are for. You don't spend six years in a succession of RAF billets without finding out about lots of things you've never seen before. He closes the box, but continues to hold it in his hand. Looking at it. Thinking of what it means.

'Your sandwich and tea are waiting for you, dear,' comes the insistent voice.

'Yeah. Ah'll just be a second.' He puts the box back in the drawer, then walks through to the kitchen in his bare feet, carrying the clean socks and his best shoes. He takes a bite of sandwich, then goes over to the Belfast sink and lifts his right foot into it. Turns on the tap. The cold water feels lovely, refreshing, as he rubs his fingers between his toes. Ahhh! Reaching for the towel, he holds it below the lip of the sink and lifts his foot out, gives it a quick dry.

'That was a clean towel, George, fresh out today. Now I'll have to put another one out.'

'My feet are hot after being on them all day. Should Ah go out to my evening job with sweaty feet?' She makes no reply. He takes a drink of tea, then another bite of sandwich. As he dries his left foot, he turns towards her. Might as well bloody have it out now. 'What are you doing with a Dutch cap?' He can tell he has caught her on the hop. She goes red; her mouth opens then closes. No sound comes out. 'So much for "I don't know why I haven't fallen, George." Or, "I do hope I'm not going to be one of the unlucky ones who just can't get pregnant!" You've had nae intention of having a baby – *my* baby – have you? You know Ah've been dying for us tae have children. So looking forward to being a dad. Fat fucking chance! What a nasty thing to do. A mean trick. But increasingly that's how Ah'm coming tae think of you. You really are getting to be a selfish bitch. When Ah look back on things, Ah don't know why it's taken me so long to see it.' He puts his clean socks on, then his shoes. 'Have you nothing tae say?' He finishes the last of the sandwich, washes it down with the tea.

'It wasn't that, George. I didn't want to have a child while we were living here. Once we'd moved to our new flat I intended to stop using it. Really.'

It's the 'really' that does it. He's heard it before. She always uses it when she lies. 'Ah! It was jist a decision for you tae make, was it? Nothing tae dae wi' me?'

She makes no attempt to reply. No further excuses. He really has wrong-footed her.

'Anyway. Ah'm away to my wee job. Be nice tae be wi' pleasant people. Ah'll see ye later.' He takes his jacket off the hook, closes the front door behind him, puts the jacket on as he walks the length of the close out to the street. His mind is in a turmoil. Four bloody years! Lying in her teeth all that fucking time!

He's barely conscious of the tram ride to St George's Cross or the trip on the subway to Hillhead. The couple of hundred yards along the busy Byres Road hardly registers. Someone passing by says, 'Evening, George.' He glances. 'Oh, hello.' Walks on, knows the guy's face, the name's gone. Concentrate. Try and take your mind off her and that bloody Dutch cap. He's a local businessman . . . Bill? Crossan! That's him, Bill Crossan. Owns a shoe shop. Immediately his mind goes back to Joan. Their marriage. What marriage?

At last he's approaching the entrance to the bar. He has a feeling of relief. Thoughts of Joan suddenly seem less dominant. He looks at his hand, with its wristwatch, as he stretches it out and pushes on the Art Deco door plate.

The door swings shut behind him. The ambience of the Bar Deco enfolds him. There are four men at the bar. They all look to see who's come in.

'Good evening, George.'

'Ah! It's George.'

'How are you, George?'

'Good evening, gents.' He smiles. Recalls the night he came in to apply for the position. These four were in for their regular end-of-another-week snifter, before going home to their wives and families. Ah barely merited a glance that night. Now? Ah'm George of the Bar Deco. Ah'm also George whose wife is fucking him about!

'Hello, George.'

'Hiyah, Alan.

Stefan, as usual, has made his way along the bar and stands holding the flap open. 'How are you this evening, my friend?' he says. His strong Polish accent is also part of the Bar Deco.

'Oh, fair tae middling, Stefan.'

He walks along the corridor towards the office door. The aroma of Black Sobranie cigarettes hangs in the air. Joan slips further into the back of his mind. He stops, raises his hand . . .

'Just come in, George.'

He pushes the door open. Loves that first sight of her every Friday and Saturday night. The desk lamp with its long green shade sends its light down on to the desk, as it should. Some of it bounces back up from the large rectangle of blotting paper. The lighting is perfect. She is in various shades of blue this evening. Where's Raymond Chandler when he's needed? You don't know whit you're missing, pal! You'd be looking around for the nearest typewriter if ye were here. George stands at the door for a moment. The continental smell of the tobacco adds to the scene. For the moment, Joan has been banished.

'Are you sure you did'nae used to be in the movies, Ruth Malcolm?'

'Ah, George. Nobody pays the ladies such compliments as you do.'

'Ah could swear Ah saw you in one of the nightclub scenes in *The Lady From Shanghai* with Rita Hayworth.'

'What a load of old tosh, George. However, don't stop. I like it. Makes me feel good. How are you?'

He pauses. 'Oh, fine, fine.' He takes his jacket off. Swaps it for the light blue barman's one.

She looks at him as he puts it on and does up the buttons. That pause before answering, then the answer itself, have given the show away. I don't think he is fine – two 'fines' aren't better than one. Just one more question might do it. She takes a draw on the cigarette through the long holder. 'How is Joan?'

He's totally incapable of hiding his reaction. His body stiffens, he looks everywhere but at her as he tries to say casually, 'Oh, she's well.'

Ruth has suspected for a while his marriage isn't very happy. He never, ever spontaneously talks about Joan. If Alan and Stefan are talking about their wives, George never contributes. If she does come into the conversation, his comments are always matter-of-fact. There are never any fond memories or funny stories. Without fail, he'll swing the topic on to something else or, preferably, hand the floor over to one of the others.

'Anyway, Ruth. Ah'll away out and show my face. Have a wee blether with the boys before we get the usual Friday-night crowd in. See you in the bar later on.'

She watches him leave the office. There's no doubt about it, he's an unhappy man at the moment. A last draw is taken on the cigarette; it's extracted from the holder and stubbed out in the ashtray. She sits back in her chair. I don't like seeing George miserable. But what to do?

CHAPTER THIRTY-FIVE

What a Difference
a Day Makes

As George Lockerbie approaches, then enters the close at 18 Dalbeattie Street, he can feel the depression bearing down on him. What a miserable bloody weekend lies ahead. Thank God it's Saturday. At least Ah'll be over to Hillhead for a few hours this evening. Being in the bar will take my mind off things for a wee while. Talk to Ruth. See her. Be in her company. His thoughts go back to last night. When he returned from the Bar Deco, Joan had already gone to bed. Appeared to be sleeping. This morning there was hardly a word said as she saw him off to work. Suppose Ah could have brought it up again. Tried to make her realise how much it hurt when Ah found that contraceptive thing. Ah don't know what's the worst part of it. To realise what she's been doing behind my back, or . . . No! No, Ah know what's the worst. Ah should have been a dad by now. He pauses for a moment outside his front door. There should be a three- or four-year-old toddling about in that kitchen, and Joan saying 'Daddy will be home soon . . .' He feels tears brim in his eyes again. A lost child.

Never been born, yet lost. Ah'll never forgive her for doing that. What a bloody selfish, self-centred thing to do. He reaches down, turns the door handle, pushes. It doesn't move. Locked? It's never locked on a Saturday afternoon. Maybe she's at the shops. He reaches into his pocket for the Yale key.

He steps into the lobby. Pauses. The house is still. The stillness you only get when there's no one in. He doesn't call her name. Doesn't want to speak her name. He takes his bag and jacket off, goes through the usual 'hame from work' routine. Surely she's not in bed? Kidding on she's distraught. He opens the room door. Empty. Bed made. Walks along the small lobby and enters the kitchen. Still. The sun is blazing down into the back court. He can hear the weans playing. Ours should have been out there with them. Imagines himself chapping the window: 'Daddy's hame!' At just that moment, he spots the letter on the table.

With a sigh he sits down on the fireside chair with its back to the windows. He pulls out the single sheet of paper. Can't stop himself racing through it.

Think we will both agree, marriage has gone stale. Things won't get any better. Gone back to Mummy and Daddy in Camberley. My fault more than yours. Realise now how much I've hurt you over not starting a family. I'm willing to admit I'm 'in desertion'. Most certainly not looking for any money from you. As there are no other parties involved, I don't think we need to rush into divorce proceedings at the moment. If, or when, that time comes, I hope it will be ended amicably. Please write and let me know if you agree with the above.

George sits for a moment, then reads the letter again, at a more measured pace. He looks at her last line: 'I do wish you well, George. You are a good, hard-working man. But somehow, not for me. Joan. PS I've taken a tenner from the Kelvinside deposit fund for train fares, etc.'

He puts the letter back in its envelope, stretches over from where he's sitting and places it on the kitchen table. Leans back in the chair. The sound of the weans playing in the sun is, somehow, relaxing. What do you think, George? Are you sad? Glad? Well, right at this moment Ah'm glad she wasn't in when Ah came hame from work. Ah really didn't want to see her. Ah'm a bit miffed at the way she's suddenly upped and left. C'mon! That's fucking male vanity. Living on my own will take a bit of getting used to. But it'll be cheaper. My wage was keeping the two of us. Now it's just me. There's about thirty pounds left in the fund. That'll make a nice wee nest egg. There's nae fear of me moving tae a posh flat now. This room and kitchen will dae me nicely. Ah don't mind sharing a lavvy in the close. You still have'ny answered the question. Sad or glad? Little bit sad. But mostly glad. It really was getting tae be pretty miserable. For the two of us. Yeah, it's definitely for the best.

He rises from the chair, takes the kettle and fills it at the sink. While he waits for it to boil, he opens the sideboard drawer and brings out the writing pad and envelopes. Hope there's enough ink in the bottle. Nae point in delaying writing to her. Get it all done and dusted. As that thought enters his head, he feels a little pang of regret. Jeez! Five years ago Ah was crazy about her. And as far as Ah know, she felt the same. Now, here we are. It's all over. Hard to believe.

*   *   *

It has just gone half-six on the Saturday evening. Ruth Malcolm sits at her desk sorting through the cash bags inside the petty cash box. Pennies, threepences, sixpences, shillings. 'Do you need any two-shilling pieces, Alan?'

'Aye. Ah'd better have a few.'

'What about half-crowns?'

'Ah think we should have enough.'

'Notes?'

'Mmmm, maybe four ten-bob notes and five ones. That should definitely be enough, Ruth.' Alan closes the wardrobe door and begins buttoning his barman's jacket.

She opens the ever-present box of Black Sobranie, pushes it in his direction. 'Want one?'

'Oh, Mammy Daddy, naw! It's like smoking a Partick tram-driver's jockstrap!'

'It is not!' Ruth laughs. 'You've no class.'

Alan reaches into his pocket. 'Ah'll just have a wee Willie Woodbine, thank you very much.' He reaches for the lighter on the desk.

'Did you find George was a bit, ohhh, sort of not himself last night?'

'Oh aye. Definitely.' Alan sits himself half on the corner of the desk. 'Top and bottom of it is, Ah don't think him and his wife – it's Joan, isn't it?' Ruth nods. 'They're not hitting it off at all this good while past. Ah don't think there's terrific big rows, or dishes gettin' thrown aboot. Ah don't think they're that kind of folk. He diz'nae really talk aboot it. But now and again Stefan and me will be talking aboot something, and we'll say, "Have you and the wife been there?" Or "Have ye done that, George?" And he either avoids giving an answer, or he'll say, "Aw, we don't go oot very often." Well, as ye probably know, they've nae family. There's nothing tae stop them going oot.'

Ruth raises a cup of tea to her lips, sips, puts it back on the saucer. 'I got a really strong impression he was quite upset last night. So quiet. As if something was bothering him. Anyhow, we'll see how he is tonight.' She looks at her watch. 'He shouldn't be long.'

'Ah'll away through in case we get busy.' Alan nips the Woodbine into the ashtray. Ruth sits watching the blue smoke curl up from its ember. She wonders how George will be this evening.

Five minutes later, she hears voices drifting in from the bar: Stefan's, followed by George's. It gives her a little frisson. Then his footsteps coming along the passage. Towards the office.

'Come in, George' She watches for the door opening, his face to appear, then the tall figure. He smiles. 'Good evening, Ruth. Been another warm June day.'

'Yes. I think it's trying hard to be a flaming June. Make a nice change.' She looks at him closely as he gets ready. 'You seem to be in a far better mood than this time yesterday, George.'

'Huh! That's for certain. You can definitely say that.' He seems to pause. Maybe trying to make a decision? He turns towards her. 'Ah suppose Ah might as well tell you; Ah'd eventually let it slip anyway.' He laughs. 'Never could keep a secret. Anyway, Ah don't have anybody Ah can tell my troubles to, so it's—'

Ruth interrupts. 'You know what they say, George. A trouble shared is a trouble halved.'

'Well, last night Ah caught Joan out in, eh, for want of a

better word, a lie! An ongoing, quite deliberate lie. Ah came home from the factory this afternoon to find she's gone back to her folks. Our marriage is over.'

'Oh!' That's all Ruth says. She doesn't add 'Sorry to hear that.' She isn't.

'Now that's the bare facts. The marriage has been failing for the last couple of years, at least. But what Ah found out yesterday. Well that, as they say, put the tin hat on it! There are lots of details to fill in; that's just the outline. There isn't the time to tell you now, and Ah really would like you to kn—'

Ruth cuts him short. 'You don't work on a Sunday, do you?'

'No.'

'Well, as there's no reason for you to rush home tonight, I'll tell Alan that you'll be my escort to the night safe at the bank with this evening's takings. He does it three nights and Stefan does the other three. And, of course, we're closed Sundays. I'll give Johnny McKinnon a ring at the Hillhead Bar and tell him I'll be along about ten thirty. He always has a few select customers in after closing time at the weekends. Then we'll find ourselves a quiet corner and you can tell me all about it over a nightcap. How does that sound?'

'That sounds good. That's really nice of you, Ruth. Are you sure you want to be bothered?'

Ruth shakes her head, a half-smile on her face. 'Yes, George. I'm quite happy to be bothered.'

It is just after ten thirty when Ruth, with George Lockerbie as escort, steps out of the Bar Deco on to the pavement. 'Hold that a moment, George.' She hands him the small locked leather bag with 'Linen Bank' embossed on its side. He watches while she double-locks the wooden street doors. 'That's it till Monday. Let's go.'

As is the way on a June night in Glasgow, especially a cloudless one, there are still remnants of light in the sky. The pavements and sandstone buildings have soaked up the heat of the sun all day and now return some of it to the night air. As they set off along a still busy Byres Road, George is so conscious of Ruth beside him. This is the first time he has been in her company outside of the bar. She steps out, high heels clip-clopping, coat open, totally ignoring the fact that every guy who passes seems compelled to give her the once-over, as do many of Hillhead's stylish women. As they walk along, George finds that only glimpsing her out of the corner of his eye isn't enough. He continually tries to think of something to say so he'll have an excuse to turn his head and look at her while he speaks.

'Ah'd think this is a perfect example of what's called a balmy night.' He steals a glance at that Roman profile. She turns her head to answer. Looks straight at him. His heart skips a beat. George! You're like a schoolboy with a crush. Except you ain't no schoolboy.

'Yes. We don't get too many of them, do we? When I was down in Kent with David, early in the war, 1940, the entire summer seemed to be made up of balmy nights like this.'

'Yeah. That was a glorious summer, wasn't it? Ah was in Staffordshire with the RAF.' He takes a few more steps. 'What exactly happened to David? If you don't mind talking about it.'

'As he would have put it, he bought it in North Africa in '42. He was a staff sergeant in the Seaforths. Just twenty-six years old. I thought he was invincible. They'd never get David. Never!'

Money deposited, they shortly afterwards arrive at the Hillhead Bar. Ruth looks around her. 'Just making sure the beat bobbies aren't around. They know it goes on, but Johnny doesn't like to rub their noses in it.' She raps twice, pauses, then three times. A bolt is withdrawn, a lock turns, one of the double doors opens a crack. 'Ahah!' The door is thrown wide. 'Get yourself in here, Ruth Malcolm!' They both step inside, then through the inner doors. Wait as Johnny McKinnon locks up. As he comes to join them, George gets a good look at him. He likes him at first sight. Maybe six feet tall, burly, wearing a double-breasted suit, hair combed back. He reminds George of the American comedy actor Jack Carson.

'Why have you no' been tae see me lately?' He takes Ruth into a bear hug, kisses her on each cheek.

'I'm a busy girl, Johnny.' When he lets go, she points to George. 'I'd like you to meet my number one cocktail barman, George Lockerbie.'

George's hand is seized in a firm grip. 'Ah! You're the new man. One or two of my regulars have told me about you. I'm pleased tae meet you.' He leans forward, lowers his voice. 'I take it you know that at this moment, you are escorting the best-looking gal in Glasgow?'

George smiles. 'Ah'm pleased tae meet *you*. And yes, Ah most certainly know Ah'm a lucky guy – even though Ah've only been escorting her to the night safe!' They all laugh.

'Come away through!' orders Johnny.

They walk into the large bar. There are at least twenty folk already installed. 'George and I will sit over in the far corner,' says Ruth. 'We've something to talk about.' As they make their way across the sawdusted floor, quite a few of the late-night drinkers greet Ruth. Two of them, to his pleasure, also acknowledge George.

As they sit down, Johnny asks them what they'd like to drink. He goes behind the bar to serve them himself. George looks along the length of the room. 'This is my first time in here. Has a nice feel to it.'

'Yes, it's a well-run place. Johnny McKinnon doesn't stand any nonsense. Runs a tight ship.'

It's an hour and a half later when they decide it's time to say good night. During that time, George has told Ruth about meeting Joan during the war. Of how soon the glamour of their wartime romance became jaded in the reality of tenement life. Of Joan's ambition to move up to a wally close in Kelvinside – with George as sole provider. Then the gradual realisation on both their parts that they were rapidly falling out of love. Finally, just over twenty-four hours ago, the straw that broke the camel's back. George's discovery of the Dutch cap – and what that meant.

It is just after 12.30 a.m. when they step out into a deserted, still warm Byres Road.

'Ah'll see you to your door, Ruth.'

'Oh, I'll be all right.'

George spreads his hands wide, palms open. 'Ruth, Ah can assure you Ah have no ulterior motive. If Ah go away without seeing you safely to your door, Ah won't sleep a wink for worrying if you got home safe and sound. And remember, it's next Friday before Ah see you. So Ah'll have nearly a whole week of worry. Do you want to put me through that?' He is slightly tipsy, and obviously tired. She knows he works a half-shift at the factory on Saturday mornings.

She laughs. 'It never entered my head you had anything other than honourable intentions. I was just wanting you to get away home. It's been a long day for you.'

Ten minutes later, they stand at the beautifully tiled entrance to 22 Agincourt Avenue, just off the Byres Road before it hits Dumbarton Road. Ruth turns to face him. 'Seeing as you're here, you may as well come in for a coffee, George.'

'No thank you, Ruth. Ah don't want you thinking that's what Ah was after all along. But if there's a next time – and Ah sure hope there is – Ah'll be delighted to come in for a coffee. Ah'll just stand at the close-mouth until Ah hear your door close, then Ah'll know Ah've delivered you safely home.'

She smiles. 'Well thank you, kind sir!' She suddenly stands on tiptoe and kisses him on the cheek. 'Good night, George.' She turns and walks into the close. He lifts a hand to his cheek.

'Ah, good night, Ruth.'

The couple of miles he has to walk home seem as nothing. Tonight Ah could walk all the way tae Mulguy and back. On my hands. The touch of her lips brushing his cheek stays with him all the way back to Dalbeattie Street. And into the week.

CHAPTER THIRTY-SIX

A Place Far, Far Away

June the 25th 1950 seems like any other Monday morning to the residents of 18 Dalbeattie Street. By nightfall it will still be just another Monday for the majority. But for some . . .

In the Stewart household, Samuel Stewart busies himself with the normal routine of getting ready for work. He has had his usual good slunge in the sink and is now through the room getting dressed. The smell of frying bacon has followed him from the kitchen.

'Will Ah put yer breakfast oot, Sam?'

'Aye. Ah'll be through in two seconds, Mary. Ye can pour the tea, tae.'

He comes into the kitchen and takes his place at the table just as the seven o'clock news starts on the radio. Knife and fork in hand, he sits very still as he listens to the first item.

'Eat yer breakfast, Sam, afore it—'

'Shhhhh!' He cocks his head to one side as though to show

how intently he is listening. The news report finishes. 'Did you huv the wireless oan for the six o'clock news, Mary?'

'Aye. Ah always dae.'

'Well why did ye no' tell me aboot that fighting breaking oot in Korea?'

She laughs. 'Ah did'nae pay any attention tae it. Whit's that got tae dae wi' us?'

'Whit's that got tae dae wi' us?' Sam splutters. 'If ye'd listened, ye'd huv found oot whit it's got tae dae wi' us. Communist North Korea has invaded independent South Korea. There are already a certain number of American troops in the south. The United Nations – that includes Britain – has got a treaty wi' South Korea that we'll go tae their aid if the commies attack. That's why it wiz the first item oan the news. They telt ye aw' that, if ye had jist listened. It's a serious situation. If we send more sodjers oot there and the fighting gets worse, the next bloody thing is mibbe the Chinese will get themselves involved. Then you'll be talking aboot a big war. And we've got oor boy in the army at the minute! *That's* whit it's got tae dae wi' us, Mary.'

'Oh Sam, stoap that. You're frightening me, so ye are. C'mon. That's awfy far away, so it is.' She pauses for a moment to try and absorb, make sense of all her husband has told her in the last few minutes. She watches as Sam, his mind obviously on other things, begins to pick at his breakfast. 'Och! It'll be aw'right, so it will.' She turns her back to the table and reaches for the frying pan. Samuel Stewart shakes his head.

Rhea O'Malley enters the office nearly ten minutes before starting time on that same Monday. 'Morning, girls!'

'Ah'll tell ye whit,' says Janet, 'as far as Macready and Company are concerned, your Robert should sign oan fur ten years. Ah don't think you've been late wance since he got called up!'

'Eeeeh! Whit a cheeky bizzum. Huv ye ever heard the like? Are you trying tae say that Robert Stewart's a bad influence oan me?'

There's a chorus of 'Aye!'

'Mind, Ah hope this carry-oan in Korea diz'nae affect him,' says Margaret.

Rhea looks up from her desk. 'Whit carry-oan where?'

'Korea.'

'Where's that when it's at hame?' asks Rhea.

'Ah think it's aboot three miles fae Pitlochry,' states Shona.

'Ma daddy says it could get a lot worse afore it's gets better,' says Margaret.

'Is somebody gonny tell me where whit's-its-name again *is*?'

'It's oot near China and Japan. That sort of wye.'

'Aw, well that pins it doon,' says Elsie.

'How dae ye spell it?' asks Rhea. Margaret obliges.

'Och, it's away oan the other side o' the world,' says Shona. 'By the time he got oot therr it wid be all over.'

'As long as it's not, as they say, all over bar the fighting!' Janet looks serious.

'For God's sake!' Rhea looks at Margaret. 'You lot urr beginning tae get me worried. Can you tell me whit's going on in . . . Korea, and why Robert might get involved? Ah huv'nae got a clue.' She listens intently as Margaret tells her what her father said about the situation.

During her lunch break, Rhea dashes off a letter to Robert

asking him if he thinks British troops, and specifically himself, could be involved in this Korea thing, then hurries out to catch the 12.45 collection. As she travels home that evening on the tram, she avidly reads, twice, the main article on the front page of the *Evening Citizen*, headed 'NORTH KOREA INVADES SOUTH. HEAVY FIGHTING'. She doesn't like the sub-heading: 'United Nations gives North Korea an ultimatum.'

The night of the 25th of June is a warm one. Samuel and Mary Stewart lie close together in the recess bed in the kitchen. It is coming up for half past eleven. In the dark, Mary lies cuddled into Sam's back. They have only a sheet and one blanket for cover; the blanket has been thrown back and lies almost at their feet. Most of the evening has been spent listening to successive news reports on the radio. The *Evening Citizen* lies on the kitchen table.

'Do ye think we're gettin' oorselves up tae high doh for nothing, Sam?' Mary's voice comes out of the blackness.

'Well, Ah hope so, hen. As long as the Chinese don't get involved it should mibbe stay, whit could ye say, sort of low key. Ah think President Truman will be quite firm wi' them. And remember, Mary, oor Robert's jist a driver. Ah'd be a bit mair worried if he wiz an infantryman. You'd be talkin' front-line fighting if it did flare up and we had tae send troops. So put it this wye. If the worst came tae the worst and he did huv tae go there – he'd jist be driving a lorry. He'd be miles ahint the front line. Well away fae any danger.' He lies quiet for a while. 'But Ah really don't think it'll come tae aw' that. It'll die doon. You'll see.'

Slightly reassured, they still spend an almost sleepless night.

*　　*　　*

On the landing above, between eleven p.m. and midnight, Rhea O'Malley and her sister Siobhan also lie in the heat of the dark. They too have kicked off their blanket and have just a sheet over them. 'He should get your letter the morra morning, shouldn't he?'

'Aye. If Ah catch that quarter tae wan collection he usually gets it next morning. God! Trust a wee war tae start when Robert's daeing his two years. Could they no' wait till he got oot? Then they can dae whitever they buggering want!'

Siobhan laughs. 'Ah don't think it works like that, Rhea. Anywye, Ah'm sure he'll answer ye straight away. And he should be hame this Friday night for his usual weekend, shouldn't he?'

'Aye. And that's a few days away. By the time he gets hame oan Friday, he should mibbe huv a better idea of whit's likely tae happen if the fighting gets worse and the United Nations get thurrselves involved.'

'Och, aye.' Siobhan stretches, yawns. 'C'mon, Rhea. Turn roond and let's get some sleep. If ye remember, oan the nine o'clock news yon man said they think that North Korea is jist trying tae show they huv some muscle. He said that wance they make their point they'll probably withdraw again.' She turns round and cuddles into her sister's back. 'You'll see. It'll jist be a flash in the pan.'

CHAPTER THIRTY-SEVEN

A Firm Hand

———

Richard Sneddon leans on the bar of the Tramcar Vaults. The two wee haufs of whisky he's already had are beginning to kick in nicely. He glances at his watch. Twenty past one. She'll have had her lunch and be back in the office by now. Ah'll give it another ten minutes. Ach, Ah'll have one for the road. 'Ah'll have another hauf.'

'Certainly, sir.' The heavily moustached barman reaches for the empty shot glass and takes the few steps over to where the various bottles of spirits stand. His customer watches, for want of anything better to do, as the man pulls the cork from the bottle of White Horse and reaches for the small pewter measure that stands nearby. He bends his knees a little so as to see when the golden liquid reaches the line for a quarter-gill, then he decants it into the glass. 'Therr ye are, sir. Fourpence, please.'

Richard Sneddon's eyes follow the man as he rings up the sum on the ornate stainless-steel and brass till. The barman then turns, crosses his hands behind his back, and leans against the long shelf on which the till and spirits stand. Richard regards the man. Takes in the waistcoat, the long white apron reaching to the turn-ups of his trousers. The pair of tackety boots.

He looks down at his glass. Ah'll have this, then Ah'll get up tae that oaffice of hers and get her sorted oot. Ah should'nae have let it go oan for so long. Probably thinks she's gettin' away wi' it. 'Hah!' The barman turns at the sound. Well she's got another fuckin' think coming! Richard downs the large measure in one gulp, bangs the empty glass on to the scrubbed white-wood counter, then stands for a moment. Ah'd better go for a pish first. Unsteadily, he makes his way to the toilet.

One arm stretched out, palm flat on the wall, Richard Sneddon leans forward and pishes into the stand-up urinal. Don't want tae splash the auld shoes. That would never dae. The small toilet smells, not unpleasantly, of pine-scented disinfectant. Right. That's me ready for the road. He looks at his penis before he puts it away. Bit o' luck that'll be in her fuckin' mooth the night. He finishes buttoning his flies. Shrugs his shoulders. Now tae get that fuckin' wee whore sorted oot. He exits the toilet, mind already working on what he intends to say, and if necessary do, if he meets with any resistance. Without acknowledging the barman, he walks the length of the bar and exits into the Maryhill Road.

'And cheerio to you too, sir,' says the barman.

The only other customer in the pub, an elderly man, laughs. 'A miserable-looking bugger, that yin, John.'

'Aye. Struck me as a nasty piece o' work.'

'Aye, ye could be right, John. Ye could be right.'

As soon as the fresh air hits him, Richard Sneddon realises he's had a bit too much to drink. Should'nae huv hud that last yin. Anywye, Ah'll manage. He shrugs his shoulders once more. A wee walk will probably be jist the thing tae help clear ma heid. Although it's early in July, the weather is unseasonable; there's a slight spit of rain and it's cool. He's glad, because this gives him a reason to wear his dark blue topcoat. Richard loves his Crombie. He feels it somehow gives him authority. There's naebody in Dalbeattie Street huz a proper gentleman's overcoat like mine. Even the boss doon at the rent oaffice huz'nae a coat like this. Slightly unsteady on his feet, he sets off up the Maryhill Road.

Turning right at the Blythswood Cinema, he walks the hundred yards or so along Trossachs Street to the red-brick Fairy Dyes factory. He pauses a moment at the door leading into the offices. Just past it, the large sliding doors of the loading bays are open. He can see the rear of a cart, hear the steel-shod hooves of the horse on the cobbled setts as it stirs a moment. He opens the door and climbs the few steps into the narrow corridor. The top half of the wall on the right consists of a large, steel-framed window. The first few panes are painted the same green as the window frames. He stands on tiptoe and looks through the first of the clear glass panes. Marjorie sits at her desk. At an adjoining one sits her workmate. Jesus! Whit's her name? Aye, Mrs Grant. Good. He smiles. This is gonny be nae bother.

At the same instant, Marjorie Sneddon becomes conscious of movement over at the window. She looks up and feels a sharp pang of fear as she sees her husband's face smiling at her.

'Oh!'

Mrs Grant looks over. 'What's the matter?'

Marjorie looks down at her desk, turns her head slightly towards Mrs Grant. Says, in a low voice, 'Ah've just seen ma man look through that windae. He'll be here tae cause—' She breaks off as the office door opens and Richard Sneddon walks in.

'I want to see you! You've not been answering any of my letters, so I've no option but to come here.' In the presence of Mrs Grant, he has remembered to talk 'pan loaf'.

In what comes out as a frightened squeak, Marjorie manages to say, 'Ah don't want tae see you, Richard. It's all over between us.'

Richard Sneddon looks at her. He can see she's frightened. 'You're coming up to the house with me now! This is no place for us to talk.'

'Ah'm not going with you. Ah want nothing tae dae wi' you!'

He walks over to her desk, leans on it with both arms outstretched. 'You're coming up to the house – the easy way or the hard way! What's it gonny be?'

Mrs Grant stands up. Both of them look at her. She gives Richard a smile 'This is a private matter between husband and wife. Ah'll leave youse alone for a few minutes.' Marjorie looks at her, doesn't want her to leave the office. How can she leave me wi' him? The fear grows in her as she watches Mrs Grant open the office door. Richard Sneddon turns his head back round to face his wife. Mrs Grant takes the opportunity to wink at her and nod her head in the direction of the inner factory. Relief floods through Marjorie.

As soon as she closes the door, Mrs Grant, on her rubber-soled shoes, almost runs the few yards through to the loading bays. Oh, thank God! Big Jack Marshall stands in the shadowy bay, arms folded, leaning against one of the concrete pillars that support the building. He's talking to Auld John, one of the railway carters. Jack stops talking and turns his head to see who's running. When he recognises Mrs G., he stops in mid-sentence and pushes himself off the pillar.

'Jack! That swine of a man of Marjorie's is in the office! He's starting tae get nast—'

Jack Marshall doesn't wait for any more information; he sets off at a run.

As he enters the corridor, he slows down. He can hear the raised voice of a man. Jack keeps his head low until he reaches the office door, puts his hand gently on the handle, then straightens up. He is tall enough to see through the first of the rows of clear panes. Richard Sneddon holds his wife by her upper right arm. He has pulled her to her feet and is in the process of dragging her out from behind the desk. She is vainly trying to resist by gripping the edge of the desk with her left hand. All the while she keeps glancing towards the door. At last! She sees Jack Marshall's face appear above the painted glass. She knows everything will be all right. With help now at hand, she begins to think clearly. Ah'll make a noise so's he won't hear Jack come in . . .

'Stop it, Richard! Ah'm no' goin' with ye. Let me go! Let go of my arm!'

'Aye, you're fuckin' going, yah bitch. You can take it from me you're going aw'right!'

While this exchange is going on, Jack Marshall, in a rising fury, opens the door and comes quickly up, unheard, behind Sneddon. In one movement he grips Richard Sneddon's upper right arm in a firm grip, then grabs his left wrist in an even stronger one, breaking the hold he has on his wife's arm. Jack whips this arm up Sneddon's back until his left hand almost touches the collar of the coat he loves so much.

'Who the fu— Awyah! Awwww!' The pain is excruciating.

Sneddon tries to turn his head to see who it is. From the corner of his eye he sees enough to know that this guy is bigger – and stronger – than himself. Years of sitting behind a desk is no training for taking on someone the size of Bruce Woodcock, the heavyweight champ.

'Ah've been hoping Ah'd meet you some day, yah fuckin' bastard! Ah hear you're good at knocking wee lassies like Marjorie aboot.' While he talks, Jack has allowed Sneddon's arm to drop from excruciating to merely painful.

'It's got fuck all tae dae wi' you. This is ma wife.'

'Marjorie is my friend. And she wants it tae be something tae dae wi' me.' Jack swings Sneddon round to face his wife. 'Do you want me tae protect you from this shitbag, Marjorie?'

She looks her husband in the eye. 'Ah most definitely do, Jack.'

Jack Marshall forces Sneddon's arm back up to excruciating. 'Awwww! Fuck!'

'Have ye got the message?' There is no answer. The arm goes past the previous record and approaches unbearable.

'Aye! Aye! Oh aye! Ahhhhhh!'

'Ah'll see him aff the premises.' Jack frogmarches Sneddon out of the office, but instead of turning left for the outside door, he takes him through into the gloomy depths of the loading bays. Auld John the carter sits on a couple of boxes full of glass phials of powdered dyes. He watches proceedings with interest. Jack suddenly lets go of Sneddon's arm and spins him round so they face one another. He punches him twice in the stomach, doubling him up, then slams him against a brick wall. He inclines his head in the direction of the office. 'Noo Ah wiz being nice tae you in their jist for the sake of the ladies. If you bother Marjorie again, in the street, at her mother's, ANYWHERE!' Sneddon jumps at this shout. Jack Marshall brings his face closer to him, looks into his eyes. 'That wee lassie jist has tae tell me that you deliberately followed her, walked past her and gave her dirty looks – or even jist walked past her and did nuthing – and Ah'll come lookin' fur ye, find ye and give ye such a fuckin' hiding. Listen tae whit Ah'm aboot tae say. Ah will do time for you. Because Ah'll make a fuckin' mess of ye! Noo huv ye got that?'

Sneddon makes no answer. He receives another dig in the stomach.

'Ooooh! Aye. Ah've got it, Ah've got it!'

'Now fuck off oot o' ma sight.' Jack points, 'Go along tae that next bay. It's empty. There's steps doon tae the street. And mind whit Ah've telt ye.'

He watches as Richard Sneddon, rubbing his left arm, literally slinks out of the factory. John the carter turns his head. 'Friend of yours?'

Jack comes back into the office. Mr Beedham, the deputy manager, has joined Mrs Grant and Marjorie. He smiles as Jack enters. 'So this is the hero of the hour, is that right?'

'Oh, Mr Beedham, Ah don't know what we'd have done withoot him.' Mrs Grant smiles. 'You handled that nasty piece of work so well, Jack.'

He blushes. 'Ah'm an ex-Military Policeman. Ah had quite a few years of handling aggressive drunks and aw' the rest of it.' He looks at Marjorie. She's sitting at her desk, pale, and obviously shaken up by the whole experience. He can see her hands are trembling. 'Ah think Marjorie could dae wi' a wee brandy, Mr Beedham. Ah'll go and—'

The boss holds his hand up. 'I've got some in the office. I'll bring her a wee snifter. Then you escort her home to her mother's, Jack, just in case that reprobate is hanging about.' He reaches into his inside pocket, takes out his wallet and extracts a new, red ten-shilling note. 'Hail a taxi. I'm sure she won't feel like going by tram.'

'Oh! Really, Mr Beedham, there's no—'

He waves a hand. 'Save your breath, Marjorie. You'll be going in a cab.'

As Jack and Marjorie leave the factory, she takes hold of his arm. 'Between all that's happened and that large brandy, Ah feel quite dizzy.'

'Aye, jist you hang on tae me, Marjorie. Anywye, it's nice tae feel you taking ma arm. Ah'll tell ye whit, Ah think a strong cup of tea or coffee wid dae ye the world of good. Jist to sit doon, the two of us, and huv a wee blether afore ye go hame. Calm yer nerves. Whit dae ye think?'

'Ah'm dying for a cup o' tea, as it happens.'

They walk the few yards over to the corner café. As it's mid-afternoon, it's almost empty. Old Peter Cocozza looks up as they enter. 'Jacko! How are you?' He smiles at Marjorie. He knows she's a regular but isn't sure of her name.

'A pot of tea for two, Peter.' Jack looks at Marjorie 'Want anything tae eat?'

'Oh, goodness no. Ah'd had my lunch no' long before he arrived. Just tea.'

Marjorie slides into a booth. Jack takes the seat on the other side of the marble-topped table. Faces her. 'Auld Peter always calls me Jacko.' As he speaks, Peter has come out from behind the counter to put the order into the kitchen. At the same time, Maria Cocozza, his daughter-in-law, emerges from the back shop.

'It's okay.' Maria waves her hand. Peter heads back behind the counter. 'Hello, Jacko. What you like?'

'Pot of tea for two, Maria.'

'Anything to eat?'

'Ah'll have a couple of biscuits. Sort of Digestive type if you've got any.'

'S'okay. I know.' She turns round and heads back to the kitchen. Old Mrs Cocozza, as usual dressed in black, her grey hair tied back, appears briefly at the kitchen door. Maria relays the order to her in Italian.

Jack places a hand gently on top of Marjorie's still trembling hands. 'Settle down, hen. Ah don't think you'll get any more bother fae the boyo. Ah took him intae the loading bays for a few minutes and telt him in no uncertain terms whit will happen tae him if he even jist crosses yer path in future. *And* gave him a wee example as a going-away present!'

'Oh, Jack! When Ah seen you coming through that door . . .' she pauses as she becomes a little bit tearful. 'It was jist wonderful. Ah thought, here's Jack! Everything will be aw'right. It was so good tae see him getting a taste of his own medicine.'

'Well, the times we've been ower here for a cuppa and you've half told me whit you've had tae put up wi', Ah must be honest, two or three times Ah've thought tae maself, Ah would'nae mind if that pig's melt came intae the office one day and tried tae gie Marjorie some bother. So, Ah know it's been awfy upsetting for you, but for me it was a golden chance,' he leans forward, drops his voice, 'tae sort the bastard oot. So Ah grabbed it wi' both hands!' As he says the word 'hands', he looks down. His large hand still covers both of hers. Neither he nor she seems to mind. He squeezes her hands. 'Ah'll tell ye something else, Marjorie. Jist tae be on the safe side, for the foreseeable future when ye go oot tae the pictures, or go oot anywhere for that matter, Ah think Ah should be by your side. Every time. Be your full-time escort.' He blushes slightly. 'Whit dae ye think?'

She places her hands on top of his. Looks him in the eyes. 'The job's all yours.'

CHAPTER THIRTY-EIGHT

A Quiet Affair

The newly-wed James and Mary Pentland step out from the doorway of the registry office in Martha Street to be met by a hail of confetti, and from the more traditional, a few handfuls of rice. Granny Thomson looks around. 'Ah'll come back and sweep that up later the night. There's enough therr tae make a puddin'!' There's laughter from the more than thirty assembled guests. Already there's a feeling that everybody is going to enjoy themselves today – and even the least of jokes will be found uproarious.

'Can I have your attention, folks!' The new Mrs Mary Pentland, smart in pale blue costume and hat – with a veil so fine it can only just be glimpsed by its pattern of fine black dots – waits until she has that attention. 'My son, John, is going to take some photos before we leave for the reception. First of all we'll have James and his sister Irene, and me and my son. Now, as John is going to be in this first photo – who's good at taking pictures?' One of Mary's cousins volunteers. This typical, yet necessary, wedding-day pose is taken in front of the registry office. As soon as the camera clicks, Billy

McClaren pipes up, 'What aboot one with all the Dalbeattie Street yins gathered roon' the happy couple?'

'Good idea!' says James Pentland. 'Let's have aw' oor friends and neighbours from number 18, please. Then we'll have one wi' all Mary's friends and relations.'

James and Mary remain where they are, with Irene Pentland on the other side of her brother.

'C'mon then, all you Dalbeattie Street hooligans. Let's be having you.'

'Anybody with bairns, make sure they're at the front,' says John Anderson. Soon, in two rows, the invited guests from the bridegroom's close gather round the happy couple to be captured, as Drena McClaren puts it, 'for posterior'. There they stand: James Pentland in his blue pinstripe suit, Mary in her smart costume. All the women in their finery, the men in their best – their only – suits. Irene Pentland, Granny Thomson, Agnes Dalrymple, Andrew and Lena McDermot, Dennis and Teresa O'Malley with daughters Rhea and Siobhan, Archie and Ella Cameron with Archie junior and Katherine, Billy and Drena McClaren with Billy junior.

A split second on a Friday in July 1950. Forever frozen. Forever happy.

'Best of order! Best of order, please!' James Pentland remains on the steps for a moment to address his and Mary's guests. Agnes Dalrymple nudges his sister.

'Ah've never seen your James in such a bouncy, bubbly mood, Irene.'

'Neether have Ah. Ah think he should get married mair often!' The two of them take a fit of the giggles. They quieten down as James begins his announcement.

'Now, if everybody can make their way round the corner

to John Street, there is a charabanc waiting to take you all to Hubbard's tea room on the Great Western Road. Needless to say, my bride, my sister, young John and myself have other travelling arrangements. And Ah bet ye we beat youse tae Hubbard's!' He receives a round of applause as well as laughter.

Agnes leans closer to Irene's ear. 'Eeeh! He's making jokes, noo! Is there nae end tae it?'

Irene links her arm through Agnes's. 'He'll no' be laughin' when he gets the bill!' Once more the two of them get the giggles and have to hang on to one another.

Eventually Agnes manages to say, 'Huv you been oan the sherry?'

'Naw. Ah weesh Ah had, Aw' Ah've had is a moothfy of Tizer afore we left the hoose.'

'Are ye sure ye did'nae lift the turps bottle by mistake?' This is enough to set them off again. As they hang on to each other, those around them begin to laugh at the state of the pair of them. Most of the guests have set off for John Street. James Pentland spots his sister and Agnes, who, still arm in arm, have almost recovered from their last bout of hilarity.

'C'mon, Irene! It's time tae go tae the car.'

'Oooh! That's ma big brother shouting oan me. Ah'd better go or Ah'll be gettin' telt aff!' Yet again, this innocuous statement is enough to make the two of them helpless.

Agnes disentangles herself from Irene's arm. 'Go on, Irene, away ye go before somebody sends for the polis!' The two now go into a near terminal state. It takes Irene three attempts before she manages to say, 'Ooooh! Imagine gettin' lifted by the polis oan ma brother's wedding day. The shame!'

'Ah'm away,' says Agnes. 'Ah'm going fur the bus.' She stops after one step 'Oh, Irene. Here's your James coming!'

'Mammy, Daddy! Don't leave me, Agnes.'

James Pentland approaches his sister and neighbour. He's aware that the two of them have got, at the very least, the giggles.

'Oh, James. It's no' ma fault.' Irene points to Agnes. 'It's her. She's a bad article, that yin.'

'Ah know whose fault it'll be.' He turns to Agnes. 'Every two or three years she has a day when, for some reason, she finds the stupidest things absolutely hilarious.' He smiles. 'So it looks like ma wedding has tipped her ower the edge.' As he speaks, his new wife comes and stands beside him. He turns towards her. 'Aye. It's just like Ah told you. She's in the middle of one of her daft half-hours.'

Mary laughs. 'Well, what better day could she choose? Shall we go for the car, Irene?'

'Aye, but Ah'll have tae go back intae the building first. Aw that laughing. Ah'll have tae go a place.' She looks round. 'And you, Agnes Dalrymple, don't come anywhere near me when we get tae Hubbard's. You're a bad influence, so ye are!'

Shortly after six o'clock, the bus drops the guests from Dalbeattie Street back at their close. James and Mary Pentland are now on their way by train to Rothesay, where they are booked into a hotel for the next week. It has been a pleasant afternoon, and unwilling to break the mood, they stand around in two interchangeable groups on the pavement outside their close. The first ones to head for their houses are those with bairns. By seven p.m., the remnants reluctantly decide to abandon the summer-evening street. As they enter the close, Granny Thomson comes up behind Irene Pentland and Agnes

Dalrymple. 'C'mon intae ma place and the three of us will have a wee cup o' tea, otherwise we'll be going straight intae empty hooses.'

'God! Aye, you're right, Granny. That's ma James away, noo. He disnae live here anymair.'

The twin gas lamps murmur away to themselves above Granny's range. The three women sit round the table. A large teapot, covered with its cosy, stands in the middle. There's a choice of biscuits and rich fruit cake.

'Well, Ah think that wiz a grand wedding,' says Granny. 'Ah really enjoyed it.'

'Me tae,' says Agnes. 'Ah've no' laughed sae much fur years.'

'Huh! Ah thought Ah was gonny end maself wance or twice,' says Irene.

They sit for a few minutes in silence, contemplating nothing in particular.

'Ah suppose you'll have tae face up tae it, Irene. How dae ye think you'll be, living on yer own?' Granny Thomson looks at her.

'Ah've been giving it some thought. Ah'm used tae having the hoose tae maself during the day. James is at work. But it'll be the evenings. And Sundays. We're the gether aw' day on a Sunday. James jist likes tae sit aroon' the hoose. He buys three papers. Always has a wee nap in the efternin. Evenings and Sundays, they'll be the worst.'

'Your new sister-in-law seems a nice wumman; says Agnes. 'Dae ye think you'll get oan wi' her? And that laddie of her's seems a credit tae her.'

'She wants us tae be friends. She has'nae got a sister, so she'd like us tae go oot the gether regularly. Ye know, pictures, go tae a show, go shopping. Things like that. So Ah told her Ah'd like that.'

'Well Ah'll tell ye whit, Irene. Often Ah quite fancy going tae a show, but wi' naebody tae go wi' Ah jist don't bother. Ah'd really like it if you and I hud the odd night oot the gether,' says Agnes.

'It definitely wid be an odd night oot if Ah went wi' you, Agnes Dalrymple.' When the laughter dies down, Irene continues, 'Whit we could dae noo and again, as well as going tae a show, you, me and ma new sister-in-law, the three of us might have the occasional trip oot. That would be nice.' She turns to Granny. 'And do you fancy coming tae a show wi' us noo and again?'

'Aye. Ah've been reading in the paper aboot somebody Ah like being oan at the Empire or the Kings. And Ah think Ah wid'nae mind seeing them. But ach, it always finishes up, when you're on yer own, ye dinnae bother.'

It's sometime after nine when Irene opens the door and lets herself into her silent, unlit house. She hangs her coat up in the lobby. Going into the kitchen, she switches the light on, then the radio. For company. She sits down on her fireside chair. Facing her is James's chair. Empty. The cushions flat from when he last sat on it earlier today. It's a comedy show on the radio. Jimmy Jewel and Ben Warris in *Up The Pole!*. She starts to cry.

CHAPTER THIRTY-NINE

On the Maryhill Riviera

―――――――

Once again the sun has brought out some of the ladies from 18 Dalbeattie Street. It is early on a Tuesday afternoon. Five chairs in a row have their backs to the wall, and Ella Cameron, Drena McClaren, Irma Armstrong, Lena McDermot and Mary Stewart occupy them.

'Is this no' a stoater of a day, girls?' asks Drena.

'Ye can say that again,' agrees Ella.

In a monotone Drena intones, 'Is this no' a stoa—'

She is interrupted as Ella says, 'Ah did'nae say ye *hud* tae say it again, Drena.'

This conversation is carried on without any turning of heads. All five women lean back on their wooden chairs, faces turned up to the sun, backs of heads leaning against the sandstone wall of the tenement.

'Well we cannae say that August huz'nae come in wi' a bang, can we?' says Ella.

'Aye,' replies Lena. 'It's good tae huv smashing weather fur a change when the weans are oan their hoalidays.'

'If it's like this oan Sunday, will we make up a wee picnic

an' take the weans doon the Low Road, Drena?'

'Aye. Good idea, Ella. Ah prefer the Low Road part of the park. There's the swings for the weans tae play oan, and plenty grass fur them tae run aboot. Ah alwiz find the bit oan the other side o' the river – roon' the Kibble Palace and that – I find it too, too . . .'

'Too posh,' says Mary Stewart. 'When Robert was wee, Ah always took him tae the Low Road. He could run aboot tae his heart's content doon there.'

'Well, when ye think aboot it,' Lena sits forward in her chair, 'the Kibble Palace end runs on tae the Great Western Road. Handy fur Hillhead and aw' the rest of it. *They* use that end 'cause it's the bit nearest tae them. So that's why it's aw' laid oot wi' formal flooerbeds and hothooses. That's the sort of stuff the toffs like. But the Low Road is near tae Maryhill.' She looks around. 'Nuff said, Ah would think!'

'Anybody know whit time it is?' enquires Ella.

There is no answer at first, then, 'It's five tae three,' says a voice from above.

Drena half turns in her chair and looks up. Granny is leaning on her windowsill, looking down.

'Are ye no' coming doon tae join us?'

'Naw, it's too hot for me the day.'

'You can have a chair from out of my house, Mrs Thomson,' offers Irma.

'Naw. Thanks aw' the same, hen. And whit huv Ah telt ye aboot "Mrs Thomson"?'

'Oh, I am sorry, Granny.'

Drena reaches into her apron pocket and brings out five Woodbine in their flimsy paper packet. She nudges Ella. 'Want wan?'

248

'Naw thanks.'

Drena strikes a match, lights a Woodbine, blows the smoke up into the hot air. She squints as she looks along the street. The heat is uncomfortable really. But who cares? The sun has moved round since they came out, and most of the street now lies under it. The tarmac seems unable to absorb any more heat. It bounces off the hot, half-melted tar and shimmers back up into the sky. The end of the street, where it runs into Blairatholl, seems to move and quiver in the rising eddies of hot air. Where the two streets meet, you would swear there was a pool of water. She remembers Billy telling her this is why folk lost in the desert think they can see an oasis. The shimmering heat causes a mirage, which, from a distance, looks as if it's a lake. Further along Dalbeattie Street two other groups of women sit outside their closes, taking the sun. In the shade of the tenement opposite, four girls are playing shops. Ten yards away her son, William, sits with Ella's boy, Archie junior. They have a broken piece of mirror each and are enjoying themselves reflecting the sun's rays on to the shadowed walls of the block opposite. But mostly into the windows of the houses, where it dances on their ceilings.

'Ooooh! Ma arse is sore sittin'.' Ella eases herself upright on her chair. 'Gie's a draw.'

Drena delicately transfers the half-Woodbine from her fingers to Ella's. Ella takes a draw, then looks down. She has her stockings rolled down to her ankles, as is usual on a hot day. Drena hasn't. Ella turns her head towards her friend. 'You got nae stockings on the day?'

Drena is sitting with her legs apart and stretched out, resting on her heels. 'Naw.' There's a pause, then she leans in close to Ella's ear. 'And Ah've goat nae drawers oan either!'

'Awwwww! Haugh! Haugh! Haugh!' Ella has been caught in the middle of her last draw at the Woodbine. She goes into a paroxysm of coughing and laughing. Mary Stewart has just dozed off and wakens with a fright. Lena and Irma turn their heads. Granny Thomson reappears at the window.

'Whit's going on?' enquires Granny.

'Oh, Ah cannae tell ye,' says Ella.

'Aye ye kin,' says Drena. 'Ah don't care.' Drena and Ella, as usual, go into fits.

'She's jist telt me,' Ella fights for control, 'she's jist telt me she's been sitting therr aw' efternin wi' nae knickers oan!'

'Eeeeh!' The assembled company, including the one in the balcony, becomes convulsed with laughter. Mary Stewart manages to say, 'Oooh, yah dirty bizzum!'

'It's jist the job oan a day like this, Ah'm tellin' ye's. Rerr and cool. And Ah'll tell ye's something else. When Billy comes in fae his work the night, if Ah jist whisper in . . .' She is unable to finish. The other five, anticipating her punch line, collapse into group hysteria. Passers-by look across the street and wonder what's been said. Drena tries again. 'Whisper in his ear whit the situation is . . .' She breaks up again, then finally, 'He'll gie oor William sixpence fur the first hoose o' the pictures!'

For the next two or three minutes all five are helpless. Ella looks up. 'Don't you be falling oot that windae, Granny!'

Five minutes later, amidst a dabbing of eyes, control seems to have been regained.

'I am surprised you have only the one child, Drena,' says Irma.

'So am Ah,' says Drena.

William McClaren comes along, stands by his mother. 'Youse were huvin' a rerr laugh, Ma.'

'Aye, it's your Auntie Ella. She's always making yer mammy laugh.' The women all smile and glance at one another. Just then Andrew McDermot comes along the street. As he nears the group, he holds a finger to his lips, sneaks up behind young William and grabs him.

'Ahah! Now Ah've got ye, William McClaren! Ah have written a letter tae the Scottish Draughts Association and telt them you've been dodging me. They've said you have tae gie me a return match, or else they'll take the title off ye!' William laughs and pretends he's trying to get away. 'You have tae give me the chance tae get ma title back this Setterday efternin. Yin o'clock at my hoose. Right? The board will be set up and there will be as much American Cream Soda as ye can drink during the game. Okay?'

'You'll huv tae gie Uncle Andra the chance tae win his title back,' says Drena. 'That's only fair.'

'Aw'right, Ah'll be there, Uncle Andra. One o'clock.'

'And Ah'll make sure there's plenty tae drink,' says Lena, 'and mibbe a chocolate biscuit, tae.'

'Oh, he'll definitely turn up noo,' says Drena. 'Ye don't huv tae worry aboot that.'

Andrew McDermot lets go of William and sticks his hand out. 'Right! Let's shake on it.'

William, slightly embarrassed, takes Andrew's hand in his. 'Ah'll no' let ye doon. See ye on Setterday efternin at one o'clock, Uncle Andra.'

It is ten minutes later. Lena has had enough sunbathing and gone up to the house with Andrew. William has rejoined Archie junior and they've disappeared through a close into the back courts. Mary Stewart has dozed off again; Irma is about to join her. Ella and Drena stretch their legs out, rest the backs of their heads against the wall, close their eyes. The sun is relentless. There is no movement in the street, only the murmur of the traffic from the nearby Maryhill Road, and a faint 'ding ding' as a tram-driver gives warning to a pedestrian. Drena leans in the direction of her pal, speaks softly so as not to disturb the other two.

'Did Ah hear raised voices coming through ma ceiling from you two last night?'

'Ye did.'

'S'no like you tae be fallin' oot, Ella. Ah take it it wiz the usual?'

'It wiz.'

Mary Stewart has come awake, caught the conversation. 'Och, well. Wait till ye get tae my age, Ella. That's the only benefit of gettin' older, your man bothers ye less often for a touch of the other. Thank the Lord.'

Ella turns towards her. 'Naw, it's no' that – for a change! It's because Ah want tae take a wee job. Noo that Katherine's started the school, Ah've got aw' this time on ma hands. Ah could get myself a job, even if it was part-time, and bring a wee bit extra money intae the hoose. But he'll no' bloody have it.' Ella puts on a deep voice, stabs a finger in the air. 'There's nae wife o' mine going oot tae work. That's final!' She sits up in her chair. 'Load o' masculine shite!' The other three laugh.

Drena leans in the direction of Mary and Irma. 'Ella's a confectioner, ye know. She can earn good money. But Archie will'nae hear of her taking a job.'

Ella has now got her dander up. 'Ah'll tell ye what started it. Yesterday, if ye remember, Christy the coalman was in the street. He knows Ah alwiz try tae huv the bunker nearly full before the winter comes. "Ah can let ye huv two bags the day, Ella," he says.' She looks at each of her friends in turn. Bristles. 'Ah hud tae say, "Thanks aw' the same, Christy. Ah can only afford wan the day." Is that no' bloody annoying? Did'nae have another four shillings.'

Drena, from her position as official confidante to Ella, decides to elucidate further. 'Archie is on short time at the moment at Howden's, so money's tight, in't it, Ella?'

'Aye.'

'Even if he'd jist let her take a wee part-time job, it wid make aw' the difference, widn't it?'

'Aye.' Ella sits on her hands, rocking gently. Simmering.

'But he'll no' huv it. Win't he no', Ella?'

'Naw.'

Irma has only listened, made no contribution so far. 'What is this "confectioner", Ella?'

'Ye know all the icing on cakes. Whether it's wee cakes like fern cakes or decorating big ones like wedding cakes. That's what a confectioner does. And no' just icing. You work wi' marzipan and chocolate, that sort of thing. Ah could get a job nae bother if that stubborn eegit would let me. But he'll no'.'

'Ah! In German, a person who does that job is called ein Konditor. It is a very skilled job.'

Drena releases further information. 'Ella served her time at Hubbard's, didn't ye?'

'Aye. That's why Ah know Ah could get a job the morra if Ah wanted. Ma former boss, Sam Costigan – he trained me at Hubbard's – he's the manager nooadays at yon big bakers' doon at the normal school, Cakeland—'

Mary interrupts. 'Oh, aye, Ah know the one ye mean. It's some size of a place, that.'

'Sam would gie me a job in a minute. Ah just have tae ask. The only one stopping me is "heid the ball".' The other three laugh. 'He says he's the breadwinner.'

'Aye,' says Mary, 'but man diz'nae live by bread alone. Ye need the odd bag o' coal.'

In the late-afternoon heat, the outburst of conversation soon subsides. All is quiet for the next twenty minutes. Drena opens an eye. Looks at her slumbering friends. It's been really nice the day. Jist sitting huvin' a laugh and a great blether. She looks to left and right along the empty street. Ye don't get many days as hot as this in the city. Too hot tae do anything except sit ootside. She quietly stretches her arms and legs out in front of her, stifles a yawn. Ah'll have tae mind and get a bottle of milk before Ah go up tae the hoose. Yon one standing in the sink will be sour by now. 'Well, girls!' They all stir; eyes are opened. 'As they say in yon travelogues in the pictures . . .' Drena deepens her voice, talks 'pan loaf'. 'And now, as the sun sinks slowly in the west behind the tenement chimneys of Maryhill, we have tae say—'

She is interrupted from above. All four look up. Granny Thomson leans on a cushion at her first-storey window. She takes up Drena's narration. 'We huv tae say farewell, 'cos it's time these lazy bizzums got thurrselves up them stairs and started getting their men's dinners ready – and Drena McClaren will have tae put some drawers oan!'

CHAPTER FORTY

The Last Casualty

Corporal Andrew McDermot stares intently at the wall of the trench. He screws up his face at the noise of the British bombardment. The large-calibre shells emit their usual half-whistling, half-roaring sound as they make the short trip towards the German lines. For all the fuckin' good it'll do. Soon as we go ower the top, the Huns' machine guns will still open up. Lads will be cut doon like corn in a field. Mibbe me this time? It's 1918. Ah've had four fuckin' years o' this. My luck's due tae run oot. Today? He looks again at the wall of the trench. French earth. Looks at the stones embedded in it. Long stretches of tree roots. The trees long ago blasted tae fuck. Andrew always follows the same routine before an attack. It's kept me alive up tae noo. Why change it? He looks to his left, then his right. There's hardly a man left who was in the company six months ago. Nearly aw' reinforcements, including the officers. Poor laddies. Ah'm the auld man o' the company at thirty-two. Maist o' the officers come tae me for advice oan routine. He looks at the young man next to him. Ah don't even know this boy's name. It's better that wye.

Ye don't feel as sad when ye don't know whit their name was. But Ah know who *should* be here. He tries not to feel resentful. Billy Strang should be here. It's nearly two months noo since Billy went missing. He'll be lying under heaps o' mud and muck somewhere oot in no-man's-land. Andrew takes out his baccy tin. We should be huvin' oor last gasper before the bombardment stoaps and we huv tae climb oot this trench.

As if his mind has been read, seconds later the guns fall silent. Oh fuck me! Here we go. He stares hard at the trench wall. The officers blow their whistles, sergeants and senior NCOs exhort, 'C'mon, bonny lads, up and at 'em!' Andrew heaves himself out of the trench. Already fellas are falling to his left and right. He can hear the chatter of the machine guns, see dirt kick up now and again. Whuzzz, whuzzz, kachink; all the time he's braced, ready for the one that'll hit him. 'Now remember, men, walk forward at a steady pace, rifle at the port.' They tell us that every time. The Germans must laugh their fuckin' socks aff. Easy fuckin' targets. The Germans don't walk towards us when they launch an offensive. They run, crouch, crawl . . . WHUZZZZ! Cor fuckin' blimey! That wiz near! Fuck it! Ah'm walking nae mair. He throws himself down, starts to crawl from tussock to hillock, to anything that sticks up in the air. About twenty yards ahead he spots part of the large circular lip of the giant crater left from the last mine. When wiz it? Aboot four months ago. The German trench-line passed along here. So the engineers and aboot two hundred men dug a four-hundred-yard tunnel, forty feet deep, under the German trenches, then hollowed oot a large cavern. Filled it wi' hundreds o' tons of explosives – dynamite, unexploded shells, oot-o'-date Mills bombs. Anything that wid go 'BANG!' Yah bugger! And it did'nae half. Like the end o' the world fur a minute. A gigantic mound of earth, like a mountain rising oot o' the grund, went up in the air. The noise, the vibration. And in amongst that wiz Christ knows how many Huns, weapons, corrugated iron, widden planks, dogs, rats. Then it fell tae earth and they were aw' buried. And we were ready. Their mates fae the support trenches came running up tae try and pull oot any survivors. We hud aw' oor best shots waiting. Must huv picked aff another twenty.

Made it! Andrew lies just below the lip. Ah'll huv tae get ower this and intae the hole as quick as Ah can, otherwise Ah'm liable tae get wan up the arse just as Ah'm rolling ower. Right! He scrabbles over the top, once again braces himself in anticipation of a German bullet. Ahhhh! Done it! He wriggles down a few feet below the rim of the crater. Looks up at the sky. Listens to the stray bullets flying here, there and everywhere. He looks down. The massive hole, like a small volcano, is nearly forty feet deep. Who the fuck is that? Right at the bottom, a figure in British uniform sits on an ammo box. He has his back to him. Thank Christ it's a Tommy! He spots a few flames, notices the blue smoke spiralling up. He laughs. The cheeky bugger's got a fire going.

Andrew sits down and, using his hands and feet as brakes, slides to the bottom of the crater. As he stands up, the man turns, smiles. 'Ah knew ye would come, Andra.'

'Billy! Aw, Billy, you're no' deid!' Andrew's heart leaps with joy.

Lena McDermot comes into the close. There's a lovely cool breeze being funnelled through from the back court and out to the street. She stops for a moment at the foot of the stairs, puts a hand on the banister. A door opens and Bert Armstrong steps out into the close.

'Hello, pet. Gettin' tha'sen a bit o' fresh air?'

'That's jist whit Ah'm daeing, Bert. It's lovely.'

'Ah'll have tae gan. Got the cab booked in for a bit service. Cheerio.'

'Aye, cheerio, son.'

Bert strides along the close and out into the street. Lena stands a moment longer enjoying the cool air. She can see some of the back court. Hear the weans playing. Occasionally catch a glimpse of one or two. Right. Ah'll away up. That auld de'il should be oot o' his bed by noo – but Ah'll bet ye he is'nae. He'll be waiting for me tae bring the *Record* in, then he'll be wanting a cup o' tea. Loves studying the horses oan a Saturday. Ah hope he's remembered that young William's coming doon tae us at yin o'clock for their game o' draughts.

Message bag weighing her down, Lena steps wearily on to the first-storey landing. She reaches a hand out, turns the doorknob. The familiar smell of her house comes out to greet her: lavender polish, dried fruit . . .'It's jist me, Andra!' There's no answer. She tuts. 'Huv you dozed aff again, lazybones?' She stands in the lobby, pushes open the kitchen door on the right. It swings wide open. All is still. 'Andra?' No answer. 'Andra! Are ye therr?' She begins to get a strange feeling. It starts in her stomach, goes to the back of her neck. She can see his trousers and shirt still hanging over the back of a kitchen chair.

Lena reaches in and places her message bag just inside the door. Doesn't take her coat off. She swallows hard, then walks into the kitchen. Somehow, she knows what she is about to find. She takes four or five steps into the room, turns left and places both hands on top of the table. She doesn't look towards the recess bed, just faces the range. 'Andra! Are ye wakened?' Silence. She makes herself look left. He has his back to her; she can see him from his shoulders down. The covers are pulled up to somewhere about his upper arm. She walks round to the side of the table nearest to the bed. All she can see is the back of his head. It is bent forward. That's an unnatural position. 'Andra!' She walks to the side of the bed and prods his shoulder with a finger. It moves slightly forward, then back. It is the stillness of him and the stillness of the room that tells her. 'Oh, Andra. Huv ye went away and left me?' She pulls out a chair from under the table, sits on it, starts to cry. She looks at him. 'Andra, ye cannae leave me. Whit'll Ah dae withoot ye? The weans are aw' up and away, there's jist you and me. We're best pals.' Lena leans forward, folds her arms on the table, rests her head on them and sobs.

Granny Thomson comes out of her house. She sees Lena's outside door and kitchen door are open. She pauses. She can hear something. That's Lena's greeting in therr!

'Oh my God! Lena! Is that you?' Granny walks into her neighbour's kitchen. She doesn't need to ask, but does. 'Whit's the matter, hen?'

Lena sits up. 'Andra's . . .' It's a word she doesn't want to say. But she'll have to. 'Andra's deid, Bella. Ah jist came back fae the shops and found him. Bella, whit will Ah dae withoot ma Andra?' She gives a great juddering sob.

'Right. Ah'll send fur the doctor. Gie me the addresses of Andy, Sheena and Maisie and Ah'll send them telegrams. There's nane o' them oan the phone, is thurr?'

Lena shakes her head. 'Naw.' She looks at the clock. 'It's

half twelve, Bella. Wee William McClaren fae upstairs is coming doon tae play Andra at draughts at wan o'clock. Away up and tell Drena, will ye? Ah don't want the wee sowel tae get a fright if he mibbe walks in.'

'Ah'll dae that the noo.' Granny goes up to the second storey and knocks Drena's door. Young William answers it, opens it wide to allow Granny in. 'Ah huv'nae time at the minute, son. Tell yer Mammy Ah want tae speak tae her oot here.'

'Ah can hear ye, Granny. Ah'm coming.' Drena appears at the door. William continues to stand, holding it open.

'It's a wee private matter, Drena. Could ye send William ben the hoose.'

Drena looks quizzically at Granny. 'Aye. William, away through the kitchen.' She ushers him through, then shuts the door behind him. Granny beckons her out on to the landing.

'Huv ye got the snib oan the ootside door?' Granny whispers.

'Aye.' Drena steps out on to the landing and pulls the door to.

'It's a bit of bad news, Drena. Andra McDermot died an hour or so ago.'

Drena's hand goes to her mouth. 'Oh, my Jesus God! Oh, naw! Aw, poor Lena, she'll be aboot demented.' Tears come into Drena's eyes and she begins to cry. 'Aw, Granny, they're such a smashin' couple. They're as happy as the day is long.'

Granny Thomson feels tears come into her own eyes. She dabs them away. 'Ah know. He's such a lovely man. Noo, there's the doctor tae get and telegrams tae send tae their three kids. Can ye come and sit wi' her while Ah dae that?'

'Aye, nae bother. Wid it no' mibbe be better the other wye? Ah'll dae aw' the running aboot.'

'Aye, of course it will, Drena. You're right. Ah'll sit wi' her.'

'Ah'll nip intae the hoose first. Billy's in. Ah'll whisper tae him whit's happened and he'll huv tae tell oor William. God! William's gonny be awfy upset, tae. He jist loves auld Andra. Right! Ah'll be doon in a minute.'

As is the custom, Andrew McDermot's remains are taken to a local undertaker to be laid out. Next day, the Sunday, his coffin is brought back to his house, where it lies on trestles in the kitchen for the next three days. The curtains are drawn on the windows in both the room and the kitchen. The lights burn all day and late into the evening. During this period, family and friends come to pay their respects and comfort his widow and three grown-up children.

On the Wednesday following his death, over a hundred folk – neighbours and acquaintances – stand on either side of Dalbeattie Street near to number 18 to show their respect as the funeral cortege prepares to leave for Lambhill Cemetery. Many old comrades from the Highland Light Infantry Association have joined the family. His coffin is carried by six present-day soldiers of the regiment who have been sent from Maryhill Barracks – where Andrew volunteered in 1914. At the graveside a bugler, also sent from the barracks, blows the Last Post.

Lena McDermot will wear black, widow's weeds, for the next twelve months.

CHAPTER FORTY-ONE

Discovered!

It's a regular routine now for Robert Stewart and Rhea O'Malley. Unless he's on guard duty, or off on a convoy to some other camp, they know that every fortnight he'll arrive at Glasgow Central on the Friday evening off the Carlisle train. And head back to Longtown Camp late on the Sunday afternoon. He doesn't even bother to hitchhike now. His army pay has increased from those first few months – and anyway, Ma and Da prefer him to come by train, so quite happily subsidise him. Life is pretty good. And getting better.

Rhea waits impatiently on the platform. She loves coming to meet him off the train. On the Fridays he is due, the butterflies in her stomach wake up same time as her. Their numbers increase as the day goes on. By the time she comes off the number 23 tram and makes her way to the Central Station, she wonders if one of these days there'll be so many of them, she'll become airborne! Especially when she enters the large concourse of the station itself and is swallowed by the bustle, the noise, the smell. Passengers and porters criss-cross as they head for various platforms. Brakes screech as trains slow to a halt. Departing locos send clouds of steam blasting up to the roof as giant wheels slip and squeal on steel rails until at last they gain purchase, the volume goes down to less than ear-splitting, and they glide majestically from the station. This all adds to Rhea's excitement as she purposefully heads for 'their' platform.

Platform ticket in hand, she stands looking along its length, anticipating that first sight, the merest glimpse, of Robert's train. Sometimes a locomotive hoves into view. Good! It's right on time. Then, och, it's no' his. Instead of coming straight on, the train veers off to left or right and favours another platform. But always, without fail, at last it arrives. This is definitely it! There's no mistake, it's on the line for this plat-form, it's too far on tae be able tae head off tae another one. This is Robert's train! Rhea feels so grown-up. The excite-ment rises in her. Ah'll be seeing his face in a minute. Squadrons of butterflies flit about in her stomach.

As ever, she stands on tiptoe, hand half raised ready to wave. For this last wee while Robert always tries to get into the carriage just behind the engine. If he hasn't been able to find a seat in there, as they enter the station he always walks the length of the train from wherever he was, and gets himself into the corridor of the first carriage. As it slows down for the last hundred yards or so, he lets the window down, leans out, and begins waving as they approach the crowd on the platform. Even if he cannot see her, he knows that Rhea, teetering on the tips of her toes, will spot him and be happy.

There she is! His own armada of butterflies takes flight. He blows exaggerated kisses as the engine crawls the last few yards and comes to a squealing halt just short of the buffers.

Great gouts of superheated steam billow up from below the platform and descend from the stack. He can taste the locomotive. Putting his beret on, he slings his small pack over his shoulder, reaches out the window to open the door and jumps down on to the platform. Rhea has run forward and stands looking up at him. As ever, he puts his arms round her and hugs her tight.

'Hello, my darlin' girl.' He looks into her brown eyes.

'Oh, Robert! Ah jist live for oor Fridays, so Ah dae.'

He kisses her three times in succession, then a long, lingering one. 'Me tae! Shall we go for a wee drink? As usual Ah've told my ma and da Ah'm going straight off with my pals for a few pints when Ah arrive.'

They walk along, arm in arm, towards the barrier. Robert hands his return ticket, and Rhea's platform one, to the inspector. The man punches Robert's and gives him it back. As they head for the exit, Rhea pulls him to a halt. 'Eeeh! Ah've jist seen it. You've got a stripe oan yer arm!'

'Ah wondered when you'd notice.'

She laughs. 'Robert Stewart. Oan a Friday aw' Ah ever look at is yer face. That's aw' Ah've longed tae see for the last fortnight. So, are you now whit they call a lance corporal?'

'That's right. And, would ye believe, it comes with an extra two shillings a week!'

'Great! With aw' that dosh coming in, we should be able tae get married next Tuesday!'

'The week efter next, Rhea. You're awfy headstrong, so ye are. It'll take at least a fortnight!'

'Eh, Robert. Good fur you!' She pulls herself up by his arm and walks on her toes for a moment to kiss him on the cheek. 'But Ah've alwiz known you're ma clever boy.'

'Ah must admit, Ah'm quite chuffed about it. Who knows, there's time for me tae get ma second up. Still got fifteen months tae do.'

They walk out into Hope Street and stand for a moment. Robert turns to her. 'Where would you like tae go?'

'Anywhere – as long as it's nice and quiet and we can talk.'

'What about walking up tae Buchanan Street and gettin' the subway over tae Hillhead? There are some nice wee bars on the Byres Road. And it's halfway home.'

'That'll be grand,' says Rhea.

Thirty minutes later finds them sauntering along a not-too-crowded Byres Road. Robert stops. 'Do ye remember the time Ah was telling you about that style called Art Deco? The Paramount cinema and the new trams are all designed in it. Very thirties.'

'Aye, Ah do.'

Robert points. 'Just look at the frontage of this bar. In fact, look at the name. Bar Deco. Ah bet it'll all be like this inside. Shall we go in and have a look? It'll be as good as anywhere, Ah'd think.'

'Aye, might as well.' They head for the entrance. 'Since you told me aboot that Art Deco style, Robert, Ah keep spotting it aw' ower the place. Cafés, ladies' dress shops. The latest wan Ah came across is the gas showroom in Sauchiehall Street, jist alang fae the Locarno. And, of course, the Beresford Hotel. Ah've always thought the Beresford looks so American. As if it belangs in New York instead of Glesga'.'

'Well that's why, Rhea. It's so Art Deco. If it was built in New York or Miami it would fit right in. We're that used tae seeing buildings like that in the movies, we always associate them with America.' As they approach the inner door of the bar, Robert stops. 'See! Look at the design of the stained glass. And the door plate. Ah'll bet you that inside the bar you'll be able to pick out lots of Art Deco features. Let's find out.' He pushes the door open.

They take two steps inside and pause for a moment. 'Aye. Just as Ah thought,' says Robert.

'Oh, isn't it lovely!' sighs Rhea. 'Ah'll bet ye Lana Turner comes in here!'

Robert laughs. 'And Clark Gable!'

There are maybe twenty folk in. More than half stand at the bar; the rest, couples or foursomes, sit at the stylish banquettes. Robert points. 'There's one at the far end. Nice and quiet. Or should Ah say discreet.' They start to walk towards it.

'Hello, you two!'

They stop. Turn their heads to the right. George Lockerbie, smart in his pale blue barman's jacket, smiles at them. Both their hearts give a leap. They've been found out!

'Oh, hello, George.' Robert smiles. He tries to appear normal. Doubts he looks it somehow.

'Hello, George.' Rhea also feels she must be looking, well, guilty.

'You go and take that seat in case somebody comes in and we lose it,' says Robert. In a lower voice he says, 'We'll have to stay now. No good walking out. That would give the show away.' He goes to the far end of the bar. George follows him. 'Ah didn't know you worked in here, George.'

'Yeah. Just Friday and Saturday nights. Ah like it. Been here nigh-on three months.'

'Eh, Ah'll have a bottle of Pale Ale. And a half-pint shandy for Rhea, please.' He puts a hand on George's forearm as he's about to leave to prepare their drinks. 'George, would you do me a favour? You haven't seen us. Nobody knows we're going oot the gether. Not even our parents.'

'Ah!' George laughs. 'The auld Catholic, Protestant carry-on, Ah presume?'

'Exactly! There's no point telling them while Ah'm doing ma two years. Once Ah come out and start work, that's when we'll tell them. Whether they like it or not, we intend tae get married.'

'Good for you! Though mind, Ah've known yours and Rhea's parents for a while. Nearly four years. They're all good, decent folk. Okay, they might not be ower happy at first, but Ah really think they'll soon come round to it. Rhea's a smashing lassie. It'll work out all right.'

'Ah hope you're right, George. We both think Rhea's ma and da will be okay. Believe it or not, it's my father who might be the awkward one. He's in the Lodge, you know.'

'Is he! Now Ah never knew that. He diz'nae exactly flaunt it.'

'Oh, right enough, he keeps it quiet. But nevertheless he is an Orangeman. So presumably he's not gonny be jumping wi' joy when his son tells him he's intending tae marry a Catholic lassie!'

'Well, you'd think so. Anywye, good luck when the time comes.'

'We'd both appreciate it if you didn't say a word tae anybody. Not even Joan. You know whit women are like – always want to be the first wi' a wee titbit of gossip.'

George laughs. 'You're a bit behind the times, Robert. Joan and I split up. Jeez! Nearly three months ago. She went back tae England, tae her folks.'

'Bugger me! Ah live next door to ye and Ah did'nae know.'

'Ah'm surprised your mother or father did'nae mention it to ye when you were hame on leave, or when they were writing to ye.'

'Well, Ah have tae give them their due. My parents have never been ones for gossip. Not even between their two selves. And definitely not when it comes to telling me anything. They'd just never dream of saying tae me, "Oh, did you know George and Joan next door have split up?" Ah've always had to find things like that out from other people.' He turns his head, laughs. 'Usually Rhea. Now there's somebody who loves a nice bit of scandal!'

'Is he running me doon, George? Anywye, is thurr a wee possibility of me gettin' that shandy the night? Ah'm dying o' thirst sitting here!' Rhea pretends she's about to topple over.

'Just before ye go, Robert. You did'nae have that stripe up last time Ah seen ye, did ye?'

'No. Brand new. Ah just got made up this week.'

'Good for you, son.'

Robert at last takes his seat beside Rhea. 'Ah've put him in the picture. He'll not say anything about us.' He starts to take a mouthful of beer, then remembers. 'Here! You never told me George's wife has gone back tae England. Did you not know?'

'Aye. Och, that wiz months ago. Ma ma telt me.'

'How come you never told me?'

'When you're hame for your weekends, Robert, Ah huv'nae time for anything else but you and me. Aw' ma gossiping is done either in the hoose or at work. When you and me are the gether, there's nuthin' else oan ma mind but us.'

Robert smiles. 'Now that's jist about the nicest thing anybody's ever said tae me. Ah come before a juicy bit of gossip!' He kisses her on the cheek.

At half past nine, one of the other two barmen calls, 'Time, ladies and gentlemen, please.' Robert watches as George speaks to the attractive woman who's been sitting at the far end of the bar since they came in. Probably the manageress. He then walks to the other end of the bar, lifts the flap and comes over. 'Just sit tight and let the rest of the customers leave. You can have a nightcap with Ruth and me. We leave about ten fifteen and Ah walk her to the night safe, so you won't be too late. That's if you want to, of course.'

'Yes, that would be nice,' says Robert. He turns to Rhea. 'That okay with you?'

'Oh, aye. Lovely!'

They watch as George goes back behind the bar to do the washing-up while the boss empties the till and cashes up. The other two barmen empty the ashtrays, then wipe down the bar and tables. Shortly after that they say their good nights and George lets them out and bolts the door behind them.

'Eeeh!' says Rhea. 'Isn't it exciting tae be invited tae stay behind efter closing time?'

'That's just what Ah was thinking,' says Robert.

A few minutes later, George comes over with another Pale Ale and shandy for them. A few minutes after that, they are joined by Ruth. George does the introductions.

After a pleasant half-hour, all four step out on to the Byres Road. George holds the small, locked leather bag, ready for the trip to the night safe.

'Well, we go this way to the bank,' he says, 'so we'll say good night.'

After a triple 'Nice to meet you' with Ruth, the two couples head off in opposite directions.

Rhea takes Robert's arm as they set off towards Great Western Road then across to Queen Margaret Drive. It's a dry, cool night. Perfect for walking. 'She's really nice,' says Rhea. 'Ah like her. And isn't she an attractive woman? She could be a film star.'

'Not half. Very classy.'

'She diz'nae half fancy George.'

Robert looks at her. 'Do ye think so? What makes you think that? Ah would have thought he was, mmmm, sort of out of her class. Don't get me wrong, George is a nice chap, and he's an intelligent fella. But Ah'd have thought she'd be after somebody . . . frankly, well-off!'

Rhea shakes her head. 'Ah'm telling ye. Will ye listen. While you were busy blethering, Ah wiz watching her. She spends maist of her time touching him, looking at him. Take it from me. She is very fond of George.'

'Well. He did'nae give me the impression he thinks he's her, well, boyfriend. He just—'

'Exactly!' Rhea interrupts him. 'He diz'nae realise it yet. The penny will drap eventually!'

'If what you say is right, how come he hasn't noticed by—'

'Huz'nae noticed! He's a man! That's why. Ah wiz crazy aboot you fur nearly a year. Everybody sitting beside us in DiMarco's café knew – except you, yah numpty-heided bugger!'

'Oh!'

'Aye, "Oh!" Ah'll "Oh!" ye.'

This is said with such vehemence that Robert starts to

laugh. A moment later so does Rhea. The two of them have to stop for a couple of minutes until they get their laugh out. Then, arm in arm, they set off up Queen Margaret Drive towards the Maryhill Road. Three times they have to stop when Robert suddenly says, 'Except you, yah numpty-heided bugger!'

Yet again their laughs ring out, young and bell-like. On up into the starry sky.

CHAPTER FORTY-TWO

Sundays Are Special

'Time zit, Ella?' Archie Cameron lies on his side, cuddled into Ella in the recess bed. She lies on her back.

'You're nearer the clock,' she says sleepily.

'But Ah've got ma back tae it, hen.' He kisses her shoulder.

'Awwww, man!' She manages to raise her head to look past his. Squints at the alarm clock. It's always placed on the kitchen table at night so as to be readable from the bed. 'Ten tae nine.'

'Good. Mmmm. Ah hope that wee yin lies a bit longer the s'moarning.' He pulls Ella in closer. Kisses her twice on the neck. 'Ah jist love Sunday moarnin's lying in bed wi' you, Ella.' She feels him getting hard; he presses it against the side of her thigh.

'Don't gie us yer patter, son.'

'But Ella. Aw' yon time Ah wiz away in the Argyles, and a POW tae. Five years. Ah've got aw' that tae make up. Five years' lost nookie. Wiz'nae ma fault. Ah wiz daeing ma bit.'

'Aye, well yer no' gettin' a bit! Anywye, Ah can hear the wean coming.'

'Awww! Ah never huv any luck.'

They hear the kitchen door being thrown open. It bangs against the wooden table. Then the patter of bare feet on the linoleum. Archie's erection vanishes; he turns round towards the room.

'Where's her daddy's wee princess? Therr she is.' With Archie's help, Katherine climbs up on to the bed and crawls over her daddy. A space is made for her in between them. Enveloped in love and bedcovers, she lies silent, her dummy moving up and down in her mouth.

'Katherine!' says Ella. 'Whit huv Ah told ye aboot that dummy? You're nearly five. You're far too big for a dummy. They're only for wee babies – no' big girls starting school.'

The dummy is shifted to the side. 'No' caring.'

Archie tries not to laugh. 'So they are, hen. They're jist fur babies. Urr you a baby?'

'Aye!'

'Oh! Oh well. That's it, then. 'Nuff said.' He changes the subject. 'Whit's Archie daein'?'

'Sshleeeping.'

'Clever boy. That's whit Sundays are fur.'

Donald McNeil comes striding along Dalbeattie Street. He's just been for his usual Sunday walk, picked up the papers from Ken's and now, appetite sharpened, is heading home. As he nears number 18, Granny comes out of the close and heads towards him.

'Good morning, Bella. How are you this fine morning?'

'Och, no' bad at all, Donald.'

They both stop. They always enjoy a wee blether. Donald looks down, Granny is carrying her shopping bag. On a Sunday? He points at it.

'I am quite certain you will not be finding many shops open today, Bella.'

'Naw, Ah ken that. Do ye know where Ah'm off tae?' She doesn't wait for a reply. 'Ah'm away for a hurl oan the tram.'

'Chust a hurl! You are not going anywhere?'

'That's right. An auld freen o' mine gave me the idea. She diz it every month or so. Sunday mornings are the best, she says, as the route's no' busy. We're lucky tae be living near the Maryhill Road, 'cause the number 23 is the longest trip seemingly. Takes ye aw' the wye oot tae Airdrie terminus and back. She says it's the best value in the city. Ye get yersel' up oan the top deck,' Granny opens her bag, 'take a flask and a sandwich wi' ye. Jist sit there and enjoy the scenery and the sights. Nearly twa hours – for jist fourpence!'

'Aye, well. When you put it like that, it is not a bad way to be passing a Sunday morning, to be sure. As we know, there is very little to do in Glasgow on the Sabbath. I might give that a try myself one Sunday. There are many districts in the city I have never set foot in. I knew all the ones round the river, with working for the Clyde Trust. But not the outlying ones. Not at all.'

'Anyway, Ah'll get maself round tae the stop. Cheerio the noo, Donald.'

'Yes, cheerio. Enjoy your wee trip, Bella.'

Irene Pentland puts some crumbs on her window ledge. Within minutes a succession of pigeons and sparrows are availing themselves of this free snack. She sighs. It's over two months now since brother James got married. She's still not used to being on her own. Sundays are definitely the worst. Even though James spent most of the day sitting reading, no, devouring the papers, he was still company. Her new sister-in-law, Mary, has been as good as her word. We've had some nice evenings out, thinks Irene. And Agnes up the stairs, too. She's called in regularly. And she and Ah have been out the gether as well. But the two of them work during the day, so it's always evenings. Or the occasional Sunday. Mary's still working in the office at the loco works, even though she's married James. Och, well. Things could be . . . She hears footsteps coming down the stairs. Could it be Agnes? There's a knock on her door, then it's opened. 'It's jist me, Irene!' It *is* Agnes!

'Aye, in ye come, hen.' Irene's heart lifts. Ah hope she suggests a cuppa.

Agnes's face appears round the door, followed by the rest of her. 'Huv ye got time tae come up for a wee cuppa and a blether? Ah brought some nice cakes and teabread back fae the shop wi' me yesterday when Ah finished. Ah put them straight in the tin.'

'Oh! Lovely. It's great huving a friend and neighbour that works for the City Bakeries. Aw' these lovely treats!'

'C'mon, then. Ah've got the kettle oan at a wee peep. It wiz near tae boiling when Ah came doon.'

Irene puts her purse behind the cushion of her fireside chair. James's identical chair doesn't face her on the other side of the fireplace any more. Too much of a reminder. It now stands four-square at the end of the range, its back against the wall. Only when she has a visitor is it moved back into its old position.

With a lighter step, Irene follows Agnes out on to the landing and climbs the stairs.

*   *   *

Down in the close, Robert Stewart sits at the table reading the *Sunday Pictorial*. His father sits opposite him. His favourite paper is the *Sunday Express*. Mary Stewart is darning a sock. Samuel speaks.

'What dae ye think about this Korean thing, son. Is it gonny fizzle oot?'

'Hah! Now that's a question, Da. We had a lecture last week from this major, up from the War Office. The fighting's been going on now for three months. The South Koreans were caught by surprise at first. But now they, along wi' the Americans and some UN troops, have managed tae shove the North Koreans back ower their border. The main thing is that the Chinese haven't got involved. But the big worry now is the fact that the man in charge, General MacArthur, is keeping the offensive going. We've already given them a bloody nose. They haven't gained anything. When's he gonny stop? Is he going to push them till their backs are up against the Chinese border? Will China stand by and let an American general humiliate the North Koreans? Or will they get involved? If they do, it won't be a so-called UN police action any more. It could turn intae a full-scale war!'

Mary Stewart looks up, stops darning. 'If it does get bigger, son, is there a possibility you might get sent there?'

'Ah doubt it. Don't forget, it's a United Nations thing, not just Britain and America. The majority of troops needed will be infantry. They'll not want many lorry drivers. But even if Ah did get shipped oot there, remember, Ah'm not a front-line soldier. Ah'd just be driving stores up tae supply depots well away from the fighting.'

'Ah hope you're right, son.'

'Really, it looks like it's petering oot. The Chinese haven't involved themselves. As long as MacArthur calls a halt soon and withdraws, it could all be over in a week or two.'

'Well let's hope that's whit happens, son,' says Samuel. He looks at the clock. 'Nearly time tae start getting your stuff together, Robert, ready tae head doon the station for yer train.'

Mary puts the sock down. 'Ah'll just make ye a wee bite tae eat afore ye go. Do ye want a sandwich tae take wi' ye?'

'Aye, Ah would'nae mind, Ma. Ah'll keep it tae later the night, before Ah go tae bed.'

As the Stewarts speak, directly above them, on the first storey, Lena McDermot sits in her kitchen. Alone. The room is dark. It's a late-September afternoon and it's cloudy outside, threatening rain. Lena hasn't switched the light on. Later, perhaps. The gloomy kitchen suits her mood. She looks at the recess bed. Andra should huv been sitting in therr this morning. Propped up wi' the pillows and bolster, his second or third cup o' tea near at hand, reading his *News o' the World*. She smiles. He loved that paper. Even though he wiz retired, he still loved Sundays best of all. She looks again at the recess bed. All neatly made up, the quilt on top. Ah'll never sleep in that bed again. The bed Andra died in. Ah could'nae. She turns her head away from it. The half-ounce of Old Holborn and pack of Rizla cigarette papers lie on the sideboard. Been there since that Saturday morning. A month now. They should have been smoked long ago. He never got the chance. The tears start to come again. Oh, Andra. Naebody knows how much Ah miss ye. Aw' yer laughing and daft carry-oan.

She gives a long sigh. Sunday is the worst day in the week. It never ends.

CHAPTER FORTY-THREE

Not in Your Wildest Dreams

George Lockerbie stands on the pavement as Ruth Malcolm locks up the bar. As usual he has the night's takings in his care. As she goes through this last routine, her back to him, he watches her every move. If only she knew how special his two evenings at the Bar Deco are to him. She turns to face him. Smiles. He wishes he could tell her what it means just to be around her. But what's the point? What if she says, 'Don't be so silly, George.'

'That's it, George. Let's go.' They set off along the Byres Road. The thing for him now is to think up subjects for conversation. Then he has an excuse to look at her. He turns his head, preparatory to speaking. She lopes along beside him. Her dark-blue cloth coat is open; it sways seductively with each high-heeled step. He takes in the dark hair. It's longer now than when he first met her. The rich red lipstick, thick eyebrows. And Ah'm getting to walk her home. Ah would'nae call the King my uncle! 'Pretty mild tonight, Ruth.'

'Yeah.' She takes another pace or two. 'This is the last Saturday in September, isn't it?'

'It is.'

'Mmmm, September's often a warm month. Can be better than June or July.'

'Yeah.'

George furiously tries to think of something clever, diverting to say. As he does so, Ruth occasionally glances at him. What am I going to do with him? she wonders. I can't just tell him straight out I have feelings for him. Well, I suppose I could. But it would be better coming from him.

George clears his throat. 'There's a good movie on at the Regal. Ah read the reviews. *The Asphalt Jungle*. Yon Sterling Hayden's in it.'

'Oh! That's the gangster picture, isn't it? They're planning to do a big robbery. Yeah, I read something about it, too. Dilys Powell reviewed it in *The Times*. I quite fancy seeing that.' She tries to hide a smile. C'mon, George! I've given you an opening. Have I got to ask *myself* to the pictures! She hears him swallow hard.

'Eh, if you really would like to see it, Ruth . . . Now, this is just a suggestion. Not really a date or anything like that. Eh, we could go together, maybe. Just sort of company for one another. Ah think a film or a show, it's always sort of more enjoyable if you're with somebody. But if you don't fancy the idea . . .'

'I think that's a good idea, George. I quite agree with you. Anything like that is far more enjoyable if you're in company. What evening were you thinking of?' She sneaks a look at him. His mouth opens and shuts but no sound emerges. At last!

'Eh, it's actually running tomorrow evening, Sunday. The full seven nights instead of the usual Monday tae Saturday. So if that would suit . . .'

'Sunday will be fine, George. We'll fix up what time later on.' They've reached the Linen Bank. She opens the night safe; he takes the locked leather bag out of his mac pocket and they listen to it slide down the chute. The curved steel door makes its usual 'clang' as it's banged shut. Ruth locks it and puts the keys in her coat pocket. They turn away and continue their promenade along the Byres Road. She realises that George has become even more speechless since she's agreed to go to the pictures. 'Have you time for a nightcap at Johnny McKinnon's place?'

'Oh, aye. Aye. Don't mind being out late. Long lie on a Sunday. That'll be smashing.'

They walk on another few paces, then, on an impulse, she links her arm through his. For a split second she fears he's momentarily lost the use of his legs; he seems to falter, go out of step. Mercifully he recovers his co-ordination. She has trouble hiding a smile.

Her sudden taking of his arm is so unexpected, George tingles from head to toe. Feels the hair stand not just on the back of his neck, but on his head. He feels sure he must appear to have a 'standy-up' haircut like Oor Wullie. He tries to think what he can say, or do, to let her know how wonderful it was when he felt her arm snake through his. All he can think of is to squeeze her arm close to his side. She'll tell him later – that said it all.

It's over an hour before they leave Johnny's Hillhead Bar. Except for the ten minutes that mine host spent at their table, they've quite happily sat together, half facing one another, talking about everything – except what is happening to them. It's just gone midnight when they bid Johnny farewell and step out on to an almost deserted, still mild Byres Road. As they head off in the direction of Agincourt Avenue, Ruth, casually this time, once more links her arm through George's. He turns his head towards her. 'You've no idea what pleasure it gave me when you did that earlier tonight. Ah thought all my birthdays had come at once!'

'Oh, good. I know what you'll want for your next birthday, then. What about Christmas?'

'Same again, please.'

'Grand! You're easily catered for.'

They amble along, lost in conversation – and each other – and eventually find themselves standing outside number 22. Ruth looks at him in mock seriousness. 'The last time – well, the first time you walked me home, George Lockerbie, I invited you in for a coffee. An invitation that the majority of my male customers would give their eye teeth for. And you refused!'

'Ah! Now be fair, Ruth. Ah said Ah was concerned in case you thought Ah was angling for an invite by seeing you safely home. And if you remember, Ah said if there *was* a next time, Ah very much hoped Ah'd be invited again.' He presses his palms together as though pleading, begging.

'Okay. I'm convinced your intentions are honourable. Would you like to come in for a coffee?'

'Ah'd love to, madam.'

Side by side they climb the stairs to the second storey. Mindful of the fact that it's around one in the morning, they don't speak as they ascend. Ruth opens her door, they enter, and she gently closes it behind them. George finds himself in a medium-sized square lobby. He laughs. 'Now, unlike my abode, Ah take it this is not a lobby?'

'Saints preserve us! I hope none of my neighbours hear

you. This is most certainly *not* a lobby. A hall, yes. Perchance a vestibule. But never, ever a Loabby! You'll have to wash your mouth out!'

She opens one of the four doors in the hall, reaches in to turn on the light, then gestures.

'Just in here, George.'

He takes a few steps into the room, stops. 'Wow!' The light switch has brought on a mixture of table lamps and wall lights. The entire room is the epitome of Art Deco. George opens his arms to embrace it. 'The first time Ah set eyes on you, Ruth Malcolm, the word that came straight into my mind was "class". And it has always remained there. This just confirms it. Imagine coming home every night from an Art Deco bar to an Art Deco flat.'

'You don't think it's too old-fashioned? Passé?'

'For goodness' sake, no, this is timeless. And,' he looks around to confirm his opinion, 'it's all quite functional and comfortable. No, Ah could move in here tomorrow and be quite . . .' He blushes. 'Ah didn't mean that to sound as if . . . Ah just meant, Ah could live with this . . . '

Ruth laughs. 'I know what you meant. Anyway, before I tell you all about it – a cup of coffee, and maybe a cognac?'

'Lovely. Go easy on the cognac, please.'

She places the tray on a small table. Pours the coffee. George lifts his brandy glass.

'Here's to good taste – which you obviously have in spades.'

Ruth inclines her head. 'Thank you, kind sir. But let me tell you the tale. I actually lived in the flat next door. Moved in in '47 when I returned to Glasgow. The couple who lived here, had done since the early thirties, were a Patrick and Christine Fraser. They had a furniture business on Woodlands

Road. They were wonderful neighbours, very much took me under their wing. And just like you, the first time I set foot in here I immediately fell in love with it.' She laughs. 'Patrick used to say, "Don't you think it's too old-fashioned, darling?" and just like you I'd say, "I could move in here tomorrow." ' She sighs. 'Well, alas, I got the chance. Poor Patrick, he was such a lovely man. Middle of 1948, no warning, he just dropped dead in the shop one morning.' Ruth takes a sip of cognac. 'So Christine decided to sell the business and go and live with their son down in Manchester. She gave me the chance to buy all the furniture. Then, we thought, to save me having to redecorate my flat to suit, why not go and see the landlord. We did, and he let me rent theirs. So I just moved from my flat into here. The fact is, I walked into an already furnished flat. I didn't design it, so I really can't take any credit for it.'

George shakes his head. 'No! You had the good taste to fall in love with this gorgeous flat the first time you set eyes on it. And when, sadly, it became available, you knew that you had to move into it. You couldn't pass up the chance to live here. As Ah've said, you are class, with a capital K.' They both laugh, then fall silent, looking at one another.

Ruth places her glass on the table. 'Yes. I've always known what I like, and what I want. Shall I tell you something?' She doesn't wait for an answer. 'If your silly wife – Joan, if I remember – hasn't got the savvy to realise what a good man she had, and as I'm not prepared to wait God knows how long until you get round to telling me how you feel about me – here goes. She might not want you, George Lockerbie. But I do!' She laughs. 'You should see your face. What do you have to say to that?'

George clears his throat. Looks her in the eye. 'Ruth, the

first time Ah walked into your office and saw you sitting behind that desk,' he shrugs his shoulders, 'Ah was smitten. But the reason Ah haven't been, well, pushy is because Ah didn't think Ah had a hope. That's why. For a start, Ah was married. And even when Joan and Ah split up, Ah still thought I'd be wasting my time. Come on! You – falling for a guy who assembles prefabs? Huh! What's the title of that Sinatra song? Yeah – "I Don't Stand a Ghost of a Chance with You". If we'd been in a musical, that would have been my song.'

'Ah, but you see, George, I soon spotted that you were quite different. You are actually in a class of your own. And what's even more important – you're a gentleman. You really are a gentle man. You said when I took your arm earlier tonight that you felt as though all your birthdays had come at once.' She raises her glass. Laughs. 'Now I'd like to drink a toast to your wife, Joan. Good luck to her. Why? Remember the night you told me she'd said your marriage was over and she was going back to England? That was the moment I knew all *my* birthdays had come at once!' She cups his face in her hands. 'So, Happy Birthday, darling.' She gives him a long, tender kiss. When she at last lets him come up for air, she glances at the clock. 'It's twenty to three, George. I take it you don't fancy a walk back to Maryhill tonight?'

He smiles. 'Even if Ah just lived downstairs, Ah still wouldn't want to go home tonight, Ruth.'

CHAPTER FORTY-FOUR

Sprechen Sie Broons?

Drena McClaren rises from the table. Billy and William junior are only halfway through their dinners. 'It's nearly seven, Ah'll huv tae get maself ready. Ah don't want tae miss any o' the fun.' She reaches up and starts to undo the head-scarf she's been wearing as a turban.

'Where are ye going, Ma?'

'Doon tae Granny Thomson's. It's her birthday the day, so she's having a wee party tae celebrate.'

'How auld is she?' asks William.

'Seventy-five.'

'Gee! Seventy-five! That's really auld, in't it?'

'Aye, she's gettin' oan, Granny.' Drena vigorously brushes her hair 'Ohyah! Ohyah! Ohyah! Ma hair's aw' tuggy bits! She pauses. 'Will you dae they dishes, Billy?'

'Aye, of course.' He looks at William. 'There's nane o' us invited, ye know. It's wimmen only.'

William has been doing his sums. 'That means Granny wiz born in 1875. Imagine that. Queen Victoria wiz still oan the throne then. Gee!'

'And Ah'll tell ye whit else,' says Billy. He holds up his left hand, fingers spread. With his right forefinger he begins to tick off. 'There wiz nae aeroplanes then. Nae motor cars. Nae fillums.'

'Whit did people dae tae pass the time?' enquires William. His father tries, not very hard, to suppress a laugh.

'Billyyyy. Behave yursel'!' Drena applies a little bit of lipstick, then a dab of Evening in Paris perfume. Her husband sniffs the air appreciatively.

'Ahhhh! Ma favourite perfume – a Thousand and Wan Carpet Cleaner!' Drena gives a loud tut. 'Whit a cheek!' She walks into the small lobby of their single-end, puts the light on and half closes the door. She opens the press door, takes out her one and only best dress.

Billy winks at William. 'That's yer mammy in her dressing room. Jist wait a wee minute and you'll see a film star emerge from that loabby.' They sit staring at the door.

Drena tugs the floral summer frock down. Jeez. She looks at her stomach. Got a belly like a poisoned pup. It'll have tae dae. She switches the light off and makes her entry.

Billy gives an appreciative wolf whistle; nudges William. 'Didn't Ah tell ye?'

'Ye look nice when ye dress up, Mammy.'

'Oh, thank you, son.'

'Whit aboot me? Dae Ah no' get any thanks fur the compliment Ah gave ye?'

'Thank you, husband.' She steps forward, plants a kiss on his lips, then breaks away as his hand begins to slide down over her hip. Gives him a knowing look. 'Right, Ah'm away doon tae Granny's.' She goes over to her Rexine shopping bag, extracts a bottle wrapped in tissue paper. 'Nearly went withoot Granny's present.'

'Whit did ye get her, Ma?'

'A bottle o' sherry. Granny likes a wee drap o' sherry. Ah got her a good yin. Three and six this wiz.'

'Three and six! Pushed the boat oot a bit, therr. If thurr's any left at the end o' the night, bring it back!' says Billy. This elicits another tut.

As Drena, bubbling with anticipation, steps on to the first-storey landing, the door to Granny's single-end lies open. A hubbub of laughter and voices spills out. The inner door is also ajar. Drena pushes it open to reveal the jam-packed kitchen.

'Hello, girls!' She enters holding her arms up in the air, waving the tissue-wrapped bottle.

'Drena!'

'Hello!'

'Where huv ye been?'

'Oh my God! Look at that spread. Eeeh, Granny, you've no' half been giving the Be-Ro book some hammer, huvn't ye?' The table is laden. Granny has opened out both extensions, put on her best tablecloth, and there's nary a space between plates and cake stands. 'Here's a wee present fur ye. Ah know you're partial tae a glass o' sherry.'

As her guests look on, Granny removes the tissue paper. 'Oooh! Bristol Cream!' With mock solemnity, she reaches over the table. 'Ella, put that wi' the rest, will ye.' The assembled company watch for Drena's reaction as Ella places the Bristol Cream on the sideboard. Beside the four bottles of sherry already there.

'Eeeh! Jesus-Johnny!' Drena lifts a hand to her mouth. 'Many huv ye got?' There's a gale of laughter.

'At the last count, five sherry and two half-bottles o' brandy. And some chocolates.'

'Aye, and Irma's no' here yet,' says Teresa O'Malley. She pauses. 'Eh, now I don't want t' worry ye, Granny, but she asked me what she should get yer . . . ' Teresa breaks off, unable to continue. Those present, anticipating what's she's about to say, also become helpless. Teresa regains a measure of control. 'And I told her . . . ' She falters yet again. 'I said, Granny's very fond . . . ' Once more hilarity takes over. It dies down and Teresa is about to make another valiant attempt when the room door is thrown open and Irma appears. She's holding something wrapped in tissue paper. Something bottle-shaped! Before she can greet them, the eight women let out a synchronised 'Ooooooh!' Irma, her mouth open, watches from the door as her friends succumb to a collective hysteria. Fingers are pointed at her; some hold their sides as they develop a stitch. Two or three attempt communication.

'Ah don't believe whit . . . '

'Huv ye ever see . . . '

'She's brought anither . . . '

Eventually, mainly through exhaustion, order is regained. 'C'mon in, hen,' says Granny. 'We'll tell ye later whit's been goin' on. But at the minute we're in nae fit state.'

'Okay,' says Irma in her heavy accent. 'Anyway, a Happy Birthday to you, Granny! A little bird has been to tell me you are awfy fond of a glass of sherr—'

'Oooooooh!' Yet again, laughter reigns supreme.

Mary Stewart looks around her. She feels a warm glow. Chairs were brought into the house from Granny's neighbours just after eight o'clock. The nine woman sat themselves down and proceeded to do justice to the spread laid on for them.

Two empty sherry bottles stand on the table. A third is in a bad way. Granny catches Ella's eye. 'Stand by in case we need reinforcements.'

Lena McDermot sits next to Mary. She's been trying her best to join in. A couple of large measures of sherry haven't helped. It's only two months since Andrew went. Ah know he'd have been saying, 'Get yer bloody self away tae Granny's party!' But och. Sitting here dressed in black. And ye know you're going hame tae an empty hoose. She looks round her friends and neighbours. Boys-a-boys! They're knocking that sherry doon them like it wiz Irn Bru. If Ah still had Andra, them two glasses would huv made me feel grand, jist like the rest o' them. But it has'nae. It's the opposite. Ah feel that miserable. Ah could jist dae wi' a good greet. She gives a deep, almost shuddering sigh. Another half-hour, then Ah'll slip away. C'mon! Make an effort. She turns to Mary. 'How's your Robert gettin' oan in the army?'

'Gettin' oan fine, Lena. He's got a stripe up, now.'

'As long as they don't send him oot tae yon Korea.'

'Aye, we were fair worried aboot that. His faither reads the papers tae keep up tae date wi' whit's going on. But we seem tae have got the better of them oot there. He should be aw'right.'

Irma Armstrong feels marvellous. That sherry is so good. Wunderschön. No, wonderful. She looks round the table. We are so lucky we come to Dalbeattie Street. These are alle – all mein friends. English, Irma. English. No! Besser ist – Scottish. Yah. Tonight is a good night to use my Scottish. Surprise everybody. She surveys the table again. Granny Thomson. And mein – my special friends, Drena and Ella.

They are so funny. She hiccups. I think I am, yes, a little tipsy. Granny's room is warm, the gas lights adding to it. Conversations go on all around her. Sometimes it's little groups of two or three, other times it goes back and forth across the table . . .

'Irma! Irma!'

'Oh!' She looks round. Ah, it's the lady from the top flat. Miss Dalrymple. She sits with Miss Pentland from two up. 'Hello, Miss Dalrymple. I was miles—'

'Now, never mind "Miss Dalrymple"! It's Agnes.' She leans over the table towards Irma. 'How are things going?' She points down.

Irma tries to recall the Scots she has been learning. 'Oh, everything is braw. It is all hunky-dory.' She is vaguely aware of Drena and Ella's heads swivelling round to look at her. Then at each other.

'How far gone are you? How many months?' enquires Agnes.

'Five months we think. Maybe a wee bit mair. The doctor says it will be December.'

'Whit are ye hoping for? A boy or a girl?'

'Oh, cricky-jings! It has tae be a wee boy, a wee laddie. Oh crivvens, aye!' From the corner of her eye, Irma glimpses Ella deftly saving Drena from sliding off her chair.

'Have ye got a name picked out for him?' asks Miss Pentland.

'Aye. He will be Arthur. This is after the bruder – brother of Bert who died in the war.'

'Mmm. A wee bit auld-fashioned, mind. If ye did'nae huv tae call him Arthur, whit name would ye choose yerself?' Agnes Dalrymple waits for an answer.

Irma takes a gulp of sherry. Holds the glass up in the air. 'Oh, freens! Isn't this so gute stoff?'

The other conversations at the table have died down. She hasn't noticed. She regards Agnes. 'If I have to choose the name. For me, I think . . . Boab! Or Eck. Yah, I like that. Eck ist good.'

'Why is she talking like that?' asks Drena. She bites her knuckle, trying not to laugh.

'Ah huv a good idea,' says Ella. 'Ah'm gonny try a wee experiment. Irma!'

'Yah?'

'Jist say ye had a wee lassie. It won't be – but jist say ye did. Whit wid ye call her?'

'Oh, michty me! That is awfy hard, Ella.' A low moan comes from Drena. 'But, och, I think she would have to be . . . Daphne!'

Ella turns to Drena – in time to stop her slipping under the table. 'Ah thought so. She's gettin' aw' they words and names fae the Broons and Oor Wullie in the *Sunday Post*. Fat Boab, Wee Eck and Daphne Broon!'

Teresa O'Malley leans forward. 'Jaysus! I t'ink that might be my fault, girls. O'ive been givin' her the *Sunday Post* this last couple o' months when we're finished with it. I told her, this'll get ye tuned in to t'ings Scottish.'

'It huz'nae half,' says Drena.

Granny Thomson stands up. 'Best of order, girls!' She rattles a teaspoon on a crystal cake stand. 'Noo, Ah'll be brief. It's nice youse have aw' turned up. The only yin missing, of course, is Marjorie Sneddon. But in a wye that's good. 'Cause as we aw' know, a few months back she finally left that swine! And nooadays, thank God, oor Setterday nights are the better for it. Ah think we've had a lovely night the night – and so will the folk that make sherry! Also, Ah hope youse realise whit a great sacrifice Ah've made by holding this wee do. Ah've had tae miss *Take It From Here* oan the wireless. Anywye. It's ten o'clock, Ah'm ready fur ma bed – so it's time ye's aw' buggered aff tae your beds. Thank you very much!'

'Hurrah! Three cheers fur Granny!'

'Whit a rerr laugh we've hud the night, Billy. And see Irma. Ah'm no' kiddin', Ah nearly wet maself, so Ah did! Ah'll tell ye the morra.' Drena stands in the middle of the floor. Billy McClaren lies in the recess bed, reading.

'We could hear ye's. Ah've heard less noise coming oot o' Firhill oan a Setterday efternin.

Drena tuts. She looks over at William. He lies sound asleep in his trundle-bed. The *Film Fun* he was reading when the Sandman got him lies over the bottom half of his face.

'Aw', look at the wean.' She walks over and removes the comic, folds it and places it on the bottom of his bed. 'Right! Ah'll huv tae make a quick visit.' She takes the lavvy key off its hook.

Less than ten minutes later, she climbs over Billy and into the back of the bed. Lies silent for a moment. Then, 'Billy?'

'Uh huh?'

'Pit that *True Detective* doon. Ah huv tae speak tae ye.'

'Aw, man, man!'

'Seriously. It's really important.'

'Ah hope sae.'

'It is.' She watches as he folds the corner of the page he's reading, stretches his arm out and places the magazine on the edge of the table. 'Ah'm all yours, darlin'.'

Drena snuggles in close to him. He stretches his arm along the base of the bolster, then round her shoulder. Pulls her closer. She moves her head into the hollow between his chest and shoulder. 'Ah'm almost certain Ah'm pregnant, Billy. That's me jist missed whit should huv been ma second period.'

'Aw' that's great, hen! Ah hope you think so tae.'

'Aye, and naw!'

'Whit dae ye mean?' He has an idea what she's about to say.

'Billy, Ah'm quite pleased, Ah think, to be expecting another wean. But William's ten noo. Even withoot a second wean, we need a room and kitchen. But Ah'm telling you now – Ah am not bringing up two weans in a single-end. Noo ye know Ah love ye. But if you love me, you'll get us a room and kitchen. Stying here is'nae fair oan me, and is'nae fair oan the two weans. If you don't make any effort tae get us oot o' here, Ah'll take the weans tae live at ma mother's until ye dae. That is a promise.'

Billy squeezes her closer. 'Ah know, Drena. It's jist Ah hate the thought of moving oot o' this close. Ah love livin' here. We've got smashing neighbours. Except fur that human shite Sneddon!'

'Shhhh! The wean.'

'He's sound.' He lies silent for a moment. 'Ah cannae see a room and kitchen comin' vacant in the close. So the best we can hope fur, if oor luck's in, is tae get wan somewhere in the street.'

'You're no' gonny let me doon, Billy McClaren, urr ye? Dae ye promise?' She raises her head to look him in the eye.

'Naw. If you're expecting, Drena, even Ah realise we've got tae get a bigger hoose.' She snuggles her head back into his shoulder. He lies for a moment. 'Right. Ah'll write a letter tae the factor the morra. Tell him the circumstances. They're

factors fur the whole block. And Ah'll find oot who's factor
fur the other side o' the street. Write tae them tae. Surely,
between noo and whenever you're due, we might get lucky.'
He lies thinking once more. Drena starts to snore gently into
his neck. He turns his head, kisses her softly on the brow.
Reaches up to switch off the bedside light – an extension
cable that hangs from a hook above their heads. The dark
embraces him. Jeez, Ah hope we don't huv tae leave Dalbeattie
Street. Bad enough the close. But tae leave the street . . .
Various thoughts and scenarios run through his head. None
of them satisfactory. There's only one thing for it. He gets
his thoughts together.

God? It's Billy McClaren. Well, You'll know that. And You'll
know whit the problem is tae. The last time Ah prayed tae
Ye, or spoke tae Ye, wiz when the Jerries marched us away
fae the camp intae the snaw tae get away fae the Russians.
Archie Cameron up oan the tap landing could tell Ye. Nae
joke, February 1945. That's ower five years ago. So, Ye can
hardly say Ah'm alwiz pestering Ye. Well, first of all, at the
very least, dae Ye think we might strike lucky and there'll be
a room and kitchen come vacant somewhere in Dalbeattie
Street? That wid be smashing.

Now Ah know Ah'm gonny push it here. But it is five years
since Ah last bothered Ye. Ah know it's asking an awful lot,
because Ah've been thinking aboot oor neighbours here in
the close. At number 18. Well, Ye know the number. Ah really
cannae see a vacancy fur a room and kitchen any time soon.
No' withoot a miracle. Now, Ah'm definitely not wanting
anybody tae die so's we can get a vacancy. That wid be oot
of order. But Ah'd really love tae get wan in this close. So is
there any chance of a wee miracle? Ah'm quite sure You'll be

able tae dae it if Ye feel like it. Finally, if You're huving diffi-culty, could Ah jist say two words: 'Richard.' And 'Sneddon.' He wid'nae really be missed. And it wid'nae need tae be done tae get us a hoose. It could come under 'smiting'. 'Cause it's aboot time he wiz. Long overdue. Anywye, Ah'll say no more. Ah hope Ye can help, God. Like Ye did in '45. Thanks for listening. Amen.

CHAPTER FORTY-FIVE

Always the Unexpected

It's a rainy morning, early in October, as Robert Stewart comes hurrying out of the Central Station. He's wearing his army greatcoat, unbuttoned because it's mild. He makes his way round to Wellington Street. Although there are a hundred thoughts racing through his mind, he still keeps half an eye open, ready to button up if he spots one of the Military Police patrols that occasionally grace the city centre. The dreaded 'redcaps'.

Ah'll be at Rhea's office in about three minutes. What am Ah gonny say? He tries again to slow his thought processes down, but can't. He feels excited because he's going to be shipped abroad, almost certainly to a war zone. It makes him feel, well, manly. Going off to war. But every time the word 'war' flits through his mind, it's accompanied by a little . . . who are ye kidding? A *big* jab of fear. He stops at the half-dozen stone steps, flanked by railings, that lead up to the entrance, the highly polished brass plate – 'W. Macready & Co. Solicitors'. He hasn't been able to put together yet what he's going to say to Rhea. All the way up from Carlisle, as he sat on the train, he ran various versions through his mind. Och. Ah'll just have to say whatever comes into my head. He's about to set foot on the first step when there's a rapid rat-a-tat-tat on the window nearest to the entrance.

Rhea has seen him. She looks surprised. It's always every second Friday when he's expected in Glasgow. Not a rainy Tuesday morning. Don't frighten her. He gives a big grin, waves vigorously. She manages a smile, but looks concerned, turns her head to speak to her workmates. Within seconds four more women join her at the window, waving, smiling, giggling. Rhea beckons him to come in.

The reception foyer is just as he expected. Wood panelling, lots of brass fitments. As he enters from the street, Rhea, followed by her nosey colleagues, exits the office.

'Robert! Whit are you daeing hame?'

'Ah'll tell you in a minute. You'll have to introduce me. Ah know it's Janet, Elsie, Shona and Margaret, but Ah don't know who's who.'

The girls introduce themselves. Robert looks at them.

'You keep talking about "the girls" whenever you speak about the office, Rhea. Ah was expecting four young lassies. Whit a disappointment!'

There's a chorus of 'Eeeeeh!' Janet speaks. 'It's surprising how quick ye can go aff some people!' They all laugh. Except Rhea. She hasn't taken her eyes off Robert since he entered.

'You still huv'nae said why you're hame in the middle o' the week, Robert.'

He feels that little stab of nerves again. Or is it fear? 'Aye. Eh, is there somewhere we can talk?'

'In here will dae fine,' says Rhea. She turns to her workmates. 'Will ye gie us a minute?'

Janet takes over. 'C'mon, girls. Give the two lovebirds a bit of privacy.' Amid calls of 'Nice tae meet ye at last, Robert,' she shoos them back into the office, adding, 'Who says it's nice tae meet the scunner! Speak for yerself.' The door closes as they giggle back to their desks.

All of a sudden the lobby-cum-reception seems extra quiet. Pin-dropping quiet. 'Can Ah chance a quick kiss here?'

'Aye.' Rhea steps forward and they kiss. She leans back to look him in the eye. 'Robert, you're frightening me. This diz'nae feel right you turning up oot o' the blue. Hurry up and tell me why you're here.'

'Come and sit down.' He takes her by the hand as they take the few steps over to the long, leather-covered bench. He notices how pale she has become. Might as well get straight to the point. 'Ah've been sent home for four days' embarkation leave.' He sees her stiffen.

'That's whit ye get when you're going abroad, in't it?'

'Yeah.' He notices he's said 'yeah' again. Not half getting into the habit of that.

'Where are ye goin'?' Her voice is a whisper.

'Well, they've actually not said. The army are stupid like that. If it was Hong Kong or Gibraltar or something, they'd tell us. Because they haven't, you can bet your boots it'll be Korea.' He has tried to say it casually. It has come out as anything but.

Tears roll down her face. To see her sit, crying silently, makes him feel helpless. Fucking army! 'Don't cry, hen. It'll be aw'right.'

'Why can they no' leave us alane? Since you've been at Carlisle it's been smashing. Hame nearly every fortnight.' As she speaks she sobs. Robert feels like crying too. Not for himself. For her.

The street door opens and a tall man enters. He obviously realises something is going on. 'Is this your young man, Rhea?'

'Aye, Mr Macready. They're sendin' him tae Korea in . . .' The sobs take over again.

'Oh dearie me.' He offers his hand to Robert, who leaps to his feet. 'I'm George Macready.' They shake hands. 'Mmmm.' He gives a rueful smile. 'Seeing the two of you is like history repeating itself. It's just nine years ago – seems less – back in '41, when I had to tell my wife I was being shipped out to North Africa.' He looks at Rhea. Smiles. 'Well, I won't get much out of my girl this afternoon, will I?' He takes out his wallet, extracts two one-pound notes. 'Now please don't give me an argument, Robert. This is staff welfare. She can have the afternoon off so as you can take her out to lunch. I suggest a good stiff brandy as an aperitif. Good luck in Korea, son.' He offers his hand again.

Robert grasps it. 'Jeez! Thank you very much, Mr Macready.' He watches as Rhea's boss opens the office door. 'Take Rhea's bag and coat out to her, Janet, will you. She can have the rest of the afternoon off.'

Thirty minutes later they are seated in Rogano's restaurant. A waiter has taken their order, and the brandy prescribed by Mr Macready sits in front of Rhea. Robert places his hand on top of hers. 'Drink that brandy, darling. Ah don't want ye greetin' in here.'

'Ah'll greet if Ah want! Ah feel like greetin'. You said it wiz only infantry sodjers they wid need in Korea.'

'Well, so it was. But what's happened is this. The South Korean and UN forces have driven the North Koreans back so far that what they call the lines of supply are badly stretched.

It's no' infantry they need – it's lorries and drivers, tae keep them supplied with food and ammo. So this is why we're being shipped out as fast as possible. Don't get worried, sweetheart. Ah'll jist be like a long-distance lorry driver.'

'A bloody long distance aw'right. Aw' the wye tae scabby Korea!'

'Honest tae God. Ah'll bet ye Ah don't even get tae see an angry North Korean!'

In spite of herself Rhea laughs. 'If you get kilt, Robert Stewart – ah'll murder ye!'

It has just gone five o'clock when Robert and Rhea walk into Dalbeattie Street from the other end. They don't go as far number 18. Instead, they slip into number 28 and stand for a while in the back close. 'Do ye realise, Rhea, Ah've now got tae go into the house and tell ma mother and faither.' He puts his arms round her. 'Ah could dae wi' a few kisses just tae get ma courage up. Ah wish it was a bit darker. We could maybe go intae the shelter, couldn't we?'

'Naw we could not, Robert Stewart! Ah'm no' going through yon again. Wi' ma luck Ah'd faw pregnant and something wid happen tae you. So Ah'm no' tempting fate.'

'Huh! That's a cheery thought.'

'At least we'll huv some time the gether. It's Saturday before ye go back tae camp, in't it?'

'Yeah. Don't quite know when we'll ship out. Probably Sunday. And the rumour is we'll set sail oan a troopship from Liverpool. That's the best Ah can tell you.'

'Naw. That's the *worst* ye can tell me.' He cuddles her in close; she lays her head on his shoulder. 'Robert, it's been smashing since ye got posted tae Carlisle. Goin' doon tae the

Central every fortnight tae meet ye has been wonderful. Why dae they huv to spoil it?'

He shrugs. 'Ah'll tell you why. It's what they call in the army Sod's Law. Just when ye think something's going fine, it aw' falls to pieces.' He looks at her. 'Now are you gonny be all right? You cannae go intae the house and all of a sudden burst oot crying, even if you don't tell your folks about us. When they find out Ah'm away tae Korea, and realise that was the day you were crying, they'll soon put two and two the gether.'

She kisses him again. Sighs. 'Naw, Ah won't gie the show away. Ah'll wait until Ah'm in bed if Ah want tae huv a good greet. Keep oor Siobhan awake.'

'Right, darling. Ah'll see ye tomorrow night, eight o'clock, round at the tram stop.'

A few minutes later, Robert watches from the front close of number 28 as Rhea makes her way along to 18. Just before she disappears into their close she waves. He waits a moment, then heads the same way. The lamplighter has been round. Robert stands in front of his door. He looks at it. He has known every chip and scratch since childhood. The gas lamp gutters and hisses away to itself, bathing the close, stairs and door in its greenish-white light.

A draught blows through from street to back court. Shadows move slightly as the light pulsates. He glances at the first flight of stairs. How many times, when he was a boy, did various pals call to swap comics? He'd come out of the house into the close and they'd all sit there, on the stairs, and nego- tiate. Barter. Two British editions of a comic for one American one. And if it was *Superman* or *Batman* – maybe three British ones. American comics were glossy, in full colour. British editions were in black and white, the paper of poor quality. Even as a boy he knew it. Why are we always so fuckin' cheap? he wonders. Five years after the war and we're still the fuckin' poor relation. Austerity. He looks again at his door. At the 'twisty' bell that hasn't rung for years. Something snapped inside it. Ma still polishes it. The combined letterbox and nameplate: S.R. STEWART. He tries the door handle. It turns. 'It's just me, Ma!'

'Oh my God! Whit are you daeing hame in the middle o' the week?'

Around the time Robert Stewart is bracing himself to speak to his mother and father, Billy McClaren is climbing the stairs to exit the subway station at St George's Cross. He makes his way along to the first tram stop on the Maryhill Road. George Lockerbie is already there.

'Hello, George. Jist gettin' hame fae yer work?'

'Aye. Funny weather, eh?'

'Aye.'

The arrival of a number 23 interrupts their less than riveting conversation. 'Going up the stairs?' asks Billy.

'Aye, Ah'll come up with you.'

'Of course. Ah'm forgettin',' says Billy. 'You don't smoke. Ah like a few draws, maself.'

'Aw' it's aw'right. Ah'll keep ye company.'

Billy takes a packet of ten Park Drive out of the bib part of his paint-stained overalls. He selects a half-smoked one. He has two whole ones left. 'Yer a wise man no' smoking. Ah weesh Ah did'nae. If ye smoke and drink,' he leans closer to George, 'the government's got ye by the short and curlies.'

'Ah used tae smoke. Packed it in when Ah was in the forces.'

Billy laughs. 'As ye know, Ah wiz a POW the full five years. Went in the bag at Dunkirk. That's wan thing we were never short of. Fags. Got any amount in the Red Cross parcels. Used tae trade them wi' Jerry fur food and all sorts. Never short of a smoke. Ah think Ah'll write tae the Red Cross in Switzerland, see if they'll let me go back oan the parcels. Don't bother wi' the grub – jist send the fags!'

George shakes his head. 'But why are they still in short supply? It's nineteen bloody fifty and we're just as badly rationed as we were during the war. The excuse then, especially from '40 tae '43, was that the U-boats were sinking loads o' ships. That's long gone – yet we're still bloody rationed up tae oor eyeballs!'

'Ach! Nae good thinking aboot it. Drive yerself demented. Anywye, how dae ye find it livin' on yer own since Joan went? Are ye managing aw'right, George?'

'Well, it's not as bad as ye might think. The marriage was burnt oot, Billy. Ah think the longer we stayed the gether, the worse it would have got.'

'Aw' well. It's mibbe fur the best.'

There's a pause, then George says, 'Well actually, Billy, Ah've got a new lady friend. And Ah think this is really the one.'

'Hey, that's good. Ah hope you're right.'

'Well, Ah'll tell you how sure we are. And you're the first one Ah've told. Ah'm going to be moving in with her next week. She lives over in Hillhead.'

Immediately, Billy feels a buzz of anticipation. He half turns in his seat to face George. 'Ah take it you'll be giving up the hoose?'

'Aye. Within the next week or so.'

'Jeez! George. You've nae idea whit this might mean fur me and Drena. There's very few know yet, wan or two of her pals, but Drena's expecting—'

George interrupts. 'That's great. It's a bit of a late yin, this one, isn't it?'

'It is. But listen, George. Huv ye definitely no' telt anybody else you're givin' up the hoose?'

'Ah definitely haven't.'

Billy feels the excitement rise in him. 'Could you dae me a big favour?' He doesn't wait for an answer. 'Wid you let me know a day or two before ye go doon tae the factor's tae tell them you're giving it up?' Again, he doesn't pause. 'And wid ye mind no' lettin' anybody else know that you're flitting? If you could dae that fur me, George, that would gie me and Drena a really good chance of gettin' it. We could huv a letter already in, asking tae be considered as the new tenants. Would ye mind?'

'No bother at all,' says George. 'If you're having another bairn, you'll definitely be wanting a room and kitchen.'

'Aye, it's Drena. She's quite happy aboot having another wean, but she's laying doon the law: "Get me a room and kitchen – or Ah'll be back living at ma mother's until ye dae!" Billy laughs. 'Ah don't even get the option of a fine!'

As they travel up the Maryhill Road, Billy falls silent. Thinks of what a good chance he'll have of getting George's vacated house. It's the same factor. He and Drena have never missed a day's rent. They've got another child coming. All of a sudden he remembers his prayer of just a few days ago. Jeez! It's only three nights since Ah asked God for that favour. At just this moment, George turns his head to look out the window at something that has caught his eye.

Billy takes his chance. He looks up. His lips move silently. God? Thanks a lot for granting ma prayer. That's really terrific. A hoose coming vacant at number 18. That really *is* a miracle!

CHAPTER FORTY-SIX

On the Move

─────────

Ruth Malcolm busies herself round the flat, tidying here, dusting there. She glances again at the Bakelite Art Deco clock on the mantelpiece. Ten past five. George really shouldn't be long now. What's keeping him? Come on, keep calm. He's had a lot to do. She knows for certain that he will be coming. A few inches from the clock stands a sepia portrait of David Malcolm, in uniform. She sighs. I remember the day we had that taken. Jerome's studio. May '42. One of me, one of David. He took mine with him to North Africa. Wonder what happened to it? Would be in his wallet that day. Probably buried with him. He's looking directly at her. You know I'm doing the right thing, David, don't you? You'd like George. He's too good to be stuck in a factory job. He and I will do all right. Together we'll think of something. After eight years, I need a man in my life. You know I'll never forget you. Even if I wanted to, I couldn't. You were my first love. My first everything. Her train of thought is broken as she hears footsteps on the stairs. Is this him? The bell rings loudly in the hall. Here he is! She and her heart skip to the door. God! I feel like a girl.

'Ah've arrived. And to prove it – Ah'm here!'

'Hello, darling. Welcome to your new home.' She stands to the side, opens the front door wide. George takes a few steps into the hall, then lays down the two suitcases he's carrying.

'This is all my goods and chattels.' He opens his arms and Ruth walks into them, puts her arms round him. They stand kissing for a few minutes. 'Seeing as it's your flat, shouldn't you have carried me over the threshold, Ruth?'

'Maybe later.'

He kisses her again. 'Remember Ah was saying the other night, if we were in a musical Ah'd be singing "I Don't Stand a Ghost of a Chance with You"?' He has his arms round her waist.

'Uh-huh?'

'Round about now, Ah'd be bursting out with "I Can't Believe that You're in Love with Me"!'

She laughs. 'Well you're just going to have to, George Lockerbie. 'Cos I am.'

He sways her gently from side to side, looking at her as he sings the first few bars. 'Ah really *can't* believe it. Don't be surprised if now and again you wake up in the morning and Ah'm lying next to you, leaning up on my elbow, just staring at you.'

She shakes her head. 'Okay. If our life together is going to be like a musical, it's my turn.' Looking into his eyes, she sings the first four bars of 'Can't Help Loving that Man of Mine'.

'Touché!'

It's an hour later. George puts his knife and fork down on his plate. 'And you can cook as well. Not just a pretty face, eh?'

'Would you like tea or coffee?'

'Tea will do fine. Ah'll see the dishes off while you brew up. May as well start doing things as they will be done in future. It'll be a partnership.'

Ruth begins clearing the table. 'George? As you'll appreciate, there will be one or two wee things that will have to be, well, sorted out. Agreed between us.' She nods in the direction of the mantelpiece. 'What about David's photo? Would you like me to take it down, put it away?'

'Why ever would Ah want you to do that? David's photo will stay there for as long as you want.' He turns his head in its direction. 'You can stay where you are, mate. Keep an eye on me. Make sure Ah'm treating our girl right.'

She holds the plates in her hands. He sees her eyes are brimming with tears. 'That's why I want you for my man, George Lockerbie!'

George pours himself a second cup. He puts the tea-strainer back in its holder. Ruth takes a sip from her cup. 'Shall I put the wireless on, darling?'

'Only if there's something you don't want to miss. Otherwise Ah'm quite happy to sit and talk. It's gone seven. Are you going in to the bar tonight?'

'I told Alan and Stefan I'd be along at half eight or so. They know you're moving in today. Did everything go all right at Dalbeattie Street?'

'Yeah. It was gone three o'clock when that dealer arrived on the scene.' George laughs and shakes his head. 'All he gave me was ten pounds for the lot!'

Ruth draws her breath in. 'Oh George! What a cheek.'

'Well, what can you do? He knows Ah'm leaving. Ah don't

want the furniture. Ah'm giving up the house. Ah just had to grin and take it. Only took him and his lads thirty minutes to load their cart.'

'And you'd already told that chap upstairs, hadn't you?'

'Yeah. Ah told them on Monday Ah was moving out Wednesday. Billy came down to see me later that night. Showed me his application to the factor. He put that in to them yesterday. After the carter cleared the house, Ah locked it up, nipped upstairs and told Drena Ah was leaving – Billy was at work – then Ah got a tram down to the factor's, paid the rent up to date and handed over the keys.' He puts on a sad face. 'And now Ah'm homeless!'

'Poor soul! Don't worry, darling. I'll look after you.'

It's the next day. Thursday. There's the usual noisy clang as the heavy brass flap of the McClarens' letterbox announces that something has come through the door. It never fails to give Drena a fright, make her jump. Oh my God! Whit's that? She goes into the lobby. A long brown envelope lies half on the well-worn runner, half on the even more well-worn linoleum. She looks at it. Usually envelopes like this mean a bill. She listens to the sound of the postman climbing up to the top landing, then the noise of one of the three letter-boxes as he puts mail through someone else's door. She continues to stand in her lobby as John, the postman, turns and starts to descend. Hardly breathing, she hears him pass her door again and head further on down. Any time now. An upstairs door is thrown open, then feet come pattering down to her landing. Timing it perfectly, she opens the door and Ella rushes in.

'Huz it come?'

Drena closes her door. Points. 'Ah think so.' The two women regard the brown envelope. Ella bends down. Tuts. 'It might huv hud the decency tae faw face up. Ye cannae tell anything fae the back.'

'Ye can turn it ower,' says Drena.

Ella bends further down and flips it on to its back. 'Oh, Drena! It's definitely fae the factor!' She reads the red meter-mark cancellation aloud. 'Turnbull, Parnie and Adam. Factors.'

'Oh Mammy, Daddy!' says Drena. 'Ah wonder if we've got it?'

Ella looks at her. 'Well open the bugger and you'll find oot!'

'Oh, Ah cannae jist open it like that,' says Drena. 'Ah'll huv tae huv a cup o' tea in ma hand.'

'Dae ye want me tae open it for ye?'

'Naw, it'll huv tae wait till there's a few o' the neebours in!'

'Fuck me!' says Ella. 'Ah'll never staun the strain!' The two of them, as usual, proceed to go into stitches. Eventually they get their breath. 'Who dae ye want up fur the Grand Opening?' enquires Ella.

Drena answers without hesitation, 'Granny and Hitler's girlfriend!'

'Hitler's girlfriend?'

'Aye.' Drena manages to keep control. 'Eva Broon!' This sets the two of them off again. 'That's ma new name fur Irma since she started wi' her *Sunday Post* language lessons!'

Twenty minutes later Granny Thomson, Irma and Ella sit round Drena's table, the letter in the centre. 'Ma nerves wull'nae staun this much longer,' says Ella. 'Ma stomach's fair churning.'

'Two minutes,' says Drena. She pours the tea, waits until

her guests milk and sugar it, then reaches for a sharp kitchen knife. They watch as she slits the envelope open. The folded, typewritten letter is delicately opened out and held between two hands. Ella leans to the side to try and read it. 'Ah! Ah! Ah!' Drena sways back in her chair, begins to read. 'We've goat it! We've goat it!' She bursts into tears.

Ella puts her arm round her pal's shoulders. 'Aw, Drena! Ah'm that happy fur ye!'

'Isn't that jist grand!' says Granny Thomson.

'Michty me!' says Irma.

Drena and Ella look at each other, then at Irma. 'Eh, there's something we want tae huv a wee word wi' you aboot,' says Ella, 'but och! It can wait.'

CHAPTER FORTY-SEVEN

In Harm's Way!

'**O**h my God!' Samuel Stewart turns the wireless off as the seven o'clock news finishes and the orchestra of Benny Goodman, backing Peggy Lee as she sings 'Why Don't You Do Right?', swells out of the wooden-cased radio. Mary Stewart hurries through from the room.

'What is it, Sam? What are ye oh my Godding at?'

'There's been a big surprise attack oan the UN forces up in the north. They're almost certain it's Chinese troops. That's the first time they've got involved. They jist came flooding ower the border intae North Korea. Ah've been saying tae ye, haven't Ah, that MacArthur has advanced right up tae the Chinese border. Does he think the Chinks are gonny put up wi' that? Stupid bugger! And we don't know if Robert's arrived oot therr yet. We've had wan letter, written oan the troop-ship. We don't know where the bloody hell oor boy is.'

Mary sits down at the kitchen table. 'Let's try and work it oot, Sam. As far as we know, he set sail aboot the seventh of this month. October.'

Samuel has calmed down a little. 'This attack has jist taken place – the twenty-fifth. So that's only eighteen days since he sailed. Ah don't think he'll be there yet. It's a helluva journey tae Korea, ye know. Quite literally, it's the other side o' the world. Noo, even if he has arrived, his ship would dock in South Korea, Ah would imagine, then they've got tae get organised and go by road tae the north – another two, probably three days. Naw. Thank God. Ah really don't think he'll have been anywhere near where this fighting's taking place.'

Mary has been listening to every word. 'Even if that's true, Sam, if the fighting's starting tae get worse noo that the Chinese are involved, sooner or later – we'll have tae face it – he is gonny be in amongst it, one wye or the other. It's nae good trying tae kid oorselves on.'

'Aye, you're right, hen.' He reaches out and gently takes her hand. She places her other hand on top of his and they sit silently for a while, lost in their thoughts.

Ten past nine in the morning. Rhea O'Malley and her four workmates are preparing themselves for another day in the service of Macready and Co. Rhea has treated herself to a small tin of Nescafé Instant Coffee. She has boiled a pan full of milk on the Baby Belling cooker and now sits savouring every sip of her milky coffee. The girls seem quiet this morning. Rhea hasn't picked up on the glances that occasionally come her way, or the knowing looks they've been giving one another. As usual, Janet takes it on herself to find out if Rhea is aware of what's been happening in Korea.

'Did you have the wireless oan this morning when ye were getting ready for your work, Rhea?'

'Naw. If ma mother hasn't got it oan when Ah come ben the kitchen Ah jist leave it off. Why?' As Rhea takes another sip of coffee, she sees her colleagues look at one another. 'Oh God! Whit? Whit's the matter? C'mon, ye might as well tell me. Whit's happened?'

'The Chinese have sent troops ower the border and attacked the UN forces!'

'Oh, Jesus God!'

There now ensues a conversation that basically follows the same lines as the one that took place between Robert's parents earlier this morning. When George Macready arrives at the office twenty minutes later, he is asked for his opinion. On being told the date on which Robert embarked for Korea, he is able to calm Rhea down by convincing her that her fiancé will almost certainly not be anywhere near the fighting. Perhaps not yet even in Korea.

Rhea watches as her boss heads off to his private office. She waits a minute or so. 'Ah'm awfy glad Mr Macready is able tae work oot things like that. He's no' half put ma mind at ease.'

None of the girls wants to be the one to point out that the fighting will worsen now that China has become involved.

'When did ye get that last letter, Rhea?'

'It wiz aboot a week ago. But he wiz still aboard ship. Mind, he had written that a week or so before Ah got it. Don't half take some time, them army letters, don't they?'

Elsie speaks. 'Do ye remember me telling ye that, Rhea? When ma Ronnie wiz oot in Hong Kong in 1948, aw' his letters were field post office yins. The forces have their ain postal service. Sodjers don't jist put their letters into postboxes in whatever country they're in. They put them intae letterboxes in the camp, and the army sees tae them. And if it's coming fae a war zone, the letters are aw' censored.'

'Whit? They get read?' asks Rhea.

'Oh, aye,' says Elsie. 'Think aboot it. You could'nae huv your Robert writing tae ye and saying, "Ah might no' get the chance tae write tae ye for the next week or two 'cause we're puttin' in a big attack, starting next Tuesday." If that wiz allowed tae be sent, and maybe somebody stole it and opened it, then told the enemy . . . See whit Ah mean? That's why you'll find Robert's letters will aw' be censored. If he says something he should'nae, they usually black it oot so as you're no' able tae read it.'

'Ohhh! That's no' gonny be very nice, somebody reading Robert's letters before Ah get them.'

Elsie looks at the rest of the girls, then turns back to Rhea. 'But they censor *your* letters tae!'

'Eh?'

Elsie laughs. 'Your letters are opened and read afore he gets them as well!'

'Oh my God! You should huv seen the things Ah was saying tae him, well, in the last two letters Ah've wrote him. Even though Ah don't huv an address yet oot in Korea, he telt me jist tae send them tae Carlisle and they wid forward them oan tae him.' She pauses, thinking, then, 'It's a good job Ah don't know anybody doon at Longtown. Ah'd never be able tae face them again!'

'Eeeeh! Rhea. Have you been writing radgy letters tae Robert? Eeeeh, yah dirty bizzum! Ah hope you'll be confessing aw' this when ye go tae chapel oan Sunday?'

'Aye, that'll be right!' All five of them now proceed to go into kinks. Helpless.

Janet manages to control herself. 'What have ye been saying tae him?'

'Oh, Ah could'nae. Ah could'nae tell anybody.' Rhea puts a hand over her mouth and goes red in the face as she thinks about her letters. 'Ah'd get the jail!'

'It jist shows ye,' says Margaret. She points at Rhea. 'Ye think you're working wi' this wee quiet Catholic lassie who wid'nae say boo tae a goose. And noo it's all coming oot! She's a right wee radgy-knickers!'

'Eeeeeh, Ah am not!' says Rhea, covering her mouth with both hands as she goes even redder.

All eyes are directed to the partners' door as it begins to open, and the laughter declines in volume as Mr Macready makes his second appearance of the morning.. He looks around before intoning, 'When I left this office quarter of an hour or so ago, it was a rather subdued group of young women I closed the door on. Now you all seem to be on the verge of hysteria. Might one enquire as to why?' He watches as four pairs of eyes turn towards Rhea. 'Miss O'Malley?' he says.

Rhea goes redder than the reddest of beetroots. 'Oh, jist girls' talk,' she manages to squeak.

CHAPTER FORTY-EIGHT

Whose Turn for the Stairs?

It is the first Saturday in November 1950. The events of this night will be long remembered by the residents of Dalbeattie Street. Such happenings are usually known as a seven-day wonder. To those who live up the close at number 18, it will become something they won't ever forget. For the rest of their lives. All of them, to greater or lesser degrees, will agree that what happened was quite fitting. Had they known what really took place this night, their approval rating would have soared!

Richard Sneddon is drunk, staggering drunk, as he approaches his close. He is also in a foul mood. Mostly because he doesn't have Marjorie to knock about any more. He really misses her. 'Fucking hoor!' he murmurs. It is cold, with a blustery wind blowing spits of rain from all directions. As usual he is smartly dressed: suit and tie and, of course, his beloved blue Crombie. 'A gentleman's coat', as he calls it. He stops on the pavement, facing the close mouth. Everything seems sharp and clear. The enamel plate with '18' in black on a white background.

From the edge of the pavement, the lamp standard shines its beam down on to the wall round the close. Successive generations have chalked the sandstone blocks up to a height of five feet. It all peters out the higher up you look. 'The Dalbeattie Boys Rule OK.' That's a fairly recent wan. Why do they always put 'Rule' and 'OK'? He sways slightly as he reads this declaration. Why no' jist 'The Dalbeattie Boys' full stop? Dozy fuckers! He looks into the close. The gas lamp spreads its weak light down on to the banister rail and the first flight of stairs. Ach! Ah might as well away up tae the hoose.

As he reaches the first storey, he scliffs his feet along the landing. Granny Thomson raises her head and looks towards the sound. The kitchen door leading into the wee lobby is wide open, so she can hear quite clearly. She knows who it is. Although it is nearly half past eleven, she is not yet abed. Still fully dressed, she sits at the table with a three-week-old copy of *John Bull* magazine lying open in front of her. She hears Richard Sneddon climb the first few stairs up towards the next half-landing, then stop. She waits for him to continue. He doesn't.

Mmmm, she thinks. Wonder why he's stopped? Another minute or so drifts silently by. In the quietness, her twin gas lights seem loud as they burn away. She can hear the gas burbling up through the pipes. She rises to her feet.

Donald McNeil has spent his usual Saturday night at the Gaelic Speakers Club in Windsor Terrace. On leaving, he walks round to the Maryhill Road and stands at the first tram stop. The next car to appear is an 18 instead of one of the more numerous 23s. Och, mix-a-matter! He boards the 18 and ten minutes later alights at the last stop on the Maryhill Road before the tram turns off right and goes down Bilsland Drive. It is a wee bit extra walk, but Donald never looks on walking as irksome. As he strides along, arms swinging, he still has the peaty aftertaste of the Laphroaig single malt in the back of his throat. He also has a bit of an appetite. I will open that tin of Spam and have a nice sandwich to myself. What's left will do for lunch tomorrow. As he rounds the corner into Dalbeattie Street, unknown to him, Richard Sneddon has entered the close at number 18 just seconds previously.

Richard Sneddon stands halfway up the flight of stairs, poised between the first-storey landing and the next half-landing. He rests his left hand on top of the wooden banister, contemplates the stairs. Huh! 'It's your turn for the stairs, Mr Sneddon. They've only been washed three times since . . . ' Ah bet she was gonny say 'since Marjorie left ye'! But she thought better of it. 'Since the end of April.' Same fucking thing. That's when that hoor left me. An idea comes to him. A beauty. He opens his coat, unbuttons his flies, takes his cock out. He sniggers. Want the stairs done, do ye's?

As Donald McNeil enters the close, he can hear water dripping. It's falling down inside the narrow elliptical well, the space between stairs and banisters, and pattering into the close. As he reaches the first half-landing, he pauses for a second to make sure he is hearing correctly. Someone is pissing up there! As he climbs the flight towards the first storey, he looks up through the rails, recognises the tall figure in the long blue coat. That man Sneddon. Donald steps on to the first landing. Richard Sneddon stands in the middle of the next flight, his back to Donald. He continues to urinate.

'That is about what I would expect from a beast like you!'

Sneddon turns his head, keeps his left hand on top of the rail, stops peeing for the moment. 'Aw, it's yerself. The wee teuchter man. Well Ah don't need a Heelander like you trying tae tell me anything. Got that, teuchter? So you can fuck off!' He begins to piss again. 'They want the sterrs washed – so Ah'm washin' the fuckin' sterrs. Aw'right?'

'I shall not be wasting my time saying any more to you. Just let me past.' Donald takes a few steps up, and stops behind Sneddon.

'Ye can wait tae Ah finish ma turn at washin' the sterrs.' Sneddon giggles.

'That is what you think.' Donald swings his left hand in an upwards direction underneath Sneddon's left hand and easily breaks his hold on the top rail. He then climbs the steps and begins to force his way past him.

'Yah teuchter bastard!' Sneddon reaches out and grabs the sleeve of Donald McNeil's coat. Donald wrenches his arm free from Sneddon's grasp, pauses, then swings it back and catches him across the chest with his forearm. This blow, mild though it is, is enough to cause Sneddon to go off balance. He begins to topple backwards. His right hand scrabbles and scrapes at the smooth paintwork of the wall on his right, but cannot find purchase. His left hand tries to grab Donald, somewhere, anywhere. The fingers of this hand despairingly grip the edge of Donald's sleeve again, but Donald tugs his arm loose, turns quickly, and starts up the stairs. Sneddon, arms flailing, begins to fall back, somehow like a tree that has just been felled. Tall and straight, he drops on to the first-storey landing five steps below. The back of his head is the first to make contact. Donald screws his face up as he hears the clear, sharp crack as Sneddon's skull splits. It is not a pleasant sound.

As Donald McNeil climbs out of sight, Granny Thomson silently closes the flap of her letterbox. Placing a hand on her hip, she grimaces as she straightens up. Oooh! Yah bugger. Ah cannae stay doon for long nooadays. She lights the gas under the kettle. Could dae wi' a wee cup o' tea efter that. She lifts the teapot. Says out loud, 'Ah knew that man would get his comeuppance.'

Outside, on the empty landing, the three front doors look down on Richard Sneddon. Lit by the pulsing gas lamp on the stair-head, he lies face up, his head supported by the back of its flat-tened, caved-in skull. His legs stretch back up the stairs, heels resting on the fourth step. His upper back and shoulders lie on the landing. The blue Crombie – on which only ten payments remain – slowly soaks up the urine. His penis lies outside his trousers. It seems to point, accusingly, down towards his face.

Granny Thomson doesn't leave her house on the Sunday morning until after the body has been discovered. Archie Cameron finds him when he comes downstairs to go for the papers. As he collects his *Sunday Post* and *Mail*, he asks Ken if he can use his phone to ring the police. He tells them that, as an ex-Para who has seen plenty of dead men, they can trust his judgement when he says an ambulance isn't needed – just the mortuary van.

After the body has been removed, most of the neighbours are talking on the stairs, or over cups of tea in one another's houses. Drena calls in to see Granny Thomson for a few minutes to tell her the latest. Minutes after her departure, Granny slips quietly up to the top storey and chaps on Donald McNeil's door. Donald opens it, wearing his braces, shirt collar tucked in. There are the last traces of shaving soap on his face.

'Oh, hello, Isabella. Been an unfortunate incident during the night, so I believe.'

'It's ma Sunday name this mornin', is it? Ah've came up tae mooch a cup o' tea and have a wee blether wi' ye.'

Five minutes later finds them sitting at the table. 'Ah'm gonny come straight tae the point, Donald. Knowing whit a good-living man ye are, Ah'm a bit worried in case ye feel ye have tae involve yerself in whit happened last night.' She pauses as she sees a quizzical look appear on his face. She carries on. 'Ah saw Richard Sneddon huv his wee accident!'

'Did you really, Bella. Man, man! Now I did not see you.'

She gives a wry smile. 'Letterboxes aren'y just for letters, Donald. Ah heard that pig's melt pishing oan the stairs. Dirty swine! Ah had a look jist tae confirm it was him. Ah knew it would be. Who else? Anywye, Ah saw him accidentally fall. And Ah've nae intention of telling the polis – or anybody else – that Ah seen it. Ah'm no' interested in gettin' involved. That's why Ah've came up tae see you. Ah hope you're gonny dae the same?'

'Well, as it happens, Bella, I was thinking of maybe calling into the polis station just to say I had been exchanging a few words with Richard Sne—'

Granny interrupts. 'Whit the hell for, Donald? Now we've been freens for many a year. Will ye listen tae whit Ah'm aboot tae tell ye? There is nae need whatsoever for you tae have one iota of worry aboot whit happened tae that . . . that human shite! Therr, Ah've said it. And Ah don't care, 'cause that's whit he wiz!'

'I know, Bella. But a man has died. I am thinking I should maybe let them know that I was there when he fell . . . '

'Donald McNeil! The polis have been and gone. They only spoke tae the folk oan the first and second landings. They're looking oan it as an accident. Drena had them in for a cup o' tea. Ye know whit she is like, loves tae be first wi' the news. The big sergeant telt her it's an open-and-shut case. Naebody on the landing above or below has reported any fights or arguments on the stairs last night – that's why they hav'nae questioned anybody in the close or up here. He telt Drena it's jist straightforward. Mr Sneddon must huv had far too much tae drink. Why else would such a respectable man be peeing oan the stairs, unless he wiz befuddled wi' the drink? He must huv lost his balance.'

'Even so, Bella, don't you think that—'

'Jeeesus wept, Donald McNeil! How many times huv we aw' listened tae that man knock his wee wife aboot? Why the buggering hell should you huv your life in the least disrupted because o' that bloody reptile?' She points a finger at him. 'If you go tae the polis and stir up a lot of unnecessary trouble for yersel', Donald McNeil, Ah'm telling ye, Ah'll never, ever talk tae ye again.' She sits back in her chair. 'Ah mean it.'

Donald smiles. 'Oh, Bella! 'Tis good of you to be so concerned. All morning I have been arguing with myself. Should I get involved? Go to the polis station? Then I think of all the weekends I have listened to that man batter that poor lassie.' He pauses. 'So, you have helped me to make up my mind. I will say nothing.'

'Oh! You have nae idea how happy Ah am tae hear you

say that.' She finishes her tea, pushes herself up from the table. 'Right. We'll no' be speaking aboot last night ever again. And as ye should know, there's nae need tae worry aboot me telling anybody aboot it. Case closed.' He walks her to the door. 'Ah'll see ye when Ah see ye, Donald.'

'Cheerio, Bella. Thank you for calling.' He stands for a moment, watching as she descends.

He's about to close his door when Agnes Dalrymple opens hers.

'Eeeh, Donald. Did ye hear aboot that Richard Sneddon?'

'Aye. That is Granny chust away. She was telling me. You never know the minute, do you?'

'Ah know.' She looks around as though making sure she won't be overheard. 'Mind, it could'nae happen tae a mair deserving case. That wee wife o' his will be turnin' somer-saults when she gets tae hear aboot it. Ah hope the bugger wiz well insured. Be a bit o' compensation for aw' the years she wiz knocked aboot.' She smiles. 'And she'll be able tae move back intae the hoose noo he's gone. Time her luck wiz changing.'

'I quite agree, Miss . . . eh, Agnes. It is true what they say about an ill wind.'

'Aye, isn't it jist. And us – everybody in the close – we're aw' gettin' rid o' a nasty neighbour.' Agnes draws herself up, looks around, then drops her voice. 'The bugger wiz'nae taking his turn tae wash the stairs, ye know.'

'Was he not!' says Donald. He tuts. 'I think he deserved all he has got, that one. Well, I am chust about to have a bit of lunch. See you, Agnes.' He closes the door, walks into his room, shakes his head. Man, man! he says to himself. By the sound of things, it is another DCM I should be getting.

CHAPTER FORTY-NINE

Decisions

Drena McClaren and Ella Cameron stand in the kitchen of Drena's new house.

'Whit dae ye think, Ella? Diz it need it?'

Ella looks around the kitchen. She knows Drena usually defers to her opinion. 'Mmmmm.' She nods her head up and down, purses her lips. 'Aye, it could definitely dae wi' freshening up.'

Drena receives this opinion with ill-concealed pleasure, does a bit of bosom adjusting with a forearm. 'Ah telt him that, but he'll no' huv it. You cannae get him tae decorate his ain hoose. People will'nae believe me. Painter and decorator – and he'll no' open a pair o' steps inside his ain door!'

'Zat no' terrible. Whit's the matter wi' him?'

'He cannae tell ye. Ah've got ma ain theory, mind. Ah think he looks oan the time needed tae dae his ain hoose as wasted effort. He diz'nae get paid fur it. So the time spent decorating this place – fur nuthin' – should be spent daeing a customer's hoose – fur something!'

Ella laughs. 'Noo isn't that a good example o' male thinking?'

'He says there's nuthin' up wi' it. George and English Joan left it in good order. Ah says tae him, Ah'm no' bothered aboot the bedroom, but the kitchen's a bit dull. And even mair important, it's no' tae ma taste. But he insists it's aw'right.' There's a pause for some more righteous bosom adjustments. 'So as usual, Ella, Ah'm gonny huv tae dae it maself – in spite o' the fact Ah'm three months gone. Ah hate when it gets near the time fur redecorating . . .'

'Don't worry, Drena.' Ella reaches out, squeezes her pal's arm. 'We'll dae it between us. What was ye thinkin', papering or painting?'

'Ah'd love tae paper it. But Ah cannae face it. Ah'm no' very good at it, so it'll huv tae be paint. But Ah want it done fur Hogmanay.'

'Ahah! Ah'll tell ye whit we'll dae. Huv ye heard o' this new thing called stippling?'

'Naw.'

'Wi' there being a paper shortage, and wallpaper being dear, lots of folk are daeing this new thing. Ye get a large tin of distemper in a light colour. Say, oooh, sort of pale cream. Then ye get a wee tin of a darker distemper. Mibbe mid-broon or red. Dae aw' the walls in the light colour, wait till it's dry, then ye get a sponge, dip it in the darker colour, squeeze it oot, and stipple – in other words, dab the wall wi' the dark colour in an even pattern. When it dries, it jist looks like the wall's papered.'

'Imagine that. Where did ye hear aboot that, Ella?'

'Read it in a magazine. They believe it's catching oan aw' ower the country, simply because wallpaper's sae dear.'

'Ah like the sound o' that. Though mind, Ah'll bet ye when Billy sees it, he'll hate it, him being a professional an' aw' the rest o' it. Hummpf!'

Ella laughs. 'Huh! Well ye know whit? If he hates it, that'll be great. 'Cause the only way he'll get rid of it is by re-fuckin' decorating the place. Either way you'll be gettin' yer kitchen done!' As is always the case with these two, the peals of laughter ring out, through the open door, into the close and halfway up the stairs.

Irene Pentland is in Andrew Cochrane's, the grocer's. She watches as Alec Stuart expertly folds the blue sugar bag and places it beside the already wrapped two rashers of bacon. Further along the marble-topped counter his young assistant, James, is just finishing serving another customer. Alec is taking his time. As soon as James's customer leaves, Alec turns to him. 'This should be a good time to get the back shop swept, James. Not too vigorous, remember. And sprinkle some water about. Keep the dust down.'

'Right you are, Mr Stuart.' James wonders why he wants it swept now. It's usually a Friday. This is only Wednesday. Anyway, no point saying anything. Must be a reason. He heads for the back shop.

Please, Lord. Don't let anybody come through that door for the next five minutes. Alec looks at Irene. She really is a fine-looking woman. He takes a deep breath, digs the wooden pat into the rich yellow mound of butter. 'Eh, did you enjoy the concert at the St Andrew's Halls last Saturday, Miss Pentland?'

Irene gives a smile 'How did you know Ah was there, Alec Stuart?'

This immediately gives him such a good feeling. She often calls him Mr Stuart; less frequently Alec. But there's something about the way she has just pronounced his name. His full name. Sort of the way you would say it if you were kidding on with a friend. C'mon! You will never get a better opportunity. Please! Just give me two, three minutes. He takes a breath, opens his mouth—

'Mr Stuart! Will Ah put fresh sawdust doon?'

Yah wee bugger, Ah'll swing for ye! He must keep calm. Don't want tae shout at the laddie in front of Irene – Miss Pentland. With a major effort of will, Alec remains relaxed; turns. 'Yes, put some down, James.' He smiles. As he does so, there are dark thoughts going through his mind: If you ask me another question, James, or linger in that doorway for any longer than one and a half seconds, Ah will strap you tae that bacon slicer and send ye hame tae your mammy the night in rashers! He turns again to Miss Pentland. 'Eh, aye. Ah was at the concert and happened to spot you, eh, sitting on your own, just as Ah was. Ah actually thought of coming over and asking if you'd mind if we sat together. Just for company, of course. Since my wife passed away a couple of years ago, there's not the same enjoyment going to things – concerts, theatre – when you're on your own.'

For some time now Irene has been aware that Alec Stuart . . . well, likes her. Likes talking to her. As she does him. She decides to be quite brazen. Feels herself blush in advance; thank goodness the lights aren't on in the shop. 'Well you should have done . . . ' there's a fraction of a pause as she decides what to call him, 'Alec. That would have been a pleasant surprise. Ah quite agree with you. Since my brother James got himself married, Ah have to go to most things now unaccompanied. There is most certainly less enjoyment when you are on your own.' She knows this is not quite true. Of late she is out at least once a week, sometimes twice, with new sister-in-law Mary, and Agnes upstairs. But under these circumstances a wee white lie can surely be forgiven.

Alec leans forward confidentially. His moment is at hand. 'Yes, Ah . . . ' There comes the sound of James's tackety boots; he is about to emerge from the back shop. Alec turns his head. The door opens, James is glimpsed. Alec straightens up, thrusts an arm out, points a magisterial, nay, Biblical finger at him. 'In that back shop NOW! And shut the door!' James scuttles out of sight. Alec turns back to Irene. He laughs. 'Miss Pentland. Irene. Ah've been wanting to ask you out for months. Without fail, every time, a customer always comes in.' He nods in the direction of the back shop. 'Today, my trainee seems tae be intent on spoiling things.' He leans forward. 'He doesn't know it, but he's dicing wi' death!'

Irene smiles. She likes this hitherto unseen side of him. She responds. 'Just in case half a dozen folk, ration books in hand, are about to descend on us, yes, Ah'd be very pleased to go to the occasional concert or show with you.'

He places a hand on his heart. 'Oh, Ah'm so glad that is over and done with. Ah was beginning tae think the time would never be right. Great!' He looks at the calendar. 'This is the end of November. Now, starting round about the third week in December, there are some Christmas choral concerts on in the St Andrew's Halls. Would you be—'

Irene interrupts. 'Ah saw the poster. And was thinking of going—'

He cuts in. 'Okay, Ah'll book us a pair of tickets.' As he speaks, he's gathering her purchases together. She opens her bag; he places them inside. 'There's an extra couple of ounces of butter in there.' He keeps a straight face. 'If you'd said no, Ah'd have taken it back!' Irene tuts. Alec takes a breath in;

he feels light-headed. 'I'm just thinking, Miss, ah, Irene. Four weeks seems an awfy long time. Ah don't think Ah can wait that long until Ah take you out. What about, eh, getting some practice in beforehand? Maybe go to a show, or the pictures?'

Irene blushes, but responds to his light-hearted mood. 'Well, that sounds like a good idea to me. Ah would think the pair of us are a bit out of practice at . . . ' She pauses. 'What would they call it at oor age? Would it still be dating?'

'Aye, why not. Anyway, Ah don't mind telling you, Ah feel as dizzy as a schoolboy at the moment. So we *will* say we're going out on a date.'

'That's exactly how Ah feel, Alec.' She giggles. 'It's many a long day since Ah last went out on a date. The years just dropped away when you asked. Ah felt like a lassie again.' They fall silent. Look at each other from opposite sides of the counter in the dark shop. There is a feeling between them. It is tangible. They'll find out later it's known as chemistry.

Alec eventually breaks this meaningful silence. 'Right, Irene.' He already feels comfortable using her name. 'Would you like to have a look in either the *Times* or the *Citizen*, and if there's a good picture or show on doon the toon that you'd like to see, we'll go. Is next week okay?'

'That'll be grand.'

'Now, Ah'm sure you'll be in for your messages next week. But just in case we're busy and we don't get the chance to talk, would you like to ring me at home to tell me where you'd like to go? Be far easier.'

'Oh, what a good idea, Alec.'

'The number's Maryhill 3223. Ah hope that's not putting you to too much trouble. Are you on the phone?'

'No, but there's a box just round the corner. It's no trouble. As you say, we might not get the shop as quiet as this next week. Well.' She lifts her shopping bag. Feels suddenly shy. 'Ah'd better away, Alec. Ah'll no doubt see you – or talk to you – shortly.' She gives him a smile. Her heels sound loud on the sawdust-covered floorboards as she makes for the door.

'Cheerio, Irene.'

She steps out on to the Maryhill Road. It has started to drizzle. It fails to dampen how good she feels. Fifty-two years of age and being asked out on a date! And by someone she's always liked. Things aren't half looking up.

'James! You can come out now.' Tentatively the boy emerges from the back shop. 'Come here, bonny boy.' James edges up to his boss. Alec puts an arm round his shoulder, clasps him to his side, smiles down benignly on him. James has never seen his usually sad boss in such a good mood. Nor in such close proximity. 'Sorry about all that, son. But you came through at the wrong time. Private conversation.' He gives his apprentice a conspiratorial wink – which is quite lost on him. Alec looks at his watch. 'Ten past four. Quiet the day. And it's started tae rain. Go on, get yerself away hame, James. Ye can have an early lowse.' He looks at him as he lets him go. Puts on his best stern face. 'But don't be late in the morning!'

CHAPTER FIFTY

Further Developments

The girls in the office of Macready and Co. watch Rhea's
face as she reads the latest letter from Robert. She folds
it up and returns it to the envelope. Her face says it all.

'How's he gettin' oan?' asks Margaret. Rhea is lost in thought.
'Rhea! How's he gettin' oan?'

'Oh! Ah wiz miles away therr.'

'Aye. In Korea,' suggests Shona.

'God! He hates that bloody place. He says it's the most
godforsaken country in the world. It's jist November and the
temperature huz already been doon tae minus twenty some
nights. And it diz'nae get much warmer during the day. By
next month it'll be even worse. Minus thirty tae forty regularly. And they're dog tired wi' all the driving they're daein'.'
Her voice fades to a mumble as she goes back into her thoughts,
worrying about her love.

The girls look at one another again. Wonder how they can
cheer up the normally bubbly Rhea. Janet tries.

'What was the date of that letter, Rhea?'

She takes it out of the envelope. 'Tenth of November. Why?'

'Things might have got a wee bit better since then. That's twelve days ago. According tae the radio, aw' yon Chink sodjers that came ower the border last month tae help the North Koreans, they seem tae have been withdrawn. Just drifted back north again. The fighting has died doon a lot. He might no' be daeing so much driving by now.'

'Jeez! Ah hope you're right, Janet.'

'Och, aye. That might be them ower the worst. Let's hope so.'

The bell rings. 'Will you get that, darling?' Ruth calls from the kitchen.

'On my way.' George Lockerbie smiles as he steps into the lobby. He can see the distorted reflections of their guests through the stained-glass panel on the door. It's almost six months now since he first met Johnny McKinnon. The night Ruth took him to the Hillhead Bar. He opens the door. 'Johnny! How the devil are you?' He steps to one side. 'Please come in.'

'George! All the better for seeing you.' Johnny gestures for his lady friend to enter first. He follows, then they both wait while their host closes the door. 'George. May I introduce Veronica Shaw. Veronica. George Lockerbie.'

George looks at the attractive brunette. 'Ah'm very pleased to meet you, Veronica.' She smiles and inclines her head as they shake hands.

'I don't know why I associate with this man,' says Johnny. 'Stole the love of my life from me. Snatched her away. Broke my heart – and the hearts of most of the men in Hillhead.'

'He never gives up, does he?' All three turn as Ruth appears at the door to the lounge. She looks svelte in a black-and-white frock, matching jewellery, which includes long, dangling earrings and her usual trademark vivid red lipstick. A Sobranie cigarette sends its pungent smoke up into the air from the end of the tortoiseshell holder. Rita Hayworth would have her work cut out to match such an entrance.

'Ruth, cherie!' Johnny shoves the bottle of wine he's been carrying into George's hands. 'Look after that. Cost nearly ten bob, ye know!' He steps over to Ruth, kisses her on both cheeks. 'How are you, darling?' He doesn't wait for an answer, turns towards Veronica. 'As you can see, at last I've found a beauty to replace you, Ruth Malcolm. I didn't think it possible that Glasgow could produce two such stunners – Hollywood, maybe – but the old home town has risen to the occasion. May I introduce Ruth Malcolm to Veronica Shaw. And vice versa.'

Ruth shakes her head as she offers her hand to Veronica. 'Old silver-tongue strikes again!' She gestures towards the lounge door. 'Please, go through.'

Both Ruth and George are gratified as Veronica becomes the latest in a long line of visitors, stretching back to the thirties and the previous owners, to take two steps into the lounge then stop dead in their tracks. 'Oh my God! This is stunning. Absolutely stunning!' She turns to Ruth. 'Is this Rex Harrison's pied-à-terre when he's in Glasgow? If it isn't, it should be.' They all laugh. The atmosphere immediately becomes light, relaxed. Set fair for the evening.

Ruth stops just before she returns to the kitchen. 'I'm afraid, welcome guests, that my charms just bounced off our butcher. I wasn't able to sweet-talk him into supplying a joint so we could have a proper dinner.' She sighs. 'It'll just have to be sandwiches. At least we've got plenty of vino. And cognac to go with the coffee.'

'Ah, well. All is not lost,' says Johnny.

Johnny McKinnon sits back. 'Now that wasn't bad at all.' He raises a finger. 'However, I must say I was rather disappointed. No Spam sandwiches? Tongue? Yes. Boiled ham? Yes. Any hostess worth her salt knows her table isn't complete without Spam. Has madam never heard of Spam fritters? With chips? You are obviously not a devotee of Elizabeth David!'

Ruth laughs. 'If Elizabeth David heard you mention her name and Spam in the same breath, she'd probably clout you with a tin of it. Anyway, darling. George and I would like to get your opinion on an idea we have. We're thinking of changing direction. Striking out on our own. We really would like to know what you think about it.' She looks at George. He takes a sip of wine.

'Ruth and Ah are of the opinion that this period of austerity, as it's been called, is at last showing signs of coming to an end. There certainly isn't plenty of money around, but from watching the way business is picking up at the Bar Deco, we feel that the number of folk with spare cash available is rising. And these people are looking for somewhere, and something, different. Your Hillhead Bar and the Bar Deco are very much the sort of place they want to relax in with their friends. In a word, classy. Ruth and Ah are of the opinion that the time is right to offer them more. The same atmosphere and ambience we already give them – plus a little extra. The chance to eat. A supper club. Not a full-blown restaurant. Rationing is still too restrictive.'

Ruth lays a hand on George's arm, cuts in. 'We think the

limited menu of a supper club, along the lines of a French brasserie, is possible to lay on nowadays. There are definitely a growing number of folk with money to spend. And a classy night spot with a simple menu – maybe even music and dancing on Friday and Saturday nights – we really do feel the time is right for that. People have put up with a lot these last eleven years. It's time for folk with a bit of spare cash to enjoy themselves after all the years of rationing and belt-tightening. What do you think, Johnny?'

They both watch as Johnny McKinnon swills his brandy round in his glass. Veronica takes the chance to speak.

'I'll just put my ha'p'orth in before Johnny gives you a professional's opinion. I, and my friends, frequent the sort of bars you two run. We're not ones for pubs. Anyway, as you know, pubs in Scottish towns and cities are very much men only. If you're in mixed company you have to find one with a lounge, or go to a hotel. I think there will most definitely be a demand for your supper club idea. I don't know how many times I've been out with friends, we're having a lovely evening in nice surroundings then, as happens, we begin to get rather peckish. What do we do? We either have to go home for something to eat – or find a fish and chip shop! How nice to be able to say to mine host, "We'd like to eat." "Certainly!" Then you're handed a menu. And all the better if it's not an expensive restaurant one, but instead, tasty, afford-able light meals. Omelettes and such like.' She turns to Johnny. 'So there! That's a prospective customer's opinion, for what it's worth.'

Johnny smiles. Looks at his three companions. 'Would you believe, George and Ruth, I haven't got much to add. Your proposal says it all.' Brandy glass in hand, he points at

Veronica. 'And my girl here has obviously wished on many an evening out that she could finish the night in such an establishment.' He sits up in his chair. 'I also very much like the idea of music and, perchance, a little dance floor. A late-night-bistro-cum-nightclub type of ambience. Find the right size of premises – in the right area – and you'll be on a winner. It must be in an upmarket area of Glasgow. You have to make sure it isn't anywhere near, what shall we call it? A working-class district. That's not being snobbish. For example, have it anywhere near, say, Govan or the Gorbals, word will soon get around. "Hey, Ah know where we can get a drink till late oan, efter the pubs shut. C'monnn, let's go!" It really has to be right in the heart of a good area. Otherwise you'll get all the local hard men taking it over as their drinking den. Put all the factors we've been talking about in place – and it'll become *the* place to go! The time is definitely right for it. At last we're beginning to shake off the legacy of the war years. There's a wee bit more money about, and people would like to have somewhere to go for a good night out now and again.'

'Well, let's drink to that!' George pours a cognac for those assembled. The glasses are raised. George looks at Ruth. 'Here's to the future, darling.'

She raises her glass. '*Our* future.'

'And I'm sure Veronica will join me in adding our good wishes,' says Johnny.

'I most certainly will. And I can guarantee I'll not only be one of your first customers, but I'll also be a regular – with my friends in tow. Good luck!'

'Have you been doing any scouting yet for premises?' asks Johnny.

'We have got somewhere in mind,' says Ruth. She turns to her friend. 'And you'll never believe where. If you remember, I took over this flat, furnished as it is now, from my good friends and neighbours, Patrick and Christine Fraser.' She pauses for a moment, turns to Veronica. 'I'll tell you the full story some day, when we get the chance.' She continues. 'If you recall, they had a furniture business in Woodlands Road. Well, the premises are vacant at the moment! Now that is what I call a good omen. It's the right size, in the perfect location. Do you agree about Woodlands Road, Johnny?'

'I certainly do. I would think it will go well there. And I'm sure you'll feel good about carrying on the connection with your friends. Do you have a name yet?'

'We do.' She smiles at George, turns back to their visitors. 'Le Bar Rendezvous.'

'Oh, certainement!' exclaims Johnny.

'Good night.' They watch as their guests leave and start down the stairs. Stand together at the flat door and give a last wave through the banisters until they descend out of sight. Then they quietly close the door. Ruth turns to face George; they put their arms round each other. 'Johnny seems very positive about our idea.'

'Yes. An endorsement from Johnny is worth having. And Veronica, too. She's not in the trade, but she knows what she likes, what she wants. Both very enthusiastic.'

'I'm so glad. Makes me feel it's a good decision. Anyway,' she stands on her toes to kiss him, 'we'll make it work.' She looks into his eyes. 'Together, we're unbeatable, George.'

CHAPTER FIFTY-ONE

Laughter and Tears

Drena's busy making the tea. It's her turn to be hostess. Granny Thomson is already seated at the kitchen table. 'Ye look as if you're well settled in, Drena.'

'Oh, aye. You've nae idea, Granny, Ah jist love huvin' a room and kitchen. Efter all the years in that single-end. We've been in here ower a month noo. When Billy's at work and William's at the school, Ah often go through and jist sit oan the bed and think, this is oor room. But it's best at night. William gets sent tae his bed aboot nine and Billy and me huv the kitchen tae oorselves. We can talk, listen tae the wireless. It's great!'

'It'll no' be long till you're showing, Drena.'

'Aye. Ah'm over three months gone.' She turns to the side, points to the zip at the top of her skirt. 'Ah can barely get this tae fasten. Ah wiz jist saying tae Billy, Ah'll need tae get some maternity wear soon.'

There's a knock on the door. 'Halloooh! It's Irma!'

'Aye, in ye come, hen.'

Granny and Drena turn to watch as Irma comes waddling

in. She is wearing a two-piece maternity outfit. 'Hallooh, ladies.'

'Bye! You're no' half big oan the road, Irma.' Granny reaches a hand out and gently strokes Irma's stomach. 'You're bound tae be jist aboot any time noo.'

'Yah. I would think within two weeks.' With a grunt she sits herself at Drena's table. 'It is nice now that you also live in the close, Drena. Saves me climbing all of those stairs.'

Drena's about to answer, but . . . 'Ah'm here!' Ella Cameron comes bustling in. She carries two paper bags with 'Scotia Bakery' on them. 'Hello, girls.' She looks at Granny. 'Did ye see oor handiwork?' She inclines her head in the direction of one of the walls.

'Aye, Drena was telling me aboot it. Unless ye look close, you'd think the wa' was papered. In't it great how folk think up these ideas?'

'Right! Pass your cups, girls.' Drena starts pouring. 'You dish the cakes oot, Ella.'

'Okaaay. Two custard cakes, pineapple cake . . . ' She looks at Irma. 'Are you on tae the Abernethy biscuits, Irma?'

'Oh, aye. They are braw!' Ella and Drena glance at one another then quickly look away. Drena emits a strange wee noise, but manages to regain control. Ella looks everywhere but at her pal.

'Second cup, anybody?' Drena asks a few minutes later. There's a chorus of 'ayes' from those assembled. Drena does the rounds. 'Huz anybody spoke tae Marjorie Sneddon since she moved back in?'

'Ah had a wee word wi' her roon' the Maryhill Road for five minutes. Telt her we're aw' pleased tae see her back,' says Granny.

'That wiz nice.' Drena stops pouring. ''Course, the trouble wi' Marjorie, she's no' used tae talkin' tae her neighbours. Aw' they years he wiz knockin' her aboot, she hud bruises tae hide. And she wid know that everybody knew he was treatin' her badly. It's amazing how wimmen try tae cover up the fact they've got a bad man. They're embarrassed. It's as if it's their fault.'

Granny sniffs. 'And have ye seen the big lad she's got herself? He's up maist nights o' the week.'

'Aye! In more ways than wan!' says Ella.

'Whitummph.' Drena tries to speak, but chokes on a Gypsy Cream. Granny puts a hand over her cup to deflect the shrapnel-like crumbs.

'Michty me!' says Irma.

'Ah stay above them, mind.' Ella looks imperiously around. She has their full attention. 'He usually brings her back fae her work. They're not in half an hour tae ye can hear them springs goin' like the clappers oan that recess bed. And the squeals oot o' her. Ah very near thocht her man wiz back!'

'Och, well. She's jist making up fur lost time,' says Drena. 'Ye cannae blame her.'

'Makin' up fur loast time? The wye she's going, she'll huv caught up by the end o' next week!'

'You're jist jealous,' says Drena.

'Bloody right Ah am!'

'He's a big fella, the boyfriend,' says Granny. 'Ah've seen him a couple o' times. He's a foreman or something doon at the Fairy Dyes where she works. Ah've an auld freen, Betty Grant, worked in the office wi' Marjorie. She's jist retired. Marjorie's got her job.'

'Eh! Ah'll tell ye,' Ella shakes her head in admiration, 'there's no' much gets past Granny Thomson. And if it diz – it's no' worth knowing!'

'There's an Ingrid Bergman pictur' oan in the Roxy next week,' announces Drena. 'Ah've been at Billy tae take me. Ah like Ingrid Bergman.'

'Huh! Ah'd never go and see another picture o' hers!' Granny sits erect in her chair, literally vibrating with indignation.

'How no'?' enquires Ella. 'Is it 'cause she ran away wi' yon Tally director? Whit's his name?'

'Well it should be aw'right now,' says Drena. 'She's married tae him. Wiz it Rossellini?'

'Mair like Ross's Dairies!'

'It's the fact she left her man *and* her daughter. How could any wumman leave her wean?'

'Maybe her husband was not good to her?' suggests Irma.

'Ah don't think so,' says Granny. 'There was yin reason and yin reason only. And ye's aw' know whit that was!'

'Aye,' interjects Ella. 'She fancied a feed o' the auld Tally sausage!'

'Cricky jings!' gasps Irma, holding her side. 'If I have this baby today, Ella, you are to blame!'

'Oooooh!' For the next few minutes they all, Granny included, are helpless.

Eventually order is restored. Granny pushes herself up on to her feet. 'Well, Ah'm gonny have tae go, girls. If there's another laugh like that, Ah'll finish up peeing ma breeks!'

'Eeee! Zat no' terrible?' says Drena. 'Lowering the tone a bit, therr, Granny.'

Granny looks at her neighbours. 'Lowering the tone, is it?

Lucrezia Borgia could'nae lower the tone if she moved intae this close.'

Drena looks at Ella. 'Who's Lucrezia Thingummy when she's at hame?'

'Ah think she used tae bide in Gairbraid Avenue!' This sets them off again.

'Oh my God! Ah'm no' kidding,' says Granny. 'Ah'm away!' She hobbles off, then, seconds later, reappears. 'Ah'll no' make it! Gie me a lend o' yer lavvy key. Hurry up!'

Yet again, the other three are convulsed. Drena manages to take the key from the hook in the small lobby. Granny heads for the toilet in the close.

Ten minutes later, Ella stretches her arms up in the air. Yawns. 'Well, girls. All good things come to an end. Suppose Ah'd better get roond tae Billy's mother's and collect Katherine. Next thing, Archie wull be back fae the school. Then get big Archie's dinner oan fur him coming in. A wumman's work is never done.'

'Aye, you're right, Ella. Unpaid slavery, so it is. In't that right, Irma?'

'Och, aye!'

Just gone five thirty, Rhea gets on a 23 tram and, as usual, takes a double seat inside the lower saloon. She looks out the window as the car, after one or two jerks, slowly pulls away from the stop. There's a heavy mist, fog really, settling down on to the city streets. She looks at the office buildings opposite. Many lights still burn inside. They illuminate the fog as they shine out. The headlights of cars and vans do the same. Now and again the tram passes a shop or showroom with windows lit. They all seem to accentuate the fog; intensify it.

As the tram pulls away from another stop, a man comes along and sits beside her. Although she doesn't take up a full half of the seat, she still moves nearer the window to make room. He unfolds a newly bought edition of the *Evening Times*; looks at the headlines. Rhea glances at them from the corner of her eye: 'Chinese Forces Storm Over Border Into North Korea'. The sub-headline says: 'UN: This is a major attack! Many divisions backed by tanks and planes.'

'Oh my God!' Rhea's hand goes to her mouth. She can feel the texture of her woollen glove against her lips.

The man looks at her. 'Are you all right, hen?'

'Ma boyfriend's oot therr. He's daeing his two years.' She feels faint. Dizzy.

'Oh. This took place during the night. The night over there. Aboot four o'clock in the mornin'. Ah listened tae the news on the radio before Ah left the office.' He wonders how much he should tell her. 'The, ah, UN forces are sort of pulling back.' He resumes reading his paper.

Rhea sits, pale, shocked, her mind in turmoil as she tries to picture what it must be like for Robert at this very moment. She is sitting on a tram as it takes her through a foggy Glasgow. So many times they've sat together on nights like this. She cannot grasp, cannot imagine, what is happening to him. *Why* is it happening to him? The only guide to what it must be like is scenes from the many war films they've watched. She knows it will be worse. Twenty times worse. His descriptions of Korea in his letters come to her. It'll probably be snowy, icy, bitter cold. If the UN is retreating, is he being shot at? Bombed? Is he maybe a prisoner? Is he maybe . . .

Twenty minutes later she comes running into the house. She's bought a *Times* at Ken's shop on the corner. 'Oh, Ma!

Da! There's a big battle goin' on in Korea. Robert's in the middle of it. Anything could be happenin' tae him!' She breaks down, crying uncontrollably.

Teresa and Dennis O'Malley can only comfort her as they try to calm her down and make sense of what's upsetting her. Mercifully, Siobhan arrives home a few minutes later. Teresa points to the newspaper headline, then at Rhea. 'In the name o' God, Siobhan, do ye know what's going on wit' this child?'

Siobhan goes over to her sister, puts an arm round her shoulder. 'Ah think we'll have tae tell Mammy and Daddy. Dae ye want me tae tell them?'

Rhea nods. 'Aye.' She dissolves into tears again.

And this is how Teresa and Dennis O'Malley find out that their eldest daughter is in love, and has been engaged to Robert Stewart from downstairs for almost a year. And now they know why she came home from work in such a state. Because, thousands of miles from home, Robert Stewart is almost certainly in danger. Mortal danger.

CHAPTER FIFTY-TWO

Life Goes On

Teresa O'Malley now and again shoots little glances at Rhea. Her daughter sits at the table, hands clasped in her lap. Thoughts far away. 'Eat yer toast, darlin'.'

'Ah'm no' hungry, Ma.'

'Well at least drink yer tay. You'll need sumtin' warm inside ye 'fore ye venture outside that door.' Teresa looks out the window. She can barely see the tenements opposite. She only knows they're there because folk have their lights on. The fire burns brightly in the range. Even so, the far corners of the small kitchen are chilly. 'Jayz, it's like a stepmother's breath out there.' The cold strikes through the window as though trying to get at her. 'Ye don't have to go to yer work if ye don't want to, Rhea.'

'Oh, God! Ah don't want tae stay off ma work, Ma. Ah'm better in the office, amongst the lassies, keepin' busy. If Ah wiz in here oan ma own, Ah'd go demented. Nuthin' tae dae but worry aboot Robert.'

'Aye, yer probably right. And wit' all them ructions going on over there, heaven knows when you'll get a letter t' put yer mind at rest.'

'Ah know.' Rhea sips her tea.

'And yer sure ye don't want t' let the Stewarts know about you and Robert?'

For a moment, Rhea comes out of her doldrums. 'Ma! Now this is important. Robert and me don't want tae tell them till Robert's finished wi' the army and is back at his job. Okay? Ye must'nae say anything tae anybody. Nane o' the neighbours. And think aboot it. Mr and Mrs Stewart huv enough worries withoot finding oot their Protestant son is engaged tae a Catholic lassie. They've got enough oan their plate at the minute. Dae ye no' think so?'

'Well if they did find out, I don't t'ink it would upset them as much as—'

'Ma! If the Stewarts get tae know and Ah find oot it came fae you, Ah'll never forgive ye. Ah'm serious! Ah'll never, ever forgive ye. Robert and me will dae it when the time's right.'

'Okay, okay. Jayz! I'm just trying t' help.'

Five minutes later, Rhea steps out of the close at 18 Dalbeattie Street. Within three steps the freezing fog strikes through her coat and scarf, into her shoulders. She shivers. Jesus wept! Look at it. The fog is green. Acrid. She feels it catch at her throat. She raises a gloved hand and pulls part of the scarf up to cover her nose and mouth.

On reaching the Maryhill Road, she stands on the edge of the pavement. Visibility is, maybe, five yards. She listens carefully, looks to left and right. There are definitely nae trams coming. Ye can hear them. It's cars and lorries. All senses straining, she decides the time is right, steps out into the road. She stops in the middle, between the two sets of tramlines, listens again, then dashes for the other side. She makes her way along the few yards of pavement until the queue, a grey mass lumped together at the stop, becomes human. She tags on to the end of it. The person in front turns. She too holds her scarf over her mouth and nose, a heavy-knit woollen hat pulled over her ears 'Hello, Rhea,' comes a muffled voice.

'Zat you, Mary?' It's a girl who goes to the same chapel as the O'Malleys.

'Aye.'

'Is this no' scabby awful! Look at the colour of it. It's bloody green. Nae wonder they call them peasoupers.'

'Ah know. It's no' half going for ma granny's chest. She's got bronchitis. Jist cannae get her breath this morning. It's really frightening watching the auld sowel.'

'Aye. It must be. It even gets tae us. Ah don't smoke, but Ah can still feel it goin' fur ma throat and chest.' Rhea sniffs. 'And this time o' the year, withoot fail, when yer at the pictures, they alwiz huv a wee bit oan the newsreel aboot London huvin' a peasouper.' She laughs. 'Ye'd think naebody else gets fogs except London. Want tae take a wander up tae Glesga wan o' these years wi' thurr cameras!'

'Aye. Oh! Here's a caur.' They watch as the tram looms out of a bank of solid fog. Its lights, upstairs and down, manage to shine out for about six feet. These lights, aided and abetted by the condensation on the windows, give a diffused, out-of-focus glow to everything inside. Those at the stop surge forward, anxious to enter. To escape the winter even if only for fifteen minutes.

The post is late this morning. It's after one o'clock when Macready and Co. take delivery. As Janet comes into the office carrying the bundle, Rhea watches her every move. Janet sorts through it right away. 'Here ye are! One for you, Rhea.'

She hands it to her. The four girls all watch as Rhea tears the envelope open and extracts the letter. She looks at the date, sits back in her chair, shakes her head 'It's no' gonny be much help. He wrote it oan the twenty-second of November. That's before the Chinese attacked.' She reads through it fairly quickly. Again shakes her head. 'Naw, it diz'nae tell me anything. Listen tae this.' She begins to read. 'This is the quietest it's been since the Chinks attacked over the border at the end of October. Our intelligence guys are quite confident they've disengaged and withdrawn back into China. For the first time in nearly a month we're getting some rest. We spent three days at a Yank R&R camp (Rest and Relaxation). Gee! They certainly look after their boys – I don't care if the censor doesn't like this – it's TRUE! Good food, and plenty of it. Lots of hot water for taking a spray – they call them showers. And we went to the camp cinema two nights on the trot. Not that we saw much of the movies. We were so bloody tired that, sitting in the dark watching the films, we kept falling asleep! I've definitely recharged my batteries. And the fact that things aren't so hectic at the moment means we are all feeling good.' Rhea looks up. Her eyes glisten. She tries to speak, but can't.

Elsie fills the gap. 'Och well, Rhea. That was the twenty-second of November. This is the start o' December. You know he was fit and well rested afore aw' the trouble started up again. So Ah'm sure he'd be ready tae look efter himself.'

Rhea nods. 'Aye, Ah hope sae.'

It's later the same day. Nearly six thirty. Agnes Dalrymple is climbing the stairs. She sets foot on the second storey and pauses for a moment to get her breath. She knocks on Irene Pentland's door, doesn't bother trying the door handle. Irene very rarely has the snib down on the Yale. She hears footsteps and music from the wireless as the kitchen door is opened. The front door opens. 'Oh hello, Agnes.'

'Ah thocht Ah'd gie ye a wee knock, Irene. Jist wondered if ye fancy going tae the pictures either the night or the morra night?'

Irene opens the door wide. 'C'mon in a minute. Have ye time for a wee cup of tea?'

'Well Ah'm jist hame fae ma work . . .'

'Ah, but Ah've something tae tell ye. A bit o' news.'

'Oh, well. Jist fur ten minutes.' Agnes steps into Irene's kitchen. She still isn't quite used to going in and out of the Pentlands'. When James was here, visits from neighbours were . . . well, maybe not frowned on. But certainly not encouraged.

'That fog isn't half hanging about. Ah was pleased to get back from the shops this afternoon.'

'It's bloody awful. See going tae work this morning? Terrible! And it diz'nae half go fur yer throat.' Agnes puts her bag on the table, delves into it. 'Here's a chocolate Swiss roll, Irene.' She places it on the table.

'Are ye sure?'

'Irene. Ah get them fur nuthin'.'

'Thanks very much. Sit yourself down. Whit's on at the pictures?'

'Well, baith the Star and the Roxy huv good—'

'Oh, I'd rather not go tae the Star. Wi' them having that tin roof, at this time of year it's always freezing in there. Ye could hang beef! And as ye know, if it starts tae rain, ye cannae hear a word they're saying for it battering off the corrugated iron!'

Agnes starts to laugh.

Irene does too, even though she doesn't know what has set Agnes off. 'Why ever are ye laughing?'

Agnes tries to control herself. 'It wiz the wye that ye said that. You sounded so refained – so Kelvinside.' She goes into another fit, then, 'Ah expected ye tae finish up saying, "It's enough to give one the boke!" ' The two of them go into kinks.

Irene wipes her eyes, then pours the tea. 'Do you want a couple of pieces of your Swiss roll?'

'Naw thanks, Irene. Ah never eat between meals. Anywye, it's foosty!' Yet again they both go helpless. Agnes eventually manages to say, 'Naw, it iz'nae. It wiz fresh made this morning.'

Order is restored once more. 'So what is on at the Roxy?' asks Irene.

'It's called *Cage of Gold*. Jean Simmons and David Farrar are in it.'

'Whit's it about?'

'It's a murder mystery type o' thing. Supposed tae be quite good.'

'Och well, that'll do us, Agnes. And the Roxy's no' very far. We can walk it.'

'But remember, we'll huv tae sit halfway doon. Huv ye ever been in the Roxy oan a foggy night?' She doesn't wait for an answer. 'Wi' it being such a big hall, the fog must seep intae it during the day. Then, wi' all the folk smoking during the show, if ye sit in the back stalls, halfwye through the show ye cannae see the screen for reek!' Yet again this is enough to set the two of them off.

'Eeeh, Agnes. Ah'm awful glad you suggested having a night out now and again. Even when you jist come in for a cup o' tea, you fairly brighten up ma day.'

'Right! Well that's the pictures sorted. So whit's yer news?'

Irene takes a sip of tea, then leans confidentially in the direction of Agnes. 'Ye know Alec Stuart, the manager in Andrew Cochrane's? The branch jist doon the Maryhill Road? It's the other side of the road from the Star, actually.'

'That's the one Ah use maself. Ah jist know him as Alec, did'nae know it wiz Stuart.'

'He's asked me to step out with him now and again. Concerts. Maybe the theatre.'

'Eeeeh! Irene Pentland. Ah'm tellin' ye. You're a wanton wumman, so ye are! It's gonny finish up you'll never be in. Yer sister-in-law Mary asks ye oot noo and again. Ah ask ye oot. Noo there's a fella in yer life . . . ' All of a sudden Agnes falls silent. Her eyes brim with tears. 'Ah'm gonny finish up being on ma own. Jist when you and me wiz gettin' tae be really good pals. Regular cups o' tea in wan another's hooses. Huvin' a rerr laugh. Huvin' nights oot. Ah've never had such a good friend since Ah wiz in the Land Army. Ah know whit's gonny happen – you'll be gettin' yerself married and movin' away and Ah'll be left . . . '

Irene takes her hand. 'Agnes, don't be daft. That's the furthest thing from my mind.' But as she says it, she is honest enough to admit the thought: is it?

CHAPTER FIFTY-THREE

A Lucky Break?

D rena knocks Ella's door, opens it, shouts, 'It's jist me!' all in one flowing movement. There is no reply. Yet she can hear a noise. She opens the kitchen door. Ella is on the far side of the room by the sink. She is bent double, her upper body out of sight deep inside the coal bunker as she scrapes its floor.

'It's me, Ella.'

'Aye, in ye come.' Ella's voice is muffled. She continues her task for another minute. Then emerges; straightens up. 'Phew!' She wipes her brow.

Drena sings, 'Don't go down in the mines, Dad, there's plenty of coal in the bunker!'

'Aye, but the bloody trouble is – there is'nae. Ah've been using the wee shovel tae scrape the gether every last iota of dross Ah can find. Try and get enough tae have a fire the night.'

'Och, well,' says Drena. 'Christy should be roon' the morra so ye can get a bag o' coal.'

'Naw Ah cannae. Ah'm skint! Ah've got enough tae keep

us eating till he gives me his wages on Friday. But that's it. Ah huv'nae enough for coal as well.'

'Jeez-oh! Is Archie still on flat time?'

'Aye. Nae overtime, nae bonus. Wi' two bairns it's no' enough. Ah'm gonny huv tae go up tae the pawnshop this efternin. An' we've only got three things the pawn will take. Ma engagement ring, his watch, or the wireless. The wireless will be the last tae go.'

'As it's aw' his fault 'cause he'll no' let ye take a job, pawn his watch first,' suggests Drena.

'Aw, Ah could'nae dae that.'

'Huh! Don't see why not.'

''Cause Ah hocked it last Tuesday!'

'Ah can let ye have a bucket of coal, Ella, and one o' coke. Yon two lads were roon' last week selling bags of coke off their cart. If ye mix it wi' the coal it diz'nae half make it last.'

The two of them sit at the table. 'Want a couple of Digestives? It'll need tae be margarine on them. The butter's ran oot.'

'Aye. Ah'll huv a wee bit jam as well. Kill the taste o' the margarine.'

Drena takes a flimsy Woodbine packet out of her apron pocket. 'Ye want yin?'

'Naw thanks. Ah'll have a couple of draws of yours later on.'

They sit in companionable silence for a while. Wordlessly, Ella holds two fingers out. Drena places her half-smoked cigarette between them. She watches her friend take a deep draw.

'Ah'm no' kidding, Drena, we jist cannae manage when he's on flat time. If this carries on for another month we'll huv pawned everything pawnable. Noo the weans are at the school there's nothing tae stop me taking a job doon at Cakeland.

Even jist part-time. Confectioners make good money. But he'll not bloody bend.' She sighs.

Drena places her cup down on the floral oilcloth. 'He's eventually gonny huv tae see sense, Ella. If he comes hame wan night and there's nae dinner waiting, he might get the message.'

'Aye.' Ella nods her head and winks. 'Well that'll happen sooner rather than later. Ah wiz at him again the other night aboot lettin' me go tae work. He jist gave me the usual shite: "There's nae wife o' mine gonny have tae take a job." Ah says tae him, "Is that right? Well Ah'll tell ye whit else your wife is'nae gonny dae. When we run oot o' money I am not going intae the local shops tae ask for tick. There's no wye we are gonny get intae loads o' debt." So Ah don't think he wiz ower pleased.' Ella sits back, shoulders square. Defiant.

'He hud a wee bit of an excuse when ye still had Katherine at hame. But noo she's at the school—'

Ella cuts in. 'Ah know. Morning and efternin Ah'm sitting in here twiddling ma bloody thumbs. Nothing tae do until Ah pick the wee yin up at the school . . . Ach!' She becomes speechless with frustration.

'He's gonny have tae give in, Ella. If that factory of his diz'nae get any more orders in and he's no' getting any bonus or overtime, he'll eventually realise you will have tae go tae work tae help oot.' She pauses, thinking. 'You should pawn the wireless the day. A few evenings withoot any entertainment might begin tae wear him doon.'

Ella sniffs. 'Well, he'd miss the wireless right enough. But if the weans are in bed and there's jist him and me sitting in the kitchen, and he's wondering what he can do tae pass the time, the ans—' She breaks off as she goes into a fit of laughter. Drena anticipates the end of the sentence, and as she watches her friend become helpless, is also infected. It takes Ella three attempts before she supplies the expected punchline. 'If he's wondering what he can do tae pass the time, the answer will probably be – ME!'

It's a few days into December. An afternoon. Ella sits darning a pair of Archie junior's school socks. He has to wear the long navy blue ones with the two white hoops at the top. They're also worn for the Boys' Brigade parades at the church hall. She is startled by a loud knock at the door. It isn't followed by it being opened and the visitor calling out who it is. Darning still in hand, she makes her way to the door, opens it. There's no mistaking the silhouette of a policeman. Her hand goes to her mouth. Oh my God!

'Mrs Cameron?'

'Aye. Whit's the matter?'

He places a reassuring hand on her forearm. 'Now don't get up tae high doh. Your man's had a wee accident at work. He slipped and broke a leg.' He pauses. 'Ah think they said the right yin. He's doon at the Western at the minute getting it plastered.'

'Oh my God! Aye, right, Ah'd better make ma way doon. Tram tae St George's Cross, subway ower tae Partick. Right. Ah'll huv tae get ma pal tae pick up the wee yin at the school. Archie junior comes hame on his own. Right! Ah'll get ma coat. Better make sure Ah've got ma keys and ma purse.' She looks at the policeman. 'Can ye think of anything else?'

'Just one.' He places his hand on her forearm again. 'Take a few deep breaths, calm yerself. It's just one of these things that happens tae folk every day. It's an accident at work. He's going to have his leg in plaster for a few weeks. In a few hours he'll be back home with you, sitting having his dinner, listening to the wireless . . . '

'He'll huv a bloody job,' says Ella. 'It's in the pawn!'

Forty-five minutes later, a nurse pulls a screen to the side. Archie looks up, somewhat sheepishly, from where he lies on a trolley. 'Aw, hello, hen. Is this no' a bloody game, eh?'

'Oh, Archie. When the polis came tae the door, Ah nearly dropped at his feet.' She goes to his side. Kisses him, hugs him. 'Is it a bad break?'

'The doctor says it's clean. Straightforward. They should be coming for me any minute tae take me doon tae where they put the stookie on. Then once it's set they're gonny run us hame in an ambulance.'

She takes his hand. 'Oh well. At least Ah'll get a wee hurl in the ambulance. So whit happened? How did ye dae it?'

He shakes his head. 'Dead bloody simple. Ah must have spilt some oil on the floor next tae ma lathe. Ah jist took a few steps and slipped, exactly the way ye slip on ice. Ma two feet went up in the air and doon Ah came. Oh!' He shivers. 'Ye should have heard the crack, Ella. It's an awfy sound when ye hear one o' your bones break. A real sickener, so it is.'

'Oh, ma poor Archie!' She gives him another hug and kiss. 'Anywye, we'll soon have ye hame. Though mind, Katherine will think it's great. Ye know how she loves playing at nurses. Ah've nae doubt you'll be her personal patient. By the end of the week she'll huv ye looking like "The Mummy".'

Archie manages a laugh. The screens are drawn aside. Two nurses enter.

'Mr Cameron? We'll take you down now and get your plaster put on.'

It's next morning. Ella awakens. She turns her head. Archie lies next to her in the recess bed, seems to be sleeping. She raises her head to look past him, see the clock on the table. Nearly six thirty. Och, Ah'll have another twenty minutes. She snuggles in, rests her head against his shoulder.

'Ah'm wakened, Ella.'

'Oh. How are ye this morning? Is your leg hurtin'?'

'Naw, it's no' bad. Ah'll tell ye whit, though. Having yer leg in stookie takes some getting used tae. Jeez! Ah don't know how many times Ah sort of half wakened, went tae turn on ma side forgetting Ah've got a stookie on – the weight of it! Ah turn, but ma leg diz'nae. The pain!'

'Awww! Ma poor man.' She kisses him on the cheek. 'Well, Ah suppose Ah'd better get up and start gettin' the weans—'

Archie stretches his arm over her. 'Jist lie still for a wee minute, Ella. Ah've been lying here for the last half-hour or so, having a wee think tae maself.' He clears his throat. 'Now, ye know what Ah'm like whenever you mention mibbe taking a wee job—'

Ella interrupts. 'Well ye do realise, Archie, we're never gonny mana—'

'Jist let me finish, hen. Noo, as you well know, we're no' quite scraping by at the minute 'cause Ah'm just on my basic. Well, even before ma accident, Ah was getting tae realise Ah'm gonny have tae let ye take a wee job. At the very least, part-time.' He can see she is dying to speak. He gives her a kiss on the forehead. 'Content yerself for a minute. Ah'm nearly finished. Now, as we know, Ah'm gonny be off work for at least six weeks – on half pay. At the minute we cannae manage on full pay, because there's nae bonus or overtime tae top it up. So there's no way we'll get by oan half wages.' He turns, looks at her. 'It's just plain common sense. Ah think you'd better go and see that auld gaffer of yours doon at Cakeland. Otherwise the four of us are gonny starve tae death!' He looks at her again.

'Oh, Archie. Thank God! When Ah was travelling ower tae the Western yesterday, Ah was thinking tae maself, Archie's gonny just be on half pay while he's on the sick. He'll have tae let me take a job, otherwise we'll finish up in a load o' debt.' She sits up in bed. 'Right. Ah'll go doon tae see auld Sam this morning. He'll definitely gie me a start. Especially as it's nearly Christmas. They'll be run aff their feet at the minute. They never huv enough confectioners.'

It's the afternoon of the same day. Ella climbs the stairs carrying a half-full message bag. She gets to the first landing, then stops. 'Bugger it!' She turns and wearily retraces her steps back down to the close. Knocks Drena's door and opens it. 'Are ye in, Drena?'

'Aye, in ye come.' As she enters, Drena turns. 'Ah thought Ah heard you go up the stairs just then, Ella.'

'Ye did. Force o' habit. It's five or six weeks since you moved doon tae the close. But Ah'm still no' used tae the idea ye don't live two-up any mair. If my mind's on other things Ah jist walk past your door withoot thinking.' She places her message bag against the leg of a chair.

'How's Archie?' asks Drena.

'He's fine.' Ella sits down. 'You'll be making tea, won't ye?'

'Of course Ah'm gonny make tea. Gie's a minute, will ye!'

Five minutes later the tea has been poured, and Drena's two biscuit tins lie on the table, lids off. She regards Ella.

'Well, come on. Don't drag it oot!' She watches impatiently as Ella selects a Rich Tea, dips it in her cup, takes a bite. 'Jesus sufferin'!'

Ella smiles. 'Ah saw Sam Costigan an hour ago. Ah start the morn's morn at seven o'clock.'

'Great!' Drena pauses. 'Ah thought bakers started really early. Four o'clock or something?'

Ella tuts, shakes her head. 'I am not a baker, pal. Try and remember. I . . .' she gives a discreet cough, 'am a confectioner!'

'Ohhh! Excuse me, chocolate knickers! Anywye,' says Drena, 'things should be aw'right while Archie's off work. He'll be there for the weans. And if he diz'nae feel like going tae pick up Katherine at the school, Ah can dae it. Archie junior's okay, he comes hame wi' his pals.'

'Lena says she'll help oot. Actually, Drena, Ah think Lena would be happy if they came tae her for an hour efter school. She loves weans, as ye know. And since she lost Andra, Ah think she'd like nothing better than tae huv them roon' her feet every day. Something tae look forward tae.'

'Oh, that's a good idea, Ella. Aye, let them go tae Lena's every day. She'll enjoy that. And ye know you've always got me in an emergency if, for any reason, Lena's no' able tae take them.' She reaches for the tea-strainer, fills both their cups. 'Is Archie gonny be able tae go tae the school tae meet Katherine while he's on crutches?'

'Och, aye. It's no' far tae go.' She takes a sip of tea. 'And Ah'll tell ye something else, Drena. Now that at last he's let me take a job, Ah'll take a bet with ye. When he starts back at Howdens, he'll no' say a word aboot me packing in. Anywye, Ah'm telling ye, Drena. Now that Ah've started, there is no way Ah'm going back tae trying tae live on one pay packet. Archie knows his wage is'nae enough for four of us. Jist you wait. Ah bet ye he turns a blind eye, lets me carry on.' She raises her cup. 'Cakeland for ever!'

CHAPTER FIFTY-FOUR

No News Is What?

A telegram boy cycling into a street on his Post Office bike is often bad news. To open your door and find a young lad, complete with GPO uniform and pillbox hat, standing on your step is enough to give the stoutest heart a stab of fear. So it is for Mary Stewart on the afternoon of the 16th of December when, as they say, 'a loud knock comes at the door'. Mary opens it. All the ingredients are there. Standing in the shadowy close looms a figure wearing a pillbox hat. Oh, Jesus God! A telegram boy! 'Good morning. Mrs Stewart?'

Mary can only nod. She watches in dread as he reaches into the leather pouch attached to his GPO belt and hands her the buff-coloured envelope. As he's been trained to do, he asks, 'Will there be a reply?'

Mary looks at the envelope in her hand. She knows she won't be able to open it here and now. Probably won't be able to open it at all. What if it contains the baddest of bad news? Sam won't be home for a few hours yet. Oh my God! The laddie stands looking at her. Waiting. It takes her two attempts to say, 'No reply, son.' On the first her voice comes out as a gasp. The second is just audible. The boy lingers for a moment longer. She wonders why. Then he says, 'Okay, missus. Thank you.' She watches him leave.

She wanders into the kitchen, her mind in turmoil, then from some lucid area of her brain comes the thought – you should have tipped the laddie! In the films, telegram boys always get sixpence. Maybe even a shilling. She grabs her purse and runs out to the close mouth. He's gone. She feels bad about that. If you'd tipped him there wouldn't be bad news in here. Should she put her coat on and go straight to the Post Office and leave a tip for him? What a stupid thought. She walks slowly back into the house, the unopened telegram still in her hand, sits down at the kitchen table and bursts into tears.

Five minutes later there's a knock at Granny Thomson's door. She has her coat on and is about to go round to the Maryhill Road. As usual, her visitor opens the outside door and announces herself. 'It's Mary Stewart, Bella.'

'In ye come, Mary.'

One glance is all Granny needs to work out why she is here. Mary's pale face, the red-rimmed eyes, the telegram clutched in her hand. Ye dinnae need tae be Sherlock Holmes.

'Bella, you'll have tae open this for me. Ah cannae dae it!'

The blackened kettle stands with about a third of its bottom over the fire glowing in the range. It's enough to keep it singing. 'The kettle's bileing, Mary. Sit yersel doon.'

The tea is made and poured. 'Right! Let's see whit this is aw' aboot.' Granny uses a table knife to open the envelope. She extracts and unfolds the telegram. Eyes wide open, heart beating nineteen to the dozen, Mary Stewart watches her every move.

'He's been officially listed as "missing in action".'

'Oh my God! Oh, ma boy! Oh, Bella! Whit'll we dae?'

'First of aw' you'll huv a dash o' whisky in that tea. Purely medicinal.' Granny rises from the table, opens the sideboard cupboard and takes out a bottle of Haig's Dimple. She pours a generous measure into Mary's cup, pauses, then puts a smaller amount into her own. She takes Mary's left hand between both of hers, strokes it. 'Mary. He's missing. Ye can get a telegram that says "missing presumed killed". Ye hav'nae got one o' them. He's missing. He might be cut aff behind enemy lines. There's a chance he's got separated fae his unit. He could even be a POW. Don't take it oan yersel' tae think the worst. Ye know whit they say – "Nae news is good news."' Even as she says that, she recalls the number of times she's thought to herself what a stupid saying that is! But if it gives any comfort to Mary, who cares?

When Mary Stewart leaves to go back downstairs, Granny knows her next job will be to tell Rhea O'Malley the bad news. Rhea has told Granny that her mammy and daddy now know about her and Robert. But no one else does. And no one else must get to know. Not yet.

It's just after six when Rhea – Robert not far from her thoughts as usual – arrives home from work. Just as she sets foot on the landing, Granny's door opens. Teresa O'Malley has also heard her daughter's footsteps, and at the same instant opens her door. She is faced with Granny about to speak to Rhea. 'Ah, Teresa. Ah'm about to tell your Rhea something. You'd better come in as well.'

'It'll have t' be quick, Granny. Sure and I've got the dinner on at the minute.'

'In ye's come.' They walk into the single-end. 'Right, Ah'll no' offer ye's a seat. Ah'll get straight tae the point. Ah've jist had Mary Stewart up wi' a telegram.' Granny stops as she sees Rhea visibly stiffen. She reaches a hand out to her. 'Don't worry, hen. Whit it is, Robert has been listed as missing . . .'

'Oh God! Ah cannae take much mair o' this!' Rhea takes a few steps and sits down on one of the kitchen chairs. 'Whit diz that mean?'

'Things are aw' confused oot there at the minute, Rhea. Oor sodjers are scattered aw' ower the place. It just means they don't know where he – and probably some o' his mates – they don't know where they are. So,' Granny shrugs her shoulders, 'they have tae list them as missing. He's mibbe been taken prisoner. He could be anywhere.'

Rhea looks up. She's gone pale. White. 'He could be deid!'

Two days later, a khaki-coloured staff car pulls up at 18 Dalbeattie Street. A captain, sent from Maryhill Barracks, knocks on the Stewarts' door. Samuel answers. As quickly as possible, the young officer tries to put him at his ease 'Don't worry, Mr Stewart. It's not bad news. I'm Captain Fraser. Fourth battalion HLI. Stationed at Maryhill Barracks. I've been asked by your son's unit to come and explain to you what is, or isn't, going on at the moment.'

'Oh, eh, aye. Aye, in ye come, Captain.' Samuel introduces Mary. 'This is Robert's mother.'

While Mary bustles around brewing tea, the three of them make rather stilted small talk. Five minutes later they sit down at the kitchen table. The Stewarts begin to relax. Sam admires the medal ribbons on the young man's battledress; almost two full rows. 'Looks like you've been around a bit, Captain.'

As all heroes should be, the captain is reticent. 'Oh, aye. I've seen the sights. Anyway. I've been asked to give you an idea of what's going on over in Korea at the moment. Since the Chinese came storming over the border nearly three weeks ago, I'm afraid it's all pretty hectic. To be honest, chaos. We estimate something like three hundred thousand Chinese troops were involved. They not only caught us on the hop, but they seriously outnumbered us. As you'll know from the papers and the radio, they went through our front like a dose of salts! They got in behind us and broke our lines up. In spite of some heroic rearguard actions, there were just too many of them. Our lads were broken up everywhere into piecemeal units. As you'll have read, we've been trying to carry out an orderly retreat back towards the capital, Seoul. In some areas it's being done as it should be, a slow, deliberate fighting retreat. In other places we've been so outnumbered, our boys are falling back in not very good order.' He stops while a second cup of tea is poured. 'Your son, Lance Corporal Stewart, as certain as his unit can be, was driving supplies up round the Chosin area when the attack came in. So far there's been no word from the convoy he was a part of. Now, what I'm about to say to you is not, I assure you, just something to try and make you feel better. Every day individual lads, others in pairs or groups, are turning up in our lines. Every day! They were all scattered to the four winds during the first few days of the Chinese offensive. Most of them were cut off behind enemy lines. But they managed to get back. Large numbers of them were wandering about, well away from the Chinese forces, trying to find a gap in the front. When they do, they cross through these gaps at night and get themselves back to our side. With Robert being a driver rather than an infantryman, there's a good chance he'll be one of the many who've been cut off – or he may simply have been taken prisoner. If he is a POW, it'll be ages before the enemy take it on themselves to let us know who they've got. It won't be until well after all the fighting's died down.' He smiles. 'So there you are. It's still chaotic out there, but there really is a very good chance he'll turn up. Either as a POW or by getting himself, along with a few of his mates, back to our lines under his own steam. There's plenty of hope yet. Believe me.'

The Stewarts are greatly comforted by the visit of Captain Fraser. 'Ah'm away up the stairs tae tell Granny,' says Mary. She knows Granny will spread the news to their neighbours and she's quite happy for her to do so.

After Mary Stewart has come up to tell her of the visit of the young officer from Maryhill Barracks, Granny again wants to bring Rhea up to date. As the time nears six o'clock, she keeps an ear open for the familiar footsteps. When she hears them, she opens her outside door.

'Rhea, ah've got a wee bit news for ye, hen.' She stands aside to let her enter.

'Jeez, Ah hope it's good news, Granny.'

'Well, it's certainly no' bad news. It's something that mibbe will make ye realise there's still plenty of hope. An officer fae Maryhill Barracks came tae visit the Stewarts the day. Mary came up tae see me as soon as he'd gone. This is whit he told them . . . '

'So there ye are, Rhea. It's still aw' very harum-scarum oot in that Korea at the minute. But he thinks there's a chance Robert might still be oan the wander oot there. At worst he might be a prisoner. At best he could still be trying tae find

a way through the enemy lines back tae his ain. Mary says
the officer wasn't trying tae say things jist tae make it sound
hopeful. He was quite definite. There are boys finding their
way back tae their ain lines every day in the week.'

Rhea sits back in her chair. 'Ah so hope that's true, Granny.
At the minute Ah'd quite happily settle fur him being a prisoner. As long as Ah know he'll be coming back tae me someday.'
She looks at her friend. 'Ah try no' tae think aboot it, but it
keeps coming intae ma heid. Whit wid it be like if Ah wiz
told Robert wiz deid? Ah cannae bear tae think aboot it – yet
Ah cannae stop it comin' intae ma mind, Granny. Ah'll die
of a broken heart if ma Robert diz'nae come back tae me.'
As they sit looking at each other, tears come into their eyes.
Granny leans forward and puts both arms round Rhea. Rhea
lays her head on Granny's shoulder. Granny gently rubs her
back. 'Wheesh, hen. Wheesh.' Then she sits up straight, but
keeps her arms outstretched, holding Rhea by both shoulders. She looks into her eyes. 'Dinnae worry. He'll be back.
Robert will get back hame.'

CHAPTER FIFTY-FIVE

Christmas Is a' Coming

'Huv ye got aw' yer presents in fur the weans, Ella?' As Drena speaks, she's sitting at the table cleaning sprouts and nicking a neat cross into the base of each.

'Aye. Hud them in fur nearly a month.'

'Aye, me tae. Whit urr ye gettin' Archie senior?'

'Och, jist the usual. A new pullover – he's needin' wan. Two perr a socks and hankies. That's aboot it. Practical presents.'

'Ah'm gettin' Billy a new perr o' shoes an' a trench coat.'

'You'd hardly get him an auld perr o' shoes!'

'Well, ye know whit Ah mean.' Drena nods towards Irma. 'Ye know whit Irma's gettin' Bert?'

'Jings!' says Irma, her interest aroused. She can't recall telling Drena what she's buying Bert.

'Naw,' says Ella. 'Whit's she gettin' him?'

'Either a . . .' Drena stops as she begins to shake with silent laughter. The other two are well used to this. They look at each other, then back at Drena.

'Wur waitin,' says Ella.

Drena seems to be regaining control of herself. She clears her throat. 'Ahumpff! She's gettin' him either . . . ' Again she breaks down, this time joined by her two companions. Finally, by a major act of will, Drena is able to start her sentence. 'She's gettin' Bert either a *Broons* or an *Oor Wullie* annual so's he can understaun' whit . . . ' Once more she can't finish. Ella now gets the joke, goes weak with laughter. They both look at Irma.

Although laughing – mostly at her two friends – Irma is looking nonplussed, doesn't get it. This causes Drena and Ella to go into further paroxysms. 'Ooooooh! Oh! Ah'm in pain,' says Drena. 'Ah think Ah've wet maself!'

There's the sound of water trickling on to the floor. 'Hah! I too have wet myself,' says Irma. 'Naw ye huv'nae,' says Drena, now all serious. 'Your watter's broke! It's yer time!'

'Oh, mein Gott! Help ma Boab! Is it happening?'

'Yer bloody right! Ella, will ye dive doon tae Ken's and phone fur the doctor. C'mon, hen. We'll get ye intae yer ain hoose. Is Bert in his bed?'

'Aye.'

'Huh, well he's no' gonny get much sleep the day, Irma. Right, up ye get.'

Ninety minutes later, Arthur Harvey Armstrong is born. It's the 22nd of December 1950.

Some two hours after giving birth, Irma lies sound asleep in the recess bed. The single-end is full as neighbours call in to give their congratulations, then linger on to drink cups of tea or glasses of whisky while admiring Master Armstrong, swaddled in a basket on the kitchen table.

'Where does the "Harvey" come fae, Bert. Is it a family

name?' asks Granny Thomson.

'Why naa, hinny. It's after Joe Harvey. Captain of Newcastle United!'

'All done, folks!' The signwriter smiles at George Lockerbie and Ruth Malcolm. 'Want tae come and have a look?'

'Oh, yes!' All three step out on to the pavement on Woodlands Road, turn and look up.

'Doesn't it look grand, George!' In bold Art Deco lettering the name proclaims the imminent arrival of LE BAR RENDEZVOUS. As they stand side by side, George unobtrusively takes Ruth's hand and squeezes it. He looks at the signwriter. 'You've made a lovely job of it, Andy.'

'What about the rest of the work? Are the boys gonny be finished in time?'

'Yeah. It all seems to be going to schedule. Seating and furniture are nearly all fitted. The kitchen equipment is installed. Lighting all done. Bar and pumps have been delivered and they're coming to fit them tomorrow. Then, during the few days between Christmas and New Year, the decorators are coming back to touch up any marks left by the other workmen. And providing nothing major goes wonky, we'll have those couple of days before New Year to sort out any teething troubles.'

'When is the actual opening?'

'New Year's Eve.'

Inside again, Ruth reaches for her coat. 'Right, George. Time to call it a day and head off home.' They stand together in the centre of the big room. She links her arm in his. They look around. At the Bechstein piano, covered with a dust sheet. The bijou dance floor curving out towards them.

'It doesn't need much imagination now to see how it will look, does it, darling?'

George smiles. 'It's going to be so classy.' He kisses her cheek. 'And with you front of house, greeting our guests, we cannae go wrong.'

'Ah! Ah! Ah! Don't tempt fate.' She presses a forefinger against his lips. He purses them to kiss it. 'Ruth. Even if Ah was down and out, as long as you stuck by me, Ah'd be the most successful down-and-out who's ever been!'

They emerge into a misty Woodlands Road. After locking up, they step back a few paces to again admire their new sign. LE BAR RENDEZVOUS. They look at each other. Smile.

'Did you just get a wee tingle then? A frisson?' George asks.

She pulls herself in close to him. 'I did.' She continues to look at him. 'You're always telling me, George Lockerbie, how much you love me and what I mean to you.' As she speaks, he can see her eyes grow moist. 'Well, you just make me feel so happy. Safe. After all these years of being on my own. Supposed to be the self-sufficient, cool Ruth Malcolm. To a certain extent I was. But, oh, all that time I so longed to find my man. *The* man. The one I was meant for. Then along you came and asked for a job. Hah! And you got a lot more than you bargained for, didn't you?' She stretches up and kisses him on the cheek.

'And boyzaboyz!' he says. 'Am Ah happy with what Ah got! But let me tell you something else – Ah can't remember when we last ate. Ah'm bloody starving!'

She laughs. 'Me too. What do you fancy?'

'Besides you?'

'Later, darling.' She looks at him. 'Do you know what I would just love at this moment?'

'Let me guess. Mmmm. A big fish supper?'

'Right first time!' She giggles. 'Let's hope we don't run into any of our prospective customers!' Laughing, they start to run towards the stop as a lone tram, a number 10, emerges from the mist.

As Marjorie Sneddon serves the food on to the plates, the radio plays softly in the background. Hot coals glow in the grate. Big Jack Marshall lifts his knife and fork and pretends to sharpen them against one another, just as Laurel and Hardy do when they're about to tuck in.

She laughs, then grows serious. 'Oh, Jack. You make me awfy happy, so ye dae.'

'So why are ye making me wait before ye marry me?'

'Well ye know whit it's like. It's no' yet two months since he went.' She still feels pleasure at being back in the flat and not having to talk 'pan loaf' all the time to keep Richard happy.

'Marjorie. If you'd lost a good man, Ah would agree with ye. Ye know, a bit of respect for his memory. But ye know whit he was like – even his brother had nae time for him! And there is naebody in this close has a good word tae say aboot him. He has'nae earned any respect. That auld wumman doon the stairs, Granny, eh, Granny Thingmy. She was saying tae me the other day, "It's nice tae see Marjorie enjoying life at last. She deserves a bit o' happiness." Do ye think your neighbours are gonny be horrified if you don't wait a year afore marrying again?'

Marjorie runs water into the pans to steep them, make them easier to wash later. She sits down opposite Jack. Then makes a decision. Looks up. 'Okay. We'll get married in

February if you want. That'll be three months since he died. Ah think that's long enough for him!'

Jack smiles. 'From what you've telt me, hen, Ah think that's two months too long! But never mind, it'll dae.' He rises from the table, takes a couple of steps to her side, tilts her chin up with his large hand and gently kisses her. The kiss becomes passionate. When they stop, she looks up at him. 'Oh, Jack!' Flushed, she takes hold of the front of his shirt, pulls him down and resumes from where the previous kiss left off. After a minute or so, Jack breaks away.

'Phew! Let me get ma dinner first, hen!'

CHAPTER FIFTY-SIX

No Call for Mistletoe

It has just gone three o'clock on Christmas Eve when young Mr Macready comes through to the typists' room. The girls have been expecting him. It's the same routine every year.

'Well, girls. I'd swear it was just three months ago since I was coming ben the office to wish you all a Merry Christmas. To you young folk it'll seem like twelve months. But believe me, the older you get, the quicker time passes. Nowadays, for me, a month is not what it used to be. Dearie me, no.' He takes out his gold pocket watch. 'Aye, well.' He returns it to its waistcoat pocket. 'Here's a wee Christmas box from the family to you all.' He approaches each of the five girls in turn, hands them an envelope, shakes their hand and wishes them the compliments of the season. They know the envelope will contain a Christmas card and a new five-pound note. In return they say, 'Thank you very much, Mr Macready, and a Merry Christmas to you and the family.'

'Any of you doing anything exciting?' he enquires.

Normally there are five answers at the same time. The words 'quiet', 'family', 'no' really', 'nuthin' much', 'jist for the weans' would be heard. Today there are only four answering his question. Rhea can't think of anything. She won't be doing anything exciting. In fact she wishes it wasn't Christmas. It'll just make her feel more miserable. Mr Macready looks at his watch again.

'Right, girls. You can get yourselves away home.'

There is now a chorus of 'Thank you, Mr Macready!' followed by a cacophony of conversation, drawers sliding shut and chairs dragging on the floor as they are pushed back to free the sitters. Mr Macready walks over to Rhea. She's putting her coat on.

'I take it there's no news, or I would have heard?'

She takes her scarf out of her pocket. 'No. Nuthing. Ah got a letter yesterday. Written the day before the Chinese attacked.' She shrugs. 'So it's nae help. Only thing it did was tae gie us an idea whit conditions are like. The previous couple of nights the temperature had been doon tae minus forty! Even during the day it had'nae been rising above minus thirty. Can ye imagine it? The cauld's enough tae kill ye, never mind the Chinks!'

'Yes. So there's no point telling you to enjoy yourself, Miss O'Malley. You'll have other things on your mind.'

'Aye. But thanks anyway, Mr Macready. Ah hope you and yer family have a nice time. Ah'll see ye the day after Boxing Day. Ah wid think Ah'll be pleased tae get back tae work. Ah'm no' looking forward tae jist sitting aboot the hoose. Anywye, Merry Christmas!'

Rhea makes her way out to the street. Her four workmates, Janet, Elsie, Margaret and Shona, stand on the pavement, waiting for her. It's almost dark. Although gloved, hatted and scarfed, they stamp their feet to keep warm. Their breath comes out in great wreaths of condensation. Exhaust fumes rise from cars and buses as though it were mist. The girls gather round her. She receives all their best wishes. Not for a Merry Christmas. That will be impossible. But in the hope that she'll have a restful time and the best Christmas present of all – word that Robert is safe.

As the tram travels slowly through the city, Rhea looks out the window, occasionally wiping away the ever-forming condensation. She feels isolated. Sometimes sees herself as from a distance. You've been watching too many movies, you. Yet this image stays with her. This lone figure, surrounded by folk who are in a good mood because it's Christmas Eve, looking out a tram window at people going back and forth along the pavement. This view of herself is the one that hurts most. A young couple, arm in arm, in step, come striding along past the brightly lit shops. They lean forward a little and she holds his arm as close to her as she possibly can. Almost hugging as they walk. That's me and Robert! Rhea thinks. Just by the way they move she can tell they're in love. And because it's Christmas Eve and they know they're going to have a lovely time tonight, they are even more in love right at this moment. She feels tears in her eyes. Oh, Robert! Where are ye? Whit's happening tae ye?

As the evening wears on, Rhea grows more and more . . . what? Not just one thing. Not just miserable. Or sad. Or unhappy. Or depressed. All of them put the gether. And more.

The wireless drones away on the sideboard. Non-stop. Even though she hardly listens, she'd still rather have it on than off. Her mammy and daddy try their best. They have a nice dinner, which Rhea just picks at. They listen to the Christmas edition of *Take It From Here*. She'd normally be falling about laughing, but tonight it doesn't raise a smile. Her ma and da enjoy it, but you can tell they feel guilty every time they laugh. It's going to be the same all evening.

'Ah don't suppose you want tae come oot fur a wee drink?' Siobhan stands beside her.

Rhea takes her hand. 'Naw thanks. Ah wid'nae be good company. And Ah'd imagine if Ah had a few drinks it wid make me either depressed or weepy. Or both. Ah'll jist stay in wi' Mammy and Daddy. You get away and enjoy yerself. Nae good the two of us being miserable.' She watches as Siobhan goes out to the lobby and returns with her coat and scarf.

'Are ye not puttin' yer boots on?' Teresa is drying dishes at the sink.

'Ma, ye cannae get dressed up tae the nines, then spoil it wi' big clumpy boots!'

'If you get a chill in yer kidneys, here's luck t' ye!'

'Ah'll take ma chance, Ma.'

Teresa uses the dishcloth to wipe the condensation off a window pane. She peers out into the dark back court. 'Jayz! It could kill ye out there, so it could.'

Siobhan looks at Rhea, then at their mother. 'Ye cannae see anything oot there. It's too dark, so how can ye tell?'

'Sure I can see enough, so I can. And don't be late back or you'll get a clip from yer da!' Dennis O'Malley, unperturbed at his name being used in vain, continues reading the *Evening Citizen*.

'This is Christmas Eve, Ma. If you think Ah'm comin' in at eleven o'clock, you've got another think coming!'

Teresa looks heavenward. 'Jaysus! Do ye hear the cheek I'm gettin' from this spalpeen?' She looks at Dennis. 'Are you just gonna sit there?'

He finishes turning a page of the broadsheet. 'Aye. 'Tis on me holidays I am.'

Rhea manages a smile. She looks at her ma and da, thinks how lucky she is to have them. Ah must remember to give them their presents in the morning. This leads her on to thinking about Robert's parents. What a state they must be in since he went missing. He's their only child. Ah wish they knew about us, she thinks. If things were normal, Ah'd have been able tae spend time wi' them. We'd be able tae talk aboot him aw' the time. Worry about him the gether. Instead, because of aw' this Catholic, Protestant carry-oan, they don't know aboot the two of us. Don't know we're engaged. They're sitting doon there thinking they're alone. Ah'm up here, bloody yards away. And we're aw' worried tae death aboot him. She begins to get angry. Whit would Robert want? Ah *know* whit he'd want. It wid be different if he wiz'nae missing. But he is! Robert would want me tae be wi' his ma and da. Try and comfort them. She stands up. She's been in the chair for almost two hours. Her mother and father look at her. Then at each other. She stands for a moment. What can Ah say tae Mr and Mrs Stewart? she wonders. She heads for the door.

'Are ye all right, darlin'?' Teresa has a feeling.

Rhea walks along the lobby and into the bedroom. She slides out the bottom drawer of the chest of drawers. Reaches into the farthest corner. The jewellery box is where it should be, under her collection of *Picturegoer* and *Photoplay* magazines. She stands up, doesn't bother closing the drawer. Extracting her engagement ring, she puts it on. The open empty box is left on top of the magazines. She goes back into the lobby.

'Ma! Da! Ah'll be back in a wee while.' She lets herself out, leaves the front door ajar, and descends the two flights of stairs to the close.

As they listen to her footsteps, Dennis speaks. 'Where's she away to?'

'I t'ink I know,' says Teresa. 'Shush a minute.' She quickly goes over to the lobby and stands at the half-open front door, listening. She hears a door being knocked. Then opened. Voices. A door being closed.

As she approaches the Stewarts' door, Rhea is totally unable to put her thoughts into words. She doesn't know what she'll say. Just knows she has to speak to them. She looks at the dark blue door. Watches as her hand comes up and knocks on it. Hears movement. The door opens. It's Samuel Stewart. He smiles. 'Hello, Rhea. Wha—'

'Mr Stewart! Can Ah speak tae you and Mrs Stewart a minute?' She feels the emotion start to rise in her.

'Aye, of course. Come in, hen.' He opens the door wide, stands back, gestures with his hand. She walks past him and into the kitchen. The wireless is playing. She remembers being in here once when she was a wee girl. Can't recall why. This is my Robert's hoose.

Mrs Stewart looks up in surprise. Smiles. 'Hello, Rhea. This is—'

Rhea starts to speak. 'Ah jist have tae come and see . . .' She chokes on it. Great heavy sobs rack her, tears flood down her face. She holds her left hand out, tucks her fingers behind one another, leaving the ring finger on top. 'Robert and me . . .' She can't say any more. Just stands sobbing with her hand thrust out.

Mary Stewart rises, goes to her, enfolds her in her arms. Swaying gently, she hugs Rhea for more than a minute, now and then rubbing her back. 'Wheesh, wheesh. It'll be aw'right, hen. Everything will be aw'right.' As Samuel Stewart watches, tears brim in his eyes. Mary leans back, looks at Rhea. Smiles. Then she turns to the side, keeping an arm round Rhea's waist, looks at her man. 'Ah hope you're no' gonny be saying anything against this?'

He shakes his head, swallows hard. They can see the tears in his eyes. He composes himself. 'If this wee lassie's Robert's choice, she'll dae for me! Come here, hen.' He puts his arm round Rhea, kisses her on the cheek, hugs her tight. His voice quavering, he manages to say, 'There are three of us waiting oan him noo.'

Ten minutes later there's a knock on the Stewarts' door. 'Goodness me. We're having a busy night, the night.' Mary answers it. She says, 'Come in.' Siobhan enters the kitchen.

'Ah thought you were oot fur the night?' says Rhea.

'Ach! Ah could'nae enjoy maself for thinkin' aboot you aw' miserable. So Ah came hame.'

'Mr and Mrs Stewart know aw' aboot Robert and me now. Thank God!'

'Siobhan!' says Samuel. 'Away up and ask your ma and da if they'd like tae come doon for a wee drink. After aw', we've got an engagement tae celebrate. Even if we are a year late. And though it might no' feel like it, it's still Christmas Eve!'

CHAPTER FIFTY-SEVEN

New Year's Resolution!

New Year's Eve. It isn't quite seven p.m. when the army staff car noses its way into Dalbeattie Street and once more parks outside number 18. Captain Fraser, resplendent in his No.1 mess dress and sporting his medals in miniature, climbs out.

'I shouldn't be too long, Corporal.' He makes his way into the close, then stands for a few seconds at the Stewarts' door. He takes a couple of deep breaths.

The Stewarts already have a visitor. Since the revelations of Christmas Eve, Rhea O'Malley has called in every evening.

'Ah'll jist bring the New Year in wi' ma mammy and daddy and oor Siobhan, then Ah'll come doon here efter the bells, if that's aw'right. If Ah stay in the hoose wi' them, Ah'll jist spoil their Hogmanay. The poor sowels are feart tae laugh at the wireless when Ah'm aroon'. Ah cannae help it. Robert's oan ma mind aw' the time.'

'Aye, jist come doon tae us, hen. Ah'm sure—' Samuel

Stewart breaks off as someone rattles his letterbox. He stands up. 'A bit early for first-footin', is it no'?' Mary and Rhea watch as he goes into the lobby and opens the front door. As the radio isn't playing they can hear the brief conversation. Mary recognises the captain's voice.

'Good evening, Mr Stewart. Let me say right away – it's good news!'

'Oh my God! In ye come, Captain.' As they hear this brief exchange, Mary and Rhea look at one another. Mary's hand goes to her mouth. Rhea gasps. They don't know it, but both their hearts simultaneously leapt on hearing those two words – good news!

As the captain enters the kitchen, Mary and Rhea stand up. Expectant. He smiles at them. 'Good evening, Mrs Stewart and Miss . . . ?'

'This is Rhea O'Malley. Robert's fiancée.' They shake hands. Even though she's anxious to hear why the captain has called, Rhea feels a tingle at being referred to as Robert's fiancée.

'Right! Straight to the point. Your son has been found alive and well!'

'Oh, thank God! Thank the Lo—' Mary Stewart's legs buckle and her eyes seem to go up into the back of her head.

'Quick!' Sam and the young captain grab her as she's about to fall in a dead faint. Rhea bursts into tears. They sit Mary down on a chair and gently pat her cheeks. She begins to come round. Sam dabs his eyes. 'Oh, Captain. Oh, we hoped against hope that we'd get this news.' He goes over to Rhea, who's crying uncontrollably, 'It's aw'right, hen. He's safe. Oor Robert's safe.' He gently rubs her back and shoulders. 'Are ye able tae give us any details?' he asks Captain Fraser.

'Yes, I can. RAOC Headquarters have received a fairly long telegraph message, a copy of which they've sent to us.'

Sam holds up a hand. 'This calls for a wee hauf. Ah don't usually start drinking till the bells, but Ah would think Ah'll probably have tae take tae ma bed long afore twelve o'clock the night!'

Minutes later, all four sit round the Stewarts' kitchen table. Mary has a sherry in front of her, Rhea whisky and lemonade; both men take theirs straight.

'Well, your son seems to have had quite an adventure. He was picked up some seven hours ago; the captain pauses to look at all three of them in turn, 'in the Sea of Japan, some fifteen miles off the coast of North Korea!'

'Eh? Oor Robert?'

'Wiz'nae still in his lorry, Ah hope,' says Rhea.

When the laughter subsides, the captain continues. 'He and five comrades seem to have, ah, "borrowed" a fishing boat. They were picked up by an American warship. Robert has been slightly – I emphasise "slightly" – wounded in the leg and side.' At this, both Mary and Rhea draw their breath in. 'Now please, there's no need for alarm. His unit got them to detail his wounds. He was hit by shrapnel in the upper right leg and in his right side. Both flesh wounds. They in no way incapacitated him. He was able to carry out his duties.'

'Will he be coming home?' asks Mary.

'Because he has been wounded, he'll be coming home for what is called convalescent leave. I would imagine at least a month. Maybe longer.'

'Oh, is that no' marvellous!' says Rhea.

'Have you any idea how soon?' asks Mary.

'They're flying people back all the time. They mostly use

the Hermes. It's a large transport plane. With stopovers to refuel at places like Hong Kong and Cyprus, it takes about forty-eight hours to do the trip. By the time it's all organised, he could be back, mmmm, around the fourth or fifth.'

Mary looks at Sam, then at Rhea 'Isn't that wonderful? I just cannae believe it.'

'And the good news coming on Hogmanay,' says Sam. 'We'll never forget this New Year, hen.'

The captain stands up. 'I'd better get myself away. As you can see,' he points to his uniform, 'I was about to go to dinner in the mess when the news came in. I wanted you to know straight away.'

Sam takes the officer's hand in both of his. 'We really are most grateful to you, Captain Fraser. As you know, we were up to high doh worrying aboot oor lad. So thank you for all your attention. Ah take it we'll be informed when Robert should arrive home?'

'Yes indeed. We'll let you know when he's due back in the UK. Then we'll also inform you what train he should be off at the Central. I'll be in touch.'

As soon as the captain has left, Mary stands up. 'Ah'm going straight up to Granny's to tell her. You'll be wanting tae be the first to tell your mammy and daddy and Siobhan, Ah would think, Rhea.'

'That's jist what Ah wiz gonny say. Eeeeh! Ah can hardly wait tae go up tae oor hoose.' Mary looks at her. At the joy in her face. She goes over to her and hugs her. 'You've no idea what a comfort you've been tae Sam and me since last week. We're so pleased you decided tae come doon and tell us about you and Robert.' She kisses her on the cheek. 'Robert could'nae have found a better lassie.'

Mary and Rhea climb up to the first storey together. Mary leans over to her ear. 'Ah'll let you go intae your house first,' she whispers. 'Then, when you're inside, Ah'll go into Granny's.'

Seconds later, she opens Granny Thomson's front door; the inner one is already open. Granny sits in her fireside chair. The soporific song of the gas lamps has worked its magic. Mary gives a loud knock. 'Granny!'

'Eh? Aye!' She clears her throat. 'Oh, Ah must huv dozed aff for a wee minute.'

Mary smiles. Without fail, every time she walks into Granny's, it's like H.G.Wells's *Time Machine*. It immediately takes her back to 1910 or so. She's a wee girl again and she's walking into her own granny's down in Bridgeton.

'Come away in, Mary. Any news?'

'Robert's safe and well. He should be hame on the fourth, maybe the fifth!'

'Huh!' Granny clasps her hands together. 'Oh, Mary! Mary! Oh, Ah'm so gled for ye!' She rises stiffly from her chair. The two women hug and shed a few tears. 'And does Rhea know?'

'Aye. She was in the hoose wi' Sam and me when the young officer came tae tell us.'

Just then the door is opened. 'It's only me!' Rhea enters and runs over to Granny. Hugs her. 'Oh, Granny, ye telt me. Ye telt me he'd be back. Ye wur right!'

Granny looks at her two visitors. 'Ah think the perr of ye should now go up and doon the length of the close and let everybody know. They'll aw' want tae ken as soon as possible.'

When Mary and Rhea have left, Granny masks herself a pot of tea and puts a couple of tea biscuits on to a plate. Before she sits down, she uses the tongs to place a few choice pieces of coal on the fire. She stares into the growing flames for a while. Thinking. So, Mary's been told he'll be hame aboot the fourth or the fifth. That's plenty o' time. She reaches out for a used envelope that lies on the table. She takes a copying-ink pencil from out of a tin that once held chocolates and celebrated the coronation of Edward VII and Queen Alexandra in 1911. Frequently wetting the tip of the pencil with her tongue, she painstakingly begins to write . . . 'See Mrs Spencer, church hall, for bunting (six rows at least). If poss, get Union Jacks and Saltires. Old sheets from somewhere for banner. Who'll paint it? Maybe Drena and Ella . . . ' After twenty minutes she sits back. A moment later, Mary Stewart and Rhea come blethering down the stairs. She slips her list underneath the tin. As expected, her door is knocked again.

'It's jist us!' The two of them come in, flushed and slightly breathless. 'That's everybody been told. They were aw' that pleased!'

'Good,' says Granny. 'Now, Mary. When you get tae know whit day Robert's coming hame, let me know, will ye? Whether it's the fourth or fifth. Ah want tae be washed and dressed tae come doon and see the laddie when ye's come back fae the station. Don't forget. Takes me that long tae get masel' ready nooadays.' Neither Mary nor Rhea suspects a thing.

Rhea looks at the clock. 'Well, Ah think Ah'd better go intae the hoose and start gettin' smartened up a bit so as tae bring in the New Year.' She links her arm through Mary's. 'Jist think. Ah couple of hours ago Ah wiz saying tae maself whit a miserable Hogmanay this is gonny be. Ah might no' even wait up fur the bells, might jist go tae ma bed early and huv a read – and a wee greet. Whit a difference, eh?'

'Aye. Sam and me will be bringing it in as well. Make up for the rotten Christmas we had.'

Five minutes later the two women have gone. Granny eases herself into her fireside chair. She places the strainer on her cup and refills it. Och aye! Ah'll have ten minutes. It's jist efter nine. She goes back to her plans for Robert's home-coming. Ah should definitely have two clear days tae collect aw' whit's needed. Oan the day it'll only take an hour, mibbe less, tae get everything up. She looks again at the clock. Two and a half hours and that'll be 1950 gone. It's finishing up a good year efter aw'. Yon reptile Sneddon's gone. Hah! He wiz nae loss, that yin. And yon nice big lad George Lockerbie, he moved away. Met a bonny lass, so they tell me. But Drena got his hoose, so she's delighted she did'nae have tae move oot the close. Och, and poor Andra McDermot slipped away. Noo that wiz a big loss. And Lena's no' getting ower it. And then James Pentland! Up and got himself merried. Confirmed bachelor! And we've got a new bairn doon the stairs. Wee Arthur. And noo, whit a grand finish tae the year. Robert Stewart's no' deid at aw'! Aye, wan o' the better years, 1950.

CHAPTER FIFTY-EIGHT

The Hottest Spot in Town!

New Year's Eve. The last day of 1950 is the first day, the launch, of Le Bar Rendezvous. Ruth Malcolm sits on a stool at one end of the bar. Legs crossed, she rests one arm on the brass rail that curves along its entire length. She reaches behind the bar for the flat box of Black Sobranie, selects one of the gold-tipped cigarettes, then nonchalantly fits it into the tortoiseshell holder. Perfectly on cue, Steve, one of the new barmen, flicks his lighter.

'Thank you.' The smoke spills from the ruby-red lips. To the customers who know her from the Bar Deco, it's as if she, and the stool, have somehow been magically transported from the Byres Road. To many of the newcomers she already appears to be the essence of front of house, even if they've never heard that phrase. She casts a professional eye around her. Takes in the busy room. Some folk sit and eat. Others talk. Many dance to the five-piece combo as it plays soft jazz interspersed with swinging big-band numbers by Ellington, Shaw or Goodman. Within half an hour of opening tonight, couples were already taking to the bijou dance floor. Glasgow folk love their dancing. Ruth takes in everything. Music, lighting, decor, even the blue haze of cigarette smoke, all add to the feel, the ambience. She glances at her watch: ten past ten. We're off to a flying start. The place is jumping.

George Lockerbie has been circulating since early on. Welcoming folk, having brief conversations with some, now and again sitting for a few minutes with those at tables or banquettes. He knows many from the Bar Deco or Johnny McKinnon's Hillhead Bar. There are also a pleasing number of fresh faces. He rises from the banquette where he's been in conversation with a couple, wends his way to the bar.

'Hello again, darling.' He kisses Ruth on the temple. As ever, enjoys the scent of her. 'You so look the part sitting there. That's all you have to do, darling – just be Ruth Malcolm.'

He faces the bar. Leans on the brass rail. She places a hand over one of his.

'Considering Glasgow folk are supposed to like bringing the New Year in at home, then going out first-footing, I'm really pleased by the numbers we've attracted tonight, George.'

'Yeah.' He looks around. 'And they're coming in all the time. Be interesting to see how many stay on to bring in the New Year with us.'

'Who are the couple you've just been talking to, George? I know his face, but can't put a name to him.'

'That's Peter Keenan, the boxer, and his wife.'

'Ah, is that him? I must have seen his photo in the paper now and again.' She looks over at the short, slim figure. His head of dark, wavy hair shining with Brylcreem. 'He has a real cheeky face, doesn't he? Very boyish.'

'Yeah. He's a good lad, Peter. He's going places. Highly rated. Even though it's Hogmanay, all he's drinking is orange juice. He's in the middle of training for his next fight. That's dedication for you. Ah bump into him now and again round the town. He walks everywhere. Very rarely takes a tram or bus. Considers it part of his training.'

'Mmmm.' Ruth takes a draw on her cigarette. 'It'll be good for business if we attract celebrities like that, George.'

'It will. And we've got another sportsman in. Over by the far wall, right in the middle. There's four of them at the table . . . '

'Is it that really big guy? Sort of craggy-looking?'

'That's him.'

'He's another one. As soon as they came in, I thought, I know your face. Who is he?'

'That's big George Young, captain of Rangers and Scotland.'

'Of course! Trouble is, darling, I only glance at the sports pages. Articles on society are more in my line. Still, never mind, between the two of us I'm sure we'll be able to recognise most of Glasgow's *Who's Who*.'

'Exactly! That's why we make such a good team.' She receives another kiss on the temple.

It's coming up for twenty to twelve. George walks over and has a word with Vince, the leader of the five-piece band, then makes his way back to Ruth. 'The next dance is a special request. By me, for us. Are you ready to trip the light whatsit?'

'I thought you'd never ask. I bet it's a foxtrot. And I also forecast it'll be "Begin the Beguine". Ten out of ten?'

George sighs. 'You know my every move, don't you?'

The number the group is playing comes to an end. George

offers a hand to Ruth as she effortlessly slinks off the stool. They make their way on to the floor, find a space. Vince turns towards the dancers. 'And the next number – a special request for our hosts – is Artie Shaw's arrangement of "Begin the Beguine".'

'Ah love this,' says George.

'Quelle surprise!' mutters Ruth in a stage whisper.

'Away and bile your heid!' counters George.

Ruth throws her head back, laughs out loud. 'Oooh! I love it when you talk dirty, darling.'

They are halfway through the dance when George stops; points with the hand that is holding hers. 'Look who's just come in.' Ruth turns her head.

'Johnny! Veronica!' They leave the dance floor, join Johnny McKinnon and Veronica Shaw. Kisses and hugs are exchanged. Johnny holds Ruth at arm's length.

'George, I don't know what you do for this girl – I probably don't want to, as I'd be inflamed with jealousy – but she's positively thriving under your tender care.' He kisses Ruth once more. 'You look great, kid.'

George turns to Veronica. 'It's a good thing you're such a looker, otherwise you might become quite jealous of the way this man is forever flattering Ruth.'

Veronica laughs. 'Huh! If Ruth was the only woman who got the treatment, maybe I would become a little green-eyed. But everybody gets it. We have two charladies come in every morning to see to the bar. No kidding, they look like Elsie and Doris Waters. When they leave an hour later, after their daily dose of Johnny's patter, he has so turned their heads they are quite convinced they're Glasgow's answer to Ginger Rogers and Dolores del Rio – and the bar is left sparkling. He's not daft, Johnny.'

The subject of this character assassination stands silent, hands folded in front of him, a pained look on his face as he slowly turns his head to look at each in turn.

Veronica eyes him with a bored look. 'That's him daeing his Jack Benny. Did ye's get it?' They all laugh.

'C'mon over to the bar,' says Ruth. 'It's coming up for ten to twelve.'

Ruth's bar stool has remained vacant. Even on this first night, without a word spoken, it has already been established that it is the preserve of Madame. The proprietress. Ruth regains her seat and the other three gather round. Drinks are ordered. A Black Sobranie is lit. 'I didn't think we'd see you before the bells, Johnny. I thought you'd be staying back with a few select customers to see the New Year in.'

'Not tonight. Veronica and I wanted to be here for at least part of the grand opening. I really am impressed. This is going to take off.'

'Me too,' says Veronica. 'I said to you, on the night we came for dinner, that I felt there was a gap for a French-brasserie-cum-supper-club in Glasgow. It already has a lovely atmosphere.'

While she speaks, Johnny has been looking around. 'Hey! What's this? Purloining some of my customers. I see big George Young and Peter Keenan are in. I'll sue!'

'Ah!' Ruth has spotted someone. She speaks into George's ear. 'Now *there* is somebody I recognise. That couple by the door. They've just come in. He's wearing a double-breasted blazer. She's blonde, with a blue and white frock.'

'Yeah. Ah see them,' says George. 'Ah don't know them. Who should Ah recognise, him or her?'

'Oh, I know who *he* is,' says Veronica.

'Tell George.'

Veronica inclines her head. 'The guy is Hugh Fraser. Son and heir to the owner of the House of Fraser department stores. Plenty of money attached there, as they say.'

'Swines!' says Johnny. 'Not only stealing my customers, but you're enticing folk in who've never, ever darkened my door. I'm getting depressed!'

They are interrupted by the leader of the combo, who, with difficulty, has made his way through the crowd thronging the floor. 'Do ye want tae bring the New Year in on the stage, George? There's jist three minutes tae go tae the bells.'

'Thanks, Vince.' George takes Ruth by the hand. 'Let's go, sweetheart.'

'No. You do it, darling.'

'It's *our* place. Ah'll do the talking, but Ah want you by my side.' He leads her by the hand and they step up on to the low bandstand. He turns to Vince. 'Ah'll do the countdown from ten to zero, then you guys can do a crescendo roll of drums type thing at twelve. That okay?' The leader nods. George looks at his watch. 'A minute to go. Ah'll get their attention. FOLKS! FOLKS!' He holds his arms up in the air to attract all eyes in his direction. The drummer gives a staccato drum roll, the trumpet and sax players blast all sorts of odd, discordant notes from their instruments. It has the desired effect. Conversations falter, the hubbub dies, folk turn towards the bandstand. George takes Ruth's hand again. He looks at his watch: about forty seconds to go. 'Ladies and gentlemen, we're going to bring 1951 in with a countdown, just like you've seen them do for years in the movies. But let me quickly say, we've had a wonderful opening night. We really have. The reason? Because we've attracted such nice people. Anyway.' He now focuses on his watch, pauses. 'Here we go – ten, nine, eight . . . ' The crowd begin to take up the count. 'Seven, six, five, four, three, two, one – HAPPY NEW YEAR EVERYBODY!' The group play a fanfare on their instruments, the drummer goes into a Gene Krupa-type solo. The crowd cheer then begin wishing their nearest and dearest a Happy New Year. After that, it's the turn of their fellow revellers.

George puts his arms around Ruth. 'Happy New Year, love of my life!' Her eyes glisten.

'Happy New Year to you, my special man.' They kiss, then kiss again. They both exchange greetings and good wishes with the band, then step off the dais and return to Johnny and Veronica to wish them all the best for the New Year. Johnny reaches out, takes both Ruth and George's hands in his. 'I know it's your first night, but I'll make a forecast now. You've got a gold mine here. This is gonna be the hottest spot in town!'

CHAPTER FIFTY-NINE

It's a Lovely Day the Morra'

———

It has been the best Hogmanay 18 Dalbeattie Street has ever known. The best in living memory. As Granny Thomson's New Years go back to before the First World War, and *she* says it is, well that's it. It must be. There's no doubt what was the catalyst for such a memorable Hogmanay – the news arriving that Robert Stewart had turned up safe and well in Korea. That fact made belonging to number 18 somehow special. When it came to the bells, and glasses were raised to welcome in 1951, there wasn't a house in the close where Robert Stewart's name wasn't mentioned. Nor did it end there. By one a.m., every adult had 'jist popped in' to the Stewarts' to wish them all the best and tell them how pleased they were when they heard the good news. That included Donald McNeil from the top storey. The normally reserved Donald usually only first-foots Agnes Dalrymple and Granny. But even he was moved to call in on the Stewarts. To the surprise of many, Marjorie Sneddon and her friend Jack Marshall were already there. Marjorie had come down to say how delighted she was to hear that Robert was safe

and well. The assembled company were all introduced to
Jack. Later on, in conversation with Drena and Ella, Marjorie
reverted to 'pan loaf' for a moment to let it be known that
'I'm afraid Jack, eh, will have to sleep ben the room tonight.
Not an ideal situation for a lady living alone. But I can hardly
cast the poor soul out into the night to walk home.' Marjorie,
however, appeared to have strayed during the early hours.
On the afternoon of New Year's Day, over a cup of tea, Ella
gives a full report to Drena. 'Ye should huv heard the noise
of them two aboot three o'clock this moarning! Whit wiz it
she said tae us, "He'll huv tae sleep ben the front room"?'

'Aye, Ah wid think that's jist aboot accurate – if, perchance,
a toaty wee bit less refined.'

Ella sniffs. 'Gie him his due, it certainly did'nae sound as
if he'd moved fae the front room. But she never mentioned
anything aboot her slipping through tae join him!'

'Giving it laldy, wur they?' enquires Drena.

'Laldy? Wi' the moans an' the yelps coming oot o' her. It
takes her longer tae come than a tax rebate!'

'Oh, don't!' says Drena as the pair of them go helpless. 'Ah
huv'nae goat the strength.'

Archie Cameron comes back from the stairhead lavatory.
The two women turn their heads.

'Urr you as bad as ye look, Erchie?' asks Drena.

'Worse. Is thurr Askit Powders and Irn Bru in, Ella?'

'Aye. In the press.'

Archie gingerly makes his way to the cupboard near to the
kitchen windows. He opens two of the life-saving powders in
their folded-paper covers, tips them into his mouth, then
washes them down with Scotland's second national drink.
'Ahhh!' He spends the next ten minutes looking down into

a sombre New Year's Day back court. Then goes back to his bed.

As is to be expected with Granny in charge, everything goes like clockwork. On the 2nd of January she goes to see the church caretaker and borrows the required strings of bunting, Union Jacks and Scottish Saltire flags. These last saw the light of day on the marriage of Princess Elizabeth to Prince Philip, Duke of Edinburgh, in 1947. Marjorie Sneddon, perhaps not surprisingly, contributes the two sheets needed for the making of the banner. She intimates she intends to get rid of all the bedding associated with her marriage to the late, unlamented Richard Sneddon. Drena and Ella, as Granny surmised, are delighted to be given the task of turning these sheets into a banner, then painting it. All that is needed now is the date on which Robert Stewart will be coming home.

While these plans and preparations are going on, they are kept secret from the Stewarts and the O'Malleys. During this time, Samuel Stewart comes up with an idea of his own . . .

It's the evening of the 2nd of January. Rhea and Siobhan are down at the Stewarts'. The conversation occasionally strays from the subject of Robert. But not for long. Although the Stewarts have known Rhea since she was a wee girl, this last week has impressed on them what a fine young woman she has become. And made them realise what their son sees in her. At twenty-two years of age, the same as Robert, she is an open, friendly young woman. At times rather naive, she is completely without guile and quite obviously loves their son very much. Adores him, in fact. Her sister is out of the same mould and both girls are from, as the Stewarts know, honest, hard-working parents. As Mary says to Samuel when they are talking about the eventual marriage of the pair, 'Anywye, what's religion got tae dae wi' Clyde navigation?' The question, perhaps, doesn't make sense – but he knows what she means!

The subject of what day Robert will arrive back in the country, followed by which train he'll be catching up to Glasgow, is being discussed yet again. All of a sudden Samuel sits up. 'Ah don't know why Ah did'nae think of it before, Mary. When we go doon tae the Central tae meet Robert, Rhea will have tae come wi' us! Everybody up the close now knows the two of them are engaged. But Robert still thinks it's a big secret.' He stops for a moment, imagines Robert's surprise if Rhea is at the station with them. Smiles as he pictures his delight. 'Oh, you've got tae be with us, Rhea. Can ye just see the look on his face, eh?'

Mary speaks before Rhea. 'Oh God, aye. It'll be just wonderful for him. Not only arriving hame, but finding oot that what he thought was a problem has been solved! It'll be great!'

'Jeez! Ah'd love tae be at the station with ye. It'll be jist smashing.' Rhea was hoping she'd be asked. If the Stewarts hadn't thought of it, she wouldn't have pushed the idea herself.

'Right,' says Samuel. 'When Ah go intae work the morra, ah'll see ma boss about getting the day off at short notice. Soon as we get tae know what day he's arriving at the Central, it'll just be a case of me phoning in and saying, "It's tomorrow, so Ah'll no' be in." Will you be able tae dae the same, Rhea?'

'Aye, nae bother. Ah'll see ma boss when Ah start back, and fix it up.'

*   *   *

It is midday on the third of January when Captain Fraser again calls in at the Stewarts'.

'He took off an hour ago from Gibraltar. It's a Yank plane that is bringing him on the last leg. Due to touch down at Mildenhall later this afternoon. He'll then come by overnight train from London, getting in to Glasgow Central early on the morning of the fourth. He should send you a telegram tonight telling you which train.' He smiles. 'So there you are. I'd like to call round sometime in the next week or so, just to meet your son, if that's all right?'

'That'll be grand, Captain. I'd think, if possible, mornings would be best. I'm sure Robert will be having plenty of long lies and won't be going out until late afternoons, at the earliest.'

'That's okay. With me being the liaison between yourselves and the army, I've become quite involved. So just to put a face to the name, it would be nice to say hello. Anyway, I'll be off.'

Less than twenty minutes after the captain leaves, Mary climbs the stairs to let Teresa O'Malley know the news. Rhea is at work. When Mary goes home, Teresa then takes herself off to Ken's, the newsagent's, to phone her daughter at the office. It's time to book her day off!

When she leaves the O'Malleys', Mary goes next door to Granny's. 'Are ye in, Bella?'

'Aye.' A cup of tea and two tea biscuits later, and Granny has been brought up to date. Only one last detail remains: what train will Robert be coming off in the morning?

'So he should be sending ye a telegram the night, Mary?'

'He should be.'

'Well, Ah'll tell ye whit. Ah take it you'll be coming up tae tell Rhea the train time when ye get the telegram?'

'Ah will. Or, more than likely, Rhea will probably be in our house when it arrives.'

'Right. If she is, Mary, jist tell her tae gie me a wee knock when she comes back up tae her ain hoose the night and let me know.'

As it happens, Rhea's services aren't needed. It's a few minutes after six when Mary, for the second time, climbs up to the first storey. She opens Granny's door. 'He's coming off the nine forty in the morning. It's the express, so it's usually oan time.'

Granny claps her hands together in pleasure. 'Eeeh! Isn't that grand, Mary! Ah'll be aw' scrubbed and polished and come doon tae yer hoose early the morn's morn tae see ye off tae the station. Are ye jist goin' back and forrit in the tram? Or are ye taking a taxi?'

'We'll just take the tram down,' says Mary, 'but we'll come hame in a taxi – 'cause we don't know how bad his leg is.'

'Aye, of course,' says Granny. 'Be best if ye come back in a taxi.'

A few minutes later she watches the unsuspecting Mary go back down the stairs. She allows five minutes before she leaves her house, climbs up to the top storey, then works her way back down the stairs, informing her troops of Robert's ETA as she descends. It will be almost entirely a female operation on the morrow, Donald McNeil being the only male available. Archie Cameron and Billy McClaren will be at work, Bert Armstrong in bed.

It all goes precisely to plan. Even the weather obliges. The 4th of January 1951 proves to be cold and clear. Granny calls into the Stewarts' at ten to nine in the morning to, as she puts it, see them off. When Rhea and the Stewarts leave the close to go round and catch their tram, Granny commandeers young William McClaren and Archie Cameron junior to go along to Ken's shop and purchase themselves a Penny Dainty each. Granny supplies the required funds. As ordered, they emerge from the shop and stand on the corner, ostensibly unwrapping the large caramels and breaking them – on the point of their elbows – to a more edible size. Their main task is to watch the Stewarts and Rhea, make certain they leave on the tram, and report to Granny when they have done so. Operations can't start until they have gone. By five past nine, the trio are safely on their way to the station.

The helpers – Drena, Ella and Donald McNeil prominent among them – set to work. Six strings of bunting are fixed from the three first-storey windows of number 18 to the lamp-post in the street. All the neighbours in the designated houses obligingly hammer nails into their windowledges so the bunting can be tied fast. In the same fashion the hand-made banner is prominently displayed. It reads: 'Welcome Home Robert Stewart. Well Done!'

All those folk who took the bunting also take a Union Jack and a Scottish Saltire and hang them out. The stage is now set. It isn't long before neighbours from other closes in Dalbeattie Street, and a few from nearby streets, begin to gather in little groups. All to await the return of the hero. It is at just this moment that Teresa O'Malley comes round the corner, returning from her early-morning office cleaning job. 'Jaysus, Mary and Joseph! What's going on?'

'Well, we could'nae tell ye, Teresa. Neither the Stewarts or your Rhea know aboot this welcome-home do. If we'd telt ye, ye might huv accidentally let it slip.'

'Oh, Jayz! Ye did right. I cannot keep a secret. Now, isn't this wonderful. Have I time t' dump me bag in the house and have a quick visit to the auld lavvy?'

'Ye have. But don't be long,' advises Drena.

At the Central Station, Mary and Samuel Stewart plus Rhea wait in a high state of anticipation and excitement. Platform tickets in hand, they stand side by side looking along the length of the platform, anxious for that first sight of Robert's train. A trolley loaded with luggage and cartons of goods stands nearby. Samuel eyes it. 'Rhea, when the train comes in, why don't you go behind that trolley and hide yourself? Robert's only expecting us. Let him come up tae us, and when the three of us are busy talking, you slip roond the far end o' the trolley and come up behind him – don't say anything, just tap him on the shoulder!'

'Oh, that'll be great, Mr Stewart. That's better than him seeing the three of us from a distance when he comes alang the platform.'

'Hah! Ah think this is the train,' says Mary. She looks at the station clock. 'They said it was ten minutes late. It's ten tae ten, so this should be it.'

All three watch until there is no doubt about it. The locomotive has entered their platform. With great gouts of steam and smoke rising up to the roof and brakes squealing, the long train begins to slow. Rhea nudges the two of them and vanishes behind the trolley. The engine comes to a juddering halt but the carriages take a minute or so longer to fully arrive, as with a repetitive 'ca-chong, ca-chong, ca-chong, ca-chong' they run into one another's buffers until the guard's van sounds the last note and the train, at last, is still. By now all the doors are opening and passengers, many with other rail connections to make, or further to go on tram or bus, are flooding along the platform. Through a gap between two boxes, Rhea watches the advancing crowd for just one face. Then she spots him! He has just caught sight of his parents and sticks an arm up in the air to wave. She can't wait! 'Robert!' She dashes out from behind the trolley, turns her head as she does. 'Ah'm sorry, Ah jist cannae wait any longer!' She heads towards her man. 'Oh, Robert! You're hame!'

Robert stops for a moment, can't quite take it in. 'Rhea! Oh ma darlin'. Whit are you daeing here?' She almost leaps into his arms. They kiss, then he says, 'My ma and da are here. We're gonny have tae expla—'

Tears streaming down her face, she looks into his eyes. 'We aren't. They already know. Everybody knows! We don't huv tae hide any mair, Robert!'

Just then his parents arrive and he's kissed and hugged all over again. Then his mother joins Rhea in having 'a good greet'.

It's quarter past ten when the taxi turns into Dalbeattie Street. Since leaving the station, they've all been talking non-stop. Just over an hour ago, the Stewarts and Rhea left their usual quiet early-morning street. It's the driver who draws their attention to the transformation that's taken place. 'Whit's going oan here?'

'Jesus-Johnny!' There are some eighty people standing around in a semicircle, beneath rows of bunting and flags. Samuel reads the banner out loud. 'Welcome Home Robert

Stewart. Well Done!' As the taxi pulls up, the crowd moves nearer. Amid cheers, the Stewarts and Rhea climb out on to the pavement. Samuel turns towards the driver, reaches into his inside pocket for his wallet.

'Is all this for your boy?' the driver asks.

'Aye,' says Samuel. 'He's, eh, jist got back fae Korea. He was missing for a while.'

The driver engages gear, waves a hand. 'Forget it, pal. On the house!' He drives off.

For Robert, the day becomes increasingly blurred. Surreal. He finds himself unable to focus on what anyone says to him if the conversation lasts for longer than thirty seconds. He keeps Rhea close by him all day. In some ways, the first two hours are the worst. The house is continually crowded with well-wishers. Mostly neighbours. He tries, but cannot concentrate on what they are saying. By late afternoon and early evening, he feels drained. No energy. Most of the time, he cannot believe that he's back home. Being lost behind enemy lines, wounded, escaping out to sea, being picked up by the USS *Akron*, flying round half the world, being back in his house again – all within such a short space of time. It is too much to take in. Far too much. Is he really back in the kitchen of his house? Really back in 18 Dalbeattie Street? It feels like a dream. It probably is. Yet it's a funny dream. He seems to have some control. If he wants to talk to his ma and da, he can. If he wants to hold Rhea's hand, he can. At twenty minutes to ten, he can't bluff it any longer. He stands up. 'Ah'm sorry, folks, but Ah'm dog tired. Ah must go to my bed.'

The last few visitors see that it's time to go. Robert pays a visit to the lavatory in the close. When he returns, there are just Rhea and his ma and da left in the kitchen. Thank God!

'Ah'll get away up the stairs too, Robert.'

'Ah'll just have a few words wi' Rhea in the lobby. We've never had a minute alone all day.'

He takes her by the hand and they go into the small, dark lobby. One of his parents turns on the radio. They go along to the far end, lean against the coats and jackets hanging from the row of hooks. He can smell the engine oil from his dad's work jacket. Finds it comforting, somehow. He puts his arms round her. She snuggles in. They kiss a few times. 'Oh, Rhea, this is the best it's been all day. Just you and me. All the time Ah was lost, Ah'd constantly think about you. Ah was determined tae get back to you. That's what kept me going.' He can see the glint of tears in her eyes.

'Robert, if you hadn't got back, Ah'd have died of a broken heart.'

He lies in his bed. All is quiet. It must be about half eleven. He switches the light on again. This is the third time. It's to check that he is in his own room. When he lies with his eyes open in the blackness, after a while he begins to doubt that he *is* back home. This darkness could be Korean darkness. The only way to reassure himself is by switching the light on. Jeez! How can you be so tired, so weary, yet not fall asleep? He lies for a while. Once more the doubts start to rise in his mind. He's just about to reach for the light switch when there comes a sound through the night. He smiles. It's a sound he never knew he'd missed – until now. Like Wee Willie Winkie, the echoes of a late tram come racing through the darkened streets. He turns on to his side, pulls the covers up. Yeah, Ah'm back in Dalbeattie Street. And Rhea is just up the stairs. The echoes of the tram grow fainter and fainter into the quiet night. Before the last of them fades, he is sound asleep.